EMERGING

THE ZOE EFERHILD CHRONICLES

E.C. LAWTON

First Edition: September 2023

Names: Lawton, E.C., author.

Artist: Xenia

Title: Emerging, The Zoe Eferhild Chronicles, Book One/ by E.C. Lawton

Description: First edition.

Audience: Ages 18 and up.

Summary: Zoe Eferhild must become the light in her own darkness to emerge as the woman she is becoming.

ISBNs: ebook: 979-8-9885648-0-5; paperback: 979-8-9885648-1-2; hardback: 979-8-9885648-4-3

Printed in the United States of America.

For those who believe they are not enough, you are worthy just as you are.

To all the Jellys of the world, we thank you.

AUTHOR'S NOTE

This story contains material that may be uncomfortable for readers. This work is intended for readers eighteen and older. While Zoe's story is one of hope and designed to empower those struggling with mental wellness, reader discretion is advised.

Content Warning: allusions and references to suicide; sexual assault (non-specific or graphic- flashbacks); self-harm scars; recovery from alcohol abuse; drug abuse; death of a family member; Post Traumatic Stress Disorder (PTSD); depression; anxiety; violence.

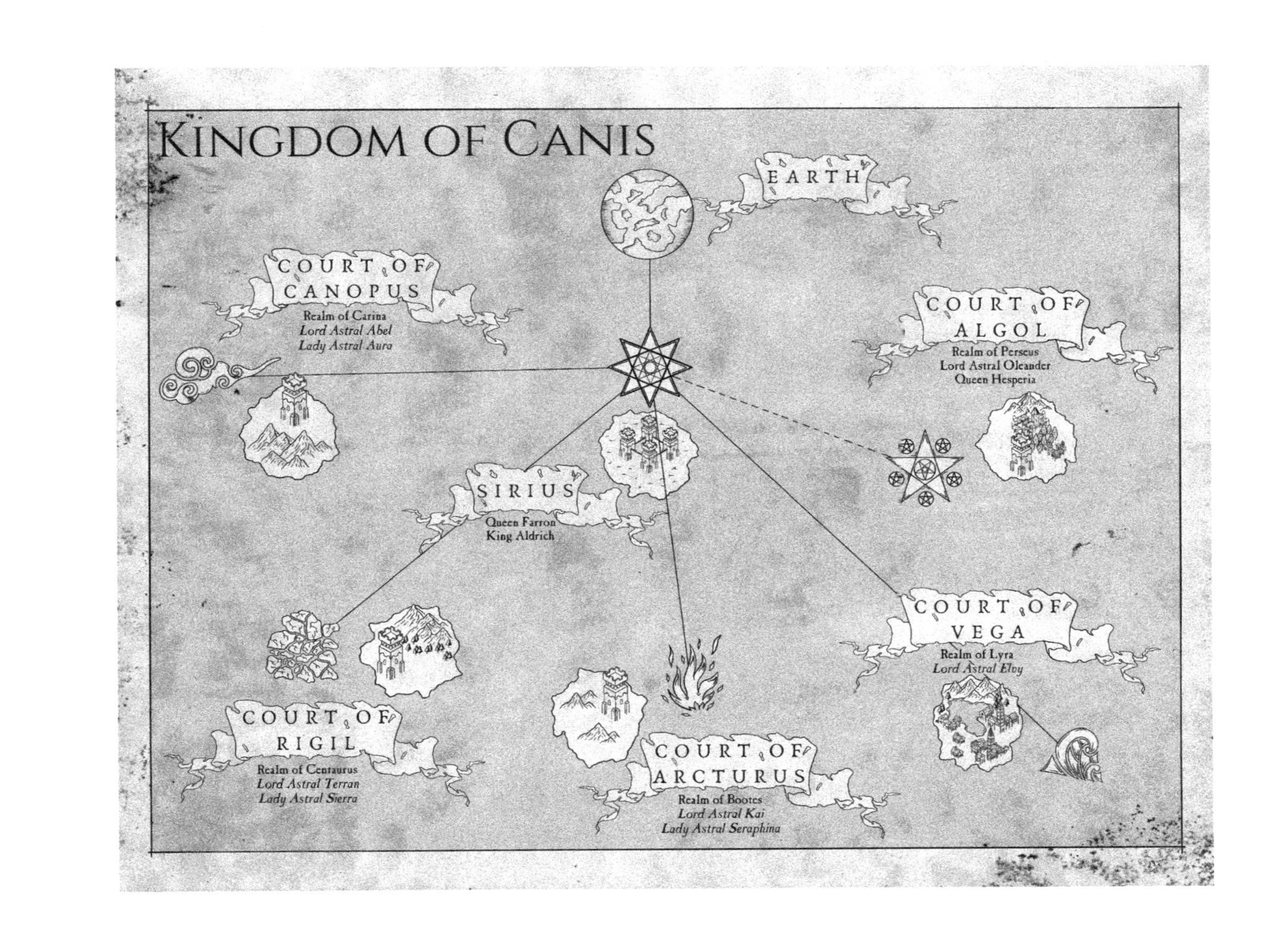
KINGDOM OF CANIS
EARTH
COURT OF CANOPUS
Realm of Carina
Lord Astral Abel
Lady Astral Aura
COURT OF ALGOL
Realm of Perseus
Lord Astral Oleander
Queen Hesperia
SIRIUS
Queen Farron
King Aldrich
COURT OF VEGA
Realm of Lyra
Lord Astral Elvy
COURT OF RIGIL
Realm of Centaurus
Lord Astral Terran
Lady Astral Sierra
COURT OF ARCTURUS
Realm of Bootes
Lord Astral Kai
Lady Astral Seraphina

Contents

1

Moments

Too often I'd heard that life was about choices, but I was of the opinion that life was really about moments. Moments that defined us. Moments that broke us. Each little facet in time intertwined together to create our end, not our life. These seconds passed us by, and we were often oblivious to the seemingly sudden change until it was too late. In the end, none of us would get out of this world alive, and I was all too aware that my life was insignificant. I would eventually leave this world with no profound legacy for those that would come after me, and I was content with that. A part of me knew that I could've been destined for something more, but that had been taken from me. Despite this knowledge, I understood better than anyone the importance of embracing life. It didn't make a difference if the moments were wrought with pain or enriched by genuine joy; it was my sole job to live because of them—*the moments*.

As a child, I'd always believed in something infinitely bigger than what my little mind could comprehend. I'd never feared the dark, and my mother would often come searching for me well after the streetlights had come on. She'd often find me dirty from the imaginative play of fantastical worlds I'd created out of the elements around me. My sister, Freyja, had never been far behind. She'd follow me out past curfew, and we would make a game out of creating the best stories for the stars. I so easily believed in the fairytales my mother read to me every night. This belief and search for more out of life carried with me into my teenage years, and I was always the first one to volunteer for the unknown. My spirit had been as unbreakable and free as the wild stallions in the west that my late grandmother was so fond of throughout her many adventures.

That all changed much too early in life. I thought my time would be filled with the adventures I'd read about in books, but those moments were never meant to be everlasting for me. As much as I grieved who I used to be, she was gone, and I had to accept that.

My life-altering moment began a few years ago when I lost my sister. Except I hadn't really lost her. Yes, I'd witnessed her death, but I hadn't been able to hold her as she took her last breath. Our captors had not granted me that one mercy as I screamed her name while they held me still. But now, she was still here with me every single day. I should've perished that night along with her. Maybe it was the survivor's guilt of this that broke my mind. Whether she was a figment of my imagination, a ghost, or something else entirely, my sister was present in my daily life. I only knew that she was as real to me as the warmth of the sun upon my tanned skin.

I supposed that was why I was in this counseling session. I'd chosen to die a year ago, unable to fight one more day for the dreamer I used to be. However, some power or voice I still didn't understand hadn't granted me the peace I sought. The last moment I remembered was waking up in the hospital, confused out of my mind. A stark white hospital room that smelled of bleach wasn't exactly what I'd pictured death to be like.

Nor was the pain.

I don't mean physical pain. Do not mistake me because there was an immense amount of anguish running through my body, but I am referring to the invisible infliction. The illness where people just tell you to get over it or think it away. The suffering that engulfs every molecule of your being. I was never completely free from it. I often longed to simply get past it, as so many unhelpful people suggested.

My little sister never left my side while I was at the hospital; however, I was the only one to notice her there. To the rest of the world, she was already gone. Long dead. Despite being three years older than Freyja, I'd always felt like she was a bit stronger than I'd ever be. I was okay with that. Freyja and I had never been competitors and had only cheered each other on. She was born in strength and courage. In my darkest times, she was the only one that could ever make me see the sun. More-so, she dreamed even grander than me. I believed in her and the conviction she had in a brighter future. Her energy and light were more healing than any drug I could take. Maybe that was why she'd stuck around. I couldn't stomach the thought of letting her go. For her, I'd agreed to unravel the mystery of the darkness that dwelled inside me. Against the odds, I hoped I would find even a sliver of light within.

"Zoe, where are you right now?" Emma, my therapist, asked, drawing me from my thoughts.

"I just miss her," I admitted. "But I'm tired of saying that. I'm tired of everything."

"Tired, how?"

"Like bone deep exhausted."

Emma was a kind woman, and the times I had actually let her help me, she'd been able to reach me. The genuineness in her soft, blue eyes was authentic. Helping others was her calling in life. It was her *moment*.

"It's okay to rest, Zoe. Your production levels aren't indicative of your worth," Emma said, pausing before changing gears. "How is Freyja?"

"She's good. I'm meeting her after this," I casually answered, pretending Freyja was alive and well. I rubbed my right thumb down the jagged scar that now took up most of the length of my forearm. Emma was the only one that knew of my relationship with my dead sister to this extent. I was certain I must have presented a fascinating case for her. Perhaps she thought I was delusional or having a psychotic break. Maybe she was right. It certainly couldn't be ruled out as a possibility.

Emma nodded her head and noted a few things on her pad of paper. I often wondered whether she did that to look busy or to fill the awkward silence. I highly doubted this as confidence radiated from her, but I knew I never really gave her much to work with. She swooped her blonde hair away from the brim of her glasses.

"Is she still someone you feel comfortable talking to about your thoughts?"

"The *only* one," I answered.

"And how is Jelly?" Emma asked, pointing to my service dog. Jelly was a beautiful black and white border collie whom I loved dearly. I'd worked hard to get her after my hospital incident. The animal therapy during my inpatient treatment had been the moments I'd felt the most alive... *normal,* if that was even a thing. Animals seemed easier to connect with than the human variety.

"She's my best friend," I said.

Jelly perked up and laid her head on my lap, sensing my faulty emotions. I squeezed Jelly's ears gently, letting her know I was present with her. Thankfully, it was time to go.

"I'll see you next week, Emma."

"Goodbye, Zoe," she called after me as I sprinted out the door.

As I stepped out into the Florida heat, I felt like I could breathe for the first time in an hour. I'd never liked the idea of telling a complete stranger my private business and old habits tended to die hard. I walked the short distance from Emma's office to my favorite spot on the beach. Despite my gloomy feelings about life, I couldn't deny that Saint Andrews was sort of beautiful. I understood why many people chose to have their moments here. Unfortunately, it would never be mine. In my twenty-five years of life, I'd never found that one true moment in time where I understood exactly why I was on this planet. Even when I'd been living a rather uncultivated life, I wasn't quite satisfied and always felt like I was searching for something else.

"Zoe!" Freyja shouted, jumping beside me and Jelly on the soft, white sand.

No one in their right mind could deny that Freyja was a joy to be around, though no one saw that now except me. She was a beautiful person inside and out. We'd both taken after our respective fathers. My parents were never married, and they'd split when I was only three. He departed from my life the same night he left my mother. I was twenty-five now while Freyja was frozen in the same twenty-year-old body she'd died in. Freyja and I both shared the same dark brown hair, but that was where our similarities ended. She had bright blue eyes compared to my dull green ones and was taller than my 5'5" athletic frame.

"How was your session?" Freyja asked, genuinely curious.

"Oh, you know, the usual. She asked questions. I answered vaguely. Pretty standard stuff."

I knew my answer frustrated her. The worry line that formed in the middle of her forehead said as much, but Freyja was not the pressing type. She always seemed to know and be just what I needed.

"So, I was thinking about going to watch the games tonight. Want to come?" Freyja asked, attempting to change the subject.

"What interest does a ghost have in intramural volleyball?" I responded skeptically.

"You know, it's just one of those great mysteries of the world," she said, punching my arm.

"Ah yes, the great philosophers and beyond will theorize until the end of time about the interests of the paranormal and only come up empty," I joked with her.

Never able to deny my sister, I agreed to go in the end.

My phone chirped as we made our way to the volleyball court a few minutes away. Mom was ringing. Again. She worried about me, but her incessant calling made me feel crazier than I already knew I was. After all, no sane person talked to their deceased sister on the daily, right? Jelly nudged my leg, letting me know she was there, which I was grateful for.

"Mom," Freyja stated. It wasn't a question.

"Of course. I know you want me to talk to her, but I just can't. It's not the same anymore."

"I know, Zoe," Freyja said, giving my arm a light squeeze. "We'll get through it."

The increased chatter and bright lights indicated we were nearing our destination as the sun dipped below the horizon. It always amazed me that no matter how loud people were, I could still hear the crash of the ocean along the shore. It was my safe harbor. As long as I could hear those waves, I knew I was alive. Sometimes, I felt like I had trouble distinguishing between fiction and reality. The waves helped me remember what was real and what wasn't, which was why I was pretty certain Freyja was not just my imagination. Jelly seemed to know when she was around, too. Dogs can't be crazy, right?

Freyja and I grabbed seats on the outskirts of the wooden bleachers surrounding the sandy volleyball court. Jelly nestled between my legs as I leaned into the sound of the waves gently cresting the shoreline. This wasn't any big tournament. If I remembered correctly, it was an intramural league that included the nearby military base and small colleges. I'd always enjoyed sports, even though I hadn't played on any teams since my world came crashing down. There was a decent crowd tonight, but it wasn't so large that it was overwhelming.

"Looks like this is the start to a weekend tournament," Freyja noted as we watched the teams line up for their pre-season games, which meant there would be games all weekend.

"Who are we rooting for?" I asked.

"Let's go with the team on the far left. They look like athletes," Freyja said, greedily sizing them up.

"You're not wrong," I consented. The team comprised both men and women, all with impressive physiques, clearly formed to be strong through tireless training. I doubted vanity had much to do with it. There were three women and three men and all except one were smiling, gearing up to have a good time.

For as many times as I'd watched volleyball while growing up on the beach, I was not that familiar with the rules. I still happily watched "my" team and got animated when they scored. One player was exceptionally good, but he didn't have a particularly friendly face. Maybe he was just focused. Either way, it was clear he was the leader.

"That guy is pretty good," I pointed out.

"You're telling me," Freyja agreed, just as the MVP made another point.

"They seem a little too good to be playing in an intramural league, right?" I asked. They moved so fluidly with each other, and it was almost as if each player knew what move the other was about to make.

Freyja said nothing, but I caught her scrutinizing MVP's team more closely. Much to my happiness, the game was close. I didn't like for one team to do significantly better than the other as that made for boring entertainment. At one of the last moments of the game, a guy who had obviously drunk a little too much veered right onto the court, causing one woman on MVP's team to go down with her leg moving unnaturally. She cried out in shock and tried to brace her fall.

The crowd seemed to hold their breath as one, as that was clearly a season ending injury. MVP reached out his hand towards her, which the woman used to help herself up. I squinted in confusion, not understanding what had just occurred. She should have left here on a stretcher, yet she was walking around completely unscathed.

"I'm not losing it, right? That should've been worse. Not that I'd want that for anyone."

"Maybe we just saw it wrong," Freyja answered unconvincingly.

I was curious. Emma always said curiosity was the ember to brighter flames. There was something about his expression that I found endearing, and what had that all just been about? He seemed authoritative, but something was off about it. MVP had not smiled the entire game. He seemed to be in the prime of his life and surrounded by joy and friends. If things had gone differently for me, I could've pictured myself there alongside him, basking in the glory of victory. It saddened me to think another person could hurt just as much as me. I knew I was likely reading way too much into it, but I couldn't let it go.

From this distance, his features were slightly blurred, but MVP's shaggy brown hair was visible. However, there was something silvery about his hair that I couldn't explain. He clearly spent time in the sun as a bit of white showed above his board shorts. Two of the women were beautiful, rich dark-skinned tones, with one a more umber brown, who had braids the length of her back and the other woman had natural, full hair.

The remaining woman had more of an ivory color to her skin, with striking violet hair. She was the one that had walked away so easily from such a catastrophic injury. One guy also had nearly identical lilac purple hair, and they looked like they could be twins. The last guy reminded me of friends I'd made while traveling in the East. He had strong, handsome features with dark brown hair, nearly black. However, the truly odd thing about this group were the flashes of silver in their hair that appeared with every shake of their head. A new trend I was not aware of, maybe? I didn't particularly keep up with the fashion these days.

"Zoe?" I heard Freyja ask, but my eyes followed MVP's retreating figure.

I eventually turned to my sister and found her staring at me in question.

"You haven't shown interest in anything outside of books and the rescue in a long time."

Freyja was referring to my job at the local marine life rescue in town.

"I'm only human after all," I laughed, standing up to walk home. "I doubt it'll last, but can you blame me? That was wild."

"Just like our old, unbridled times," she joked with me. "I don't suppose you want to watch the games tomorrow?"

"Alright," I consented. I wanted to find out the mystery behind the supernatural elite team that I'd never seen before. This could be an Agatha Christie novel in the making.

The rest of our walk home was silent, which I appreciated. That was one thing I loved about my sister more than anything else. I didn't feel like I had to keep a conversation going like I did with most of the population, though most locals avoided me most of the time. Even at my brightest, I still found constant talking mentally exhausting because of the mask I so often wore. Recharging in solitude was a necessity.

Freyja disappeared to wherever she went when not with me as I unlocked my front door. My quaint bungalow was within spitting distance of the beach, and I'd made a true effort to make it my safe haven. The living room was tiled and topped with a large, fluffy rug to make the area more inviting. I rarely turned on the small television that sat opposite the white couch. Bookcases that overflowed with my heavily used books were the main focal point in the room. They were really the only remnants of my former life that showed I could believe in the worlds of fantasy.

The living room led right into the kitchen, which had dark blue cabinets with silver features and appliances. The only tool I really used here was the coffeemaker, which did most of the work itself. Somewhat out of place, a standing punching bag took up most of the designated dining room, which was a generous word for the space. Not long after my hospital stay, I'd taken up boxing classes, vowing to take back some control in my life. I would never be caught physically weak again.

My bedroom and bathroom were off to the side of the living room, and I sighed in relief as I shrugged off the wear of another day. As I laid down for the night, I waited for the flashbacks to start. This was usually when I needed Jelly the most. She never fell asleep before me in case I needed her to get me out of a panic attack.

Sometimes they came, and sometimes they didn't. You knew you were mentally unstable when your brain seemed to deliberately think about things that would trigger a PTSD-induced panic attack. Post traumatic stress disorder is what Emma had diagnosed me with, along with some other things that brought on extraordinary hallucinations—Freyja. That's why I longed for the sound of the ocean. As long as I could hear those waves, I knew I was in reality. Needing to hear that noise was why I stayed outside as much as I could and kept all the windows open when I was home. Silencing my racing thoughts, I drifted off to sleep as the waves called me home.

***

I woke up the next day to the rumblings of the ocean's good morning and feeling refreshed. I yawned in pleasure at the waft of coffee coming from the kitchen. That meant there had been no flashbacks to the night I'd like nothing more than to forget. I was always grateful when I got a full night's rest, and I think my brain agreed with me.

The world of dreams had not been empty for me, though. I distantly remembered dreaming of six shooting stars falling from the night sky and becoming one with the ocean's horizon. I had this sense of familiarity, like I had dreamed it before. My gut seemed to scream of its importance. I quickly noted it in the journal on my nightstand, then shook off the feeling to begin my day, promising to skim through my journal later.

Unlike most of the world, I abhorred Saturdays and Sundays; hence the reason I volunteered to pick up the weekend shifts at work. Even when they did not need me, Jelly and I came in anyway, free of charge.

I started working at Gulf Marine Rescue when I was sixteen doing the dirty work. I was fortunate enough to work up to a full-time position when I graduated from high school, and I simply never left. Every animal in this facility was rescued from lethal situations. We didn't do shows, but allowed visitors to learn about the work we did, which usually helped us get more donations.

They released the animals that were well enough back into the ocean, and the rest would stay here safe from future harm. I enjoyed being part of their getting better and healing from the potentially fatal wounds. Now, if only I could do the same. I knew dolphins were intelligent creatures, but I still wondered if they remembered the pain of their hardships. Sometimes, I secretly hoped their healing would rub off on me.

"Hey there, Rafe," I said to our youngest dolphin. He had severe scarring from a boating accident, but he'd fought through it. He was a survivor. "How are we feeling today?"

Rafe answered by giving me a beautiful jump, which made me smile. This was the only place I actually felt truly warm on the inside. It was as if my body was trying to get hot enough to melt the broken pieces together so that I'd be whole again.

Jelly lay in the shade off to the side of the pool as I perched on the edge with a bucket of fish for Rafe. The trust I had in animals was unlike any other. I could trust Rafe in a way that I'd never be able to trust a human. Rafe would never hurt me or let me down. Watching him show off in the pool allowed me to feel a piece of that wildness, and for a moment, I believed I could overcome this darkness inside of me. I knew this feeling was short-lived, though. As soon as I stepped away from the water, the crushing weight of reality would envelop me again.

"Let's go, Rafe," I said, giving him a treat. "Let's get you checked out, alright?"

I went to work cleaning the equipment while our veterinarian, Dr. Malik, gave Rafe a checkup. Freyja joined me, which was not abnormal for her. She kind of came and went as she saw fit. At first, she only showed up when I was in some sort of self-inflicted danger or reckless behavior, which often coincided with giving me a gut-wrenching bad feeling. She had been like an alert system of sorts. It was a tool I was still trying to master.

"I feel like you're always lurking until you know I'll be caught off guard," I said pointedly.

"Well, I wouldn't be much of a ghost if I didn't startle you sometimes," she joked.

I paused for a moment, stretching my ears to hear the sound of the waves. Much to my happiness or maybe my dismay, I could hear them. I was not hallucinating.

"Time for us to take off, Zoe. I have a good feeling about today."

"I've only been here a few hours, Freyja. I can't just leave," I noted as I finished cleaning.

"We both know that's just a lame excuse. It's time, Zoe. You've got to start living."

"Not this again, Freyja. I told you. I can't be who I was. Not anymore and not without you. No one wants to be friends with the crazy girl who talks to her dead sister. All anyone gives me now are looks of sympathy. I'm too far gone," I said with sincerity.

"So what if you can't be who you were? Be someone totally different if you want. Just don't stay in this. It'll kill you, Zo."

I feared I'd never be *normal* even though I wasn't sure what normal really was, but I knew *I* wasn't it. I'd accepted the fact that I probably never would be and grieved the wild girl I used to be. God, I wanted that euphoria again more than anything.

"You know I haven't given up. Not really."

"I believe that, Zoe. I'm just afraid I hold you back sometimes."

I started to argue, but she cut me off.

"Enough for now. Go take a shower and change. I'll be waiting in the car," Freyja said dismissively. "Don't forget your headphones and shades."

I didn't have the energy to argue with her and did as she asked.

Unfortunately, part of having PTSD meant that I was sensitive to light and certain sound frequencies, particularly in crowds. If I wasn't careful, I could go into a panic attack. Last night's group at the game hadn't been nearly this big, and it'd been at night, which was a much more suitable environment for me. I knew Jelly could pull me out of an episode if needed, but I didn't want to put on a display for the audience, either.

Jelly calmly circled me as we made our way to the wooden bleachers. Bystanders wouldn't think she looked aggressive. It was obvious she was creating a space for me. Jelly sat politely between my legs on the sand, poised for intervention if needed.

"Looks like it'll be twelve teams playing today," Freyja deduced before I cranked the volume up on my music. The constant buzz of the crowd was getting to me. Sweat pooled at the base of my back as my mouth became dry. I drank from my water bottle, trying to pacify my trauma response.

"Think our team will play again?"

Knowing I couldn't hear her, Freyja nodded her head.

To be honest, the allure of the games had worn off some, and I didn't much care to be here now. Curling up with a book sounded better, but I found my eyes drifting towards the sidelines as new teams came to warm up. I hadn't forgotten about MVP's miracle save, and I had every intention of keeping a watchful eye on him the entire time. I was zoning out from the games, jamming to some classical beat, when Freyja nudged my side. MVP and his team had arrived. I turned down the music to hear her.

"So, are you going to talk to him today or just drool?" Freyja questioned.

"Certainly not," I said with mock surprise. "To both. My observations are purely for scientific research."

"Oh yeah, totally. Science," she teased.

As much as I tried to reason with myself that I was indeed trying to catch him in the act of something *other*, I couldn't seem to help the traitorous butterflies that filled my stomach every time he made a save. I didn't know a single thing about this guy, yet I was pulled to him like a moth to a flame. I found myself baffled by his demeanor. All of his interactions with his teammates still seemed very stiff and formal. There was still no smile to be found, not even a smirk. How could he be surrounded by such clear joy and look like that? Did people think the same about me?

"You're analyzing, Zoe."

"Yes, one does analyze while conducting research for a hypothesis," I said, smiling. Freyja only rolled her eyes in response. Thankfully, she didn't press on what that hypothesis was.

The other members of his team circled around him, almost as if flanking in rank. MVP's next game began, and much to my irritation, there were no mysterious healings performed. Yet I remained committed to understanding him. I wasn't sure what I hoped to find, but I knew I would press forward.

Amid all the excitement, someone behind me grabbed onto my shoulders in celebration of MVP's point. Little did they know, they'd just triggered a flashback. At the same moment, MVP seemed to spin his head in my direction with eyes locked on mine, but I was losing my grip on reality too fast to be sure.

It was suddenly dark—and not just from the lack of illumination. My face was smashed into the concrete and a hand was choking my neck. I felt the pavement burning against my knees as something wet pooled around me, but I couldn't fight back. Something sharp was slicing through my side. I felt my heartbeat slowing, and I knew what was coming. The horizon was spinning... where was I?

Jelly pulled me back to the present by tugging on my hand to lead me away from the game. No one around me seemed to realize I was having a crisis except Jelly and Freyja. I could barely focus on walking, but I forced myself. One foot in front of the other. I refused to crumble in front of this crowd. Jelly calmly but swiftly led me to the edge of the water and continued rubbing her head against my leg until my heart calmed down. I hated that I lacked control over my flashbacks. It made me feel weak and, well... insane.

When I'd calmed down enough, I sat beside Jelly on the beach and hugged her neck. Freyja stood near, giving me the space I so craved. A sudden burst of noise from the volleyball game indicated MVP's team had won yet again, but I could barely get myself to care. My body was in a different time. It no longer belonged to me.

This was my moment, and I despised it.

2

Curiosity

That was my routine for the next couple of weeks. Therapy. Flashbacks. Panic attacks. Jelly. Freyja. Work. I couldn't seem to function outside of these realms. I only went to the games for Freyja.

Even the pages of a familiar book couldn't lull me to some sort of peace, nor did the usual comfort of the punching bag ignite the light buried deep within me. I kept trying despite this, and that had to count for something. The sound of the ocean was one of the few things that kept me grounded. The water and the animals reconnected me to the gravity of reality.

I still watched MVP and his crew from a distance, and I tended to make up scenarios for his life, like I could fit him into some character from one of my favorite fantasy books. He still didn't smile, and he'd usually jet off after a game. Occasionally, he'd stick around and watch a match or two. I got the sense that he was searching for something, likely scouting the competition. As far as I could tell, he never made eye contact with me again, so I must have been mistaken about that.

I couldn't explain the pull I had towards him other than my curiosity as to why he seemed to suffer, even though his companions clearly adored him. Some would say the same about me, though. I had a supportive family, a good job, and a roof over my head, yet that all seemed insignificant when my mind was my enemy. Since helping myself seemed impossible, I found I got some sense of purpose when I could be part of the healing process for others. Did he feel the same? Emma hadn't discouraged my interest in MVP in therapy, so I took that as a good sign. To be honest, he'd become an enigma, something quite unattainable or real.

I gathered through watching the team's interactions that the two darker skinned girls were a couple. A sense of longing pulled at my stomach as I watched the pair be so clearly in love. The stolen kisses and gentle touches stirred something inside me I couldn't quite identify. Even if it seemed impossible for me, I sent them well wishes in my shattered heart. After everything that had happened, I didn't think I'd ever trust someone with that part of me again.

Just as I started to feel myself emerging from the most recent numbness, I got a rather uncomfortable phone call. It was Freyja's father. He was a kind man, and he'd adopted me as his own with my mother, Vivian. I still wasn't overly close to him, even though he tried. He made my mother happy, so that was enough for me. My mother never spoke of who my biological father was, and I didn't care to ask.

"Hello, Grant," I answered my phone hesitantly.

"Hey, Zoe. How are you doing today?"

"I'm alright, I guess. Same old stuff. Just got off work."

That was only partially true. I'd actually just settled in with a decent book and a boiling hot cup of coffee with a ridiculously soft blanket wrapped around me. I dreaded the inevitable disruption to my peaceful world of fiction.

"Well, you know I'm not one to beat around the bush, so I'm just going to ask you."

I braced for impact, clutching Jelly hard.

"We're having a charity event tomorrow. Your mother and I want to sponsor the rescue as the major beneficiary. Viv tried to reach you a few days ago about it."

"That's generous," I answered cautiously, ignoring the subtle hint about my mother.

"We would like for you to accept the donation in person."

NO.

"Do you think you can do that?"

NO.

I sighed longingly at my cup of coffee, wondering why life could be so cruel. Jelly humphed her head on my lap in solidarity.

"Of course, Grant," I said with only mildly gritted teeth. I couldn't very well tell him no. The rescue needed the funds badly. I could already hear Emma challenging me on my boundaries and people-pleasing nature in the next therapy session.

"Your mother can pick you up before the ceremony if you'd like."

"No, thanks. I know where to go, and I'll need some alone time with Jelly to get ready."

"Zoe, this is a big thing for us. Does Jelly—"

"Yes," I said, cutting him off. "Jelly is a necessity for me. She either goes or I don't."

How about that for boundaries, Emma?

"Of course. Sorry, I even thought about it."

I finally felt myself relaxing a bit into my blanket burrito and lessened my grip on Jelly. Freyja now sat on the other side of me.

"I'll see you tomorrow, Grant. Send my love to Mom. Goodbye," I said, hanging up.

"Shit," I whispered to myself, rubbing Jelly's head. "Why did I say yes?"

"Because you're a good person, Zoe," Freyja insisted.

"What did being good ever get me? Besides, I have nothing to wear," I said, frowning and unfazed by her appearance. My wardrobe was pretty basic, with mostly work clothes and comfortable athletics.

"Good thing we can fix that," she said, reminding me that not everything was the end of the world. Despite my best efforts, I knew I could be dramatic when I didn't want to do something.

Before I could convince myself otherwise, Freyja had all but dragged Jelly and myself out the door.

***

I was in a changing room at one of the local dress shops, the shop owner handing me dress after dress through the tiny curtain that did not close enough for my liking. Seriously, could they not afford to put a few more yards of fabric on this thing? If the owner seemed bothered by Jelly, she didn't let on. I wondered what she'd think of my dead sister sticking her tongue out in disgust at some of her choices. Personally, I found it amusing and incredibly difficult to stifle my laughter.

Freyja sifted through some dresses, and her face lit up at one in particular. It was a floor length, emerald green dress with lace, long sleeves, and a subtle spark. The sleeves would also cover my scar. I'd mostly grown past the shame I had of it, but I didn't enjoy flaunting it either. The dress was elegant, but still hung around all the places you wanted it to. I had worn nothing so extravagant or form fitting since Freyja's death.

My neck flushed red as I analyzed the stranger looking back at me in the mirror. She was objectively beautiful, but the hollowness in her eyes was marred by the dark circles beneath them. More importantly, there were signs of life there in the flush of her cheeks and the freckles that proved too much time in the sun.

"That dress makes your eyes pop," Freyja said, pulling me out of my negative thoughts, and I found that she wasn't wrong. I'd always loved my green eyes, but they didn't shine quite as bright as they used to.

"It's gorgeous," I agreed, returning to the reflection I didn't quite recognize. I could almost believe that the woman staring back at me knew how to have fun and lived a life full of adventure. I gently touched the crow's feet that had formed from all the years of deep belly laughter. Then, there were the scars barely visible on my knees from my fall while rock climbing in Central America. I'd lived a life of dreams, and before this moment, I'd almost pushed those memories so far into the abyss of me that I'd forgotten them.

I went to sleep that night hoping that the woman in the mirror would emerge from the pit of me, even if it meant she had to scrape and claw her way out. I silently whispered to the stars and the moon that the path to the authentic Zoe would break free.

My dreams were filled with the warmth of the sun and the beauty of a rainbow after a thunderstorm. Six shining stars danced in the moonlight, and a streak of darkness seemed to intertwine with them. Neither overtaking the other, but moving in harmony to the beat of the waves below.

I woke up feeling rested, but with another sense of Déjà vu. I grabbed my dream journal and noted what I could remember of the dream, trying not to let the fear of this reoccurrence rattle me today. More pressing matters required my attention tonight. Not only did I have to be in a very public setting, but all eyes would be on me. What if I went into a panic attack? I just had to somehow force myself not to, right? I could do that.

"Alright, Jelly. You'll have to keep a very watchful eye on me tonight. Don't let me break down in front of all those people."

Jelly seemed to nod her head in promise. She wouldn't let me down.

"I got you too. I'll be there the whole time, if that's what you want," Freyja said from behind me. There was a softness to her voice and in her eyes, which kept from startling me.

"Yes. Please come," I begged.

"Always. Now, come on. You need some food, and you need to burn off some energy," she said, motioning towards the punching bag.

Since I was dreading the evening so much, the hours zoomed by before I even had time to properly talk myself out of it. I was sitting in my rarely used vehicle in my gorgeous green dress, unable to put it in drive. Jelly was crammed in the front seat with Freyja. They were both looking at me expectantly.

"Well, are we going to go?"

"I'm not so sure about this," I confessed, my bravado from earlier faltering slightly.

"We are here with you. All the way. You'll have your headphones just in case. You can do this. I believe in you," Freyja coached.

"I can do this," I agreed, reminding myself that I had done much harder things.

Jelly barked as if in agreement.

"Let's go," I said, driving away towards the convention center in my decrepit two-door white Jeep Wrangler.

Upon arrival at the convention center, I noticed that the line to get in was taking much longer than expected. It looked like the security guards were requiring all passengers to exit their vehicles for a more thorough search because of some professionals in attendance; I guessed. While annoyed, I complied and slipped out of the vehicle with Jelly when it was my turn. Freyja defiantly stayed put.

"Welcome to Elysian," the young security guard said, scanning me up and down in the way my curves had always seemed to incline males to do so. Another guard used a mirror to look under the Jeep.

"Thanks," I said with a forced smile. As usual, he took note of Jelly, probably wondering why someone like me would need a service dog. Before he could satisfy his curiosity, the other guard gave the all clear, and I sped off, finding a parking spot away from everyone else. I needed time to relax before walking into such a high-profile place with Jelly and Freyja.

I took five deep breaths and blasted a soothing jam to decrease my heartbeat. I can do this. I have to do this. Not only for the rescue who desperately needed the funds, but to prove to myself that I can.

"Well, it's now or never," I mumbled.

I opened my Jeep's door and let Jelly and Freyja out.

"You never know. You might have fun," Freyja said, looping her arm through mine.

I grabbed on tightly to her and Jelly's leash and stepped forward to the place I desperately did not want to enter.

As I'd feared, most eyes fell on me as soon as I breached the threshold. Service dogs just did that. Apparently, the phrase, "staring is rude" disappeared from people's minds when a cute animal was involved. I scanned the area for Grant and my mother. Thankfully, they quickly found me and welcomed me to their table.

However, there was noticeably not a place for me at this table as overly priced suits and dresses and the people who wore them took every seat. I swallowed the rage boiling beneath the plastic mask I'd put on the surface of my face.

"You know how these things are, honey," my mother smiled kindly, seeing the terror in my eyes. Or maybe terror was the wrong word. Hurt was more accurate. Emma had once told me that anger's true name was grief. I believed her.

"Then where the hell am I supposed to sit?" I asked through a fake smile, ever so cautious not to cause a scene in front of some of the wealthiest people in town.

Grant pointed to the table right beside them. "You'll be sitting with some of the best, Zo. Come on, I'll introduce you." Mom squeezed my hand, trying to ease my anxiety.

All the lovely gentlemen and women in their gala attire stood when Grant and my mother approached the table. I internally rolled my eyes. Freyja was loquacious in her own way with her displeasure at the situation.

"This is my daughter, Zoe. I know you'll treat her well," Grant said, as if it was an order.

My face burned red with embarrassment. Ordering people to be nice to me? That settled it. Whatever hope I'd had of getting through this night unscathed was gone.

I surveyed the people I'd be having dinner with and found the one person I did not expect to see: MVP. He'd be sitting across from me, which might as well be miles apart at this ridiculously large, clothed round table. I quickly averted my eyes on instinct.

I felt my heart fluttering like a tiny hummingbird beneath my chest, so I quickly took my seat and rubbed Jelly's head to calm down. Freyja let me know she'd be in the back of the room if I needed her.

"Don't let this moment get away from you, Zoe. Talk to him. I know you want to," Freyja whispered before skipping off.

Grant and my mother, Vivian, each gave me a kiss on the cheek, careful not to touch me anywhere on the back of my neck and went back to their seats. Great. Now I had to deal with small talk. I silently regretted not bringing a book with me, even though it would have been bad manners to look bored at an event like this.

MVP was talking to a gentleman beside him who seemed pretty tipsy. They all did, except for MVP. My wine remained full, and I sat there awkwardly watching the condensation trickle down the glass.

After things went down with my sister, alcohol had become my favored coping skill—and not in a good way. I shuddered at the memories that tried to break through and the mistakes I'd made while trying to escape my pain. After I got out of the hospital, I never touched the stuff again and found I didn't miss it most of the time. So instead of replaying those fun times, I nursed my lemon water and silently wondered how long was appropriate before I found an excuse to leave.

I casually scanned the crowd as I always did, observing the exits in case I needed to use them quickly. I was also looking for the group of people who were usually with MVP. Eventually, I found them spread about the convention hall, but none of them actually sat together, which made it difficult to locate them all. How odd not to all sit at one table?

"So, you run the marine rescue?" the person next to me I had no interest in knowing asked.

"No, I just work there," I said, not bothering to explain further.

"Lived here long?"

"Pretty much my whole life, but I traveled a lot."

He seemed to wait for me to elaborate. I didn't.

I knew these were all relatively normal topics of conversation, but I didn't enjoy talking about my personal life. MVP seemed oblivious to my existence, and I tried not to read into that feeling too much.

The chatter was getting to me. These damn frequencies bothered me especially badly. When people were trying to talk over one another, it was particularly bothersome, which was what everyone was doing right now the more they drank. I was sure I sounded curt and unkind, but I was also trying to keep it together.

Much to my happiness, the ceremony began, so I could finally rest easier for the time being. When it was time for me to accept the donation check, I did it flawlessly. Jelly was by my side the whole time, and I kept my eyes on Freyja as much as possible. However, when I was finished with that, I needed to get out there, if only to breathe fresh air for a moment. My flight response was increasing every second I was in this crowd.

As soon as they announced the beginning of dinner, I made a beeline for the door to the patio where there was an inviting fire pit waiting to warm my frigid body. I whipped out my headphones as quickly as possible and found a more secluded part of the outdoor space with Jelly. I just needed a break from the buzz of human interaction, so I focused on the beat and lyrics, trying to pretend I was anywhere but where I was. The ocean was too far away for me to hear, which frightened me. There was no way for me to know what was real or not.

Then he showed up beside me.

MVP.

I don't know what caused the words to come out, but somehow courage roared inside me and led directly to my mouth.

I pulled off my headphones and blurted out, "Who are you?"

That was probably the most direct question I'd ever asked a stranger.

He reached out to shake my hand, which I stared at for a breath too long before taking it.

"Elvy Kimble," he answered, voice warm and a far cry from the stoic face I was accustomed to.

"Zoe Eferhild," I offered back. "Elvy is... unique."

"That all depends on your perspective," he answered, smiling.

"Do you fit the name, then?" I asked, continuing to be bolder than I could have ever guessed.

"I don't know. Maybe you can tell me."

I thought back to his superior athleticism and his Apollo-like healing abilities, and decided unique was one word for it.

Jelly nudged between us, making sure I had the distance I needed.

"Sorry, this is Jelly," I said, pointing to my companion. "She's a bit overly protective."

"Hi, Jelly," he said, examining my beloved. She seemed to show off at his gaze, prancing around with a puffed-out chest. Figures.

"So, what brings you out here?"

"Just a bit crowded in there," I brushed off.

I quickly scanned him, and something warmed in the pit of my chest. He wore a simple black tuxedo and looked damn good in it. He was like Apollo in more ways than one.

"I've seen you before," he casually mentioned. A shock rippled through me. Had he noticed me at all the games? I felt my cheeks reddening at the thought.

"Yeah?"

"A fan of volleyball, are we?" he asked, with a smirk playing on his lips.

"Something like that."

There it was. A smile. Finally. I doubted I'd ever forget that smile. Now that I could see him up close, I appreciated his intrigue even more. He still had that authoritative air around him, but there was a gentleness and sense of safety about him I couldn't pick up from a distance. However, I hadn't been imagining the silver streaks in his hair. They matched the gray of his eyes, reminding me of storms over the sea.

"I've never seen you around here before," I said, attempting to pry.

"I'm new to the area," he explained.

"Are you some kind of doctor?" I asked.

His brows raised at that. "No, I wouldn't quite say that. What makes you think that?"

"Well, it looked like one of your teammates got injured on the court pretty badly, but after you helped her, she seemed fine."

"Mmmm, that's observant," he said, not denying what I'd seen but also clearly not going to offer anything else.

The purple-haired girl appeared and tapped him on the shoulder, drawing his attention, which had not left my face.

"Until we meet again, Zoe Eferhild," Elvy gave a small bow before leaving me alone with Jelly and the crackling of the fire.

I tried not to smile at that. I shoved my headphones back in and focused on the music. Deciding not to push my luck any further, I quietly exited the building and headed home, but with a secret smile on my lips. I welcomed the feeling of hope like an old friend. I didn't know how long it would last or what it meant, but I burned that moment into my heart and slept peacefully that night.

3

Dreamers

"How was your week?" Emma asked as I stared off into nowhere.

"I attended a benefit for charity and kept it together pretty well."

"Why do you think that is?" she probed.

"I don't know. I took precautions to not break down in front of people."

"Because what would it mean to 'break down' in front of everyone?"

I knew where she was going with this, and I didn't really feel like facing my truth today.

"It would mean weakness."

"I challenge it would allow you to be vulnerable."

"I don't know that I'm ready for that, but—" I hesitated.

"This is a safe place," she reminded me.

"But I hope to. I think it's possible," I said, not elaborating on Elvy. I'd keep him to myself for now. "What do you think about dreams?"

"What do you mean?" she asked.

"Like actual dreams. Do you think they're real?"

"I think our dreams can be our subconscious talking to us or trying to process things," she offered. "What do they mean for you?"

"I'm not sure," I said, shaking my head. "I've just been having the same dreams a lot."

"Perhaps that's your brain's way of trying to tell you something."

"Maybe," I agreed noncommittally.

"I'll see you next time, Zoe," she said, smiling brighter than normal.

I hadn't told Emma that I'd unexpectedly met the mysterious MVP. Not that there was much to tell. I hadn't been back to see a game since then. There was something about him knowing I was watching that had me running for the hills. I'd probably never hear from him again, but deep down, I didn't believe that. Freyja had been around less, which seemed to make my nightmares return. If ever I went too long without her, I feared never seeing her again. No amount of time would make me wish for that.

***

I sat by the ocean, letting the saltwater burn my nose as I focused on the sound of the waves. This was real. I was safe at this moment. Freyja would return. I briefly let myself wonder what it'd be like to face my past and regain control of what happened to me. I could only hold on to this wonder for a second before my heart rate started increasing and my chest throbbed with the ache I was not ready to conquer. I clutched my side as the phantom pain of being stabbed radiated within me. *Moments.*

Before I realized how much time had passed, I was bearing witness to the sun sinking below the horizon. The magnificent hues signifying the end of the day or the beginning of night. Beachgoers were departing as the last rays of sun left, but I wasn't ready to leave the comfort of this ocean while it cared for me in its melodic embrace. I leaned back on the sand to better see the stars trying to break through the clouds that so often covered this ocean. I tried to find the stories of old in the stars, which wasn't too difficult with how brightly they shined tonight. I was grateful for this moment.

Suddenly, I felt nauseous. Jelly jumped up, hackles raised. I whipped my body into a crouched position, pleading for Freyja to appear, but she didn't. I knew this feeling all too well—this was my body's alarm that something bad was near. This was a side effect of surviving near death, I think. Being brought back from the edge of death had left a mark on my soul.

The first time this happened, I thought it might have just been residual uneasiness after my attack. However, I quickly realized it was deeper than that. Whether it was God, Freyja, or fate, I now knew when something truly horrific was going to happen, and I needed to get out of here. While I felt prepared for a fight, if it came down to it, I'd rather avoid one.

Quickly, I surveyed the area around the beach, trying to locate the potential threat. Nothing jumped out at me and my home was only a few blocks away. I realized how alone I was, even with Jelly. I quickly gathered my bag and started jogging towards my house. I didn't bother to brush the sand from my legs as I made my way past the shops along the boardwalk that was now covered in darkness with the sun sleeping for the night. The sickly feeling only intensified as the ocean got further away, and it took every bit of willpower to keep a level head. Panic only made situations like this worse. I'd learned that the hard way.

Finally, out of the corner of my eye, I saw a figure cloaked in darkness waiting for me. The ache in my stomach was nothing like I'd ever felt before. His body was not fully formed, seemingly part of the shadows in the alley I would have to cross to get to the safety of my home. Readying myself, I took an extra breath. I could fight or I could flee. I had to make a choice, and I had to make it now. With one final steadying breath, I tore off as hard and as fast as I could stand it. The legs in my muscles burned, but I silenced them.

The sick feeling never left, and I knew without looking back that he was behind me. Jelly was tight on my tail; and I knew she would defend me if it came to that. The thought of someone hurting her pained me, though. We had to make it home. The sea-blue house came into view, and I ordered my legs to continue pressing on. I just had half-a-mile longer.

The hair on my neck raised, and gooseflesh covered my skin. Just as I was approaching the front porch, the sickness abruptly left.

I whirled around to find nothing but a quiet street. I heard the ocean against the panic in my mind, so I knew I hadn't imagined the pursuit. In the distance, I saw a flickering of lights. I knew it wasn't possible, but the lights looked like the colors of the rainbow colliding.

The curious part of me wanted to chase those lights. I yearned for their warmth, as if they were calling me to join them. I felt the first foot fall to move towards them, but Jelly brushed up against my leg, pulling me back to the realm of safety. Swiftly, I entered the house, locking the door behind me. All the windows were open, and I took one last moment to hear the waves crashing against the shore before locking them, too.

As added thoroughness, I picked up the softball bat by the door and crept through the house, checking every closet and under the bed just to make sure I truly was alone. Jelly dutifully followed along beside me, sensing something was still off.

"Zoe," a familiar voice whispered behind me.

I whipped around to find Freyja standing in front of me, but her image wasn't as solid as she normally was.

"Where have you been?" I asked, the concern evident in my voice.

"I don't know what happened, Zoe. I just couldn't seem to get through the barrier from the otherside. Like something was blocking me. Or someone."

A worry line formed between her brows as she solidified more around me.

"I can't lose you, Freyja. Not again," I murmured, shoulders easing their tension. I knew I'd be sore the next day. I wanted to sink to my knees, but I kept my feet planted.

"I know."

"Did you see that guy following me home?" I questioned.

"No," she answered, turning from me, as if concealing something.

Too disoriented to question her, I didn't press.

I grabbed my journal from the nightstand drawer and quickly noted the events of tonight. My gaze landed on the last entry—the rainbow dream. My blood seemed to freeze over. Those lights from only minutes ago had felt so warm and familiar. I flipped back further and skimmed through the recurring theme of the six shooting stars—six. The same number of Elvy and his teammates. I tried to remember how many colors were in the lights from the alley, but I couldn't be sure.

My spine shivered at the unnerving experience and the unmistakable connection of it all, even though I wasn't completely sure what it all meant. I had no explanation for tonight, but I knew I wasn't mad.

I stripped from my sandy clothes and hopped in the shower. I took my time, scrubbing my skin raw until it was pink. The flashbacks were on full throttle tonight because of the extreme stress, and I was fighting to lock them back up. I knew subconsciously that I scrubbed to rid myself of someone else's touch. No matter how long I stood under the scalding water, I could still feel unfamiliar hands on my body. I swallowed, forcing the bile from my stomach down.

"Just breathe, feel the water on your skin, smell the lavender soap in your hair. You are safe," I whispered to myself.

I stayed in the shower until the water ran cold. Feeling like I'd just fought a physical battle, I shrugged into my pajamas and snuggled into bed in victory. Jelly warmed the covers near my feet, and I felt Freyja creep onto the other side of the bed.

"Sleep well, Zoe. We'll be watching over you. Promise."

***

I slept through the night without ever waking or dreaming of nights better forgotten. Freyja was nowhere to be found, but it wasn't abnormal for her to be gone in the morning. I woke to the smell of fresh coffee coming from the kitchen as my coffee pot finished brewing today's batch. I savored the taste of something comforting and took out my journal from the night before.

It hadn't been a dream.

I was chased, but I was safe now. Something or someone saved me, or maybe he got spooked. I flipped to the page before and trailed my fingers along the six shooting stars I'd sketched out. I quickly looked through earlier entries to find six stars several times throughout and jotted down Elvy's name with a question mark beside it. Something big seemed to lurk in the small town of Saint Andrews. Whatever it was seemed to be making me its primary target.

I nursed the coffee as I got ready to head to work, forgoing a round with the bag. I'd been right about my muscles feeling sore. Gingerly, I stretched them out, and I felt guilty for enjoying the pain just a little.

Jelly and I arrived at the rescue as refreshed as possible, ready for our workday. I hoped no one noticed the purple bags under my eyes. My boss, a plump older woman, who had seen one too many days in the sun, greeted us on our way in.

"If it isn't my two favorite worker bees," she said with a strong southern drawl.

"Hey June," I answered with a smile. "Got anything exciting on the schedule today?"

"Actually, we do. We have a group that requested a private tour. Potential investors. Would you mind taking over today? I've got a pile of grant paperwork with my name on it."

"No problem," I said, shrugging. I liked June. She never asked about my scar, even when I let it show in the Florida heat. She'd been more than gracious and understanding when everything happened. Today, I wore the short-sleeved blue polo shirt of the rescue, and she didn't so much as glance at my arm like most people did, which was why I frequently wore long sleeves. She never treated me any differently than any other employee. In fact, I think she saw me as her transplant granddaughter in a way. She'd never had kids, as far as I knew. The animals were her life, and she seemed okay with that.

"They're waiting in the conference room," she called, rushing to her office.

"Conference room" was a lavish description of what it actually was. It was maybe a bit larger than a smaller sized bedroom with fold-away chairs and collapsible tables. A stained white board took up most of one wall with the other walls plastered with educational posters that were probably a decade old.

I took a generous swig of coffee before stepping into the room, but not even my favorite brand of the sacred bean could've prepared me for who waited inside. Elvy and his usual crew were all sitting around, chatting with each other easily. Their presence seemed otherworldly in this tiny room, and I felt so small. Were they always this... massive? I gulped, reminding myself that I'd given this tour many times. It was no big deal.

"Welcome to Gulf Marine Rescue," I stated, with a forced smile.

Elvy rose from his chair with an outstretched hand.

"Hello again, Zoe. I couldn't help but come for a visit after hearing all about this place at the event," he replied, to explain the question I'm sure was written on my face.

"Is that so?" I asked, brow raised.

"Among other incentives," he answered.

"Well, I'm glad we could work you in," I said calmly. "Who else do we have here today?"

Elvy turned his attention to his entourage, not hesitating to introduce them.

"This is Delmira," Elvy said, motioning towards the ivory-skinned female with brilliant purple hair. I took a mental note again that all of them had silver streaks in their hair. Delmira's eyes almost seemed violet.

"Unique," I murmured.

"Zoe has a fondness for unique names," he explained, smiling at the one named Delmira.

"Then she is in for a treat," she said, laughing.

Elvy turned to the other two females. The stunning woman with the braids was named Clodovea. Her eyes were bright blue while the other woman, Imelda, had honey brown eyes. I smiled at their closeness, but I felt minuscule in their powerful energy, even though their expressions only held kindness.

"And my name is Finnian," the twin to Delmira said. I assumed so anyway. They looked identical, with the same violet eyes.

"Nice to meet you," I said, shaking his hand. Finnian did not seem to notice or care about my marred arm. "And you are?" I asked the last of the group.

"Blaz," he grunted. There was an intensity to his dark eyes, but not unfriendly.

Jelly sniffed around them and seemed unsure, like she couldn't quite place them. I also noted they had identical black tattoos of an eight-point star on each of their right wrists. I stored this information away to explore later.

"It's nice to meet you all. Come follow me then," I said, turning towards the main facility.

All eyes were on me as I explained rehabilitating the animals. Currently, we were treating sea turtles, otters, bottle-nosed dolphins, reptiles, and a few native birds. Most of these animals were too damaged to be released back into the wild, but that was always our intention with the animals we accepted into our rescue. We were desperate to build an expansion to further help more wildlife while also keeping our current marine animals healthy and happy.

I tried not to notice Elvy clinging to every word I said, but it was distracting. Never allowing myself to fumble over my words, I resolved to give them a great tour. I also noticed the way the group interacted with each other. Delmira was always to the right of Elvy with Clodovea to his left. Finnian, Blaz, and Imelda created a semi-circle beyond the central three. Elvy kept the company of a protective bunch, though I wouldn't mind having this group at my back. Before long, any unease left me, and I found myself enjoying the tour. I was passionate about the work being done here, and I could never hide my excitement about it well.

I paused at one of the isolation pools with a new sea turtle admitted to the center.

"This young male is struggling with a buoyancy disorder, which basically means he has an excess of gas built up and can't submerge beneath the surface. This makes him easy prey, and it's difficult for him to feed."

"Will he be able to go back to the ocean?" the one named Clodovea asked.

"No, most likely not. It really depends on what is causing the buoyancy, but they are, unfortunately, typically un-releasable once this happens."

"May I?" Elvy asked, motioning towards the turtle.

I directed him to the sanitization station, then showed him how to handle the turtle.

Much to my surprise, the turtle immediately came to him, struggling to swim the entire way. It almost reminded me of a dog greeting its long-lost owner.

"He hasn't wanted to eat much," I said sadly. "We are going to have to start IV fluids."

Elvy only nodded and gently used the tool to brush the shell of the turtle.

"Can I try to feed him?" he asked.

"Sure," I said, handing him a small fish from a nearby feeding container.

The turtle didn't hesitate to take the food from him and almost seemed to sigh in relief. He continued to brush him and feed him fish while I stood mesmerized. The sun seemed to shine brighter than it had moments before.

"Are you some kind of turtle whisperer?" I asked.

"Something like that," he answered as he washed his hands in the sink.

"Maybe unique does fit you," I admitted.

By the end of the tour, it was around my lunch break, and I was ravenous. I hadn't eaten anything after being chased and was in too much of a rush this morning to eat breakfast.

"I hope this was educational, and you enjoyed your time with us today," I said, smiling, but ready to be left alone to sort through my own thoughts. "Please let June know if you need anything else."

Elvy gave a silent nod and the rest of his circle dispersed, leaving just the two of us. Jelly laid down near enough to be at my side if needed.

"I was hoping I could take you to lunch," he said. "To say thank you."

"I'm sorry. I only get 30 minutes. I usually just eat here."

"That works for me," he answered, eyes curious.

June conveniently came by as I was silently deliberating and insisted I take lunch with the potential investor. Sighing in exasperation, I dragged Elvy to the break room to grab my food. Then I led him to a couple of plastic chairs around one of the rehabilitation pools to eat. Jelly, my constant shadow, followed close each step of the way. I sat in silence, unsure of how to be a functioning human. Where were the instructions?

My heartbeat hastened, and Jelly's ears perked in anticipation. I concentrated on my breathing and the sounds of the ocean. This was real. I was safe. My heart eased its pace.

"What are you thinking?" he asked.

"It'll sound crazy," I admitted.

"What if I told you what was on my mind, and you can do the same in return if you'd like? No judgment from either of us. Deal?"

I only nodded as I tried to decide what my best course of action would be.

"I'm thinking that I'm glad that our paths have crossed, though I wish it didn't have to be under these circumstances. It's a bit unfair, really."

"I'm not sure what that means. What circumstances?" I asked.

"In my line of work, I'm only rendered necessary when the worst happens," he explained. "This is a special case. I know that doesn't clear things up, but I'm trying to be as honest as possible."

"So, you are *unique* then."

"No, Zoe. *You* are," he answered.

The warmth in my chest grew, but I didn't shy away from him. Not now.

"Do you believe in dreams?" I asked.

"I believe the world is created by the dreamers who dared to be brave enough to do something about it."

"And you? Do you have dreams?"

"I dreamed of a girl cloaked in darkness who kept reaching out her hand, and just as I was about to clasp it, she'd disappear just out of my touch."

"What did you do?"

"I kept showing up," he smiled. "Hoping she would reach out again."

"Did she?"

"I'll let you know."

"I'm thinking..." I paused. *Be brave*. The conviction of vulnerability ran through me like a knife. I swallowed my desire to stay hidden. "That I'm afraid."

He didn't ask what I feared. He only studied me openly, as if trying to read me and understand me in the same way I'd been trying to with him. I wasn't sure I understood everything he was saying, but I found myself enraptured by him anyway. Had he felt pulled to me the same way I'd been called to him? I'd never understood why I couldn't seem to pull myself away from the lure of him.

"Fear can be forged," he murmured. His eyes seemed to go off to a far-away place. "Whether that is a good thing or not is entirely up to the person holding the fear."

"Have you ever had that kind of fear before?"

"Yes," he answered, but did not explain further.

"This is all a little strange, isn't it?" I hadn't meant to ask the question out loud.

"I have a feeling you're good with strange."

"Because you think I'm a dreamer?"

"Because *we* are dreamers."

"I don't really know anything about you." I trailed off, hesitating on the words I wanted to say. I leaned into the heat rising in my core. "But I'd like to."

His stormy gray eyes held mine for what felt like just a moment too long, but not long enough at the same time.

"I'm thinking you are a woman worth knowing, Zoe Eferhild. And I'd like to know you."

For the first time in ages, I felt seen.

I felt a familiar tug in my chest. It wasn't fear or panic. It was warm and welcoming, like the first time I saw the sun rising after I'd been lost to the infinite darkness of that tragic night. Maybe Elvy really was Apollo, my personal sun god.

He suddenly froze, staring back at me, and took a deep inhale through his nose.

"Sorry," I murmured apologetically. "This place reeks of fish."

He seemed to ignore the comment and kept staring so deeply; it was like he could see directly into my soul. He took another sniff and his eyes seemed to go darker, curious.

"There's something about you," he said, those stormy eyes on me. "I'll see you soon, Zoe."

Before I could get out a reply, he was walking away. I had the distinct feeling I'd just had my *moment* that could change everything. I felt in my gut that there was something off about Elvy in the way there was something off about Freyja, but she was conveniently not around to confirm or deny my suspicion.

In the back of my mind, I knew that interaction had been more than a casual lunch, but I couldn't find it in myself to be bothered by it either. Good or bad, I felt a new path emerging in front of me.

"Zoe, you won't believe it!" June exclaimed, running through the door.

"You know that buoyant turtle we got in a couple of days ago?"

"Yeah," I said cautiously.

"He's submerged to the bottom of the pool. Dr. Malik is floored. He's getting him in for x-rays now. Can you help assist?"

"Sure thing," I said, but I knew in my heart that he wouldn't find anything.

4

PROPHECY

It had been a week since lunch with Elvy. I found myself sprawled out on the living room floor with the ocean scent and breeze wafting through the open windows. Freyja sat in the rocking chair with an amused look on her face, and Jelly laid next to me, snoring soundly.

"You know it's Saturday, right?" Freyja asked.

I had recognized that it was Saturday. I'd also realized it was the first Saturday in months that I hadn't picked up an extra shift at work. I wouldn't necessarily call it a healthy thing, and I definitely still didn't want to sit with my feelings. However, I had a major project to distract myself with. I'd decided figuring out who or what Elvy and his friends really were as my top priority. I was embracing my inner Hercule Poirot.

"Why are you reading these occult books?" Freyja pressed.

I looked around at the number of books on mythical beasts with notes adorned in highlights and scribbles jutting out everywhere. My journal was opened to the dreams of stars and rainbows. I wondered what Emma would make of this new hobby of mine and if she'd try to refer me for immediate hospitalization. I wouldn't blame her if she did. It'd truly take a dreamer of the strange kind to believe that this could all be real.

I knew it was a leap, but I felt it deep in my gut that there was something not of this world about Elvy. He and his group were just... *other*.

Then, there were the unexplained healings with his teammate and the turtle. The first could've been a fluke, but I knew marine life. That shouldn't have happened, and it conveniently coincided with Elvy's visit. No, that did not add up. I didn't find it completely irrational to find him and his group of friends a little off. They'd shown up out of nowhere in a town where everyone knows everybody and had taken an interest in me, of all people. No one took an interest in the crazy, sad girl of Saint Andrews. His energy was unparalleled to anything I'd felt before. Well, except the darkness that had followed me home the other night and scared me half to death.

"Just a hunch. If you aren't actually a figment of my imagination, and I'm pretty sure you aren't, then who's to say what else might be out there?"

"What, like the supernatural?" Freyja asked.

"Technically speaking, you are supernatural, my dear sister," I pointed out. "They aren't ghosts. That I know for sure, but there's all kinds of lore out there. Some of it has to be based in reality, right?"

I'd all but given up on the hope that there was some higher being out there that determined my fate or happiness, but I also couldn't help believing in the vastness of the universe when I looked up into the night sky. So often I'd found my hope in the stars when everything was quiet and still.

"It's okay to hope, Zo," she conceded, seemingly on board with the paranormal theory.

I acknowledged I could actually be losing my mind right now. My grip on reality was such a delicate thing, but I felt the conviction in my heart, nonetheless. For once, I decided to believe in that instead of the doubt that tried to take over.

I gulped down another swig of coffee as I surveyed the lunacy around me. If any of the lore was to be believed, I could rule out vampires, since Elvy was so fond of sunlight. I couldn't entirely rule out werewolves, but it didn't feel right, either. The Apollo theory was feeling more accurate by the minute. Then there was the Fae or Folk. That could be a possibility, but I was fairly sure I would've noticed pointed ears. None of the books had said anything significant about star tattoos or silver hair. Maybe a fallen angel, but that was just a complete guess.

"I don't suppose you have some insight into this?" I asked curiously. "You know, since you exist between both realms of life and death."

Freyja only stared back at me, as if willing me to ask her anything else.

"You know something," I stated.

She only continued staring back, challenging me.

"But you can't tell me," I suggested.

She gave a slight nod and continued scanning the scattered mess of papers. I'd never given much thought to where Freyja went when she wasn't with me. I'd just assumed it was *beyond*. I was also frequently trying to understand if she was real or part of my subconscious speaking to me, so trying to unravel the dynamics of the afterlife had not been on my priority list. She and I had come to an unsaid understanding that I wouldn't pry about where she went, and I wouldn't press so long as she kept coming back. For argument's sake, let's say she was real; I wondered if the world of the dead had rules to follow, too.

As far as Elvy and his group, I had little to go on. I knew that they all had matching star tattoos. I knew the group felt *off*, and they *may* have some baffling healing abilities. The more I sat here thinking about it, the more I felt like I was indeed absurd. So what if his group had matching tattoos? A lot of organizations distinguished themselves this way.

Right, but the average club didn't go around miraculously saving sea turtles.

No longer willing to argue with myself, I had to acknowledge that there was a yearning and tugging in my chest that told my intuition I was onto something.

"I think I need some air," I said, standing up and stretching for the first time in hours.

Freyja, Jelly, and I walked along the boardwalk on the pier, checking out the vendors selling mostly tourist souvenirs. I hadn't done this in ages, and it felt nice to do a non-sequential human activity. Amongst the street sellers sat an older woman, skin weathered by the sun, with hair so black it looked almost purple.

In front of her sat an upturned wooden crate with a stack of cards on the side. I'd never been one to want a reading or mess with fate, but I was curious. I felt a tug towards her as if she'd been waiting for me.

"Free reading?" she asked as I approached her a bit warily. Jelly and Freyja didn't seem bothered by her presence.

"I don't mind paying," I answered.

"First one is on the house," the older lady answered.

She put away her cards and asked me to show her my palms. I gently sat down on the pillow on the opposite side of her, allowing her to take my hands. As always, I was a little self-conscious of my jagged scar, but the woman didn't seem to pay much attention to it.

She closed her eyes and became so still it was almost unnerving. The wind blew through her inky hair, and I focused on the sound of the ocean, breathing to the crash of the waves on the shore.

Her dark eyes opened to find me waiting, eager to hear what she had to say.

"Discernment's blood is part of you, a gift from the master of spirit itself. The elixir of life's breath cannot fully manifest without the other. There is conflict within you as light moves through and around you, but the darkness is above and anchoring you. One creates while the other shows the way to destiny. The stars demand a choice to be made, but your path is unclear. Forged in a true act of embrace, the course can mend that which was broken. Be warned, without true creed, defying the celestials will end in eternal darkness."

With those alarming words, she dropped her hands and her empty eyes held mine.

"What does all of that mean?" I questioned. It felt a little mad to believe a word this lady just told me. I glanced at Freyja, who was staring off into the distance, biting her lower lip in thought.

"The stars do not tell me such things," the woman answered.

"What about dreams? Can they tell you the future?"

"Do not ask me what is already convicted in you, child of the cosmos. My words cannot assuage the truth."

I knew I'd get no further information from the gypsy woman, and her words rang true to the deepest crevices of my soul.

"Thank you for your gift," I said with a nod of my head, wondering what she'd meant by "child of the cosmos."

I seared every word into my mind. I didn't know how it related to what I was experiencing, but it was more information than I had this morning, though I was left with more questions now.

A conflict within me, and I would have to make a choice. The elixir of life and eternal darkness? What a vast contradiction. And what about my blood? I quickly gathered my journal from my pack and wrote her words down to further analyze later. I wondered what Emma's opinions of fortune tellers were. I doubt she'd find them reliable sources of information or healthy influences on my fragile mind.

When Jelly and I arrived back at the small sea cottage, an envelope was wedged into the door. Freyja had gone her own way after the gypsy's revelation, despite my protests. You can't really argue with a ghost, apparently.

Slashing the note free, a small smile played across my lips. It was from Elvy.

I came by the rescue earlier to ask you to dinner. June seemed to think it was a great idea and gave me your address. I'm thinking I'd like to see you tonight. If you're thinking the same, meet me at Maggie's at 8. I hope to see you soon.

E

I'd have words with June about this. It was unlike her to do something like this, but I knew without hesitation I'd go to him tonight. The tug in my chest was too strong, and the sensation that I was just on the verge of a major revelation was overwhelming. I didn't know what tonight might hold, but I was determined to face it head on.

I had an hour to get ready to head to Maggie's, a well-known local joint with the best seafood in town. It had one of those vibes that stood the test of time despite its heavily outdated interior needing some TLC. There was live music every night it was opened and you could always count on the food being fresh. I slipped on some sturdy jeans and a nicer black top. It would not hide my scarred arm, and I felt content with that. I loosened my long hair from its usual braid, letting the waves flow down to my waist. I intentionally left my headphones behind and motioned Jelly to follow me into this new moment.

Jelly and I made the short walk to Maggie's and found Elvy there waiting outside. I stifled a small laugh as I noted our matching outfits. He wore jeans and a black t-shirt that left little to the imagination of what his physique underneath looked like. Not that I hadn't memorized it by now, watching it work in the Florida sun during the games.

"Zoe," he said with a breathtaking smile on his lips.

"Elvy," I nodded in return.

"I'm glad you came," he said sincerely.

"Did you ever have any doubt?"

"Doubt—maybe. Hope—endlessly," he said, taking a step closer to me. "Shall we?"

Elvy led us to a table outside with a view of the dark ocean, but it was still positioned to provide some privacy. The ocean acted as a mirror to the stars and full moon above. I ordered my usual water with lemon and crab claws for the appetizer. I tossed on a black coffee as well because I had a feeling it was going to be one of those nights. He seemed to follow my lead and ordered water, too. Jelly lay between my legs on the floor, understanding that she was at work.

"So, any specific reason you asked me here tonight?" I asked, inclining my head.

"Must I have a reason... I thought we'd just get to know each other," he stated simply, running a hand through his curly hair. "For instance, you ordered coffee at 8 o'clock at night. Won't that keep you from sleeping?"

"I'm a little supernatural when it comes to coffee. I drink it as much as I drink water, probably. So, no. It won't keep me awake. And—" I hesitated for a moment, but plunged forward, wanting to get this out of the way. "I've always been a coffee drinker, but I started drinking it a lot more after I stopped drinking alcohol."

"You don't have to explain," he said patiently.

"There's nothing to explain, really. I just didn't always make the best choices with it."

"Thank you for sharing that with me. I get it. I much prefer getting drunk on other things myself," he said, eyes serious and mischievous at the same time.

I hadn't gone on a date in years. Well, I wasn't entirely sure this was a date, but it certainly felt like one. I wasn't sure if that had been too much information, but he didn't seem bothered by it. I felt like we were well past holding back with each other at this point.

"So, your friends, how do you know them?" I asked, changing the subject.

"We go way back," he answered easily. "They're my family. That's the best way to think of them. My most trusted confidants. Blaz, I've known for most of my entire existence. Imelda and Clodovea found me in a bad way many years ago, after I'd lost someone close to me. Delmira and Finnian, I've worked with for a long time."

"Are they close by now?" I asked, suspecting the answer. I noted the phrasing of his words 'entire existence' instead of 'my life' and stored it away for later.

"Yes. They follow me like shadows," he said, laughing at something I didn't understand.

"What brings you to Saint Andrews? I don't think I've ever seen you before."

If he noticed the few local glances that went my way and down to my arm, he didn't give it away. I briefly felt a hint of shame flow through me, but I swallowed it down with determination to stay present in this moment.

"You," he said, as if that was supposed to be a socially acceptable response.

I looked at him, dumbfounded. I'd expected a bullshit answer, something vague and without meaning. Maybe Emma was onto something about vulnerability.

"I'll never lie to you, Zoe. You are free to make your own choice about believing it or not."

There was that word again. Choice. I had a feeling this was one of those moments that would go down in my personal history book. I wanted to remember this moment of mine and protect it from my fragile reality.

"Thank you for your honesty," I said finally.

"You must have questions," he insisted.

I did have questions, but I didn't know where to start. I closed my eyes, ensuring the ocean was crashing around me. I was not dreaming. This was real. I glanced up at the moon, praying to whomever was up there that they were with me.

"You'll tell the truth?"

"I will."

"Did you really need June to know where I lived?"

"In truth—no. I already knew before she told me."

I swallowed, weighing how I truly felt about that. For some reason, I did not fear him.

"What if my questions make you scared of me?" I questioned.

"They won't. I could never be afraid of you, Zo. Maybe *for* you, but never *of* you."

I paused for only a moment at the way I enjoyed him shortening my name.

"Are you human, like me?" I asked.

"No, I'm not."

"Are you a ghost?"

This garnered a deep laugh.

"No, Zoe, I'm not a ghost. My flesh is as warm as yours."

He held out his right hand to prove a point. I cautiously grabbed his calloused hand in mine, basking in the warmth it provided. Safety. A touch I didn't fear. The buzz of the crowd went away, and then it was just us.

As soon as he pulled his hand away, it was like waking up from a dream, and I was painfully reminded that I was in public.

"That is unusual," he murmured to himself, almost in a whisper. He'd noticed it too.

"I don't suppose you'll just tell me what you are?"

"It's not that I want to keep it from you. Some truths are better left revealed in time. But I must ask. Why was a ghost your first guess?"

As if on cue, I heard Freyja breathe a laugh beside me, but I knew she didn't stay. I somehow managed to not flinch at the interruption. I wondered what Elvy would think of me seeing my dead sister. If he would not lie to me, maybe I could learn to trust him. Maybe I could tell him a dark truth of mine that no one but Emma knew.

"I sometimes see and talk to my sister, Freyja."

"Why is that so odd?" he asked.

"She's been dead for a while now."

He didn't balk at my words. Elvy didn't mock me or call me crazy. He just continued with the conversation as normal. Perhaps that should have been a glaring red flag, but it wasn't for me.

"Was she important to you?"

"She's the most important," I stated firmly.

"Then I wish I could have met her," he said sincerely.

I hadn't realized we were leaning closer to each other until he reached for my arm—my scarred arm. I steeled myself into a statue. No one had touched it since it healed from my life saving surgery.

"May I?" he asked, before proceeding.

I couldn't speak, so I just nodded, praying I wouldn't go into a panic attack. His touch did trigger me, but not in the way a panic attack did. He gently caressed my arm in his and lightly moved down the length of the scar, pausing at the edge of my wrist. I felt cold and warm all at the same time as my mind tried to keep up with what my body was emitting.

"You're beautiful," he stated. "So painfully lovely."

I wanted to look away. Shying from compliments was something I'd grown familiar with. I was equally unnerved by the unabashed attention he was giving me. He looked at me like he really saw me... and liked what he found. The sincerity in his expression kept me looking at him, desiring the comfort of his gray eyes on me. The tug in my chest grew deeper, and I knew the absence of him in my life would crush me. I wanted to chastise myself for feeling this way, but the Zoe who used to repel from the summit of mountains always leaped towards the unknown. Fear wasn't in her vocabulary.

I needed to know him. Whomever or whatever he was. Enduringly, to whatever future.

"I am sorry you have experienced this kind of pain in your life. I would like to know the soul who is more than this," he said gently, tracing the scar.

"It's been a long time since I thought about anything else," I admitted. "But ever since you came colliding into my life, I've started to remember what it was like to live freely."

"I believe you are in there," he said. "I see you, Zoe, and I want to know you."

Hesitating only a breath longer, I started telling him about my moments. I described the way I longed for grass beneath my bare feet and the magical imagination of the kids Freyja and I once were. I told him about the time I'd gotten hopelessly lost in Athens, Greece, and many more stories of wrong turns that somehow ended up right. Most of all, I told him about how I missed the exhilaration of the wind in my face and the stillness that came with parasailing or windsurfing. His eyes seemed to light up at that.

He would occasionally pause and ask a clarifying question. Mostly, he just let me talk, and he simply listened. It'd been so long since I'd invited someone to know me, and it felt almost thrilling to have a connection again. I got so lost in my light that I didn't go into my darkness or even think about it, and he didn't ask. I forgot about my original mission this morning of learning the mystery behind Elvy and just let myself be fully present with him. I didn't need to know that part of him, not tonight.

For the rest of the night, we talked about our favorite foods, smells, and everything in between. Each craving more information about the other, as if we could not get enough of it. No panic attacks came that night, and I noticed no tension in my muscles, no constant surveying of exits. I wouldn't say I felt free, but I felt light.

Elvy walked me back to my house on the beach after we were finished, and for the first time in my life, I wanted someone in my safe space, in my home, but he didn't pry. I fumbled with my keys as I turned to face him.

"I felt like I did most of the talking tonight," I mentioned.

"I think I know a solution to that," he answered, smiling playfully. "I'd like to take you for coffee in the morning, and I'll do all the talking if you'd like."

"I'm thinking this is all a dream," I whispered, closing my eyes and stretching my ears to the crest of the waves in the near distance.

I felt him move closer without opening my eyes. My body seemed to be attuned to him now. He cradled my head in his palm, gently stroking the dimple in my right cheek.

"What a wonderful dream, Zoe."

My heart fluttered as I thought of his lips pressing against mine. Before I could fully form the thought, my feet stepped back. I opened my eyes with an apology ready on my lips.

"Good night, Zoe," he said softly, stopping me.

"Good night, Elvy," I said, closing the door behind me.

Jelly nudged my legs, urging me to sit down, and I plopped onto the floor, leaning my back against the front door.

"What have we gotten ourselves into, girl?" I asked, while scratching behind her ears. Jelly's only response was to place her forehead against mine, giving me the level ground I needed to keep pressing on.

5

Flying

Elvy and I walked side by side on the pier with all the vendors, which was the same place I'd received my reading from the older woman. We walked close enough to one another that the occasional brush of our fingers sent me stirring every time I felt a whisper of his skin on mine. I liked to think I noticed the same reaction in him.

I sipped my cup of coffee, gazing in wonder at this perfectly normal moment.

"What are you thinking?" he asked.

"I thought I was the one asking questions today," I teased.

"Of course," he conceded. "What would you like to know?"

"If I guessed what you were, would you tell me?"

"You won't," he said, pausing. "Would knowing what I am change things?"

"No," I answered firmly. "Sometimes, I even forget that you aren't human."

"It's not just my story to protect. There are greater works, far more powerful than you can imagine. A part of me feels guilty for disrupting your life."

"That's not up to you," I pointed out. "I get to decide what I can handle."

"I can't protect you from what's coming, Zoe," he answered, frustration written on his face, lips pressed together.

"If I've learned anything, Elvy, it's standing on my own two feet. Keeping the truth from me could do more harm than good."

"You still have time. We can still have today."

I sighed, resigned to know that he wouldn't let up right now, but we both knew that could change at any moment. I redirected the conversation back to him, and he obliged my less intense curiosities. He explained that the smell of rain, just as it was about to fall, was his favorite, but that he loved the feel of the sun on his skin even more. He spoke about the sun as if it was something just out of reach for him, which made me laugh because, to me, he was the sun rising after a never-ending night.

The conversation paused as something caught his eye, and he left me while I examined a painting an artist was working on of the ocean. She must have gotten here at sunrise, as it looked like she was nearly finished. For a fleeting moment, I desired to truly dream again. To be creative. This was a feeling I'd thought I'd lost forever, but it was taking hold in my heart after all this time.

Elvy came back with a small wooden box about the size of my hand and mischief in his eyes.

"For you," he said casually.

I took the box from him and opened it excitedly. I couldn't remember the last time I'd been given anything from anyone who wasn't blood related.

Inside the box was a simple brass necklace with a flat coin sized pendant that depicted a colorful constellation and a bright star in the middle over the sea. It was beautiful.

"Can you help me put it on?" I asked, sweeping my long, braided hair back to allow him access. I froze as the realization of my offer dawned on me. I'd freely offered my neck to him, which was something I hadn't done since long before that dreadful night. Focusing on my breathing, I stayed in the moment with him.

He carefully snapped the necklace in place, careful not to come in contact with my skin. How did he know not to do that? Could he possibly be that observant?

"Thank you," I said, turning to face him.

"What do you want to do today?"

"I think I'd like to meet your friends."

"I was hoping you'd say that."

"Maybe they'll actually tell me something useful," I said, hopefully.

"I wouldn't count on it."

Elvy lit up with a brilliant smile. He wanted me a part of his world too, whether he or I wanted to acknowledge that yet or not. He grabbed my hand, leading me down the pier, closer to the ocean. I knew where we were going as the familiar setting greeted me. We were back at the volleyball courts where his friends were casually playing a game with each other.

They seemed to sense his presence and stopped what they were doing to greet us.

"It's nice to see you again," Delmira said with a knowing smile. "I've been pestering him about it for weeks." Her lavender hair seemed to lighten in the rays of the sun. Everyone seemed happy to have me here, as if I belonged.

"Weeks?" I asked, brow risen.

"Delm," Elvy cautioned. "We don't want to bombard Zoe."

"Little ole us, Elvy?" Blaz said teasingly. "You don't find us intimidating, do you, Zoe?"

"Not at all," I answered a little too quickly.

Before Blaz responded, the nauseous feeling flooded me, and sent me to my knees. *Shit.*

I whipped around, searching, yet praying that it would go away. It was the same feeling I'd had the night something chased me home. Jelly, sensing my unease, let off a warning growl with hackles raised. She couldn't seem to pinpoint where the threat was coming from, either. I clung to her fur and tried to focus on deep breaths.

Elvy stepped in front of me with Delmira to his right and Clodovea to the left. Imelda, Finnian, and Blaz created a crescent moon along our backs. Jelly and I were in the center and protected on all fronts. I wanted to speak, but I was petrified to breathe too loudly.

"Breathe, Zoe," Elvy whispered. "Focus."

I listened and shut out the noise of the crowds, thankful I had plenty of experience in doing this already. Pushing back on the sound of the ocean, I focused on the feeling in my gut screaming at me to run and hide. Against my instincts, I ordered my mind to cling to the feeling of sickness instead of running from it. I couldn't explain it, but I had a feeling it would lead me to what I was looking for. I may not look like much, but I'd made a vow to never be weak again. A fight was not something I would easily shy away from.

The air was so tense I felt like I might suffocate, but I held resolute.

Dark spots were clouding my vision, which meant passing out was soon to follow. Amongst the dots, a path of flowing light seemed to ebb in and out of focus along the sand that had definitely not been there a second ago. I had to be hallucinating, but I couldn't tell for sure.

"There," I said, pointing in the direction I thought I'd seen the light.

"Delmira, take Zoe back to the house. Imelda, Finnian, flank them. Blaz, with me."

"No," I stated. Sweat was pooling in my eyes and the world was spinning.

"Zoe, let go. It's not a weakness to survive today to fight tomorrow."

I held back the bite I wanted to lash out.

"Now or never, Zo," Elvy said as he wiped the wayward hairs from my eyes.

If I wasn't on the verge of fainting, I would've argued. I didn't want to be separated from him, this wild man I'd just come to know. What if I woke up, and this was all a dream?

"I still see you," he whispered so low that only I would hear him. "You always have a choice, Zoe. If you don't go with them, then I'll stay with you. Tell me."

"Go," I whispered, barely able to keep my eyes open now. "I can't hold on much longer," I admitted.

"You don't have to hold on anymore. We can take it from here," he answered, eyes pleading for me to rest, but I knew he would carry me on his back if that's what I desired.

"I'll go with them, Elvy."

Delmira outstretched her arms as if to cradle me like a small child. I knew she was asking permission, and I mustered a nod before collapsing in her arms. I was only partially aware that Imelda and Finnian collected Jelly before my eyes gave into the lull of the draining of my body.

Then, I was flying. At least, I thought I was flying. I strained to hear the ocean to see if this was real, but the sound of air whipping all around me proved too loud. My heart pounded as I tried to get my bearings, but I knew I was only moments away from succumbing to my exhaustion. The last thought before I closed my eyes was of Elvy and the fear of losing the ember of hope he had diligently been stoking since I'd first laid eyes on him.

***

What felt like days later but couldn't possibly be, I woke up in an unfamiliar room. I sensed that I wasn't alone, and my heart began a rapid ascent as I recalled the moments before I blacked out. The familiar warm body of Jelly lying beside me calmed those racing thoughts. Jelly was at ease, and that allowed me to relax some. I glanced around, still fearful of being in a foreign place.

I was in a large open room with windows for walls. I could see the ocean for miles and realized with a start that I had to be in the lighthouse to the north of my bungalow. There were no buildings tall enough to be anything else. There was a kitchen in the center of the room with modern features and a living area where I currently laid on a teal blue couch. This place looked lived in and well loved. I dropped the remaining tension from my shoulders and surveyed the outside. I could see my home off in the distance, and I didn't know if the shudder that blasted through me was pleasure or not.

"You're awake," Elvy said.

"And all in one piece," I answered. "And you?"

It took every inch of self-control to not run into his arms to check for any injuries. I stood firm, holding my breath for an answer.

"I'm okay," he assured. "So are the rest."

"Where are they?" I asked curiously.

"They'll be back soon. I wanted to speak with you alone first."

He started walking closer to me with hands raised, as if he might scare a wild animal. I wasn't running, though. I stayed still as a statue until he reached me. He gently lifted my scarred arm, tracing the lines up and down. Where he touched, my skin burned gloriously. I couldn't help the tremor that shot through my legs. I expected a laugh from him, but none came. He seemed to be trembling, too.

Life was about moments, right? This one, I could live in infinitely.

"Who are you?" I asked, a mirror to the first thing I ever said to him. The underlying message sounded more like, *"Where have you been?"*

"I'm Elvy," he answered, as he continued stroking my arm. "And I've been waiting a very long time to find you."

"I think I need to sit back down," I said between labored breaths.

He helped prop me up on the pillows but did not stop touching me, which I only welcomed, defying all the odds against me.

"Whatever you're holding back, tell me. I'm in this," I said, my face serious.

"I can see that," he agreed. "It seems some external *complications* are forcing my hand." He seemed to almost snarl at the word.

"Then maybe you should quit fighting it," I pointed out.

"I want you to know that if you do not like what I tell you, you can leave at any time. No questions asked. My family and I will leave your life for good if that is the choice you make."

I clung to the star pendant on the necklace he'd given me just earlier today. I listened closely to the waves. This was real. I was safe. I could be whole again. Good things could happen to me. Emma and I had gone over developing trusting relationships over and over again. I didn't think this is quite what she meant, but that was only semantics.

"Thank you for that, really, but there's no moving forward without taking the first step. Today proved that keeping me in the dark could put me in more danger."

He must have sent a silent signal because the rest of his friends appeared through the trapdoor on the floor. In this small space, their presence filled the room to an almost suffocating level. Elvy and I remained alone on one couch with Jelly. Blaz sunk down in the gray beanbag chair on the other side of me. Delmira and Finnian claimed the other teal couch while Imelda laid her head in Clodovea's lap on the floor.

"It's not only my story to tell," Elvy said, waving to his companions. "If you don't mind?"

His family seemed to nod their heads in agreement.

"The universe is far more vast than most can imagine."

"The stars have always heard my hope in that," I replied.

"Sometimes, the stars talk back, Zoe Eferhild."

6

The Shadowed

"We are the Shadowed," Elvy started, motioning towards his friends. "We come from the land of Lyra."

I racked my brain around that name. Apart from some vague memories in the astrology books I'd read, it didn't ring any significant bells. Neither did the term Shadowed.

"It wouldn't be anything you know of, Zoe," Elvy stated, answering my own thoughts. "It's a separate realm from the world you know of as Earth. We hail from the Court of Vega under the Kingdom of Canis, which Lyra is a part of; what humans know as one of the brightest stars in the northern hemisphere. We are born from it and serve it. In return Vega, our star and power source, brings us immortal life and extra abilities."

The crash of the ocean broke through the fear I felt building in my chest. Me, an ordinary human who could barely function on a daily basis, was sitting before beings from not just another planet, but a whole other realm. I took a steadying breath, filling my lungs with the comforting taste of ocean water and oxygen.

"I think I need a cup of coffee," I said seriously. Finnian handed me a cup from seemingly nowhere. I took a lingering warm gulp and nodded my head.

"Extra abilities—like healing?" I asked, thinking about the events I hadn't been able to explain away.

Elvy only nodded, not elaborating on how that was even possible. *One mystery solved at a time, Zoe.*

Seeing my resolve, he continued, "You are currently experiencing what we call *Emerging*." He methodically traced the scar on my arm. "You died on this night, Zoe."

It was a subject I never brought up. On the night I tried to end my life, I was feeling so many emotions at once that I just wanted to shut it all out. I couldn't take it anymore, and I was desperate to stop the flashbacks, to end the agony that they made me live after what those bastards had done. I didn't care that I still had parents or people that loved me. I only cared that the pain stopped and that I'd be reunited with Freyja, who I should have died with.

What I struggled to admit to myself was that at the moment the darkness was about to consume me, as I lay on the bathroom floor, I mourned what I'd just done. I wanted to live. I feverishly wanted to fight for just one more day, but I knew I was too late. The paramedics would not reach me in time to save me. I wish I'd been able to scream to them I wanted to live. I wanted to struggle every day if that was the price to keep breathing.

And then I did.

I'd woken up in the hospital in great pain from the surgery that had repaired what should have been a fatal injury. I don't remember my time between life and death. I shouldn't have ever woken up, but something had given me a second chance. Maybe that's why I took the abnormal in stride. My sister's ghost and now the Shadowed. I was living proof that the impossible is possible. Was it so hard to believe in Elvy?

No, I decided. It wasn't. I'd always fight to have my moments, my choices, and my life.

"Yes," I answered, returning to the present.

Elvy nodded knowingly. "When you were between worlds, your soul was gifted another life under the power of Vega, but Vega was not the only life source that touched your soul. The Court of Algol, whose powers come from the death star, also granted you rebirth. It is your choice to make in which path you follow."

"Why me?" I asked, voice shaking. I was struggling to wrap my head around everything he was saying, despite my willingness to believe him.

"Even I don't pretend to understand the ways of the celestials. But we think those who have endured the atrocities of their world and who have fighting spirits in death are at times granted rebirth from one of the ruling stars. It's yours to accept or decline. It's part of our destiny, the Shadowed, to help you on this path."

"People die every day, Elvy," I said, shaking my head, trying to grasp everything he was telling me. "And in a lot more honorable ways than what I did." I refused to shy away right now. Emma had challenged my self-loathing many times, but there was a piece of me that hated the path I'd chosen.

"It's not about how you died," Blaz said, handing me a fresh cup of coffee. "It's about how you *lived*."

My heart stilled as I was taken back to the feeling of standing on top of a mountain with the wind whipping my braid around, and the feel of dirt caked onto my arms after a brutal hike. The absolute joy and stillness as if the Earth had paused for just a moment for me to take it all in. That moment had felt so surreal. The spirit of a dreamer. That's who I was underneath it all.

I was Emerging. I could choose my path. I could choose life or death all over again.

"And if I defy the stars' gift?" I asked, guessing the answer.

"Then your mortal body will die," Elvy replied.

"When must the choice be made?" I asked.

"The Winter Solstice is the first day of your trials."

"Trials?" I asked nervously.

"It's part of the process of Emerging. The ultimate test of your spirit."

I had two months to make my choice. Two months to decide to accept my human fate and die or take a true leap into the unknown via the path of the powers of Vega or Algol.

"So, if you guys are from the Court of Vega, should I be expecting Shadowed from the Court of Algol?"

"Yes," Elvy stated, running a hand through his shaggy brown hair. His gray eyes gave himself away. He didn't seem to care for the idea of me meeting them. "They've already tried to contact you. Twice now."

I thought back to the feeling of despair after being chased to my house and at the beach just earlier today. Had that been the Court of Algol?

"Are they like you?" I asked.

"They are not like us," Delmira spat. "We are Earth's guardians."

"There is a balance in this world, Zoe. Light and darkness. Algol is shrouded in darkness. Vega is in the light. Neither is good nor bad, but fate saw potential for the Emergence in either gift for you."

"Why would anyone ever choose the darkness?"

"The darkness can be just as alluring, Zoe. The darkness is just as necessary and everlasting as the light. Mortal souls who have the capacity for greatness can also have the same potential for vengeance."

I understood what he meant. There were times that I'd thought about hunting them down. The men who had savagely assaulted me and killed my sister. I often smiled and fantasized about their blood dripping from a knife I'd just dragged through their guts. I desired that darkness all too well, and I knew how easily it could entice me to its side.

"You once told me that my fear could be forged," I said. "What did you mean?"

"You can let it forge your fury or your grace," he replied.

The words from the gypsy woman flashed through my mind. Maybe she wasn't full of it after all. It still didn't fully make sense, but things were falling together more now than they were. Algol and Vega seemed to be the stars that wanted me to make a choice. I tucked the information away to study later and continued on.

"Why are you called the Shadowed?"

"We can move between realms, through the shadows or the fissures that bind all worlds together, but not all immortals can."

"You're their leader," I stated.

"Elvy is Lord Astral of the Court of Vega and commander of the Vega Shadowed Legion," Delmira said, with pride in her voice. "And we have sworn to serve him and protect the peace of realms."

I believed every conviction in her voice. She would die, throwing herself in front of anyone that might harm her Lord Astral.

"And Delmira is my second," Elvy stated with matched intensity. "Clodovea is third in command. All five here are part of my immediate court, the Luminaries. My advisors and generals. Imelda, Blaz, and Finnian are my emissaries to the other three ruling courts in Canis."

"And is it typical for a Lord Astral to come meet a new Emerging?" I asked, already suspecting the answer.

"No, Zoe, it is not," he said, gripping my hand firmly, tethering me to this fantastical reality. I didn't pretend to understand much of anything he said, but I didn't doubt him either. Whispers of what the gypsy woman said flooded through my mind again. I definitely regretted not, at least, tipping her.

It was a miracle that I was sitting here, breathing, living. It wasn't hard for me to believe and accept that there was more to this life than what was so easily seen. In fact, every breath I took was a sign that something greater lurked in the vastness of the stars above. Books were for the dreamers of this world, and here I sat, in the greatest story never told—in *my moment*.

All eyes were on me as I took in the magnitude of the Shadowed.

I had a thousand questions, but I didn't know which to ask as I tried to keep up with the complete change of my life. If Elvy was this Lord Astral, what was so special about me that he would leave his court and realm to help me on this journey? I felt so small, so insignificant amongst the six faces studying me. I needed to feel *human* for a minute, so I reached down to scratch Jelly's ears, wondering what she would say if she could speak.

"I need a moment," I conceded, as I made my way to the sounds of the ocean waiting to greet me outside on the balcony.

Elvy only nodded and leaned back, sinking into the couch further, allowing me my space. I desperately needed to hear the ocean and let the saltwater air around me fill my lungs. No one followed me outside, which I was grateful for.

However, my solitude didn't last long. Freyja stood beside me, grabbing my trembling hand, which rested on the flaking railing. I embraced the familiar gesture of my sister with questions in my eyes.

"Did you know about this?" I asked her. It wasn't accusatory.

"Yes," she answered. "But I'm bound by the rules to a power far greater than you can possibly understand. We have a gag order on telling mortal souls what is beyond. But I knew Elvy could help you."

"That's why you kept pushing me to talk to him," I said with understanding.

"Among other things."

"You're real," I said with finality.

"Did you ever really doubt that?"

"Never in my heart," I whispered.

"I'm so proud of you, Zo."

"Freyja," I began. "If I can be reborn into an immortal despite all the shit, do you think we could do the same for you?"

She squeezed my hand with tears in her eyes. My heart sank at the sadness I found there.

"No, Zoe. My soul belongs to the spirit world." She paused, as if struggling to find the right words. "My life was taken by someone else, not given in the pain and sorrow you felt. Do not feel sorry for me. This is where I was always meant to be. You are on the right path now. That's all that matters."

"Not all that matters," I challenged.

That deep, shameful part of me wanted to envelop me. Knowing that I had this chance, and she didn't because some star decided so enraged me. If anything, Freyja had been more full of life than I had. She was always the more selfless one and the one people looked up to.

"I know what you're thinking. And don't you dare think for one minute that you aren't good enough. If I had lived and you had died that night, I don't know that I would've made a different choice. You did what you felt would help you survive. As for me... you don't know everything, Zoe, so don't be a martyr for me."

"I should have been stronger for you."

"Stop right now, Zoe. It was my idea to go out that night. It was me who pushed you to do something you were uncomfortable with. We should never have been there. I appreciate that you've glossed over all of that, but that is for me to shoulder. Not you. You don't get to take on that burden for me."

Her words cut me deep. If she'd suffered, I wouldn't have known it by the way she seemed to live her life. I didn't agree with what she said now; however, I would honor her.

"So, what do I do?" I asked.

"Live, Zoe," Freyja said, disappearing into thin air.

I was *Emerging*. A broken, human girl, barely an adult in the eyes of the law, and some other world that I still had no concept of understanding, saw my soul and recognized its value—*my value*. I'd never felt like I belonged in this world, and maybe there was a reason for that.

"Are you okay?" Elvy asked, dragging me from my inner turmoil.

"I think so," I croaked out.

He joined me on the balcony, gazing at the sun brushing against the ocean. Lord Astral. I was standing next to probably one of the most powerful beings of the universe, and he'd come searching for me. I flushed, feeling oddly satisfied against the weight of how large this galaxy was.

"Do you want to go home?"

"Not yet. I have more questions," I answered.

"I'd expect so."

"Did all immortals used to be mortals?"

"No. Most of our bloodlines come directly from Vega."

"And you?" I asked, realizing that my Emergence might be rarer than I thought.

"I had immortal parents. My bloodline has held the Lord Astral title since its conception," he answered, looking as if he was remembering something from a long time ago.

"Had?"

"They died," he said firmly. The stiffness of his posture gave away how hard this subject was for him.

I'd hate to think what could kill something that was supposed to live as long as an immortal. Even more, I despised the hurt in his eyes. I felt protective of him and knew I would go to great lengths to be there for him.

I decided that was enough questions for the day.

"I'm thinking," he started. "That I'd like to show you something."

"I'm not sure how many more world-shattering things I can take in a single day, Elvy," I said seriously.

He led me back down the lighthouse to the private, rocky beach it rested on. The waves were roaring into the rocks as a storm brewed in the distance. Jelly stayed behind with the others.

"I'd like to show you my true form. Well, the most a mortal can see anyway," he stated. "If you are okay with that, of course."

I only nodded, bracing for whatever might come.

He tossed his shirt to the ground and closed his eyes. I rested my gaze on his face, even though I felt my eyes wanting to wander. He seemed to remove a glamor around my eyes while willing his true form into this realm at the same time. As he appeared to grow a foot in the blink of an eye, breathtaking wings sprouted from his back. The wings looked almost translucent, as if water was flowing through them. I silently wondered if my hand would become wet if I touched them.

Black tattoos slowly formed across his firm chest and down both the lengths of his muscled arms. Across his chest, the tattoos depicted five stars that connected to one larger star, and other constellations flowed down his arms. When he opened his eyes, they were more otherworldly than I'd ever seen. It was as if his eyes held a sea storm in them, becoming more of a rich blue-gray, but he was still Elvy.

My mouth parted as I took in the one who had come for me. I hadn't craved someone's touch in so long, and I realized just how lonely I'd been. I slowly lifted my scarred arm, such a juxtaposition to his ethereal beauty, and traced the tattoo, beginning at the eight-point star on his wrist. He held his towering frame as still as the rocks beneath us and let me explore his true form. I traced my fingers up his bicep and let my hand rest where I felt the warmth of his beating heart beneath his skin.

"Is this my future?" I asked, breathlessly.

"If you want it to be," he answered.

Uncomfortable with the intensity of his gaze, a smile crept on my lips as I thought back to the occult books still sprawled out on my living room floor.

"So, you're definitely not a vampire?"

Elvy roared with laughter, and I loved that sound.

"Are you very disappointed?" he asked.

"No," I answered honestly. "I don't suppose you'd tell me if they were real?"

"There's some truth to every myth, Zoe. I would not call them that though, no."

"I also thought maybe Elf or Fae," I teased him. "Like maybe your name was some giant hint."

"Those guesses are at least closer to the truth than a blood-sucking creature," he continued, laughing. He tucked his hair behind his ears as if making a point to show they were not elongated.

His hands hovered over my hips, and his eyes asked a question. I nodded eagerly, desiring the feel of him on me.

"We are the stars and the stars are us. Some would say we are just mortals who have achieved a higher level of consciousness. At one time, we would have been much like you are now."

"So you're an alien," I joked.

"Technically, that's not wrong," he said, amused.

"I've always loved the stars," I admitted. "I actually dreamed of getting abducted by an alien when I was a kid. I was so convinced that they were real, I persuaded my grandma to take me camping in the desert in New Mexico for several nights, but we didn't see so much as a flying saucer."

"Wait until you see how realm travel really works. Much cooler than spaceships."

"Eh, at least the stars granted me a handsome alien," I said, laughing.

"You're really taking this in stride, aren't you?"

"Laughter is the best medicine, right? Don't worry, I'm sure I'll freak out, eventually."

"That would be normal," he agreed.

"I'd like to see what these feel like," I said, motioning towards his outstretched wings.

He brought his angel-like wings closer, as if cocooning us around our small but perfect moment. Cautiously, I reached out to trace his gigantic wings. As my fingers made contact, I felt a tremble escape Elvy's resolve. They didn't feel wet at all, but still held that same watery glow that was feather light.

"That feels... nice," he whispered, as he brought my exploring hand back down to his chest.

"Is this what I'll look like?"

"Only the Shadowed have wings and these," he said, motioning towards his tattoos and streaks of silvery hair. "But if you become Shadowed, your wings will look similar. Vega is the life source for the water element and we are bound to it."

"You can manipulate water?"

"Water is not a power to manipulate, Zoe," he answered, placing a finger over my lips. "No more questions. Let's see how wild you really are."

The crashing sound of the waves sounded in the distance. This was real. I was safe. I smiled that the star who had found me worthy of life was connected to the water just as much as I was. Maybe this was my fate.

He outstretched his hands in question. Understanding what he wanted, I nodded and allowed him to pick me up in his arms. In what felt like less than a second, we were soaring above the ocean, flying so close we could feel the mist splashing our faces. My heart pounded so joyfully that it almost hurt.

Freedom. I would savor every moment of this life. A seductive feeling of darkness shivered through me, reminding me I could choose a different path—that I might want to give in at the right opportunity. I shoved the thought away, determined to choose the light. I owed it to not only myself, but to every human being who thought they weren't worth the fight. If I accepted this immortal life, I knew my mission would be to heal the suffering—to help others find hope. To live a life where they could dream as large as they wanted to and believe those dreams as possible.

We could've been flying for days, and I wouldn't have cared. I noticed I did not squirm or cringe where Elvy held me in his embrace. In fact, I welcomed it. I lifted my eyes to find him gazing back at me, as if in awe of what was in front of him. Much too soon, he landed us back on the balcony of the lighthouse, never taking those gray eyes off the pale green of mine.

"You have work tomorrow?" he asked.

It took me a moment to realize what day it was. I did have work tomorrow, and therapy.

"Yes," I answered.

"Let's get you home then. It's getting late."

The sun was setting around us; the sky creating a painting of oranges and purples.

"Can we watch the sun go down?" I asked, wanting to prolong the moment.

"I'll watch as many sunsets with you for as long as you'll have me," he promised.

I felt a burning deep down in my soul that clung to those words like a prayer. I leaned my shoulders against his chest, allowing him to wrap his arms around me as we watched the sun sink below the horizon. We stayed like that until the moon graced us with her presence and the stars filled the night sky as if to welcome me home.

"The wonder of it all," he murmured, placing a gentle kiss in my hair.

7

Encounter

Work had been a blur of cleaning up after animals and assisting Dr. Malik with the patients that still required physical therapy. I occasionally found myself wondering if being connected to Vega and the power source for the water element would also connect me with the creatures that lived there. It certainly had with Elvy.

It felt odd to do something as mundane as working, but I welcomed the normalcy of showing up and getting my hands dirty. I fondly listened to the rumblings of old June. This didn't mean that I'd pushed my new reality aside by any means.

When I was certain no one else was around, I tried to see if I could do the same thing Elvy had with the animals. After a few tries and feeling a little ridiculous, I decided I hadn't become a master of this new ability overnight, much to my disappointment.

After work, I nervously walked to Emma's office, unsure of what to tell her about my newfound predicament. I'd debated with myself into the night on whether I should cancel all together, but I hadn't been able to press send on any of the lame excuses I'd come up with. I knew Emma was open-minded. She'd proven that in the way she spoke with me about Freyja as if she was still alive. However, I'm not so sure she would quite jump on board with realms and star trials. I definitely would refrain from telling her I was an Emerging immortal. That might land me in a psychiatric ward, and I didn't have plans to go there today.

"You seem preoccupied with something today," Emma noted, as I picked a non-existent piece of lint off my jacket.

Understatement of the entire year.

I sat across from her on the couch while she sat casually in her chair, notepad, ready to dissect my every word. Jelly laid dutifully beside me. I twiddled my thumbs, refusing to make eye contact with her. I couldn't tell her about any of it without sounding completely mental, but I decided on one part that she actually might actually help with.

"I met someone," I said, deciding that was safe enough.

"Like a friend?"

"No... maybe. I'm not sure."

"I think this is the first time you've mentioned meeting someone since I've known you. This must be significant for you to tell me."

"I think it could be something big," I admitted, careful of how much I gave away.

"How have your anxiety levels been around him? Flashbacks?"

It was a fair enough question. We had determined touch to be a main trigger for my flashbacks and panic attacks. The budding of a new relationship typically involved all those things, or so I assumed. I wouldn't classify myself as an expert in the subject these days. Most of my previous experience was more fleeting and sensual than a genuine connection.

"I've actually been doing well on that. Less panic attacks and flashbacks. I noticed my shame came up a few times, but with him..."

Emma sat in silence, allowing me to form the thought on my own.

"With Elvy—it's like... effortless and feels right, cliché as that sounds."

"I'd like to acknowledge how wonderful it is to find this connection with someone," she began. "But I'd also caution you to make sure you feel whole on your own, too."

"I'm starting too," I admitted. "It's more like he's in my corner. A safe place to start trusting and expressing all that I am."

"What does he help you believe about yourself?"

I paused, thinking about the root of it all. How he'd chosen to empower me instead of fix or choose things for me. He'd seen past my shame when I couldn't. How he saw me for everything I am and everything I could be.

"That I'm worthy."

"Do you embrace that belief?"

"Right now, in this moment, yes. I think I do."

"Recovery isn't linear, Zoe. Sometimes, it's a literal roller coaster of twists and turns and sometimes even backwards. That's normal and more than okay."

"That checks out," I agreed, laughing.

"So, how do you see yourself navigating the physical or emotional things that might come up with this new person?"

"Um." I paused. "I haven't really gotten that far."

Sure, I'd thought about how his hands would feel on me—on *all* parts of me. Despite every truth he'd given me and I him, I still hadn't actually considered going that far. Even now, I wasn't sure I was capable of that level of intimacy, and it made me a little angry to know that longing had been ripped away from me.

Jelly nudged my clenched fists, forcing me to redirect my behavior.

"Well, let's think a little through that now, so you are ready to have that conversation if it happens. If you're comfortable with that," she added.

Was I really going to talk about my sex life with my therapist?

"Okay, where do we start with that?" I asked. Apparently, we were going there today. God, I wish I had a cup of coffee, an energy drink, or *something.*

"Let's talk about the basic boundaries. What touch is okay and what isn't okay?"

Emma brought out a laminated copy of a woman's body. We had done this exercise a few times before, but never got into the intimate details because I'd never had a reason to before now. I suddenly felt heat rushing to my cheeks, staining my skin pink. This seemed so silly. I knew nothing about immortals or really if Elvy was interested in that sort of thing, but his body language had indicated that he would indeed be intrigued by something like that.

"This is about you and your level of comfort," she said, seeing my hesitation.

I took a few deep diaphragm breaths like she'd taught me, and I circled the areas I thought I'd feel okay with and put X's on the ones that did not. The back of my neck seemed to be the primary no-go zone.

"And do you feel comfortable setting these boundaries?"

"I do with him," I answered, and I meant it.

She made a few notes on her pad and locked them away in her filing cabinet. I thanked her for the time and headed down to the coffee place near the beach with Jelly. I'd decided it was best to satisfy the caffeine craving.

I inhaled my frozen mocha so fast I winced at the brain freeze surfacing. After shaking it off, I stared at the vastness of the sea. I'd always found the ocean to be so infinite, but now it seemed small, measurable. If I let myself fully embrace the realm of Vega, Earth would probably feel tiny to me.

I found myself fantasizing about how it would feel to fly on my own and what my wings might look like when the wave of nausea flooded my senses. It came so fast and ferocious; I didn't even have time to think through my flight or fight response. Just as I turned around, a tall, dark figure was standing before me with a familiar sensation emitting from him.

He was an objectively handsome man who looked to be in his late twenties. Well, immortal, I assumed. His skin was several shades lighter than my sun-kissed skin, and his platinum blonde hair was a stark contrast to my own. I noted the streaks of gray spread throughout—the sign of a Shadowed. His piercing blue eyes were unnerving, and they were staring into my soul.

"Oleander," a familiar voice sounded, now standing beside me. Elvy and his Luminaries formed a circle around the figure, blocking his direct path to me.

"Ah, Elvy, it has been too long, brother," the stranger spoke.

"I'm not sure brother is entirely accurate," Elvy replied calmly.

"Maybe so, but you know the laws of the Emerging. I have just as much right to court our newest addition as the Lord Astral of Algol."

I had no intention of going anywhere with the one named Oleander. The nauseous feeling did not diminish, making it difficult to stand.

"Sorry about that, love," Oleander said directly to me, snapping his fingers. The sickness went away. "Algol has a cruel sense of humor. That sickness was a gift, though I'm afraid you haven't learned to use it yet."

He looked at me like that should've cleared things up.

"What do you mean?" I asked, wiping the sweat from my brow. Jelly circled protectively around me. Not that Oleander seemed to notice.

"A fiery one, you are," he observed. "You would be most welcome in the Court of Algol."

"Be quiet, poison," Delmira snarled.

"What did you take from me?" I asked, more sternly, ignoring Delmira. While I didn't particularly want to be sick, if it was a gift, I wanted it back.

"It's still there, Zoe Eferhild. I only tucked it away for a short while."

Elvy and the others were moving in closer, so smoothly it was hardly noticeable. I was feeling claustrophobic. As if sensing my unease, the Luminaries stopped with a nod of Elvy's head.

"I'm sure Elvy's told you there is a balance to the universe. A give and take, if you will. Algol seems to have gifted you with foresight. Sickness is the price paid for such a power while still in your mortal form. Ironic really," Oleander explained.

"Discernment," I breathed, remembering the leathery woman from the pier.

"You're smart, too," he noted.

"If I only get sick when bad things happen, what must that mean about you?" I questioned.

Oleander laughed comfortably. The lurking Court of Vega did not seem to concern him.

"Who said it was only when bad things happen? That, love, is because you are still Emerging; you don't know how to wield it yet. Discernment is neither good nor bad... I think it is telling, though, which path you will choose if Algol's gift is already manifesting this strongly."

Elvy's wings sprouted, but he remained where he was and silently ordered the rest to stay put. As far as I knew, no gift from Vega had manifested in me yet, and I wondered what it meant about me if Algol's was showing before Vega's.

"You know you cannot make this decision for her, Elvy," Oleander taunted.

"It's always been her choice," he replied, his stance never faltering.

"I have no intention of going anywhere with you," I said, finding my voice again.

Oleander only smiled at that and leaned in closer to me.

"You will, and I will welcome you with open arms despite your unpleasantness now," he said with a wink before walking away.

I hadn't realized I'd been holding my breath until I felt the exhale in my lungs. I looked around at my newfound friends, and their postures remained tense. Delmira, in particular, looked like she could tear through someone's flesh with her gaze alone.

"Calm, Delmira," Elvy ordered. "You know this is the way."

Blaz and Imelda were deep in conversation, planning the stars only know what. Finnian seemed to be calming his twin down with the help of Clodovea.

"Vega, help us all," Elvy muttered.

"I don't have to go anywhere with him, right?" I asked, eyes fearful.

"No," he stated. "But it's okay if you decide to change your mind."

I could tell he meant his word, but clearly it was difficult for him to admit this to me. Even if I knew nothing else about him, this confession alone endeared him to me. The tug towards him in my chest grew at that moment, and my desire to close the distance between us flourished through me.

"Do you know what Vega's intended gift for me is?" I nearly begged.

"It has remained hidden from me," he sighed, taking my hand. "Water is in all forms of life. We know it to be the breath of life. Your gift could be many things."

His words felt familiar to me, but my thoughts were racing too quickly to search for the connection.

“Elvy, how do I even go about making this choice?”

He guided me away from the bustling crowd of his friends and seemed to search for the words that would answer the question without freaking me out.

“If you choose to accept an immortal life, on the night of the Winter Solstice, you’ll go into a deep meditative state to expand your consciousness to our realms. You won’t be aware that your mortal body is asleep. It’ll feel just as you are now, fully present in the realm of the trials. There you will be presented with obstacles to prove you are worthy and accepting of your immortal existence.”

“What kind of trials?” I asked, wanting to prepare for the fight for my life.

“No one really knows, Zo. Anyone who went through the trials themselves to become immortal never remembers when they are over. It’s a sacred, truly ancient ritual.”

“Were any of your Luminaries former mortals?”

“Delmira and Finnian were the last mortals to be granted a new life with Vega,” he explained. “That was a very long time ago. It’s been a couple of centuries since the last Emergence.”

“But why wait so long?” I asked, a little angry. “There’s been plenty of mortals to choose from in the last two hundred years. Have they missed the literal *wars*?”

“There’s something that happens in the inbetween where the scent of an Emerging comes out and the stars choose to give new life to them. It's kind of like the evolution of the strongest that shines the brightest to them. Not only do the stars need to choose the Emerging, but the mortal needs to choose them back. Sometimes, the Emerging does not choose to be returned. You must have or you would not be standing here right now. Maybe they were searching for you.”

"So while I was in the inbetween... I must have chosen Vega and Algol back?"

"Yes," he confirmed. "To be chosen by one star is magnificent on its own, but two... that's unheard of."

I strained my brain, wanting to remember my time in the inbetween even though I knew I wouldn’t be able to. I wanted to scream and shout and grieve for all my fellow humans suffering. Tears escaped my eyes in the shame and weight I felt for having been chosen. It was like living while Freyja died all over again. I felt Elvy wipe a tear away and tuck my hair behind my ear.

"They are at peace too, Zoe," he said, attempting to comfort me. "The ones who chose to stay in the world of the dead."

"I know this is stupid, but it just doesn't seem fair," I said, heart full of sorrow for the souls I didn't even know.

"It's not about fairness, it's about acceptance and embracing the course you truly want to take. You can choose to fight for them now," he said, lifting my scarred arm away from my stomach. I gripped even tighter, as if to keep my essence from exploding.

I would fight for them. I couldn't control much, but no one could control the fight in my spirit except me.

"But what do the stars really want from me? What's so special about me that they waited so long?"

"To me, *everything*," he said softly. "I don't have the explanations you want about the celestial's motives, but what I can say with confidence is that you, Zoe Eferhild, are magic. Screw the stars and what their agenda is for a moment. Some spirits as wild and free as yours should've been cannot be held back by something as small as fate. Believe in that."

I took in the weight of what he was saying and nodded. My spirit settled for now.

8

Enough

I found it difficult to stay in my routine with work, but I continued to show up, which I knew June appreciated. This ordinary task was still a crucial part of my life, and I wasn't sure what Dr. Malik would do without me. As I fed Rafe treats, my heart felt a little sad knowing my days were numbered with him and the rest of the animals I'd grown closer to. Death, Algol, or Vega awaited me. Rafe splashed water on my face as if he knew my thoughts were a jumbled mess.

"June will take care of you," I said, throwing him another fish.

The Winter Solstice might be a couple months away, but I knew time would pass me by too quickly. Oleander would undoubtedly show again, and a secret part of me felt drawn to him. Maybe not him exactly, but the power of Algol. I swallowed that feeling down as I tried to focus back on my tasks.

I sighed, running fingers through my wild hair. I would miss this place no matter what I decided. June had let this be a home to me when I'd forgotten what that word meant. I glanced at the clock, noting that it was the end of my shift, and I had an appointment to keep. I was finally having dinner with Elvy and his court tonight.

I waved my goodbyes to June, and Jelly followed me on the short walk home. I really only used the Jeep when going outside the city limits. Not wanting to smell like fish at dinner, I quickly showered, but still took the time to methodically massage my head while rinsing my hair out.

I wasn't sure what one was expected to wear at this sort of thing, but I had a feeling it would be more casual than anything since we were all hanging out in the lighthouse. I decided on a pair of black leggings and teal blue, long-sleeved athletic shirt, and quickly braided my hair into a loose fishtail.

"Ready?" I asked Jelly.

She barked in response as Elvy knocked on the bungalow door. He'd graciously agreed to escort me to the dinner.

Only it wasn't Elvy. It was Oleander, and the sickness immediately flooded my stomach.

"Well, hello, Zoe. You do look divine."

I would have rolled my eyes at the fake flattery, but I was too focused on not vomiting.

"I thought you got rid of this," I stated, clutching my stomach, willing the nauseous feeling to expunge itself.

"That was a onetime thing, love. Perhaps, with proper training, it will go away. If you ever give me the honor of knowing you," he stated, eyes seemingly sincere, but I didn't trust them for a second.

"I'd rather not," I said through gritted teeth. The feeling would not ebb.

"I didn't think you would be one so quick to judge someone you know nothing about," he said, brows raised.

His point was reasonable and hard to argue with, which made him all the more infuriating.

"I can't help it that I'm enduring a Pavlov experiment every time I look at your face," I said, gagging.

This seemed to only amuse Oleander further.

"Is there anything I can do to make you feel more comfortable hearing me out? That's all I and the Court of Algol desire, Zoe."

I felt like I was playing a dangerous game. I was the toad, him the scorpion, but I knew something deep in the pit of this sickness urged me to go to him.

"You've felt this before. With another," he said, eyes full of mischief.

I had felt this before. Not this intense by any stretch, but I vaguely remembered the feeling when Freyja first started showing up after she died. It had trickled away, though with the passing of time.

"Not just Freyja, Zoe," he said, but I couldn't think through the sickness.

"I can tell you why. Come with me," he suggested, with an outstretched hand.

If he knew something about Freyja, then I was tempted. Very. I'd made a commitment to someone else tonight, though.

"Zoe," Elvy said cautiously as he approached the porch.

"Always ruining the fun," Oleander sighed.

"I'm sorry, Oleander. Not tonight," I said, but the intentions were clear in my voice.

"But another," he promised, vanishing into the shadows.

"I leave you alone for a few days, and the enemy descends," Elvy said, laughing.

I'd appreciated him giving me a few days of space to process, but I'd found myself missing him all the same.

"Is he really the enemy?" I asked, truly wanting a straightforward answer. I licked my dry lips, the nausea finally gone. "I need some water. Would you like to come in for a minute?"

Internally, I understood the severity of what I'd just asked. I hadn't allowed a man in my home since the attack, not even Grant, my stepfather. I feared what this meant for me in the deepest, shattered parts of myself. Maybe I was Emerging in all kinds of ways.

Elvy cautiously followed behind me as I went to the kitchen for a glass of cool water. My cottonmouth thanked me for it. He declined a glass of his own, and I waited for him to come up with an answer to my question.

"You really don't like him, do you?"

"*Enemy* is a difficult term to define. The darkness isn't bad. Some say that darkness is just the parts we reject. Without it, there would be no reason to appreciate the light. Algol has not been part of the Kingdom of Canis in a long time, and it has had some devastating consequences," he explained.

"I assume they did not leave on good terms?'

"Oleander's predecessors severed themselves from the life force of Canis, creating their own ruling realm."

"Why would they do that?" I asked, mind spinning.

"You understand Vega is the life giver of the water element." He paused, and I nodded for him to continue. "All courts are bound by and protectors to one of the elements: fire, ground, water, and air. Algol was steward to the spirit element, arguably the strongest of them all."

I'd read about the elements in the occult books, but I only knew vague information.

"Then what happened?"

"Let's go meet with the others. I'd like for you to hear it from them as well."

"Let's go then," I said, putting my glass down. "Can we fly there?" I asked excitedly. "Can you carry us both?"

"Of course I can," he scoffed, morphing into this more true form. Jelly hopped into my arms while Elvy settled me into his own embrace.

"Hold on," he said, darting off into the night sky.

***

I was sitting around the dinner table staring back into the eyes of the immortal Shadowed, wondering just how lethal they could be. In the center of the table was a huge shrimp and crab boil laid on parchment paper. It smelled heavenly. Everyone piled a helping in front of them, and I followed suit while waiting for Elvy to begin. Jelly lay at my feet, trying to seem innocent, but I suspected Blaz was feeding her under the table. I didn't mind since she was off duty.

"As a rule, immortals don't make a habit of going to war with other realms. The results can be grave with worlds ending needlessly," Elvy began, with all eyes on him. "When Algol left Canis, the split was felt across planes and had a lasting ripple effect. It's steadily gotten worse."

"Ripple effect where?" I asked, fearing the answer.

"All that energy had to go somewhere, and the mortal realm of Earth is tethered to Canis. What happens there affects Earth, good or bad."

I stilled, angry that the world I'd always known had not always been its own master. I knew that feeling all too well.

"We think that plays into the Emerging mortals—nature trying to balance the chaos of the ripple. Spirit being untethered to Earth is affecting mortals negatively... so the stars are leveling the playing field," Delmira theorized.

"When something is taken, something must be given," agreed Finnian.

"If I had to guess, you are going to be the most powerful Emerging across all realms. That's the only reason that both Vega and Algol would be vying for you. What you choose could literally change everything."

"No pressure, Zoe," Imelda said, slapping Delmira on the back of the head. "Delm gets a little dramatic sometimes."

"I think they've waited purposefully for you, Zoe. I'm not exactly sure what, but it has to do with the tether to Earth," Elvy added.

While that might not be true, I couldn't argue with that logic either. I remembered the twins were the last Emerging mortals in Vega. I wondered if they had any recollection of their former mortal lives and how it compared to their lives now.

"What about you two?" I motioned to Delmira and Finnian. "Did you serve the star's greater purpose?"

"If it is to kick absolute ass, then yes, I've served them well," she replied, smiling maliciously. "However, you cannot compare my truth to yours."

"Always so serious, Delm. Lighten up," Clodovea said, punching Elvy's second in command. Apparently, punching Delmira was a frequent occurrence.

"Touch me again, Clove, and we can give the human some real entertainment," Delmira taunted.

"Ladies, ladies, I can think of other ways to spend some energy," Blaz piped in, breaking the stoic mask of the warrior I knew he was.

"Prick," Imelda snapped, but there was humor flickering in all their eyes.

"You can joke," I said, eyes on Blaz.

"Blaz prefers to keep his scary, serious face on in front of strangers," Imelda explained, rolling her eyes.

"Am I not a stranger?" I asked.

"Elvy trusts you. That's all I need to know," Blaz answered. His loyalty was unnerving, but I could see they all felt the same.

"I could always choose a different path from Vega," I mentioned.

"You could, but how could you say no to all of this?" Blaz responded, motioning to his friends. "We are irresistible."

"I might actually gag," Imelda said, sticking her tongue out, feigning sickness.

I glanced over at Elvy, and he just shrugged as if to say, *"You get used to it."*

"You all seem so informal with each other," I observed. "It's different from what I expected."

"Even immortals have loving, dysfunctional families," Elvy explained. "We just happen to rule a realm, too."

"Thank, Vega," Delmira laughed. "Immortality would be boring without your pains in the asses."

"So, if Algol became connected with Canis again, what would happen?" I asked.

"It would restore the natural order," Elvy said thoughtfully. "I don't know if that will ever happen, though. When the split first occurred, all the Shadowed Legions of Vega, Arcturus, Rigil, and Canopus invaded Algol in an attempt to repair the damage. So many lives lost with nothing to show for it."

"Vega was hit hardest of all. So many of our strongest healers died in vain to restore the connection," Finnian said solemnly.

Delmira, Elvy's second, placed a comforting hand on his shoulder. There was a sort of intimacy about it that made me want to look away. Not from jealousy, but I could feel their unshakeable bond.

"We will be ready next time," Clodovea responded. "We were all so confused and disorganized over what happened."

Imelda picked at the tattoo they all bore, lost in thought.

"Why do you all have those?" I asked curiously.

"You haven't tried to show her?" Imelda asked Elvy.

"You know I can't. Not yet," he answered with warning in his voice.

"It can only be seen with immortal eyes," Blaz offered.

"So many vague answers," I noted. "I assume there's a good reason for it?"

"Your mortal eyes would probably burn straight from your skull," Delmira said as she stabbed a potato with a fork.

"Never mind then. I've grown fond of my eyesight."

"I like you," Blaz said. "I think you'll fit right in."

Blushing, I looked away. I'd forgotten what it felt like to feel so incredibly at ease. I could picture myself happy with this group, this family.

Family.

I felt the tears well in my eyes, realizing what I would be leaving behind. I would miss my mother and even Grant. What would I tell them? Or would I just die all over again to them? I couldn't put my mom through that. Jelly nuzzled my leg, sensing my unease. *And what about Jelly?* I couldn't just leave her. Freyja's face flashed through my mind. If I chose this immortal life, would that mean never seeing my sister again? That was a reality I wasn't sure I wanted to live with.

And just like that, my thoughts ruined a pleasant evening.

When my mind returned, I found myself alone with Elvy, patiently waiting for me to come back to him. I closed my eyes, straining my ears to hear the barely audible ocean.

"Would you like to go outside?" he asked.

"Yes," I said, trembling.

The part of me that was embarrassed hated Elvy for seeing me like this.

"Never for one minute be ashamed or feel like you have to hide in front of me. I want to know all of you, the pieces of you that no one else sees," he confessed under the stars shining down upon us.

"I'm working on that," I admitted.

"I've got nothing but time," he breathed.

"But I don't," I said, tears sliding down my heated face.

"I'll be with you every step, no matter what you choose. Even if it isn't this," he said, his expression giving nothing away. The tug in my chest pulled me closer to him.

"I've decided nothing, Elvy."

How could I explain to him that I felt like I was choosing between a future with him and leaving everyone else I loved behind? I would never have to see a day without Freyja if I stayed and accepted my mortality, but I wasn't sure I could accept that path if it meant others suffered because of it.

"Let's live for right now, Zoe," he said, taking my scarred arm and placing it over his heart. He gently examined my palm, and I was suddenly aware of some pain there.

"I must have been clenching my fists," I said, pulling away.

"May I?" he asked.

I nodded as Elvy placed his hand over mine and a soft blue glow emitted from his hand, healing the minor scrapes that had just been there.

"Incredible," I whispered. "Can you all do that?"

"No. We all have some healing abilities because of the water element. Some are stronger than others or function a little differently. Some can barely heal, but can use the element in extraordinary ways. Water is tied to more than you think."

"Could that be me, too? Healing?"

"Anything is possible," he admitted.

Live, Zoe. Freyja's words whispered through me.

"I'd like to try something," I whispered, gazing into those stormy, kind, patient eyes. It was not a *want,* but a *need*. The ache in my chest had to know what his lips felt like on mine. The burn within me had to close the small space between us.

I placed one of his hands on the side of my face, and the other on my waist. He didn't let his hands wander and waited for me to make a move. There wasn't a trace of doubt within me as I set out to claim my moment.

"No sudden movements, alright?"

He nodded, understanding my instructions.

"Tell me what you need, Zoe," he mumbled, voice deepening.

I wanted to shout from the rooftops how badly I desired him. I wanted to scream at the fire in my chest and the heat between my legs to leap into his arms, but I remained calm—focused. I would take this slowly for my own peace.

I pressed on my tiptoes, showing him with my body what I wanted. His lips met mine gently—this beautiful man and his soft lips achingly caressing mine. As I kissed him, the need to get as close to him as possible flowed through me. I'd had many lovers throughout my travels, but none had come close to evoking the electricity I felt with Elvy. I'd thought it impossible to feel this way after what had happened to me.

His hands never wavered from where I'd positioned them, but I let him trail his lips along my jaw, a soft moan escaping me. If the waves weren't crashing around me, I would have sworn this was a dream. I couldn't seem to stop from fisting his hair in my hand as I greedily took more of him. This only seemed to rouse him more and his desire for me was clear against the press of my body.

His control was much more impressive than mine.

By the time we were finished, my lips were happily swollen, and I leaned my head on his chest, listening to the steady beat of his heart and found a sense of peace there.

For a moment, life was still and calm. Elvy brushed his nose against my hair, nuzzling me closer.

"I think I love trying things with you, Zoe," he said, smiling mischievously.

"I'm sorry," I whispered. "This is all new to me after..." I trailed off not wanting to explain.

"You are enough just as you are, Zoe Eferhild."

He placed a lingering kiss in my hair, inhaling the sea breeze.

Life was about moments, right? I chose to live in this one.

9

Sight

"For what it's worth, you seem happy," Freyja noted, as we walked side by side along the beach. The weather was becoming cooler as we approached the beginning of November. The wind was particularly violent today, whipping our hair around just aggressively enough to be a nuisance. Jelly seemed unperturbed, trotting happily along beside us. Occasionally, she stopped when something caught her interest in the shallow water.

I sat down on the damp sand, pondering her observation. I felt like a completely different person from who I was just a few months ago, watching stunning strangers play volleyball. The Winter Solstice was near the end of December, so time was running lower than I'd prefer.

To admit to myself that I was happy felt scary, as if at any moment it could be taken away from me. Emma had driven into my stubborn skull that I was worthy of good things, but believing it wasn't always the easiest thing.

"I think I could be," I admitted, thinking of Elvy and the rest of the Vega court.

"Yet you are hesitant to say yes to Vega's gift."

"I don't even know what it is."

"The thought of the unknown is intimidating, but the real magic is on the other side of courage," Freyja said with wisdom in her voice.

I traced the scarring on my arm in thought as I let her words sink into me.

"I have to consider what I would be leaving behind," I reasoned.

I expected her to argue or say some selfless, philosophical statement, but she didn't. She only clasped my hand and leaned her head on my shoulder.

"I love you, Zo. No matter what you choose, but I want you to live... for you. Not for the stars or Elvy or anyone else. You are meant for so much more than this."

I squeezed her hand tighter, again wondering what the stars had in store for me. I could let that question fester until it drove me mad, or I could accept it for what it was. *Unknown.*

I felt the wash of nausea roll over me just before I heard him speak.

"Such a heartwarming sight," Oleander said, smiling before us.

"You can see Freyja?" I asked, full of surprise.

"Of course," Oleander said, sitting down beside me. I wanted to squirm away from the proximity, but I refused to let him see me move an inch. "Algol is master of spirit."

I tucked away that information for later questioning.

"What do you want, Oleander?"

"I'm coming to collect," he said, winking. "You didn't think I actually missed the desire to see me away from the prying eyes of Elvy?"

"It's not like that," I said, riding the waves of my stomach, needing to find release soon.

"Your motivation means nothing to me," he stated. "I'm here to give Algol a fair chance at an Emerging."

"You'll tell me what this is about?" I asked, sweating through the sickness.

"I don't make a habit of lying to you, Zoe."

"Alright," I conceded through gritted teeth.

"Follow me," he said, standing.

I gave Freyja a last wistful look and begrudgingly followed Oleander's retreating figure. Jelly, my faithful companion, was hot on my tail.

"How do you expect me to stand near you with this?" I said, pointing to my heaving stomach.

"Through discipline," he answered simply.

Oleander had led me to an alleyway in the town center. The small businesses and restaurants were bustling about with people slipping in and out. The hum of the crowd was growing uncomfortable as I stood there trying not to dry heave.

"But what does it mean?" I managed to get out.

"I can show you," Oleander said. "But I'll have to touch your head."

I wasn't overly fond of that, but I nodded, deciding to follow my gut.

Oleander gently placed his palms on either side of my temples.

"The beginning."

At his words, flashes of the first time I saw Freyja buzzed across my mind, then the first time I'd seen Elvy playing volleyball. The night I first felt Oleander burned through my mind... I hungrily followed the thought to deeper waters, knowing something from much longer ago was hiding in there.

"No, no, no, Zoe. Let's walk before you fly," he said, removing his hands. "Going too deep could kill you while still mortal."

"What were those besides my memories?" I asked.

"They were moments your gift of discernment was trying to warn you of something that would change your destiny. You must learn to *see* others outside of yourself"

"But why was Elvy there? I don't remember feeling this way with him."

"Sometimes, it presents differently... think, Zoe."

I recalled the seemingly unnatural pull I'd had towards Elvy from the moment I'd first seen him.

"But what does that mean?" I asked, still fighting the sickness.

"Do I look like a big ball of gas in the night sky?" he asked sarcastically. "Now, as much as I'd love to dissect your feelings for Elvy, I actually don't."

I rolled my eyes and met his gaze with as much stubborn defiance as I could muster.

"Now focus," he commanded. "It will be difficult at first, but lean into the uncomfortableness, Zoe. Let it guide you."

"You want me to get sick, don't you?"

"No, I want to show you what Algol can do for you and for others," he whispered. "Silence. Focus."

I closed my eyes and focused on the dampness of my palms; the sweat running down my back, and the pain in my stomach. I embraced the feeling, retching on the ground beside us, my poor body finally finding release. Oleander seemed to want to help with my hair, but my glare kept his feet in place.

"Now, close your eyes again. What do you see? Lean into the feeling."

This guy was really infuriating, but I closed my eyes obediently and willed a burning image into my consciousness. For only a breath, an image flicked by before I lost hold of it. All I'd seen was a man following another man to a vehicle. Call it intuition, or maybe it was this discernment gift, but I knew he was up to no good.

"Get a lock on it, Zoe," Oleander stated firmly.

I expanded my will, like flexing a muscle in my mind. The image flared across my vision again. The man was still being followed.

"Expand your consciousness out. Find the location."

I did as he instructed and found a familiar sign. I knew where they were.

"I've got it, but it's a few miles away. We won't make it."

Making a grand gesture, Oleander's wings sprouted from behind him. They were a translucent black, but still seemed substantial. Whispers of darkness encircled him, moving organically. He outstretched his arms, clearly wanting to carry me.

"No," I said, still feeling a little nauseous.

"We'll never make it on foot," Oleander pointed out, and I knew he was right.

"What about Jelly?" I asked seriously.

"She can come too," he said simply. "She's trained, right?"

"Of course, but—"

"Time is of the essence, love."

"Damn it to hell," I said, rolling my eyes, striding towards him. "You will do nothing other than carry us, understand?"

"Your low expectations of me are always so thrilling," he said, voice full of sarcasm. "It'll be over in a flash."

Surprisingly gentle, he carefully caressed me in his arms and flapped his enormous wings, bounding us into the sky. In what felt like a heartbeat, he descended upon the two men, gliding just behind them. They did not glance up at our presence, and I looked at Oleander curiously.

"They cannot see us, not without my permission," he whispered, most likely for effect. The shadows seemed to conceal us in a mist.

It was clear what would happen to the man being followed. He was going to get mugged if I didn't stop this right now.

"Make me visible," I said, angrily.

"There are other ways to help," Oleander reasoned, all too casually for the situation.

"No time. Make me visible now," I demanded.

"Your call," he said, snapping his fingers. The mist vanished.

"Hey, asshole!" I bellowed, startling the pursuer. Jelly was swiveling her head between us, analyzing the situation.

He didn't seem happy with my interruption. The potential mugger looked like any other guy, but his eyes were on me, full of hatred. *Shit.* He was coming for me now.

The guy I'd just saved had run off, sensing a fight. How heroic? I quickly thought through the best plan of attack and braced myself for a fight. As I steadied my breath, I could hear the ocean faintly in the background. This was real, and I would choose to fight. Jelly stood beside me, hackles raised, ready to go right alongside me.

Just as the assailant launched for me, Oleander's steel arm quickly blocked him.

"Now, didn't anyone ever tell you it's rude to hit a lady?"

"I can take care of myself," I spat.

"Oh, I have no doubt," he said easily. "This is more for him than for you."

He was still holding the attacker back as he struggled to break free. Not a drip of fatigue could be seen on Oleander's face.

"You are boring me," he told the man while pressing two fingers on his forehead. "Sleep."

The man collapsed at our feet in a peaceful slumber. I silently hoped he'd dream of nightmares.

"The nausea is still there," I said. "Why?"

"Because you're still learning. It's prompting you to develop your gift. I also may have given you a little boost before you began tracking," he explained. "Look beyond your fury."

I gazed closer at the man, seeing the signs of hunger there. He was malnourished and his facial hair unkempt. The smell coming from him indicated it had been a good while since he'd been able to properly clean himself. My eyes passed over the telltale signs of drug use that had started to run rampant in the area over the last year. I suddenly felt guilty and empathetic about his motivation. This man was suffering, trying to survive in the only way he knew how. I could relate.

"Darkness isn't always as it seems," I muttered.

"Your human race is the most sick population I've witnessed in centuries. Drugs, violence, torment, such brokenness. Though humanity is, perhaps, not to blame entirely," he said, looking down at the man. A glimmer of guilt flashed in his eyes, but he quickly concealed it.

"How can I help him?" I whispered, heart racing at this turn of events.

He seemed to debate for a moment on how much he wanted to say.

"You've already helped him in one way. You've saved him from bearing the burden of having hurt someone else. Those consequences build up and lead to the damaging of souls," Oleander cautioned. "If you choose Algol, your gift can intensify, helping him change his heart from within."

"What do you mean?"

"You know your stomach is your second brain?" Oleander asked.

"Like a gut instinct," I said. "Like the way I've felt when something bad was going to happen."

"Right. Among other manifestations, Algol can allow you to project that into others, giving them the opportunity to pause. You can never force though. It's like reading someone's soul—their aura. You can read someone's true intentions."

"You seem confident that I will choose your star."

"A guy can dream," he said, smiling.

"Can we at least get him something to eat?" I asked, eyes pleading.

"Oh, I think I can do better than that," he answered. "I picked up on his scent a while ago. He'd been deliberating this choice for some time now. I've already made arrangements to help him."

"What if that doesn't work?" I asked sadly.

"It's his choice to decide what to do with it, Zoe. We can't save everyone. If it takes generations to make true change, he could need help again. That's part of it. We keep showing up for them, even then."

So quietly I wasn't sure if I heard him correctly, Oleander whispered, "I have to make up for what's been done."

"Where are we taking him?" I asked, deciding not to confront him about what I thought I heard.

"*We* aren't taking him anywhere," Oleander informed. "*She* is going to take him."

A brilliantly beautiful woman strutted through the alleyway. Confidence radiated all around her, and I'd been completely unaware of her existence. She had fiery red hair and pale, flawless skin that nearly seemed translucent.

"Lord Astral," she gave a silent bow.

"Don't pretend you have any manners, Zadie," he said, rolling his eyes. "Please take him to his new accommodations."

"I'm glad to finally meet you, Zoe," she said, before lifting the gentleman up in her arms as if he was as light as a feather. "I'm sure I'll see you around."

"Friend of yours?" I asked curiously.

"Zadie is my second," Oleander offered. Two Lord Astrals had a female as their second in command. Humans would cringe at the thought.

"One day I'd like to know how all this works," I said, wondering how their government of sorts functioned. "But right now, I'd like to get back."

"Would you like to fly or walk?"

I shuddered at the idea of being in his arms again, but agreed to fly back with him. Upon our landing, Jelly sniffed and circled me a few times to make sure I was in one piece.

"That's quite the loyal companion you have there," Oleander noted.

"I don't know if I can leave her," I admitted.

"Maybe you don't have to," he said with a sparkle in his eyes.

Before I could question him further, he asked me the question he knew would distract me the most.

"Is it gone, the nausea?"

It was still there, but not nearly as intense as it was earlier.

"It's faded. I guess the sight of you no longer makes me want to vomit," I said with a smile playing on my lips.

"Funny girl."

"So, Algol's gift... it can give me the *sight*? Like, prophetic sort of? I'm not quite understanding everything."

"You mean you don't understand every little thing about a universe you had no idea existed until the very recent past?" Oleander answered, voice full of sarcasm. "That is a very simple explanation for something so complex. It remains to be seen what all Algol has gifted you. I can tell you it helps you see into the spirit of someone you're called to by the stars. You can see someone for who they truly are. Like tonight, stopping that human could have a positive ripple effect. Counteract the negative ripples coming from Algol's severing and great things could happen. Mistakes could be fixed. Mortals and immortals alike need the goodness that spirit can be, Zoe." He paused a moment, then proceeded. "Because this gift is incredibly powerful, it has the ability to be used in disastrous ways, turning someone or keeping them trapped within their own mind. It can be its own kind of torture."

"I don't suppose you want to tell me why Algol would leave the world I love without the power of spirit?" I questioned.

"Algol put its faith in the wrong being. It's a complicated story for another time." He seemed to hesitate, but decided not to elaborate.

"So one day, I could be strong enough to read you?"

"Yes, you could read me now if you truly wanted, Zoe. If you dare."

Oleander opened his arms in invitation.

"Give it your best shot," he challenged.

Closing my eyes, I centered myself into the pit of my being, leaning into the uncomfortableness of the nausea. I was met with a mist so thick I couldn't see my hand raised in front of my face.

"You're hiding," I murmured.

"I never said I'd give it easily."

"Afraid of what I might find?"

"Always," he replied, moving closer to me. "If Algol allows, I can teach you this, too. How to hide yourself."

"I'm tired of hiding who I am," I admitted.

"I see. Hide was the wrong word. *Protect* yourself," he murmured, voice breaking slightly. "Open your eyes, Zoe."

I obeyed and found him standing close enough to me that I jumped back at the proximity.

Oleander hadn't been what I expected. He didn't seem like a bad guy, and I wondered what conflict must be there between Canis and Algol. More importantly, maybe he didn't fit into this equation the way everyone thought he did.

"I think I'll go home now," I said, heading towards my sea bungalow.

"Give Freyja my well wishes," he said, moving closer. "She seems like a lovely person... I see why you wouldn't want to leave her behind."

"She wants me to be happy," I said, voice faltering. I knew he saw through my resolve.

"What if you could have it all... choose Algol and you get an immortal life and Freyja. You don't have to die to have her with you. Not if you choose Algol."

I stood frozen, my body seeming to forget how to move.

"It would be as it once was between you two," he promised, whispering so close I felt his breath on my ear. I knew that wasn't true, though. She'd still be dead and not fully with me.

Jelly nudged against my leg, pulling me from the trance of Oleander. I thought of Elvy and the Luminaries... of Jelly and my mother. No matter what I chose, I could not have them all. No, it would not be that easy as much as he may wish it could be.

"I'll see you around, Oleander."

"I'll see you soon, Zoe," he promised, disappearing into the shadows.

Not wishing to think of anything really, I walked home silently. I listened to the crash of the ocean against the shore and allowed the mist of the sea to fill my tired lungs. I was shocked that I had more or less enjoyed my time with Oleander today, but the tug in my chest ached for Elvy. I hoped to see him soon. I had so many questions, but more so I just craved to be near him.

Wedged between my screen door, an envelope fell as I pried the rickety door open. As if he longed for me too, Elvy had left me a message.

I'm thinking... I'd like to get more practice at trying something. We'll be at the volleyball court tomorrow at 6. I hope you come.

E

"A bunch of immortals playing volleyball," I muttered, laughing to myself.

Jelly and I slipped into a peaceful sleep that night, dreams full of the ocean and flying.

10

Practice

I was methodical in every task at work today, taking extra care to scrub everything twice, hoping it would make the time go by faster. It only made the hours go slower. I tried to practice the skill Oleander had taught me the previous night, but it was difficult to control without his guidance. I also wasn't getting any waves of sickness and wasn't sure if that was a requirement to read someone or not. He'd also mentioned that the gift presented differently at times, which only added to the difficulty in mastering it.

Eventually, it was time to clock out, and I raced home to freshen up before heading to the courts—the first place I'd ever laid eyes on Elvy. I opted for my favorite jean jacket and leggings. My hair was already in its signature braid from work, so that saved even more time.

The pull in my chest and butterflies in my stomach nudged me and Jelly out the front door and towards the awaiting Court of Vega. The stormy weather was holding off, and it looked like it would actually clear up soon.

"Hey, Jelly!" Blaz shouted, as we closed in on the playing field.

"What about me?" I teased back.

"Can you blame me?" he asked, scratching Jelly's upturned belly, a big sign of trust.

I found my eyes searching for Elvy and tried to ignore the sigh of happiness when I found those gray eyes staring back at me. I felt like I'd been waiting my entire life for him to find me, long before I knew that the ghosts and monsters I'd always read about were real.

"I'm glad you came," Elvy said, as if he'd actually considered that I wouldn't.

"I don't scare that easily," I replied.

"Clearly not, since you seem to think hanging out with Oleander is safe," Delmira chimed in, eyes full of ice.

Elvy shot her a warning glare, silencing her. I wasn't sure she obliged out of respect for her brother of sorts or from following the command of her Lord Astral.

"So, you all know about that?" I asked.

"You don't need to explain yourself," Elvy said simply. "But if you want to talk about it, we can."

"I'd already planned to," I admitted.

Internally, I could feel the trauma response—that's what Emma had called it—trying to surface. I could feel the explanation on my lips about to break forth, worrying that I'd upset him. Heat flooded my cheeks, and I felt my head hang down in false shame. Jelly nudged her head on my leg, attempting to disrupt my thought patterns from spiraling.

"Breathe, Zoe," he whispered. The rest of the group had faded away. "Do you hear the ocean?"

I closed my eyes, listening closely. Yes, I heard it. This was real. I was safe. My chest warmed at knowing he'd picked up on my need for the ocean and its significance to me. Jelly continued to make her presence known, further allowing me to still my racing heart.

"If I could promise death to your demons, Zoe, I would. Until you slay them on your own, I'll be right here," Elvy said, a flare of righteous anger in his voice I'd never heard before. "You are your own person. I'm protective, yes, but it's always your decision in the end. Delmira gets... territorial over the safety of her court."

I wasn't angry at Delm. In fact, I wondered what hurt might linger underneath that icy gaze. I knew from my own lived experiences that the inner workings of the mind were far more complicated than what we presented on the surface.

"Would you like to leave?" he asked.

"No," I answered, shaking the feeling off. "I'd still like to play with you guys."

"This should be interesting," Finnian said, eyes gleaming. Delmira stood next to him, body language a little less stiff. I saw regret in her eyes. I gave her a small smile, letting her know that all was forgiven.

"She'll get over it," Clodovea said, pulling me onto the court.

"I'll make the teams uneven," I pointed out.

"We don't care," Imelda said, shrugging.

"Why volleyball?" I asked the group.

"Hitting Delmira with the ball is fun," Blaz answered, wickedness in his eyes.

"Because we knew you might come here. We had to be sure who the scent of the Emerging was, and we traced it here. Immortals only get a general sense of where an Emerging is until we get a true lock on it," Elvy explained, then continued. "Plus, we needed a normal human cover story for being out in the public eye so much. We strategized it would be the best place to start looking."

"I have a scent?" I asked, self-conscious.

"Oh yeah, you reek of an Emerging," Blaz offered.

"Don't worry, it's enticing," Elvy whispered, placing a kiss on my forehead.

"If it wasn't for Freyja—" I paused, catching myself.

While I had confessed my relationship with Freyja to Elvy, I hadn't to the rest of the Luminaries. I wasn't sure if he would have told them about her. They all had stopped what they were doing to hear what I was about to share. I cleared my throat, resolved to share my truth.

"My sister, Freyja. She'd been insistent that I go to those games. She seemed to know you all would be there."

"Where is she now?" Delmira asked, gaze piercing.

"I'm not sure," I confessed. "She died a couple of years ago, but she didn't exactly leave."

None of them batted an eye at this news. They seemed to analyze, trying to figure out how this could fit in with their mission. I had to agree it was significant.

"How would she know? Someone from Algol?" Delmira asked.

"I'm not sure," Elvy answered, a little too nonchalant.

"Are we going to play or what?" Finnian asked, anxiously tossing the ball up and down. "We won't figure it out tonight."

"As long as Zoe is on my team," Imelda announced. The rest of the group relaxed at her easy words.

"Just so you can blame the mortal when you lose," Blaz taunted.

"Women against you boys then," Delmira declared.

With those final words, we divided the rest of us into two teams. Imelda, Delmira, Clodovea, and I were on one team. Elvy, Finnian, and Blaz took the other. Elvy gave me a sympathetic look just before Blaz sent his first serve soaring over the net straight for me. Shockingly, I got underneath it, popping it up for Clodovea to spike it too quickly for Finnian to counter.

"A point for the ladies!" Imelda cheered.

Hating to admit it, the guys were just as good and the game remained neck and neck the entire time. My mortal body was growing fatigued, but I willed my stamina to keep going to the end. Jelly seemed content to lie down and watch us bicker and challenge one another. She occasionally vocalized her opinion and wagged her tail in excitement. Jelly was quite the cheerleader.

"Final point," Clove announced.

"Tired?" Blaz, asked.

Refusing to respond, Clodovea served the ball straight at his face, but he put it in a perfect position for Elvy to spike it right at me. I poised my body, ready to return the attack. Elvy gave me a wink before slamming the ball down over our side, but I dove, reaching the ball at the last second. Delmira used the opportunity to earn the ladies their winning point.

We erupted into cheers, and the men joined in, good-naturedly. Well, most of them.

"It's just because you had a fourth player," Blaz whined.

"Now, the mortal is an unfair advantage. Make up your mind," I joked with him.

"Alright you guys," Elvy said, still with a smile on his face. "Scram."

"You got it, boss," Delmira said, leading the others away.

Elvy offered his hand to me, which I happily accepted. I grabbed my jacket off the ground before he led us down to a spot out of the way of prying eyes close to the water.

"I've missed you," he said.

"It's only been a day," I replied, teasing.

"Ah, but I've been waiting many lifetimes for you."

"Surely there have been others," I responded.

"No, Zoe. I had companionships, but not this. Not with anyone," he said, brows furrowing together. "You'll understand it better when—*if* you choose Vega."

"Speaking of Vega," I began. I launched into everything that had happened with Oleander yesterday, not leaving any detail out. Well, I left out Oleander's unnecessarily close proximity. I figured a war between realms would be slightly inconvenient and disastrous. His interest peaked when I mentioned the gift from Algol, and he asked more questions around it.

"Your Emerging gift is presenting much stronger from Algol," he noted. "The nausea makes sense then. Your mortal body doesn't have the ability to contain it as well. It will eventually fade to something more manageable."

"Do you think something like that will happen with Vega?" I asked, curiously.

"Yes, every Emerging is gifted something from the stars that choose them. Mortals who have gone through the Emerging process are usually more powerful than birth immortals. Extra blessed," he said, poking at my shoulder.

"What about you? Oleander hinted that he had multiple powers. Are all immortals gifted the same in their realm?"

"Life is not biologically possible without the water element, so as you know, most of us have some form of healing ability. Some heal very complex diseases and injuries, while some can only heal minor scrapes. Others can exclusively heal animals, while some immortals can bring life back to plants or other smaller life forms. Others work the vibrations of water in interesting ways."

"Would that mean... you could bring someone back—if they died?" I asked, but I felt in my heart that it would be a disappointing answer.

"I've never known anyone powerful enough to bring a life back from the spirit world," he said softly, trying to ease the pain I felt etched on my face. "The closest I've seen to someone creating new life is in our farmers and botanists—they've been able to create more viable strains on a very small scale."

"How do the gifts get decided by Vega?"

"I think it has something to do with the bloodlines. Before Algol's separation, an immortal could have a parent from two different elemental realms. I've never heard of an immortal having more than one gift from multiple stars; one always wins out. Typically, the immortal will swear allegiance to the gift that does manifest."

"What about the ones that don't?"

"They're called the Sublunars. Rebels. Master of none and answer to no one. A powerful ally and even worse enemy."

"That doesn't sound so bad."

"Sometimes, I agree with that," he acknowledged.

The weight of ruling could be exhausting, I'm sure.

"Does it mean something that Algol's gift is already present?"

It made me nervous that Vega's gift has not manifested in me yet. I'd had choices taken away from me before, and not being able to choose again was my greatest fear.

"Maybe, maybe not. You said you see Freyja, your sister."

"Yes, it started almost immediately after I woke up in the hospital after the night of the attack..." I trailed off, not wanting to finish the thought.

"With Algol being the realm of spirit, the gift could have been manifesting since that moment, strengthening it initially," he theorized.

"Are Algol and the world of the dead the same thing?"

"Linked, but separate," he explained.

"Master of spirit," I muttered. "I've heard something similar before."

I told him about the woman on the pier and the reading she had given me, which made more sense now, but still left questions.

"Maybe one gift is clouding the other?" he speculated. "Now that Algol's gift is more *settled*, Vega's can emerge and reveal itself."

"I would like that, but I don't think that's all. There's something big that we're missing. *The path to the truth of your blood has been revealed,*" I muttered, remembering the gypsy woman who had become an unwanted figure in my mind.

I briefly noted that Elvy had not revealed his powers to me, but I figured there was a reason for that. I wouldn't push tonight. The longing gaze Elvy gave me proved to be the distraction I needed. The burn in my chest pulled me closer to him, lips parted just shy of his.

"Want more practice?" he asked, barely audible.

I answered by closing the gap between us. He never lifted his hands, allowing me to take control of the moment. His lips tasted like sea salt, but were still sweet. I collapsed a hand through his curly brown hair and pulled him down to the sand beside me so that we both lay on our sides. As I guided his hand to the curve of my waist, I pulled his body flush with mine. I wanted to feel every inch of his warmth against me. He raised himself up so I could guide his other hand to the base of my neck, along my collarbone.

He skimmed his fingers up and down the front of my neck, never letting his touch move to the back of my neck—the boundary I had set for us. He gently nuzzled my ear with his mouth, whispering my name like he enjoyed hearing it. A whisper of anticipation escaped my lips, and he squeezed my waist in response. He expertly drew my chin to look towards him until my eyes met the storm of desire in his.

"You know, Zoe, I do think your eyes are sparkling green right now. This seems to make you happy," he smiled, continuing his slow, intentional movement up my side. "I long to see you that way."

"I never thought it was possible—to feel this way."

And I meant that. I'd had a few casual boyfriends in high school and many purely carnal relations while traveling on my adventures, but there had been no real love there. I hadn't been with anyone since the night so much had been taken from me, even when I'd been drinking heavily. I couldn't stop the feeling of hope from gently caressing my scarred heart.

"You've been healing long before you met me, Zoe. Never forget that," he said, seriously, like he wanted me to believe in myself, in my ability to be my own hero.

"Then can I say I enjoy knowing that I have you to stand by me and remind me of that," I said, meeting his gaze.

Elvy traced his thumb across my heated cheeks.

"More than my equal," he whispered so softly I could barely hear it.

"I'd like to practice a little longer," I said, pulling his lips back down to mine. He never wavered in staying within my limits. Even when my kissing became needier, he only chuckled and let me seek him.

We eventually pulled ourselves apart, and Elvy walked Jelly and me back to my house. As he kissed me goodbye, I briefly imagined him in my bed, wondering what it would be like to have all of him between my sheets, holding me as I slept. I smiled sheepishly at the image.

"The wonder of it all," I whispered to the universe.

11

Bloodpath

I dreamed of darkness. I was looking frantically into the night sky trying to find the familiar stars that I'd grown accustomed to watching over me. They never came. Darkness continued to shroud me, but a sense of calm washed over me as the ocean suddenly appeared in front of me and the sand softened beneath my bare feet.

A figure came walking slowly towards me. I couldn't make out anything distinguishing to identify him, but something about him was familiar. I didn't run, and I wasn't afraid. I began walking towards him, but with every step I took, he seemed to get further away.

"What do you want?!" I called, standing still. My heart pounded as I waited for him to respond.

"The path of blood can soon be found if only you look in the stars."

The words of the gypsy woman flashed through me.

"To Vega? To Algol? Which one?" I cried out.

"In the stars, Eferhild."

The sound of my alarm woke me violently. I was drenched in so much sweat that I was almost gleaming in the softness of the rising sun breaching through the curtains. I downed the glass of water on my nightstand and rubbed Jelly's belly, calming myself.

"I don't think that was a dream," I muttered, noting what I could remember in my journal from what I was certain was a vision. Perhaps it was a gift from Algol. I shivered at the cool breeze against the sweat of my body. I gripped the pendant Elvy had gifted me, hoping to feel closer to him in that moment.

The comforting waft of coffee distracted me long enough to find the courage to get out of bed. Jelly trotted happily behind me.

"Coffee, then we punch things," I said, eyeing the bag. Jelly seemed to think this was acceptable as she wagged her tail happily.

Two hours later, Jelly and I arrived at the rescue. I prayed to the stars for an easy day. It seemed the universe was not ready to give me a break.

"This is a bad one," June said sadly, filling me in on the new rehab intake. A sea lion had gotten caught in some fishing wire, cutting off blood supply to his outer extremities. His prognosis didn't look too good, but we would do everything for him or make him as comfortable as possible if it came to that.

"A sea lion? Why on Earth is a sea lion in this area?"

"Not sure. He seemed to be alone, though."

"When do they get here?"

"Should be any minute," June said, glancing down at her watch. Dr. Malik stood nearby, pacing, his station ready to go.

Finally, the large moving van backed into our loading area, carrying our patient. Only two people had come: one driving and another in the back of the van with the animal. The sight of him made my heart break. By the looks of it, the poor little guy was just a pup, but the wire had been wrapped around him for a long time. He'd probably been the victim of some irresponsible human. The skin around the wire was bleeding and raw. The coloring of the flippers didn't look right either.

It only took four of us to hoist the pup onto the stretcher and into our operating room for the vet to check him out.

"Will he be okay?" I asked.

"Only time will tell," Dr. Malik answered and began his work.

His fingers were precise and gentle while freeing the pup from the lines. June and I worked to keep the pup from moving too much since we didn't have time to put him under anesthesia.

A couple of hours later, my body was stiff and tired, but the pup was free of the bindings. Dr. Malik seemed to breathe a sigh of relief as the last of them came off and the sea lion responded to his sensory exercises well. He placed salves on the open wounds to hopefully help prevent infections, along with IV antibiotics.

"We'll need to keep him in quarantine for a bit until we see how he does," he declared.

"Want to give him a name?" June asked, eyes on me.

"He seems like a Brodie to me," I said, softly caressing his trembling body.

"Well, let's get Brodie to the shallow pool," June directed.

'Pool' was an exaggeration. It was maybe the size of a standard hot tub. We wanted him to comfortably rest until he was a little stronger. June left me with Brodie to make phone calls to rehabs that were better equipped to work with sea lions while I cooed nonsense to our mysterious patient.

"You know, Brodie. If you get big and strong again, we can get you back home," I said, my hand trailing in the water near the pup. "Or, at least, to some other little lions."

Brodie nudged my hand with his head, much like Jelly did when she wanted me to give her more attention and head scratches.

"Alright, alright," I laughed. "No need to be so sassy."

I closed my eyes, letting my ears drift off to the sound of the ocean, and wondered if Brodie was doing the same, thinking of his home or family. The familiar tug in my chest pulled on my heartstrings violently, a similar feeling to when I was around Elvy. I whipped my eyes open, but he wasn't around anywhere.

However, to my utter astonishment, the pup was *healed.* Not entirely, but the red skin was now a soft pink, and Brodie was moving around more easily. I rubbed my eyes, doing a double take. Had I just *healed* him?

I closed my eyes again and tried to emulate the same state of mind I'd just been in, and peeked at Brodie only to find him staring at me. No other signs of healing had happened. I don't know why I was in such disbelief. After all, the world of magic was something I'd learned was very much real.

But why was Vega's gift manifesting *now*? I hadn't had so much as an inkling of anything like this before. I shuddered, remembering my dream from last night, and sat down beside the pool with Brodie.

I flipped through the journal I'd brought from home and read through the gypsy woman's reading again, imitating my best mystery detective. There had to be a link between the two, and I prayed my budding gifts would help me without bringing me more questions.

Discernment is part of you, a gift from the master of spirit itself. The elixir of life's breath cannot fully manifest without the other and the path to the truth of your blood has been revealed. There is conflict within you as light moves through and around you but the darkness is above and anchoring you. One creates while the other shows the way to destiny. The stars demand a choice to be made but your path is unclear. Forged in a true act of embrace, the course can mend that which was broken. Be warned, without true creed, defying the celestials will end in eternal darkness.

The first line was pretty self-explanatory. That was talking about my gift from Algol. The stars would demand that I choose between Vega and Algol. I got that much. I had no idea what I was meant to mend. The elixir of life's breath could be Vega's gift, but what did it mean that it could not manifest without the path of my blood? Did it mean I had to make some kind of blood sacrifice, or something less literal than that?

The figure from last night's dream said I had to look to the stars soon to find the path to my blood. Not to Vega or Algol, but the stars. Maybe something to do with the constellations? I'd have to check a chart for that later.

"I don't suppose I could just get a simple answer for once?"

I finished up my work for the day, waving goodbye to June before I left. I hoped no one noticed the healing on the pup or, if they did, they'd just chalk it up to good medicinal practices. I was scheduled to meet Emma today, unsure of what we would talk about. That's usually how it went; I would always go in there having nothing to say and come out with something, even on the days I despised being there.

"Good to see you today," she offered in a way of greeting.

She sat in her usual chair across from me, waiting for me to begin.

I had to look down at my fidgeting thumbs to begin talking about what I felt safe enough to say. Magic and realms might be out of the question, but good old-fashioned relationships had proven to be a safe subject.

"I kissed him," I said, flashing a brief glance. "The guy I was telling you about."

There was only kindness in her eyes, and maybe a hint of a smile on her lips.

"What was that like for you?"

"Um, I liked it," I started, "A lot, actually. He stuck to the boundaries I set with him and didn't do anything else."

"Was it hard to have that conversation with him?" she asked, noting a few things on her pad of paper.

"Well, I didn't so much as speak it as I showed it." I explained further on how I'd shown him my limitations.

"And how do you feel about moving forward in similar situations with him?"

"It's kind of scary," I admitted. "I don't want to freak out on him or anything, but really I kind of feel like if I go there with him, I'm letting someone see all of me, the good and bad stuff."

"And in thinking of our cognitive distortions, where does that specific feeling come from? Letting someone really see you."

"I guess deep down, I'm still afraid of feeling like I'm not enough, damaged goods."

"Let's examine the evidence for that thought," she offered.

For the next thirty minutes, we went through the exercises of challenging these thoughts rationally. It was helpful to see it on paper, even when my gut wanted to scream at me for pushing it away.

"Zoe, I want to normalize what you are experiencing. Survivors can sometimes be hypersexual after their trauma or sometimes they can close off. Neither is better nor worse than the other, but I want to remind you of something. You are in control. For some, sex is a very fun, satisfying part of their life with many people, and for others, it's a serious thing. Whatever it is for you, it's valid. You aren't broken because you choose to evaluate before leaping."

"Thanks, Emma," I said, sincerely. I don't know how she knew I needed to hear that, but I had. I longed for that desire to just be normal in that area, but this reminder was helpful. I *was* being healthy about it in my own way.

"I'll see you next week, Zoe."

I glanced at the calendar behind her and saw that we wouldn't have much longer left. We had four weeks until the Winter Solstice—just before Christmas—which marked the first day of my trials.

"See you then," I answered, leaving through the door with Jelly on my back.

Nearly startling me, Freyja joined us on the walk back home, but she said little. I had a little over a month before I had to choose the rest of my life. For the first time in a while, the buzz of the crowd was getting to me. My heart raced, and Jelly began circling us, creating space and safety for me.

"Your headphones," Freyja said, motioning towards my satchel.

I nodded, slipping them on and allowing the comforting beat to reverberate through me. I bopped my head along to the music, murmuring the song as I followed the familiar path to my home. There were so many things I wanted to talk to Freyja about, but I had to get into a good headspace first. Freyja stayed silent behind me, patiently waiting for me to speak with her on my own terms.

We finally reached the safety of my living room, and I collapsed onto the fluffy rug. I paid close attention to the feel of the material, so buttery soft beneath my fingers. I lingered on the smells coming from my home, the smell of earth emitting from the plants by the window was the most centering. A few moments later and I was back in my own body, much calmer.

"Hey Freyja," I said, acknowledging her presence.

"Zoe," she smiled.

I hadn't seen her since my Emerging gifts had manifested with Oleander, which felt like a lifetime ago, but it'd really only been a week or so. Her lack of presence had bothered me, but I felt like she'd been intentionally hiding from me.

"It's weird, Freyja. Not seeing you every day," I admitted.

"You're moving on," she said. It wasn't a slight, but an accurate acknowledgment of reality. "I was never meant to be here forever, Zoe. Now that you have *others,* you don't need me like you used to."

"But I could have you in my life. If I chose Algol. I could be connected to spirit just like Oleander can see you now."

"Oleander talks too much," she muttered.

"And you don't talk enough!" I shot up, angry.

"I'd never ask you to choose me over your own happiness, Zoe. You should know that by now."

I did know that, but I was too frustrated to give a shit right this second.

"At least Oleander is giving me an accurate depiction of *all* my options. It's not fair to keep things from me."

"You're right, it isn't. And it also isn't fair for him to leave things out," she said, matching my frustration.

"Leave what out, Freyja?" I probed.

She became mute at my question, so I tried another one.

"Who told you about Elvy?"

"What do you mean?" She was never good at feigning innocence.

"Who told you to persuade me to go to him?" I clarified.

Freyja stood up, pacing in front of my well-loved bookshelf. She started biting her nails, which also showed she was getting antsy.

"Please believe that I want to tell you everything, okay? But I can't and you can be pissed about it if you want. It's all there in front of you though, Zoe. You just have to put it together."

I sighed, plopping down on the couch. I had no real reason to be angry with her. I knew deep down that I was only projecting my anger onto her.

"Please don't go," I said sadly. "Promise?"

"I'll stay tonight."

"I don't know what to do," I said, voice shaking.

"I'll always be right here," she said, placing her hand over my heart. "No matter the distance, you'll keep my spirit alive."

Slinging my arms around her neck, I sobbed into her shoulder. I didn't know who or what I cried for, but a little piece of me seemed to heal with every tear shed.

12

Hairbrush

The chime of my cell phone pulled me out of my slumber. I glanced at the clock to see I was late for work, and expected to see June's name on the screen. Being late was not something I was known for. However, it wasn't my boss; it was my mother.

"Mom?" I questioned, answering the phone.

"Oh, good. I got you," my mother's shrill voice came through the speaker. "Did I catch you at a bad time?"

"No, now is fine," I answered, stifling a yawn. Freyja had already disappeared, much to my dismay.

"Well, you know Grant and I just returned from a holiday over Thanksgiving, and we wanted to get together for dinner tonight."

With no coffee in my brain, I couldn't think of a good reason to avoid going. I'd been aware of the holiday in passing, but hadn't found the capacity to give it any of my energy.

"Sure, can I bring someone?" I asked, thinking of Elvy.

"Of course," she answered, voice faltering only slightly.

"Seven?" I asked.

"That works just fine, darling. I'll see you and your guest then."

I quickly sent a text to June expressing my fervent apology and leaped out of bed to head to work. I threw on the first clothes I touched and tied my hair back into a messy bun. It wasn't my best look, but there were no scheduled tours today, so it'd just be me and the animals.

On my way to work with Jelly, I silently swore, as I had no way to contact Elvy to ask him about coming tonight. I really would have to rectify our one-sided communication problems. The letters were sweet, but a little inconvenient at times.

I rushed into work, experiencing a bit of coffee withdrawal, and slammed into the angel himself, coffee in hand.

"It's a little cold," Elvy said. "I thought you'd get here earlier."

"I usually am," I admitted.

"Is everything okay?" he asked, doing a once over of my body.

"All fine, just slept through my alarm. Thank you for the coffee. If it has caffeine in it, I'm happy," I answered, taking a swig.

"It's decaf."

I almost spit it out until he started laughing.

"Only joking," he winked. "I wouldn't dare."

"You cruel man," I answered, taking another generous sip. "Well, I have to get to work or June will have my ass, I think."

"Of course," he replied, placing a quick kiss on my cheek before leaving.

I swore again, chasing after him. I really was off my game today. I quickly told him of the dinner with my parents tonight, and he agreed suspiciously quickly. I'd expected him to be nervous or weird around it, but he seemed good at rolling with the punches.

Throughout the day, I tried practicing the same healing gift I'd accomplished with the sea lion pup. I focused on the tug in my chest, trying to breathe life into the harmed or broken parts of the animals. Every now and then, there would be a flicker of relief from them, so I thought it might be working. I just wasn't visibly seeing much change.

If Elvy and Oleander were right, my mortal body wasn't really the best vessel for this magic. Since my body was carrying two gifts, I could only imagine what that meant. No wonder I was so exhausted all the time.

Jelly dutifully followed me to my different stations, never straying in her care of me. Brodie, the sea lion pup, seemed interested in Jelly, and she only returned the sentiment. Dr. Malik had noticed the change in Brodie and mentioned that his prognosis was exceptional. Brodie would be transferred to a better equipped facility once he put some weight back on and healed completely. I smiled at that, silently wishing I could have done more.

Before I knew it, the workday had come to an end, and I bounded off to my home with plans to meet Elvy there before we headed to my parents.

My heart soared to find him waiting for me on my screened porch with a piping hot cup of coffee in his hand. My savior.

"The service around here is great," I mused.

"Your words wound me," he laughed, handing me the coffee. I took a sizable sip, allowing my twitchy hands to settle down once they got their vice.

"I still need to shower and change, then we can go."

"I can wait out here if you want," he offered.

"No, come inside," I answered, letting him into my safe space. He let me guide him into the living room, and I briefly wondered what I would provide to entertain an immortal. Before I could fester over the expected pleasantries, he found his way over to my overflowing bookcase and began perusing.

"I'll be right here," he called, running his fingers over the spines of my collection.

"Actually, I'd like you to read this," I said, showing him the pages of my journal. "I had this dream two nights ago. Then you won't believe what I *think* happened at work yesterday, right after the dream."

Elvy quickly skimmed the pages, brows raised. I took the journal back and flipped to the pages of the prophecy.

"Now get this—I swear, Elvy, I healed one of the animals at the rescue. I tried to do it again today, but I couldn't replicate it."

He whipped me into his arms, embracing me in a crushing hug.

"Sorry," he said, sheepishly, setting me gently down. "I hope that was okay."

"More than okay," I nodded. "What do you think it means?"

"I've got a couple of ideas, but nothing concrete. One thing is for sure, we are all correct in suspecting there is something special about you, Zoe. What that truth is, I'm not sure."

"Let me guess, the mystical stars will reveal their truth when it is the right time?" I said in a mocking tone.

"Something like that," he agreed. "Now we've got plans tonight, right?"

My hair desperately needed a good washing, but I needed to get through the tangles first. Oh, the joys of having thick hair. I left him to explore my book collection while I set to work detangling the mess. Much to my embarrassment, the brush got snagged to where I could not get it out on my own.

Today is the day I lose my shit.

I briefly thought about just shaving my hair off, but I was fond of this stubborn head of hair. I hated to ask for help, but with seemingly no other choice, I faced my fears and wandered into the living room.

"I need help," I said, unnecessarily pointing out the disastrous mess.

"My goodness," he responded with a small chuckle. "I'd say so."

"Don't laugh," I said, hiding my face in my palms, but peeking through my fingers.

"Laughing with you is my favorite thing."

Elvy put down the book he'd been skimming through, and patted the spot on the floor in front of him. I was a little nervous at the position, but allowed my trust in him to overrule this fear. I sat crisscrossed between his legs and my back leaned on the sofa as he worked the brush out of my hair.

His fingers were gentle and methodical while working through the tangled disarray, and his hands never strayed from the task at hand. Once he had worked the brush free, he brushed out the rest of my hair, which was a happy surprise.

I felt so entirely safe and cared for in this moment that I closed my eyes, leaning into the feel of him expertly smoothing and taming my long hair. He took care not to touch the back of my neck, but brushed my hair out with his palm instead. It felt so euphoric; I had to stifle a groan, desperately trying to break free.

"I think that should do it," he said, drawing me from my thoughts. "I can wash it if you'd like."

The words caught in my throat, but I nodded, eyes full of desire.

He led me to the empty kitchen sink and positioned a chair and towel so that it comfortably leaned back, flush with the sink. I quickly grabbed the shampoo and conditioner from my bathroom and brought them out to him.

He let the water warm up, eyes never leaving mine. Those beautiful, kind gray eyes were so full of... *something.* As if I was the most important thing in the world to him at that moment. With all the magic I was sure radiated beneath that muscular, tan skin, he was incredibly tender.

I leaned back into the sink and let him massage the shampoo into my wet hair. We didn't speak throughout the process, but there was a silent electricity coursing through the air between us. I couldn't help the smile that played on my lips as I enjoyed the care of Elvy.

"You are a truly stunning creature," he noted. "Especially when you smile like that."

"What's the first thing you think of when you think of Lyra?" I asked, desiring to know the land he called home.

"Art. It's more mesmerizing than simple words could adequately describe. No matter where you are in the city or countryside, you can see billions of stars. It's so clear, it almost seems like you can touch them. It's a land of healing and a place where visionaries come to fulfill their dreams."

"Do immortals have wishes?"

He leaned so close to me; I felt his breath on my ear while he continued kneading my scalp. "Even Vega listens to the dreamers, Zoe."

"Have you wished on the almighty Vega, Elvy?"

He stopped working through my hair and turned on the water again.

"After my parents died, there was an unfathomably dark hole inside of me… it was the first time I wanted to wish for something."

"Did it come true?"

"Not in the way I expected, no. Maybe in the way I needed, though."

He finished his task with a final rinse and helped me towel off the dripping hair.

"Thank you, Elvy… I could get used to that," I murmured.

"I don't think I'd ever get used to you." He placed a soft kiss on my smiling lips. "Do you need help drying your hair?"

"No, I think I got it from here, but thank you."

He gave me one more kiss, then resumed his position on the couch with Jelly.

I quickly rinsed off in the shower and took the time to blow dry my hair out afterwards, something that was a rarity for me. I left my face natural and decided on a nicer pair of black jeans and olive-green shirt.

I emerged from my bedroom to find Elvy and Jelly cozying up to each other. Jelly's head laid in his lap, looking perfectly at home.

"Traitor," I said, pulling him from his book. "Can't say I blame her."

"Ready?" he asked with a gleam in his eyes.

"We're about to find out."

13

Dinner

My heart was pounding so loud I thought Elvy might hear it with his immortal ears. If he did, he didn't give me away. My mother greeted us with a winning smile as she opened the door.

The space was not homey, nor did it elicit any childhood memories. In fact, it felt sterile, filled with whites and grays. Grant and my mother purchased this home not long after Freyja passed away. The memories were too much for her to bear in our old house.

"It's a pleasure to meet you, ma'am." Elvy held out his hand. It was odd to see him so formal now.

"Please call me Vivian," my mother answered, shaking his outstretched hand. "I don't get to see enough of you, Zo. Come on in."

We followed her retreating figure with Jelly in tow behind us. My heart rate only increased, wary of what kind of behavior my parents would have around him tonight. So far, so good. Bringing him with me had to have thrown them for a loop.

"Just breathe," Elvy whispered, squeezing my hand briefly. "I have faced down evil incarnate, I got this."

"If you say so," I said, letting out a big breath. I couldn't allow myself to go down the rabbit hole of what evil he'd seen in his life and refocused on the task at hand.

We followed Mom past the foyer and into the living room. Grant sat in the large leather armchair with a beer already in hand.

"Good to see you, Zo," Grant stated, nodding his beer to Elvy. "Want anything?"

"Water with lemon is fine, thank you," I said.

"Make that two please," Elvy replied. "It's nice to meet you, sir."

"I wondered when our Zoe would finally bring a man home," my step-father said, making my cheeks flush in embarrassment. "I'm Grant."

"Elvy," he said, shaking his hand.

"Elvy? That's a little...unique," Grant pointed out.

"Grant, where are your manners?" Vivian chastised.

"Oh, it's completely fine, Vivian. It's an old name," Elvy offered in explanation. "Can I help with dinner or anything?"

"Thank you, Elvy, but it's almost ready, actually. Just a few more minutes. You and Zoe could help finish setting the table, though."

"Absolutely," he beamed.

Vivian and Grant sauntered off to the kitchen to finish up dinner while Elvy and I went to the adjacent dining room to finish arranging the table.

"You're surprisingly good at this," I noted casually. "Meeting the parents." A slight twinge of jealousy shot through me, but I swallowed the irrational thought down.

"I've never done it before," he said, as if answering my unspoken question. "Just years of court manners and diplomacy. Delmira and Blaz also gave me a pep talk before coming."

"Blaz knows how to impress parents?" I scoffed.

"Oh, no. His suggestions were terrible," he laughed.

"I can't wait to hear them later," I said, trying to stifle my laughter. "I'm sure Delmira was just as hilarious."

"Dinner is served," Vivian announced, ceasing our conversation. She set freshly grilled steaks and vegetables on the table in front of us. "Our guest picks first."

Elvy didn't hesitate and made his plate; however, like a true gentleman, he waited until everyone had food before digging in. It was probably good, too, since Grant decided to lead us in a brief prayer before eating. Elvy quietly grasped my hand under the table, eyes closed. I silently wondered whether he believed in the God Grant was praying to or if this was just for show.

"So, how did you two meet?" my mother asked before I could even swallow my first bite. Here it comes. All the questions.

"Actually, at the benefit you two hosted for the rescue," he answered, not missing a beat. "My friends and I took a tour of the rescue afterwards."

"You were at the benefit?" Grant asked curiously. "What's your last name?"

"Kimble, sir," he answered.

Grant and my mother went pale and flushed with apologies.

"I am so sorry I did not recognize you. Zoe, did you know Mr. Kimble provided the largest donation to the rescue?"

"I'm afraid he forgot to mention that," I said, glancing at him. I speared a vegetable a little too aggressively.

He only smiled broader, stealing a secret squeeze of my hand under the table again.

"It was no problem at all, Vivian. I believe in Zoe's cause," he explained. "I've seen her work. She's excellent at what she does. June is also a delight."

"It was still very generous," Grant acknowledged.

"Very," Vivian agreed.

I knew Grant and Mom would be on their best behavior the rest of the night after learning this information. They were good people, truly, but money spoke to them. I quietly slipped Jelly a piece of steak while the parents were busy ogling over their guest.

"The steak is grilled perfectly," Elvy offered, stifling the onslaught of compliments.

The rest of dinner went about the same, non-sequential questions and pleasantries, asking nothing too deep or personal, much to my relief. A pain shot through my chest as I stared at the empty chair across from me where Freyja should be sitting. I silently wished for her to present herself, even if I was the only one who could see her. She never joined us, though, allowing me to *move on* as she had claimed.

"Zoe?" my mother asked, pulling me from my thoughts.

"Yes?" I must have missed a question.

"Do you have any plans for the holiday season?"

Finally, a question I'd hoped to avoid had manifested itself. I stumbled, trying to find the right words to explain my mortal turmoil without sounding utterly insane, but I failed.

"I was going to wait," Elvy began. "But now is as good a time as any."

Oh no, where was he going with this? He noticed that fear in my eyes and squeezed my hand reassuringly, asking me to silently trust him.

"I actually booked us a getaway to my home in Alaska over the rescue's downtime in December. That is, if you'd like to go, Zoe."

"Why in this world would you want to go to Alaska?" Grant asked, too ignorant of the rescue's work to understand that the rescue did not have downtime ever.

I wasn't listening to Grant. My focus was on Elvy's endearing gray eyes. I realized what he was offering me. More time to figure out how to part with my parents. I doubted he'd really booked us this trip, but I knew he would if that's what I wanted from him.

"I'd love to," I answered. "As long as Jelly gets to come."

"Wouldn't dream of leaving her behind," he agreed.

I hadn't realized how close we'd leaned into each other before my mother cleared her throat. "I was hoping to spend Christmas with you, Zo."

"We can celebrate before we leave," Elvy offered.

Mom, never wanting to disrupt the societal pleasantries, nodded in agreement.

After we cleaned up the table, Grant pulled Elvy back into the living room, and I shot him an apologetic look. Mom filled our glasses with coffee and guided us to the outdoor patio. I'd gotten my taste for coffee with Vivian as a mother.

"I never thought I'd see you happy again," she noted, with the silver of tears in her eyes. "You are happy, right?"

"Yes, Mom. I really am." I realized the truth in my voice as I spoke the words.

"And you are still seeing Emma, talking about things?"

"Yes," I answered, unwilling to discuss that further.

"Good. I just worry sometimes," she explained. "But you seem different now. Lighter."

"I hope it lasts," I admitted honestly.

"Freyja would be so proud of you," my mother whispered, eyes shining.

"I think you're right."

Mom and I drank our coffee in silence, enjoying the peaceful moment. I allowed myself permission to be fully present, knowing that my time with her was limited. I found myself with a belly full of laughter at some of my mother's gossip about her group of friends. I was glad to know she was happy in life and with a strong support system, no matter what happened to me.

"This is my favorite time of year," Vivian said, staring up into the stars. I followed her gaze, but found nothing particularly moving about it tonight.

"Why is that?"

"You see those clusters of stars, just to the left of the moon? Then down a little?"

I squinted, trying to see the image she was pointing out.

"That's the Archer," she said, almost fondly.

"Like as in the zodiac sign? Sagittarius, right?"

Vivian only nodded, sipping her coffee.

I knew very little about the meaning behind zodiac signs. I knew I was a Pisces, having been born in March, but that was about it. I didn't know the significance this time would hold for my mother.

"What's so special about the Archer?" I asked, curiously.

"Your father used to tell me the story of Chiron in Greek mythology. He was obsessed with the stars. He always said that the Archer never missed his mark because he could see the future."

My heart was pounding. One, my mother never spoke about my father, not even his name. He wasn't even listed on my birth certificate, but I knew I held his surname. Two, I felt like this could be part of the answer I was looking for in the stars, but I had no idea who my father was.

"You've never talked about him before," I said.

"It's weird, Zoe. He's just been on my mind lately. I know he left us, but I was in love with him. It was a great love," she said, the last word breaking just slightly.

"What was his name?" I asked, holding my breath.

"His name was Archie. But I always got the sense that there was more to him than he let on."

A rasp on the patio door interrupted our gossip.

"It's getting late," Elvy noted.

I glanced at my watch, seeing that he was right. I would need to sleep soon.

"It was good to spend time with you," I told my mother genuinely.

"You too," she said, wrapping me in a bear hug, as if she knew this might be the last time she'd get to. "Just be happy, Zo."

14

Scars

Elvy stood beside me outside my front door, giving me the play-by-play of his interaction with Grant while I'd been with my mother.

"He said what!" I exclaimed.

Apparently, Grant had taken it upon himself to let Elvy know he'd hurt him if he ever did anything to break my heart.

"He was just doing the dad thing," he smiled. "As he should."

"Maybe so, but I'm not overly fond of the idea of someone hurting you," I admitted.

"I'm not that fragile, Zoe," he said, allowing me to snuggle into his chest.

"Vivian told me about my biological father tonight," I whispered, as if I didn't want to acknowledge what she'd said. "It was kind of weird. She's never spoke about him before. Apparently, he and I are both fond of the stars."

"What do you know about him?"

"Nothing. I wouldn't recognize him if he came up to me right now, and I know that he's not on my birth certificate. I remembered it caused a big fight between them."

"Seems like that is a path worth looking into," he answered.

He leaned his chin on top of my head, swaying to a song I couldn't hear.

"So you didn't really book us a flight to Alaska?"

"No, but I can if you want me to," he said, playing with a strand of my hair.

"I'd rather do the trials here," I said after some thought.

"Then no Alaska."

"I don't want to be alone tonight," I said, shyly.

I felt him still beside me. Perhaps, realizing the weight of what I was saying.

"Are you sure?" he asked.

"I just want you near me."

"Okay," he said, smiling. "Lead the way, milady."

"Lord Astral," I nodded, teasing him.

Jelly and Elvy trailed behind me as I locked the door for the night. Jelly seemed content to flop down on the living room couch, belly full of illicit steak, and I guided him into the bedroom.

"I've never had someone in my bed since that night," I admitted, attempting to be honest, even though I'd never gone into detail with him over what happened.

"You're in control here," he said, not moving an inch closer.

"I have a spare toothbrush in the cabinet," I said, motioning to the bathroom.

He only nodded and followed me to the bathroom to get ready for bed. We stood in silence as we brushed our teeth, but I caught a few gray glances at me peek beneath his brown, silver curls. When we finished, I led him back out to the bedroom.

"Do you want me to stay in these?" he asked, motioning towards his jeans.

"They don't look very comfortable," I said, stepping closer to him. "May I?" My intention was apparent.

He nodded as I moved my fingers to the button of his jeans, easily pulling them down his heavily muscled legs. I helped him step out of them and stood back up, eyes burning.

"And this?" he pointed to his shirt.

"Seems unnecessary," I said, grabbing the bottom of his shirt and pulling it over his head.

Elvy tossed the shirt in a discarded corner, never breaking eye contact. Before my eyes, he allowed his tattoos to break through the glamor and mark his skin. The only thing that remained were his boxers.

"I think my pants would be a little uncomfortable in bed," I noted, guiding his hand to the zipper of my jeans. His fingers gently grazed the skin of my stomach, warming where it touched. The tug in my chest ached to have him all over me, but I settled with brushing my fingers through his hair and along the stars across his chest.

His hands seemed to tremble as he slid my jeans open, and he knelt on his knees before me, pulling them past my hips down to the floor. I saw the desire in his eyes, strong as mine, and I had to admit that I liked him in this position.

His fingers lingered at my ankles, his eyes looked up at me in question. I only nodded, craving his touch just as badly. He swept his fingers up the length of my legs, painstakingly slow. My breasts peaked painfully against my bra, and I arched my back at the sensual circles he created with that incredibly light touch that seemed to hold a hurricane beneath the surface.

Not taking his hands off me, he stood in front of me, waiting.

Without looking away, I unclipped my bra underneath my shirt, expertly taking it off while my shirt stayed put.

"Shirt stays on," I said, leading him to the bed, not nearly finished surveying him. He continued to let me have control of our progress. His patience and kindness were unparalleled to what I could have hoped for.

Elvy was flat on the bed but propped up with pillows behind him, and I slowly eased myself so that I straddled his hips beneath me. He growled softly as I made contact with him, but he didn't move an inch, waiting for me to make my intentions clear.

For a moment, I was worried about ruining the mood, but I knew I had to be honest with him. I had to speak my truth.

"I'm going to show you where you can touch me," I said.

Elvy nodded—the desire had not left those gray eyes.

I took his hands and guided them to my waist, slightly touching the fullness of my backside.

"Here is okay," I breathed. My stomach fluttered as I guided them higher on my body until each hand cupped my breasts. "And here."

He swallowed, eyes darker, and I took pleasure in the heat that filled between my legs and the hard length of him beneath me.

I continued leading his hand to the front of my neck, not the back, then finished by going down the front of my shoulders and arms.

"Clear?" I asked.

"Yes," he said, breathlessly.

Elvy saw the *okay* in my eyes and leapt into the desire of what we both wanted—*needed*.

He sat up and kissed my mouth fervently, desperately needing to fill himself with me. I slung my arms around his bare back, digging my nails in as he moved his hand to explore my body. He groaned in satisfaction as I breathed his name frantically, repeatedly.

He flipped me over so that I was on my back, gazing into my eyes to make sure I was still comfortable and fully present with him. I nodded, eyes pleading for him to continue. He murmured my name like a prayer, burning kisses on my hips and up my side. I pulled my shirt up slightly, giving him more access to my skin, and my toes curled in pleasure.

His body became rigid, and I searched for his gaze, wondering what I'd done wrong. His eyes were caught on the scar that had come from the stab wound. Elvy's entire frame trembled, and his eyes held death in them.

"Who did this to you, Zoe?"

I pulled his chin up to meet my eyes. "Don't let them take this moment from us."

With a true show of strength, he shook the rage from his expression and placed a tender kiss along the scar, claiming this moment once again.

His entire body was over me now, nuzzling under my jaw, and I clung to him as my hands explored the length of his muscled back and down to his hips. He flipped me again, so that I lay flush on top of him, careful to leave his hands wrapped on my lower back, near my waist. We just laid there breathing, listening to each other's heartbeat.

"I don't think I'd ever tire of touching you," he said, placing a kiss in my hair. "You are so beautiful, Zoe."

"Even with these?" I asked, pointing to my scars.

"Stunning," he breathed.

"Is this enough?" I asked, a little nervous.

He cupped my cheek, turning my face so that he could see into my eyes.

"You are enough. Just as you are," he stated. "Now, sleep."

It didn't take me long to slip off into the world of dreams. I'd never felt safer in my own skin than I did tonight. I never strayed far from his touch as we both drifted off into sleep, hearts seemingly beating as one.

***

I woke up before Elvy the next morning to find him peacefully sprawled out on the bed. The Lord Astral sound asleep in my mortal bed. I hadn't forgotten the words he'd spoken to me when he first told me that I was Emerging—the rarity of the Lord Astrals being the ones to find their star's Emerging mortals, and I had two—Oleander and Elvy. There was a reason for it, but I would worry about that later. For now, I would breathe in this moment, and thank Vega, or whoever was out there listening, that they had brought Elvy into my life.

Jelly leaped on the bed, waking Elvy from his slumber.

"Good morning," I said, smiling, with two cups of coffee in my hand.

He met my smile and happily accepted his cup of jet fuel. At least, it was with the way I made it.

"Good morning, gorgeous," Elvy winked. "Are you working today?"

"Yes," I said, not entirely sad. I enjoyed my work.

"I have to tend to a few things in Vega," he began. "Don't give me that look. I'll only be a call away."

"You have a cell that can cross realms?" I questioned, remembering my inability to call him. "I can't even call you while on the same planet!"

"No, but my court all have a direct link to me. I can have one of them stay close to you if you'd like."

"That would be okay," I conceded.

"Clodovea, Delmira, and Finnian are going with me. What about Imelda?"

"You don't want Blaz staying with me?" I asked, laughing.

"Your choice," he chuckled. "I'm sure he'd love it."

"Maybe I'll let him hang with me and Imelda then."

"They'll be here soon," he said, getting dressed. "We are leaving straight from your place."

On cue, I heard a knock on the door, and I welcomed the familiar faces inside my home.

"Fun night?" Blaz asked with playful, taunting eyes.

"Pipe down, grunt," Imelda said, rolling her eyes at him.

"It's okay," I said, laughing at them.

Delmira, Finnian, and Clodovea were off to the corner, engaged in a heated discussion.

"I've instructed Imelda and Blaz to be anything you might need while I'm away. I shouldn't be gone more than one day, but things could change."

My heart ached at the thought of being away from him for even that short amount of time. He seemed to think the same thing and lingered a little longer on our kiss than normal.

"Will it be just a day for me, too?" I'd never given much thought to the concept of time there.

"Time moves much the same in Lyra," he replied, attempting to pull away, but I held on, biting my lip.

"You're stalling," he said, placing a playful kiss in my hair. "I'll see you soon, Zoe."

Elvy and his three Luminaries spread their wings, getting ready to travel to their realm. All of their wings were that same watery translucent color as Elvy's. I hugged him tightly, remembering the last time I'd flown with him.

To the corner of my eye, I noticed Imelda giving Clodovea a passionate kiss goodbye, seeming just as sad as I was to be separated from her partner. I pulled my eyes away from them, giving Elvy one last kiss before he disappeared from my embrace.

"What now?" Blaz seemed excited.

"I guess you're coming to work with me?" I looked at Imelda, worried.

"Blaz will be on his best behavior, won't you?" Imelda questioned.

"I always am!" Blaz exclaimed, feigning hurt.

"Let's go then," I said, calling for Jelly to follow us on the short walk to work. I certainly had my hands full today.

15

Sleepover

June saw no problem with my two companions coming along, which was the response I expected from her. Not only could we always use extra hands, but it was just the way she was. Today, we'd have to get into the shallow pools to work on the physical therapy exercise with the animals.

"You'll need to put this on," I said, handing Blaz a tiny wetsuit.

He held the suit up to his larger-than-life frame, and I tried to stifle a laugh.

"You've got to be joking," he said, sizing the suit up.

"It's stretchy," I said, laughing with him. "Get a move on. We have things to do."

Blaz gave me a low, goofy bow and headed off to the men's locker room while Imelda and I hurried off to the women's.

"How long have you and Clodovea been together?" I asked, slipping off my clothes, not feeling a hint of shame for the scars that she would surely notice.

"Around a century, if I had to put a number to it. We didn't get along at first, but Clove was persistent," she said smiling, eyes in a memory, long before my existence was even thought of in this universe.

"It must be hard to be away from someone you've been with that long," I mused.

"It can be," she admitted. "But being the Lord Astral's third comes with its expectations. She is gone a lot. So am I for that matter."

"Right. Elvy mentioned you were an emissary for him."

"Yes, I'm the emissary to the Court of Arcturus—fire nation," Imelda explained, pulling her arms through her wetsuit.

"Water and fire... doesn't seem like they'd get along."

"It's delicate, but I have such a winning smile," she beamed, and I believed it.

Seeing that she was finished, I led us back outside to meet up with Blaz. Like I'd known it would, his wetsuit had fit him fine, but it left little to the imagination. So dramatic. We found him squatted next to Jelly, rubbing her belly.

"Slackers," I said, shaking my head at the pair. "Come on, we're going to the pup first."

I led Imelda and Blaz to the shallow pools where we would conduct the physical therapy. Brodie was doing much better, and I tossed him a couple of fish when we arrived.

"Hey there, bud," I said, splashing water around him.

"Should we get in?" Blaz asked.

"Not yet," I directed, stepping into the pool, letting Brodie decide I was a safe person for him. "Are you ready to get better?"

I gently lifted Brodie into my arms so he could practice moving his flippers without carrying the weight of his body. The water was about waist deep on me, and I sunk into it further until it covered my shoulders.

"What happened to him?" Imelda asked.

I explained what was going on with our patient and shared what I'd been able to do for Brodie. I also shared my frustration with struggling to duplicate it, and Blaz seemed to analyze my words, asking for clarification. Neither seemed surprised by this development in my gift from Vega, but happy that it was finally revealing itself.

"Go back to what you were thinking of when you first did it. Picture your source of magic like a thread attached to Vega. You have to pull on the string, and allow it to fill you, then redirect it where you want it to go," Blaz explained.

"I was thinking of Elvy," I admitted.

"Then go back there," Imelda said. "Your gift is part of you, not something you are ever separate from. It will come when called."

"Don't be discouraged if it takes a while to get the hang of it," Blaz offered.

Closing my eyes, I allowed the tug in my chest to fill every atom that resided within me. I let my mind be consumed by the thrash of the ocean in the distance, and I felt the sweat forming on my brow despite the cool water around me. Imagining the wounds on Brodie healing, I tried to take away his pain. I let my mind be transported to what I could fathom Vega to be, and I gently plucked on the strings of energy, redirecting them to my target.

"Zoe, you're glowing," Imelda said, breaking me from my trance. "A bright white around you."

"What?" I asked, blinking my eyes back into focus.

"It's fading now, but you were definitely glowing, Zo," Blaz said, studying me.

"That should be normal for immortals, right?" I asked, turning my attention back to the pup. "I've seen Elvy glow, like a blue before." Brodie's wounds had all but healed, and he was wiggling to break free of my hold. I obliged, and he used his flippers without pain for probably the first time since the accident.

"You healed him nearly fully—a mortal wielded extensive magic," Imelda said, eyes questioning.

"You guys are freaking me out," I said, climbing out of the pool. "You literally just told me what I was supposed to do to use my gift. I just did what you said."

"I thought you were exaggerating about your first healing with Brodie," Blaz admitted. "This is far more advanced than what a typical Emerging would be able to do."

Even Jelly was sniffing me like something was off about my scent.

"Zoe, Emerging mortals shouldn't be able to use their gifts like that. And you are *healing*—better than any young immortal. I've never seen an Emerging do that," Imelda explained.

"There's something different about you," Blaz agreed.

"Is that why Elvy really came to find me?" I asked, my body unsure of how it felt about that. "He knew I'd be different. He knew I could be a powerful asset for Vega. We all know there is more at stake with my Emergence."

"No, Zoe," Imelda said, honesty in her eyes. "It's for him to tell you, though, not us."

"So there is *something*."

Blaz only nodded, confirming.

"But there's a good reason he hasn't revealed it yet?"

"Yes," Imelda said, warily. I'm sure she thought I might get upset.

"I'm not mad," I reassured her. I knew all too well the need to let things come out when they needed to, or I was comfortable enough to tell them. I had no issue extending that to Elvy.

"I mean, Imelda and I both have some pretty gnarly healing gifts, but if you are already healing... you'll be a force to be reckoned with as an immortal," Blaz said. "That is—if you do choose Vega."

"More importantly, Zoe. You have two Emerging gifts manifesting," Imelda said. "Elvy told us what happened with Oleander. You have to be careful until the trial. You don't want your mortal body to burn out."

"Now that you mention it, I am very tired," I admitted, eyes heavy with sleep. I felt like I'd just gone rounds on the punching bag.

"Let's get you some coffee then and we'll help take over what you need to do today," Imelda said, with concern in her eyes.

"Please don't tell Elvy about the healing today. I'd like to myself," I said, and they agreed. I could tell it was difficult for them, though, not wanting to keep anything from their Lord Astral. I was certain Elvy would be happy that Vega's gift was emerging strongly in me, but I wasn't sure he'd like the toll it took either.

When Imelda brought me to the rescue's office, June came in, making a fuss over me. She went on and on about me working too hard and expressed her guilt about the extra time I'd put into the rescue. With the help of Blaz and Imelda, we finally calmed her down enough once they offered to help finish off my shift for the day.

I sat on the tiny couch still in my wetsuit, but I'd rolled down the top half. I briefly noticed Blaz glance at the scar on my abdomen, and his eyes flared with anger. One look from Imelda, and he shook it off. I covered myself in a blanket, gingerly sipping on yet another cup of hot coffee. Jelly had squeezed herself beside me, laying half her body on top of me. I needed the weighted therapy she was providing by doing so.

Despite the caffeine, I had apparently fallen asleep, because I was woken up by the loud laughter coming from June and Blaz as they came to check on me.

"How are you feeling, honey?" June asked.

"I'm feeling much better," I said, stretching my muscles to find them feeling rested. "Did you guys get everything done?"

"Yes, you have some wonderful friends," she said, smiling at both Blaz and Imelda.

"That I do," I said, genuinely.

"Go ahead and head home for the day, Zo. Take the rest of the week. You deserve some rest."

"June, I couldn't possibly do that," I said in disbelief.

"The pup is doing so much better, and we'll handle the rest. Don't you worry about it."

"June, what are you and Dr. Malik going to do without me?" I questioned.

"If we could have a moment, Blaz," she said, sitting down beside me. Blaz nodded and walked towards the entrance. "Listen here, Zoe Eferhild, I love you. I think you know that. You're like my own flesh and blood, but you were meant for more than this. I'll die here at this rescue. It's my whole life, but I don't want the same for you. Call it the wisdom of an old woman, but you need to go find your purpose, child."

I stared at her, stunned, going mute at her words.

"I've seen you at your lowest, kid, but I've also seen you start to bloom. Keep on blooming, Zo. It's alright."

I slung my arms around her neck and breathed in the familiar scent of lilies that always accompanied her. I knew there was no arguing with her at this point, and I resigned to let her have her way.

"I'm not ready to say goodbye."

"So don't yet, Zoe, but I swear I'll fire you if I have to," she said, grinning.

"Thank you, June. For everything," I said with sincerity.

"Now run along, Zoe. I'll see you soon," she promised.

I quickly changed clothes in the locker room and followed Imelda and Blaz out the exit. We stopped by some hole-in-the-wall taco shop before heading home. My healing gift must also make me ravenous because I downed three tacos before even reaching the front door of my bungalow.

"Damn, Zo," Blaz said, laughing. "Maybe we should have gotten more tacos."

"Don't judge," I answered, turning my nose up at him. "Come on in."

We all settled in on the couch, enjoying the feast of tacos. I turned on some background music while we finished eating.

"So, are you both staying here tonight?"

"Yeah, I can sleep in the reclining chair," Blaz said. "Imelda, you can have the couch."

"Sounds good to me," she shrugged. "You better control your snoring, Blaz."

"I don't snore," he said, feigning offense.

Imelda responded by slamming a pillow in his face.

"Have you heard anything from Elvy?" I asked, drawing them from their battle.

"No," she said, shaking her head. "But no news is good news."

I had a feeling Imelda was only telling me that to reassure me, but either way, they didn't seem concerned about it themselves, so I would take their lead on it.

"Is that a punching bag in your dining room?" Blaz asked, like he wanted to keep me distracted, and I decided to go along with it.

"Yeah, want to go a few rounds?" I asked, pulling him and Imelda towards my makeshift gym. Jelly followed naturally.

"Let's see what you've got, mortal," Blaz answered, arms crossed. Imelda smiled encouragingly and flicked him on the ear.

"She's a strong one. I can tell," Imelda said as I finished wrapping my wrists.

With a breath of courage, I got into my fighting stance and began working the bag. I incorporated different kicks and punch patterns, forgetting that I had an audience for a moment. It felt good to sweat and be in control of something in a world I so often felt powerless in.

"Nice form, Zoe," Blaz commented. "You would do well in the Shadowed Legion. Let me show you a few things?"

I nodded and let both Blaz and Imelda show me new moves, and my body seemed to conform to everything they taught me. Blaz strengthened my kicks and made them more lethal, while Imelda improved my flexibility. I felt like I was learning from Athena and Ares themselves, and I clung to their every word, committing it to memory. Eventually, my mortal body tired, and we resumed our seats in the living room.

"So, both of you were born immortal, right?" I asked.

Both of them nodded.

"What's it like?" I asked. "Vega, immortal life?"

"Nothing is truly immortal, but we age slow enough that we might as well be," Blaz said thoughtfully. "I don't think it's really any different from a human life. Just a little more razzle dazzle."

"Did you really just say 'razzle dazzle'?" Imelda asked.

"You know what I mean," he said.

"It's a poor way of explaining it, but it's just *other*. We feel things more intensely, which is both better and worse."

"The sex is epic," Blaz chimed in, earning him another pillow to the face.

I couldn't help the flash of what Elvy and I had done the other night fly through me. If he was feeling that even more intensely than I was, then I suddenly appreciated his patience with me even more.

"Can you not for five seconds?" Imelda continued, "It's hard to explain, really, but Vega is the source of water. The heart of our nation is right on the coast, kind of like Saint Andrews is but a lot bigger. The stars are infinite and the air feels so good to breathe. There are colorful lights flashing all around, starlights," she said, motioning toward her tattooed wrist.

The flash of the memory of the light show following my unknowing first encounter with Oleander popped into my mind.

"That was you guys, wasn't it? The first time Oleander followed me home."

"Yes," Blaz answered. "It's our truest form, too dangerous for mortal eyes."

"That's why Elvy said I had to wait," I said, putting the pieces together.

"Elvy's just looking out for you," Imelda replied.

"Well, if it's going to burn my eyes out or whatever it would do, I appreciate the protections," I said, laughing. "So Blaz, if Imelda is emissary to the fire nation, who are you emissary to?"

"Air—the Court of Canopus. Finnian is an emissary to the Court of Rigil—ground," Blaz answered, freely offering the extra information.

"Keeping the peace between realms seems exhaustive," I mentioned, feeling my eyes getting heavy with sleep.

"In all seriousness, Zoe," Imelda began. "Yes, we immortals feel things more intensely, but our actions have much bigger consequences than mortals. Selfishness cannot be part of our nature. It is always about the greater good."

"But power is seductive," Blaz replied. "Power can corrupt those without true creed."

Creed. That word had stuck out to me in the prophecy of the gypsy woman.

"Creed—what does that mean to you or to immortals?" I asked, a little too intently.

"For me, it's about remembering that no matter the summit of a mountaintop or the depth of a valley a person is in—we are all one, interrelated universe. It's my conviction in the stars," Blaz said, almost poetically. "My creed guides my path."

"My path," I said with sleep in my voice.

"Go to sleep," Imelda said, noting the stifled yawn. "I'll keep him straight."

Too tired to argue, I called for Jelly to follow me and drifted off to sleep with the sounds of Blaz and Imelda quietly bickering at each other.

16

Lagoon

Much to my dismay, Elvy had not returned when I'd awoken. I'd gotten up just before five in the morning to find Imelda and Blaz passed out. Blaz was snoring loudly, after all. Not wanting to disturb them, Jelly and I walked to the local coffee shop a few blocks away for some much-needed caffeine.

As I was flipping through a well-worn book while waiting for my coffee, the familiar wave of nausea rolled over me. 'Wave' was too strong of a word. What had once felt like a tsunami was more like a trickle in a stream, enough to be uncomfortable but not overwhelming.

I turned around, expecting to see Oleander, but another familiar face greeted me. The gypsy woman gave me a knowing smile and sat down beside me without me extending the offer. Her blue-black hair seemed to glow in the morning sun.

"Have you been following me?" I asked bravely.

"No, Eferhild. I wouldn't say that," she said, sighing as if she had the weight of the world on her shoulders.

"Eferhild?" I asked, only ever called that once in a dream that had been plaguing my waking thoughts. My gut seemed to scream at me to follow this path. "Who are you?"

"You can call me Phoebe."

"Should I know who you are, Phoebe?" I asked, trying to concentrate.

"Child, you reveal too much," she said, almost chastising. "You must learn to shield or you will not survive the trials."

"How do you know about that?" I asked, heart racing.

"I come on behalf of blood, Eferhild. You must embrace who you really are. Their own desires blind the celestials. Time is running out."

"What do you mean blood—do you know my father?" I asked, gripping her shirt, which did not seem to intimidate her at all.

“You should know by now. It’s all in the stars, Eferhild,” Phoebe said, before walking away as I let my hands fall from her. I nearly raced after her when a fresh wave of nausea wafted through me.

“Hello, Oleander,” I said, not taking my eyes from the retreating figure.

“Why the cold shoulder?” he asked, seemingly in earnest.

“I’m cranky before I’ve had my coffee,” I explained, still not looking up and choosing to keep the interaction with Phoebe to myself for now.

“I can always come back later... you are a hard woman to find alone, Zoe Eferhild,” he said with an almost smugness in his voice.

“And I’m sure it's a coincidence that you found me while Elvy is away?” I asked, finally looking up at him. His expression told me what I’d already realized. Oleander had orchestrated some reason for Elvy to return to Lyra.

“He was never going to let you near me again,” he stated, shrugging his shoulders.

“He may not like you, Oleander, and you may hate him for whatever reason I’m too exhausted to hear about right now, but you should give him more credit than that.”

“Perhaps,” he said, not unconvinced.

“It’s not his decision, nor does he own me,” I said, irritated. “If you wanted to meet with me so bad, you could have just asked.”

“Nonetheless, it had been far too long since I’d poked the lurking beast beneath his cool facade,” Oleander replied playfully.

“You shouldn’t do things like that—whatever it is you did,” I said, glaring.

“I assure you no one will be hurt,” he said with promise in his voice. “I just wanted to see and check on you.”

I rolled my eyes in exasperation. He seemed sincere, and I’m sure whatever history there was between Oleander and Elvy probably made him feel this way, but that was still no excuse for him to corner me like this. Especially given my fear of that very thing.

“Well, you’ve laid eyes on me. I’m just fine. Satisfied?”

“I thought we might also do some training, practice the gift Algol gave you,” he stated.

“You’ll burn her out,” Freyja spat, springing up in the chair next to me and across from Oleander.

“Ah, Freyja,” he purred. “So lovely for you to join us.”

“If I wasn’t dead, I’d tear out your throat,” Freyja said, matching the intensity of his gaze. This only made him smile more broadly. I knew this kind of fury was always in Freyja, but it was a rare occasion that it surfaced.

Refusing to let these two hot heads tear down my favorite coffee shop, I led them outside, just as the sun was breaching the horizon. I still hadn't gotten used to the idea of someone else other than myself being able to see Freyja, but given the instability of Oleander, I'm not sure that really boded well for my own sanity. I looked longingly back at the coffee shop, twitching for another fix, but I had to save it from the two supernatural, stubborn souls in front of me.

"She's right," I said to Oleander once we were out of earshot of any prying eyes. "This magic—or whatever it is—it's fatiguing me. I basically passed out the last time I tried."

"You've been practicing the gift of Algol?" he mused.

"No," I said simply.

"Then Vega's gift is finally coming out to play?" he guessed, but I said nothing, unsure of how much I could trust him.

"Your mortal body could burn out, yes," he agreed. "But mastering them as much as you can before your trials will only help in the long run. You can balance it."

"You don't know that," Freyja said sternly.

"Do you doubt your sister?" he questioned.

Wrong question to ask. Freyja launched at Oleander, but he had already vanished where he stood and was now standing behind her.

"Do you really think you're going to overpower a Shadowed Lord Astral?" he asked, almost patiently.

Freyja's eyes had venom in them, but Oleander did not falter in meeting her gaze. Even in her human life, few stood against her. Oleander seemed to see that same fire I did in her. At last, Freyja cooled and came to stand beside Jelly and me.

"Now that we can all act like adults," he began. "My offer still stands. You understand the risks and benefits. It's your choice whether we move forward with it."

"What benefits?" I asked, considering.

"There's more that can be wielded with the discernment gift than the *sight*," he said. "You are already showing more advanced control than most immortals from Algol."

"You mentioned I could learn to protect myself too, right? Like you do."

"We could see if that is possible for you," he conceded.

"Now," I said, almost too desperately. If Phoebe was correct, I had to learn how to do this very quickly, even if I didn't understand why yet.

"Alright," he agreed hesitantly. "Then we have to practice the *sight*, okay?"

I nodded, ready to pounce.

He led us to a patch of grass even further from the public eye.

"You cannot have proper *sight* without discernment. You can have endless dreams or prophecies, but they mean nothing without your ability to interpret them accurately," he explained. "Reading minds and seeing the future are not the same thing, love. One is far easier but much less reliable than the other. Intent doesn't change, but thoughts can be deceiving."

"That actually makes sense, Oleander," I said, slightly amused. I briefly thought about the dreams I'd written in my journal, promising to look at them later.

"Yes, I frequently know what I'm talking about. Now, think strongly of something you want to do. Truly believe in it."

I nodded, smiling at the desire I had.

"Imagine your mind as an impenetrable void... locked and guarded by a being that only answers to your commands. Give it a color, texture, smell, invite energy in from the stars above if you wish," he said, guiding me through the visuals.

I imagined an infinite number of stars around my mind, guarded by beasts with wings with all the strength of the cosmos providing them aid.

"Let me know when you are ready," he said.

I nodded, brow beading with sweat as I kept the intent of my actions hidden beneath.

I felt Oleander's power like a dark onslaught of giant waves, probing my mind for a weak spot. Biting my lip in defiance, I refused to give in. I could feel myself fatiguing, but the nausea was gone. I clenched my fists, begging the winged beasts to keep him away, remembering what Imelda had said about my magic always answering my call.

"You can't hold on much longer, Zoe," he said seriously. "Let's stop."

"No," I said, voice unbreakable, but deep down I knew he was right.

"Let go, Zoe!" Freyja screamed.

Without wasting anymore time, Oleander broke through my shield as I lost my grip, slouching to the grass. Jelly was frantically licking my face in worry.

"Really, love?" he asked, amused. "You really want to punch me that bad?"

"Even more now," I said, drenched in sweat but coming out of fatigue.

"You could have killed her," Freyja said angrily.

"I wouldn't dare," he replied, just as mad. "She's stronger than any of you recognize."

"Help me up, you bastard," I said, gripping Oleander's hand. I shook the use of my magic from me.

"Again," I said.

"Not now, Zoe. You'll need to recharge before attempting to shield again. You did well, though. Keep practicing that. Just be careful though, alright?"

"Okay," I whispered. If this would ultimately help me get through the trials, I'd do it.

"Excellent," he answered happily. "Now, can we go do what I originally came here for?"

"Sure, as long as Freyja is present, and I want you to call Elvy back here. Now."

Neither party looked happy with the thought of being around each other, but I knew Freyja would do it for my sake. I trusted her to keep me safe. Oleander knew he had little choice if he wanted me on his side.

"Come on, you two, this will be so much fun," I said, slinging my arms around the duo. "You know, unless I fail the trials and die."

That earned me a laugh from Oleander, but Freyja only nodded, eyes focused elsewhere.

"It's a deal," he said, snapping his fingers.

Zadie appeared next to us, hands on her hip, looking annoyed at being summoned.

"Please let our friends in Vega know I changed my mind," he said, smiling.

"Anything else, Lord Astral?" Zadie asked, turning her gaze on Freyja with a curious look. "Not immortal or mortal. You must be one of the dead."

Freyja snapped her attention to the stunning woman standing beside Oleander.

"Congratulations on the detective skills," Freyja answered.

"Isn't it wonderful to be blessed by Algol? To see the living and those beyond," he said, seeming to want to remind me of this fact. "I'd hurry Zadie. Zoe isn't as patient as I am."

She only laughed and turned into the darkness, disappearing.

"Now, shall we move to our next lesson while we wait or do you need Elvy present too?" Oleander asked, with knowing eyes.

"I do not, but I should let Blaz and Imelda know where I am. They might worry."

"Fine, fine," he said. "Then let's go."

We stopped by my house to find Blaz and Imelda pacing around my tiny bungalow, and relief flooded in their eyes when I walked through the door. I explained what had happened, and Blaz looked like he wanted to rip Oleander's head off. I wasn't sure if I minded or not. Freyja hung in the background, unseen by the pair, which she seemed to prefer.

"Where are we going exactly?" I asked Oleander, so that I could relay the information to Blaz and Imelda.

"I don't know yet. We'll have to follow that gut of yours," he explained.

"I'll have to lean into the nausea again, won't I?"

Oleander only nodded. Algol's gift made me nauseous. Vega's made me extremely fatigued. I wasn't sure which was worse. If I made it through the trials, I really hoped these side effects would go away. An eternity of either sounded exhausting.

"We'll come with you if you refuse to rest like you should after summoning so much power earlier," Blaz said.

"I don't need a babysitter," I said, annoyed at the overbearing protection but secretly satisfied I had someone looking out for my well-being.

"It's more than that. We just want to *see* it—Algol's gift," Imelda replied.

I had an unwelcome flashback to a public speaking class in high school and shuddered. I wasn't a fan of having an audience, but I knew their intentions were genuine.

"Okay, but no fighting," I said, looking at all four of them. "Or I'll stick Jelly on you."

Everyone smiled at that as we headed out the door to nowhere in particular. Leave it to animals to bring even the worst of enemies together.

"So, do we just walk around and see what happens?" I asked.

"We could do that, but it will take all day. And I'm sure you'd like to be done with this by the time Elvy gets back," Oleander said.

"Go on," I said to him while I caught the faint heat of rage welling within Blaz.

"I helped you trigger the sickness last time. I won't now. Eventually, you won't need the nausea to do this... you'll be able to pick up the essence of someone, a scent of sorts. The nausea will go away completely as an immortal."

This seemed to make sense to Imelda and Blaz, so I just nodded.

"Close your eyes and focus on the feeling," he instructed. "Let it guide you like last time."

I quickly recapped what I did the previous time I'd summoned Algol's *sight*. I'd gotten flashes of images, but I'd only known where the person was because I recognized the street. I wouldn't always be able to rely on that, I realized. For a while, nothing happened. I stared into the darkness behind my eyelids, focusing on the faint nausea in my stomach. For once, I wished it would intensify, so I could feel its vibrations better. Emma would probably say that it was just psychological. I tried to ignore my audience, though. I imagined if I moved past my embarrassment and stole a peek, I'd find them perfectly patient.

I was drenched in sweat again by the time I finally had that "gut feeling" surface about someone and an image flashed in my brain. I could tell it was a pier out on the ocean, but there was nothing particularly special about it.

"Focus," he whispered confidently.

I strained and flexed my mind so hard; I felt like a vein would pop out of my forehead.

"She's burning out," Freyja said, worried.

A burst of energy flowed from me, creating a path of light in its wake, guiding me to my destination. I faintly felt like I'd manifested something like this before, but there was no denying this power.

"Remarkable," Oleander praised.

I'd barely heard him utter the words as I took off down the path, Jelly on my right flank. I knew the rest were trailing behind me now.

The correct pier finally came into view, but nothing struck me as out of the ordinary. The burst of energy hadn't led me to a specific person, and the pier itself was pretty crowded with people. I whipped my head around in the crowd trying to find something bad happening.

"Stop the panic," Oleander whispered dangerously close to my ear. "No one else can see us. Breathe."

I listened, taking in the ocean's scent and the crashing of the waves. Finally, the image I needed flashed through my mind. She was an older woman, probably around my mother's age. She had a terrible sense of sadness about her.

I found her sitting by herself at the very edge of the pier. She was looking off into the distance, and I wondered if she planned to jump or something.

"Look deeper," he said, instructing me.

There were tears in her eyes, and the circles under them showed she hadn't had a restful sleep in a long time. No one bothered to stop and talk to her, and it made me furious.

Flashes of loneliness and sorrow engulfed me as I stared at the woman. There was an emptiness so great that would lead to a void of hopelessness if her course was not changed.

"How do I help her?"

"How do you want to help her?" Oleander asked. His line of questioning would have made Emma proud.

"Make me visible. I'd like to talk with her."

He nodded and snapped his fingers in the air.

I shyly approached the woman and sat down next to her on the uncomfortable wooden bench. There were probably hard and fast rules about messing with fate, but I had to do something, though I would not force her hand.

"It's a beautiful morning," I noted, turning more towards the woman.

She seemed surprised that I'd spoken to her, and I felt like I'd interrupted her solitude. However, I don't think I would have been called here if she didn't need help.

"The sunrise was very nice," the lady agreed. The hint of an accent I couldn't quite place showed itself in her words. She must have been sitting here for a while.

"Are you from around here?" I prompted.

"No, I'm from up North. I got here yesterday evening."

I really hoped she'd taken a flight. I'd hate to think of her driving here all alone.

"Well, I'm from the area if you need help with anything," I offered.

The lady burst into tears, and I just sat there with her, waiting for her to finish. It wasn't uncomfortable for me, and I hoped not for her.

"This sounds so silly, but I got a little turned around. There's something I need to take to the lagoon, and I can't find it," she admitted. I was familiar with the lagoon she was speaking of and quickly offered to walk there with her. She pulled out a small backpack from underneath the bench and began hoisting it onto her back, but I stopped her.

"Please, I'll carry that for you," I said, with outstretched hands. If I could carry the burden of what she was facing internally, I would have offered to carry that for her, too.

She obliged and began following me down the pier and along the sidewalk to the lagoon she was seeking. I was keenly aware that the rest of my entourage was following us silently and invisible to the rest of the mortals. This act seemed so insignificant, yet some higher power had deemed it necessary.

"You have a beautiful dog," she said pleasantly.

"This is Jelly, my service dog," I said proudly. Jelly gave her a lopsided grin.

"I'm Madison," she told me.

"Zoe," I replied.

"Zoe... do you know what your name means?" Madison asked.

"No, I've never thought about it," I admitted.

"It means 'life'," she answered, smiling. "I have a thing for names and etymology. I'm an English professor at university back home."

Life. I could feel the tears brim in my eyes, but I shut them down, refusing to let this be about me.

"Thank you for telling me that," I smiled back. "Is there anyone I can call for you?"

"No, Zoe. I have no family," she said, wiping away a few more tears.

We walked in silence the rest of the way to the lagoon, and her sadness seemed to only grow the closer we got. My heart silently broke for her to have no family left. She must have had a family at some point. I wondered what happened to them. As we reached the edge of the lagoon, she began rolling up her pants to wade into the water. I followed suit and joined her in the frigid ocean. She motioned for me to open up the backpack, and inside, I found two aquatic plants.

"The larger one first," she said.

Curious, I handed it to her.

Her fingers trembled violently as she held the plant close to her chest.

"This was where my husband and I met. He said he wanted to leave his favorite memory here when he passed. So, I got these plants. He'd hate the idea of putting his ashes in the ocean. He passed three months ago," she explained, voice cracking on the last words.

"What a beautiful testament to him," I said.

I stood there patiently despite how cold the water was. The ice was a small price to pay to help this woman heal. She let the first plant float away into the tide and motioned for the second plant, which I quickly gave her.

"My daughter," she said, with tears in her eyes. "My beloved daughter."

My heart pounded in my chest, and it took everything in my power not to break down right along with her. The water felt like little knives poking my skin, but I ignored it, knowing this moment was more important than my comfort.

"They died within a few days of each other," she explained. "We had a house fire. I was the only one to live through the ordeal. They both initially made it out, but their burns were so bad they succumbed to the wounds."

I stood there, allowing her to get her story out in whatever way she needed to. I couldn't imagine the guilt this woman must feel. I wished I'd been able to heal her family and wondered if I'd ever be strong enough to do something like that, to spare someone like her this kind of pain.

She hugged the plant tighter before letting it drift into the infinite abyss of the ocean. Her tears flowed endlessly now, and I stood resolute in the water, waiting for her to finish grieving.

Out of the corner of my eye, I saw Elvy standing on the beach, motioning towards the sky.

"Madison," I breathed, "Look at that." A rainbow had formed in the crystal blue sky, something that couldn't have occurred without the help of something *other*.

"Let's get you out of the water," I said, and she followed me back to shore.

After we reached the beach, she asked the question I didn't know the answer to.

"What now?" Madison's eyes were pleading, and I sensed the overwhelming sadness in her. This was a pivotal moment in her future path. I knew Algol's gift would allow me to help others, but I didn't know in what way yet.

"You can take some of it from her, Eferhild." The voice from my dreams whispered right through me. *"You are strong enough for this."*

I let my instincts guide me and my gut told me what I needed to do. I spread my arms open for her, and she happily allowed me to embrace her in a hug. Listening to the ocean, I closed my eyes, focusing on her pain, and I pulled it into me—my soul. The wave of emotion hit me like an avalanche, but I stood my ground, crying with her.

"One day at a time, Madison. That's what we do. We keep going. We keep their memories alive in us. We don't let the hard days claim us. We remember them for how they lived, not how they died. They were more than their death."

Madison clung to me so desperately that I refused to let her go.

"Life," Madison murmured into my tear-soaked shirt.

"Moments," I bowed.

17

Truth

"You were glowing."

Elvy, Jelly, and I were now back at my modest home after taking care of Madison. Oleander and Freyja had promised they would watch over her for the next couple of days to make sure she was okay in the only way they could. I couldn't imagine those two spending any quality time together.

"I took so much from her," I said, with a heavy heart. I guessed that was a side effect of taking on someone else's emotions just enough to make it easier for her to bear. I felt like I was spiraling in Madison's grief now, and the internal screams residing deep within me were scraping against my core. If I let the wailing woman tucked deep in the midst of me break free, I feared I'd never stop crying until my last breath was stolen from me.

Breathe. Such a simple action that held infinite power.

Rational thinking came trickling back through my mind, but the desire to fall into an eternal sleep held strong.

Elvy explained it was morally wrong to take someone's hurt completely away—that it was theirs to have, and I agreed. He also didn't think it was possible to heal a spiritual wound the same way one could heal a physical hurt, which made sense. One was far more complex than the other, and I was living proof of that reality.

"You were brilliant," Elvy whispered as I let him cradle me to his chest.

"You're not angry I was with Oleander?" I asked, knowing my uneasiness came more from the overwhelming emotions versus fear of angering the man holding me.

"No, Zoe. I'm a little pissed that he tricked me into leaving your side, but I understand why he did it. I disagree with the methods though," he replied, the poster of patience.

"You are always so calm, collected," I mumbled, wishing the same for me.

"I don't know if that is true," he answered seriously, clasping my hand. "I feel like I'm always on the verge of losing control, Zoe. My fury has cost me in more ways than I'd like to acknowledge. I'm afraid it will take what I value most from me one day... if I let it."

I squeezed him tightly, understanding that feeling, and his power seemed to rumble deep in his core. It was as if lightning was about to strike.

"Will I ever get to see your true power?"

"I hope not," he said, a shudder running through him. "That part of me stays caged."

He was stroking my hair, trying to calm the despair within me and the questions lurking. I knew he was capable of dangerously unimaginable things, and that was enough for now. I tried to focus on the feel of him and the smell of the ocean. This was real. I was safe.

"What color did I glow?" I asked, curious if it would be the same white Imelda and Blaz had seen.

"It started out the purest white I've ever seen, but then faded to a rich black," he answered. "As if you were taking the darkness from her."

"Have you talked to Imelda or Blaz?" I asked, heart beating steadily.

"No, they only said you had some things you wanted to tell me."

"I was able to heal again back at the rescue. The pup I was telling you about... I healed again with some guidance from Blaz."

Elvy nodded for me to continue.

"I've been experimenting, practicing. With Oleander, I always felt nausea around him. With you... it's always felt like a powerful ache here," I said, pulling his hand to my heart. "So, I followed it, leaned into it like Oleander taught me to do. In an almost meditative state, I healed him. Imelda and Blaz both seemed surprised by it."

"Was the healing extensive?" he asked, lost in thought.

"Yes," I admitted. "He's almost fully well now, and he shouldn't have made it."

"I understand their surprise then. No Emerging has done that before or done what you have with Oleander. Any Emerging who has wielded their gifts on even a small scale typically burns out before the trial. While I am stunned by your strength, it makes me worry about what might wait for you in the trials."

"Freyja wanted to snap Oleander's neck... she thinks he pushed me too hard."

"She could be right, Zoe. You need to be careful."

I hesitated before continuing. "I wish you could meet her. Freyja."

"You understand Zadie and Oleander are gifted in seeing the dead?"

I nodded, wondering if this was a hard subject for him.

"Most immortals of Algol can do that since it's tied to the spirit realm directly, just like with Vega and its healing gifts from the water element. Every Algol immortal has some connection to a gift from spirit—prophecy, death, soul, and the stars only know what else."

I began a circular motion with my thumb on his still resting hand on my chest as I thought about the possibilities.

"How am I supposed to choose? How can the stars ask that of me?" There was a taste of venom in my tone.

"Maybe the trials will help guide you to the star meant for you. When the time comes, you'll know which one to leap towards. Everything you've learned and will learn before then will be with you in that realm."

"But what would it mean for us if I chose Algol?" I asked, not liking the sudden shake in my voice.

"We would figure it out," he said, but I heard the uncertainty in his voice.

"What aren't you telling me?"

"I told you about the bloodlines? How there has been plenty of intermingling between the star realms? Whenever that occurred, the couple had to choose which star to serve and the partner that was not from that realm had to swear new blood allegiance to that star, which then became their source of life and power. Ever since Algol severed with the Kingdom of Canis, the stars have been angry, unwilling to grant anyone who was not born of them to swear their life to their power source... I think this is why your Emergence is so important. But never in our recorded history has their been an Emerging touched by two of the celestials."

"If I chose Algol, then you would no longer be in my life?" I asked, heart pounding.

"Nothing is for certain, but I'm not sure of that, no."

"Even if you could, you would never swear allegiance to Algol," I said, tasting the truth of my words. "And I would never ask that of you. You have sworn an oath to serve the immortals of Vega. There's no breaking that."

"I believe in you and me," he whispered defiantly. "Somehow, we will find a way."

The conviction was strong in his voice, but I wasn't a fan of letting fate decide my future. I had to figure out this prophecy before the Winter Solstice and give everyone their best chance. I wanted to spring out of bed and find answers, but fatigue was lurking beneath the surface of my eyes.

Elvy cupped my face with his callused hands and placed a gentle kiss on my lips. I sighed, snuggling into the comfort of his arms.

"Are you ever going to tell me about your beef with Oleander?"

Elvy stroked my hair absentmindedly, lost in thought.

"Oleander is not my favorite person. I suppose I'm jealous of him; not to what he might mean to you or do for you," he trailed off. "But that he can see Freyja. That he can share that with you. I wish I could know her, know someone who is so important to you. There's a history between Oleander and me that is... unpleasant, though I don't know that he is really responsible for it in the end. I believe in you though, Zoe, and if it's within my power, I'll follow you anywhere."

I couldn't help the tears that formed in my eyes, and I briefly wondered if he wished he could see his parents like I could see Freyja. He wiped the moisture away, holding me close, but still respecting the limits I had set for him.

"You've never told me what all happened to you and to Freyja, and it's your choice to tell me in your own time, but I am patient."

I decided to tell him about *her* instead of about what happened to us. "She was—is—so full of life," I said, voice low. "I was as adventurous as they come, but my name is probably more fitting for her than for me. She was always laughing and seemed wise beyond her years. She never said no to a fight and wasn't afraid to piss our parents off. Freyja stuck up for me when I didn't do it for myself."

Those gray eyes watched me, appreciating the trust I had in sharing this with him.

"The night everything went down, when she was killed, they were going to kill me first," I said, voice cracking as the flashes of that terrible night swarmed my mind. Jelly leaped on the bed with us, nudging my arm. I kept one hand on Elvy and the other stroked Jelly's soft fur. The phantom pain of where I'd been stabbed made its presence known.

Breathe.

"You don't have to tell me."

"Emma, my therapist, said that sharing my story with those I trust lessens its power over me... and I agree with her."

I swallowed, debating what to say or not.

"She begged them to kill her first," I breathed, my voice unrecognizable. "They had... used me up already and forced her to watch it all happen. I was so badly beaten that I had no fight left in me, but she did. She still had that fiery rage in her that couldn't be blown out so easily. She made enough noise that they had no choice but to leave me alone before they turned on her."

This was my greatest shame about that night. Something I hadn't really ever expressed to anyone, certainly not Emma.

"Do you know why they targeted you and Freyja?" His eyes had gone dark with a pledge of death to the men who had harmed us.

"We were bar hopping. Freyja had wanted to go and had just gotten her fake I.D. The police think they followed us from the last bar. They'd probably been watching us for a while and figured we'd be easy targets."

Elvy's grip on me tightened, and I glimpsed a flash of power emit from him with vengeance in his eyes before I turned away, unable to look at him until I finished.

"It should've been me that died," I said, taking a steadying breath as he caressed my broken heart. "Law enforcement and paramedics arrived just after they killed her. I still don't know who called them."

I was shaking, but I was proud of myself for revealing that truth. I was afraid to look into those stormy eyes, unsure of what I would find. Would he judge me or pity me?

He did neither. Elvy grasped my temples with his strong, safe hands, and leaned his forehead so that it connected with mine, allowing me to breathe and center myself.

"Thank you for trusting me with that part of you, Zoe," he whispered. "I vow to keep it safe, and I thank Vega every damn day that you were placed in my life—no matter the length of time. Selfishly, I am so thankful you survived that night—both nights."

"I didn't think immortals were supposed to be selfish?" I asked, remembering Blaz's words.

"I'll never pretend to be perfect. Not with you."

"I don't always feel so strong," I admitted.

"I am always willing to remind you of just how much strength you have, Zoe Eferhild. You need no one to save you. You are the chosen hero. You are the one the stars have been searching for all this time."

I couldn't believe the words that had just fallen from his mouth... the words I'd longed to hear someone say. I didn't want anyone to save me. I wanted—needed—to save myself. After the attack with Freyja and the night I wanted to end my life, everyone walked on eggshells around me. I felt like everyone saw this broken person who wasn't capable of getting better, that I was too far gone. Sometimes, I'd chosen to believe those lies. All I ever wanted was for someone to stand by me while I glued the pieces of my broken soul together without pitying me or offering empty words of condolences.

"Every hero needs someone to stand with them," I said, smiling.

"As long as I have breath in my lungs," he promised, kissing me again.

This beautiful, wonderful man was the first person I felt understood and heard by. He had literally crossed realms to find me himself. The Lord Astral of Vega had washed my hair, cried with me, and sought to know me—*really* know me. I'd never considered that I'd be able to love someone after what happened to me because I never believed I could find the courage to love myself first. But I felt the words caught in my throat, seemingly not ready to come forth yet. I would trust that.

"So, why did you come for me?" I asked, needing to know. "If it's so rare for the Lord Astral to find Emerging mortals."

"There have been rumors that the next Emerging would be *significant*. There is a hope you will be the one to heal what has been broken, and there's been legends of someone like you being chosen by two conflicting stars to do this." He paused. "But for me, it was a little more personal."

I'd never seen Elvy seem so flushed or nervous.

"How so?" I probed further, deciding to get back to those rumors later.

"If I tell you, there's no going back. I don't want it to influence your choices."

"I'm all in," I said with finality.

"I'll tell you what I can for now. That tug, you explained, when you're around me or healing… I feel it too. When we first caught the scent of Vega's Emerging, we didn't know that Algol had chosen you as well yet, not until we caught wind of Oleander being in the area. Your scent was so strong for me, I had to come see you for myself. It was like a pull that I couldn't ignore."

"What do I smell like to you? Or do all Emergings have the same scent?" I asked, not bothered that he had tracked me that way oddly enough.

"Like rain forming over the ocean. Powerful, consuming," he explained, smiling down at me. "And no, you smell unique to me, which was confusing at first because the rest of my Luminaries said you smelled like any other Emerging—a lily—though they said the scent was stronger than they'd ever experienced."

I could ignore the longing in my chest no longer, and pushed him down into the bed, needing a physical connection with him desperately. Jelly, thankfully, had skirted her way to the living room.

He sat up on the bed, waiting to see what I wanted him to do.

Standing between his legs, I placed his hands on my hips as I took his shirt off. I would never tire of seeing that strong, tattooed chest that he always had on display now. As I ran my fingers through his hair, he closed his eyes, savoring it. I made quick work of the joggers he wore, leaving him in just his underwear.

Elvy helped me out of my leggings, his hands tauntingly slow in returning to my hips. Taking a steadying breath, I quickly lifted my shirt over my head and tossed it to the floor beside us. He did not take his eyes off me, waiting for me to make clear what I wanted.

I turned around, back facing him, the most vulnerable position for me, a sign I truly did trust him.

"Can you help me?"

He said nothing, but quickly undid the clasp of my bra as I slipped the straps past my arm, letting it fall to the floor. The necklace he'd given me dangled between my breasts. This was the most vulnerable I had been since everything, and I almost feared turning around. Not looking back at him, I leaned my back flush with his and guided his hands to my hardened nipples.

A low rumble escaped his lips as he mercilessly explored my body. I guided his hands further down to the apex of my pleasure, and my entire frame trembled at the warmth of his strokes against my clit. He moved my ass on top of him as he kissed my neck, while continuing the onslaught of tortuous pleasure with his hands. I felt him harden as I ground against him, needing as much friction as possible.

"I'm yours," Elvy whispered, gently biting my neck, breaking me all at once. I loudly rode his fingers into the pulses of my orgasm, shaking.

Unable to stand it any longer, I shyly turned to face him, but I couldn't bring myself to look into his waiting eyes. He moved one hand from my hip, and I felt him gently lift my chin to meet his piercing gaze.

I was met with a soft, tender expression and desire shining through.

"Breathtaking," he said, voice husky. "Ethereal."

"I still don't think I'm ready," I admitted.

"That's okay… I'm thinking I'd like to hear you make that sound again, though."

My only answer was to plant an aggressive kiss on his lips and jump into his arms so that I could straddle his hips with my legs. He stayed true to his promise and made me feel things I didn't even know were possible with limited access. We were lost in a tangle of limbs and temptations I wasn't sure what to do with. He proved to be a master at creativity, and I found myself lost in euphoria.

Anytime I tried to return the favor, he'd flip me back over, devouring my protests with his sinful lips.

"You are incredible," he breathed, finally laying down beside me with a smile on his face.

"Me?!" I exclaimed. "That was all you."

"Maybe knowing I'm pleasing you is uniquely satisfying," he said, smiling into my hair.

"Why wouldn't you let me?"

He clasped his hand in mine, kissing the back softly. "I want you to know that you should be worshiped. That you don't have to give to receive. That's more important to me than anything else. That you feel... safe."

"I'm enough," I recalled him saying during our last *practice.* A sliver of tears formed in my eyes.

"More than enough," he kissed my cheek. "Realm saving enough."

"Realm saving?" I asked.

"Zoe Eferhild, Realm-Healer," he muttered. "It has a ring to it."

I only hoped I could live up to the title if I ever learned what he meant by it.

18

The Archer

I used the next week off work to do more *practicing* with Elvy, but we also took time to work with my gift from Vega. Elvy and Oleander managed to come together at the distaste of both Delmira and Zadie, who seemed even less fond of each other than the Lord Astrals. I didn't dare question them further about their feud, and they kept their cool, mostly. When things started to become dicey between the two, Finnian would step in and act as referee. Apart from Elvy, Finnian was the only one Delmira would really listen to.

So much for immortals being on a higher plane of consciousness. They acted much like humans, but they were, perhaps, a little more dangerous when they exploded. Clodovea and Imelda were the only two with any sense, and they did a good job at keeping Blaz in check when his sarcasm wavered between offensive and funny.

"How do you keep up with them?" I asked Elvy one day after training with Oleander on my shields. I was steadily improving, and I could block him for longer periods of time.

"They mean well," he answered, probably questioning the answer himself.

As promised, Freyja was present every time I was around Oleander, and the snarl never left her face. Zadie seemed to find Oleander's squirming amusing. So did I. I had to give him credit, though. A lesser man would have caved at Freyja's onslaught of protection and snide remarks.

"Your sister is infuriating," he said through gritted teeth. "Doesn't she understand that I'm trying to help you?"

"Don't talk about me like I'm not here," she snapped.

"How could we possibly forget that?" he growled back.

"She means well," I said, emulating the same response Elvy had given me. "Besides, we both know it's more than just helping me."

"I have no idea what you mean," he said, smirking.

"So there aren't rumors in the other realms about some legendary Emerging immortal?"

"Elvy shouldn't speak on things he doesn't understand," Oleander said dismissively.

At night, Elvy would come to bed with me, never requesting more than I was willing to give. He continued to surprise me by finding unique ways to work within the boundaries I'd set, easily finding my bliss in him. Afterwards, I slept soundly. Not one nightmare entering the peaceful slumber I'd grown accustomed to with him by my side. Jelly didn't seem to mind sharing the responsibility with Elvy, but Blaz had proven to be her favorite. It was probably the treats I slyly caught him slipping her when he thought I wasn't looking.

I tried to ignore the ticking of time as the Winter Solstice approached. I wasn't sure what I feared the most. When I used to struggle with making a decision, Freyja always suggested flipping a coin, not to leave it to chance, but to see what I hoped it would land on. It seemed silly to try this around something so potentially monumental, but truthfully, I didn't know what my decision would be. Each gift from both stars was something precious to me, and I despised the idea of parting from either.

However, the idea of no longer being able to see Freyja again if I gave up the gift from Algol hardened my heart. I wanted to choose her just as much as she had chosen me that fateful night. I needed to put her before my own wants, but I knew she would never want that for me, either. She would want me to choose what was best for me and humanity in the end. Much like Elvy, she wouldn't want me to factor her into the choice, but that was much easier said than done.

We were sitting in the lighthouse and my legs were casually placed in Elvy's lap as he gently massaged my aching feet. Clodovea and Imelda were snuggled up on one couch across from us, and Finnian was trying to keep Delmira and Blaz from killing each other over a game of darts. Whoever gave them access to sharp objects had very poor judgment.

"It's only two weeks away. I hate this waiting," I said.

"I believe in what will be," Elvy replied, vaguely. "I believe you were chosen for a reason, Zoe. I have faith in that." The rumble of his true power gave his fury away, though.

"Sounds like a bunch of bullshit," I answered, punching him playfully in the arm.

"How about some coffee?" he asked, stepping towards the kitchen.

I nodded my head, always desiring the sweet nectar of comfort it provided, and sprawled out on the couch, thumbing through my journal.

"He's not as calm as he seems," Clodovea said, eyes serious. "He's terrified, actually."

"I can't imagine Elvy scared of anything," I said, knowing he could probably hear everything we were saying with those immortal ears.

"He wasn't, before you," Clove replied, stroking Imelda's arm lovingly while she snuggled closer in her lap. "He'd never tell you this because he's truly one of the most selfless people I've ever known, but I'm not."

I swallowed, bracing for the words Clodovea, Elvy's third, was about to say.

"Choose Vega," she said. "I know you don't want to leave Freyja. I know it feels like an impossible decision, but you have become family to us. It's more than what you mean to Elvy—you mean something to all of us."

The room had gone stiflingly quiet.

"I would hate to live the rest of this life without you in it," Imelda added.

"I don't know what to say," I admitted. I didn't hate them for their words as I knew they only spoke their truth and needed to tell me how they felt.

For a brief moment, Freyja's figure manifested beside me, wanting me to know she heard what they'd said and agreed with them.

"Be happy. Live. Whatever that looks like for you," Freyja whispered, squeezing my hand before disappearing again.

The rest of the group shuddered, as if they had felt the coldness around Freyja's spirit among them. Only Elvy seemed to realize this, and he gave me a knowing glance as he resumed his position next to me, where Freyja had just been.

"You'll have to excuse Clove. She thinks she knows what's best for me sometimes," he said, giving his third a stern but kind glance.

"I always welcome honesty," I muttered, thanking Clodovea for saying what she felt compelled to.

Blaz, Delmira, and Finnian joined us in the living room, having decided darts were a little too dangerous with their heated arguments.

"As if she could say no to this face," Blaz joked, waggling his eyebrows.

I took a note out of Imelda's book and slammed a pillow in his face.

"Nice one," Delmira laughed, picking up her own pillow to slam into Blaz as well.

Somehow, we erupted into a massive pillow fight, stuffing flying everywhere. Jelly seemed to enjoy herself and easily joined in the fray, seemingly siding with Blaz. I relished in this simple, joyous moment, committing it to memory. I allowed myself to forget the pressing trials and just *be*—for what it was right now. No matter what I chose, I would remember this moment and cherish it.

I snapped a picture of the moment on my phone, fearing that I might somehow lose it, but the sound of my cell ringing was the only force able to draw me from the fun. I stepped outside, leaving my friends to continue at their whims.

"Hello," I answered, knowing who was on the other line.

"Hey, Zo. How are you doing?"

Such a conversational question; little did she know how deep it hit me.

"I'm good, Mom. What's up?"

"Grant and I are traveling over Christmas, and we wanted to throw a charity ball on the weekend before. We would love for you to come. And Elvy."

"I've got a few more names to add to that list actually," I said, deciding that I would do this for my mother. One last memory to fill her with. The ball landed just one day before the Winter Solstice, and I would enjoy every minute of the last night of my mortal life.

"Of course, honey," she said happily. "As many as you like."

I gave her the names of Elvy's court, and I added Oleander and Zadie to the list, hoping I didn't regret that decision later.

Waiting eyes greeted me when I went back inside, the mess already cleaned up somehow.

"So how do you all feel about going to a charity ball?" I asked, smiling. "I'm hoping it's a resounding yes, because I have already told my mother you'll be there."

"We would be honored to come," Elvy answered, moving beside me, with one arm wrapped around my waist.

"If you think the mortals can handle my stellar dance skills," Blaz said, demonstrating his moves.

"Please, spare us, Blaz," Finnian answered, rolling his eyes, but his tone was playful.

Everyone seemed happy to go, which was an enormous relief. Now, I just had to ask Oleander at our training later. I winced at the thought, plopping back down on the couch to flip back through my journal.

"What do you have there?" Elvy asked, peering over my shoulder.

I turned the journal towards him so he could see the page I'd landed on. It was the first entry of the dream I'd had of the six shooting stars.

"What's the date on that?" he asked, and I adjusted so he could see what I'd written.

A small smile crept onto his face.

"That's the day the Court of Vega arrived in this realm," he said. "May I?"

I nodded, heart thundering in time to the crashing of the ocean waves cresting the shore. He glanced at the previous pages, pausing to read the entries that caught his attention.

"It appears you knew we were coming before even we did," he said, silencing the rest of the room with those words.

"Does that mean Algol's gift was manifesting that long, then? My *sight*?"

"Maybe," he replied, unconvinced. "It could be something else entirely."

He turned the journal back to the entry of the dream around my blood. I'd made notes around it about what my mother had told me about my father and bits and pieces I'd been trying to put together.

The Archer never misses his mark. Chiron was my father's favorite story to tell my mother. Someone had told Freyja to go to Elvy—connected or just Oleander playing tricks? Archie is the fake name my father gave my mother—connected to Chiron/Sagittarius/the Archer?

"The Archer?" Elvy asked, puzzling over my words. "That's what Vivian said about your father? I wonder..."

"Yeah. Apparently he went by Archie, but I don't know much else," I said, pulling out a book on different mythologies around the constellations.

"Finnian, that sounds familiar, doesn't it?" he asked.

"Yes, there's mention of the legend of 'The Archer' in the archives back home. It's been said to be primordial—only a myth to us."

"What's the story?" I asked, intrigued.

"The Archer is allegedly a direct descendant of Algol, making him one of the most powerful immortals in existence. I'm not sure I would even classify him as immortal if he is the son of a celestial. It is said that with his bow and arrow, he tethered the five elemental realms together, creating the first cohesive dominion of the stars."

"Is there any truth to this?" Elvy asked.

"I can't rule it out. Once we are back on Vega's plane, I can research it, but the lore is vast around the creation of the elemental kingdom."

"But what are the chances I'm connected to The Archer?" I asked.

"I highly doubt it," Finnian replied. "However, it might explain why your magic is so impressive."

"If we are talking about *The* Archer, he would be older than I can even comprehend," Elvy agreed.

I couldn't let this go. The clench of my gut told me this was significant information, and I had to follow it down whatever path it led me.

***

Later that evening, Oleander was all too pleased to agree to come to the ball I'd nearly forgotten about amongst the revelation of The Archer.

"I wouldn't dream of missing it," he answered, eyes full of mischief. "Zadie has been itching to wear something other than black leather."

"You'll be on good behavior, right?" I asked, eyes pleading.

"I wouldn't count on it," Freyja muttered behind me.

"Again, your faith in me, Zoe Eferhild, is so heartwarming," he said, pleasantly. "I can't wait to see what you look like dressed to the nines, Freyja."

She met him with an icy glare.

"There's no point," she answered. "No one will see me."

"I will see you," he purred.

"Leave her alone, Oleander," I said, understanding the discomfort in Freyja's eyes.

He only nodded and turned his full attention back to me.

"You are doing remarkably well, Zoe. A *star* student, if you will."

"Did you just try to make a joke?" I asked, laughing.

"I'm actually quite funny," he said. "Now, focus. You can see me for all the glory that I am at a later date."

Oleander guided me back to the task at hand, making me flex my mental muscles, training them to understand the gift of Algol without burning through my mortal body. Anytime I got too close to the edge, he pulled me back before I began free-falling into the abyss of darkness.

"You're giving too much, Zoe," he whispered, reminding me of the present. "Let the whispers come to you."

I nodded and continued practicing until the moon rose over the ocean. Elvy appeared on the beach, and I knew it was time for bed. Tomorrow, I'd have to go back to work and see Emma.

When we finished, I built up the courage to ask Oleander what he might know regarding The Archer. Freyja had already left us for the night, and I'd resolved to tackle questioning her later.

"The Archer—yes, I'm familiar with the legend. He used his bow and arrow to tether the five elemental realms together," he said, repeating information I already knew.

"Anything else?" I prompted.

"Why do you want to know?" he asked, and I threw up my mental shields to protect my theories. I felt his mind creeping along mine, but he could not pierce the barrier.

"Do you know anything else?" I asked, not answering him.

"The stars punished him for what he'd done, initially. They didn't want to share their gifts with each other. You see, the legends say that immortals used to wield gifts from both stars, and we shared our magic with other immortals. All immortals had a little power from each of the five realms. You wouldn't have to choose between Algol and Vega—you could wield both. They made him reverse the bonds that made this sharing possible, and it nearly cost him his life. The legends have lost where he is now."

"No immortal has wielded both realms' magic since The Archer?"

"Not without paying with their life," Oleander confirmed.

It appeared The Archer was the right path, but I may not survive the course it led me on.

19

SAFETY

Work had been uneventful, but Dr. Malik let me know Brodie had made a full recovery. He would just need to put on a little more weight before being transported to a rescue with other sea lions. It brought so much joy to know that he would get to be wild and free again soon. If he continued to gain at his current rate, he would be transferred sometime next week with plans to do a wild release not long after that.

I now sat in front of Emma, truly stumped for what words to even say. How do you tell your therapist that you would be disappearing to another realm soon or die trying? How do you tell your therapist that she has helped you so much, then just drop from the face of this planet—literally? How do you say goodbye to someone who has stood by you without an ounce of judgment?

"You seem like you are somewhere else today," Emma noted.

"Yes, I'd say that's fair," I answered.

"Are you still seeing Freyja?" she asked, knowing that was usually a safe subject to broach.

"Not as much," I acknowledged.

"Maybe you are feeling lost around that," she offered. "Maybe you're letting go and you aren't sure you are okay with that."

Little did she know how close to the truth she was.

"I don't really want to talk about it," I said firmly.

"That's okay," she replied, handing me some art supplies. It was a blank sheet of paper and an assortment of different colored markers. "Let's try this then."

"What am I supposed to do?"

"Sometimes, it can be easier to talk about what you really need to when you can put it on paper or distract yourself by doodling while talking."

I nodded and picked up the turquoise blue marker and began tracing swirls along the paper, lost in thought. I'd never been much of an artist and didn't have a plan for where my nonsense was going.

"Do you believe in good and bad?" I asked, focusing on the paper before me.

"Whatever is real for you, is real for me... do you believe that there's good and bad?"

"I believe most people live in the gray," I answered, continuing to use the blue marker to make different swirls.

"Is that where you live?"

"I guess I'm still trying to figure that out." I picked up the black marker, slowly incorporating the black to intertwine with the blue.

"You seem heavy today," she noted. "You've been lighter the last couple of sessions."

"It's the holidays," I brushed off. "They've been hard since Freyja died."

"And what about your male friend?" she asked. I'd never told her Elvy's name, like a guarded secret I kept for my heart.

"He's still around," I said with a small smile.

"And how are you feeling about talking to him?"

This was a semi-safe topic.

"I haven't told him every little detail of everything," I admitted. "But he has the gist."

"That is a healthy boundary, finding that balance of trust, yet still allowing yourself to experience it. Not everyone deserves the right to know everything about you."

"I quite agree, but I think he's worthy of it," I said, almost in a trance as I continued tracing nothing special on the paper. "Do you think there's something bigger than all of this?" I asked, waving my hands around the room.

"What do you mean?"

"Like God? Or something like that," I clarified.

"Yes, I do," she said, giving me a straight answer for once. "Does that make a difference to you?"

"No, I just... a lot has been coming up. Like my biological father. He left before I can really remember anything about him, and I think he's trying to maybe make contact again. I don't know, it just seems a little too coincidental."

"Do you want to reach back out?"

"I wouldn't know how to get in contact with him," I said, pausing my drawing. My heart sank to my core as the constellation of The Archer stared back at me.

"How do you know it's your father reaching out to you?"

"I don't," I said honestly. "Call it intuition."

"Zoe, I want to remind you of your courage. You've stepped out in your bravery so much in the last few months. Whether or not this is your father, only you can decide your worth."

"I want to believe you, but I'm afraid it could change everything—better or worse."

"Whether you know him or not, he is already a part of you," she reminded me, and I felt the truth of her words.

"I've never really thanked you, Emma. So, thank you. For believing me. For everything."

She seemed to pick up on the goodbye there, but I was unwilling to explain further. Not yet. Our session didn't change much from this. I just didn't feel like talking or working at it today. I know part of it rested in the fact that I knew I only had one more session with her. I felt guilty about that, and I didn't want her to worry about me. I'd have to find a way to tell her that next week without sounding like I was going to go jump off a bridge or something.

Elvy was waiting for me outside Emma's office, coffee in hand.

"Is it strange that I will miss my therapist?" I asked.

"No, I don't think it's weird. It sounds like she has been helpful to you... when you've let down your stubbornness enough to let her," he said, smirking.

"You're not wrong. Where are we off to?" I asked, wondering where his Luminaries were.

"Well, Delmira, Clodovea, and Imelda insisted on stealing you for the evening," he answered, eyes apologetic.

"Do you think I can afford to miss the practice?" I asked, only half serious. "Every day counts right now."

"I don't think any force of nature would keep my sisters from their mission," he replied playfully.

"So, I don't think they'd let me just stay with you," I said, giving him a deep kiss.

"Later," he whispered, just as the girls arrived to whisk me off somewhere unknown.

"We'll take care of her," Delmira promised, before Elvy could get a word out.

Clodovea held her arms open, ready to fly me to our destination. I gave one last glance to Elvy as Clove gracefully cradled me in her arms, gently lifting us airborne. Much to my surprise, Jelly did not protest when Delmira lifted her into her arms, following us. I appreciated they considered Jelly and me a packaged deal. Jelly actually seemed to enjoy the wind in her fur as we soared over the sleepy town of Saint Andrews.

We were only in the air for what felt like a few minutes before I felt Clodovea descend to the ground. I didn't recognize the city we were in and noted that it was much larger than Saint Andrews.

Imelda led us to a large shop in what looked like the center of a sprawling downtown city center. No one else seemed to go in or out of the building, and when we arrived at the door, I saw why. A sign that said the building was closed for a private showing was displayed proudly on the glass frame.

We didn't wait long before a strikingly short woman greeted us and led us into the main room. A runway ran through the middle of the room, and it was so brightly lit that I almost wanted to squint. The building was encased in what seemed like marble, interlaced with sparkles. The tiny, gray-haired woman led us to enough chairs for each of us, and offered us champagne or cucumber water.

"Welcome to *Designs by Isabella.* I am Isabella," our host introduced herself. "The store is free for you to explore, but all dresses that leave my threshold are one of a kind, nothing off the rack."

"We have less than two weeks," I said, confused.

"Your payment ensures it will be done on time," she assured me.

Isabella just now noticed Jelly. I wondered if it was because of this payment that she said nothing or if she was a genuinely kind person. My gut favored the latter.

"Courtesy of Elvy," Imelda whispered, out of earshot of the owner.

"Please let me or one of my assistants know if you need any help," she said, inviting us to see the basics of her dresses.

I longed for Freyja to be here with me, and my eyes felt heavy as I remembered the last time I'd needed a dress. Even though it hadn't been that long ago in the grand scheme of things, it felt like a lifetime in the small shop in Saint Andrews. That moment had been so full of life and laughter. She didn't come though, and I wondered if she wanted me to create memories without her. My heart seemed to crack slightly at the thought.

"I don't do dresses," Delmira informed Isabella.

"No problem," she said, moving her into a different section of the studio where I think I saw lots of leather. I couldn't help the laugh that escaped my lips. Delmira was one to always live her truth and courage—even with fashion.

I perused some samples, but nothing seemed to catch my eye. I wanted it to be special, as my last night as a mortal, whether I lived or died or chose one of the stars. I wanted to be intentional with my choice and nothing seemed to convey what I wanted it to.

"Trouble?" Isabella asked, at least a head shorter than me.

"Nothing really seems to fit," I said, hoping she didn't find it offensive. I recognized the art of dressmaking as something powerful.

"I pride myself on a challenge," she said pleasantly. "I thought the purple-haired girl would be the biggest obstacle, but no. I can see that you will be."

Isabella studied me with her pointed look and glasses that kept sliding down her nose. I wondered what she saw in me. Would she see the inner turmoil raging within me? Would she recognize that maybe I was potentially dressing for my funeral? That's in part what it felt like.

"You've got a shine to your soul, my girl. Hard won too," she said, sketching a drawing on a pad of paper. When she was satisfied, she produced a few types of fabric and asked what spoke to me.

I was immediately drawn to the soft texture of the satin fabric she held, and she nodded, adjusting one of the drawn designs.

"And these?" she asked, showing me different strips of colors.

I pointed to what looked like sea-foam green and a rich black.

"Interesting," she said, but I saw the light go off in her mind. "May I?"

I let her take my measurements, then she quickly changed a few things on her sketch pad. She proudly showed me what she'd come up with, and my heart was thrilled with what she'd been able to imagine so thoroughly. She'd captured what I'd always pictured as the two stars raging a war within me as a more fluid piece.

"I thought so," she said, pride ringing through her voice. "Excellent, I will get these made right away in time for your event."

"Let me see!" Imelda exclaimed, but Isabella swiftly tucked away her pad before Imelda's eyes could take a glance.

"Designs should only be shown when the creation is finished," she said, smiling towards me. "They are works of art in their own right."

"Then I look forward to seeing it," Clodovea replied, stepping forward.

Jelly barked and twirled excitedly as well.

"Yes, yes, I did not forget you, sweet girl," Isabella said lovingly towards Jelly.

"Did you all find something to wear?" I asked.

"Oh yes," Delmira said with a gleam in her eyes. "Vega, help whoever stands in my way."

"Let's go," Clove commanded, shaking her head.

Once we were outside, I climbed back into Clodovea's arms, and we soared back to the comfort of my own house. Much to my delight, Elvy was already there waiting for me, leaning against the doorframe.

"Thank you for bringing her back in one piece," Elvy called, as the rest of them turned to leave.

"Of course, Lord Astral," Delmira answered, rolling her eyes as she set Jelly down before jetting off into the darkness with the others.

"Did you find something?" he asked.

"Mmhmm," I murmured, still clinging to his embrace.

"I requested Isabella match us," he confessed. "If that's alright with you. I haven't formally asked you to be my date."

"Technically, I invited you," I reminded him.

"Would you do me the honor of going to the ball with me, Zoe Eferhild?"

"Of course," I answered sweetly, following him into the living room with Jelly behind us.

"And you too, Jelly," he said, bending down to give her ear scratches. "Though I suspect Blaz is the one that has truly won your heart."

"I'm just surprised you got Blaz in a tux," I said, laughing. "You are right, though. Jelly is in love with Blaz."

"He can complain all he wants, but we all know Blaz likes to look good," he replied, grinning along with me.

"I like the idea of you matching me," I said, placing a kiss on his soft, waiting lips. "It feels right."

Elvy's body seemed to sag slightly with relief.

"I missed Freyja tonight," I whispered, as if afraid of the thought surfacing.

He only gripped me tighter, creating a safe space for me to feel what I needed to without judgment. Despite knowing that missing Freyja could lead me to choose Algol, Elvy didn't try to sway me either way. He just held onto me, my resolve keeping me together as I felt the fractures scream to crumble inside me.

I held strong, not allowing myself to break tonight. I'd shelve that for later. I let him guide me to the bed as I drifted off into my first fitful sleep in a long time. I dreamed of

The Archer, and his sorrow for what the celestials had made him do. I couldn't be sure if I was dreaming or awake, at times, but I thought I heard Elvy murmur that I was safe anytime the dream wanted to take me prisoner in the darkness.

Eventually, Elvy couldn't keep the monsters at bay in the nightmarish hell my mind tortured me with.

"Come back to me, baby," he pleaded, breaking through my terror.

I woke with a start, drenched in sweat and trembling violently.

"I've got you," he whispered, wiping the sweat from my eyes. "Always."

Awareness slowly and painfully came back to me. Jelly was on top of me, grounding me to reality. Elvy held me close, whispering words of comfort directly to my soul.

"Are you with me?"

I nodded as the lingering fear leisurely left my body. I didn't have it in me to speak.

"What do you need?"

I pointed to the bathroom, and he swooped me in his arms, waiting for me to tell him what I needed. I motioned to the bathtub, and he turned on the faucet to fill it with scalding water.

"Are you still with me, Zoe? Do you want me to leave you alone?"

No.

I gripped him painfully and shook my head feverishly.

He nodded and began peeling the sticky clothes from my body. I didn't care or think about being bared to him and kept clinging to his solid frame. Jelly watched dutifully from the threshold of the bathroom, not letting me out of her sight.

Elvy must have slipped out of his clothes while still holding onto me. I only felt his bare skin against me as he got into the bath with me, turning off the flow of water. He gingerly placed my back against his chest, tenderly massaging life back into my frozen body.

Without a word, he began washing my body with care and the scent of lavender helped ground me to this moment even more.

"Thank you," I mumbled, with deep fatigue in my voice.

"You never have to face this alone. Never again," he swore.

Exhaustion consumed me, and I felt myself drifting off comfortably in his arms.

"Sleep, beautiful. I'll keep you safe."

And I believed him.

20

Sacrifice

Since Elvy had cared for me through one of the worst night terrors I'd ever experienced, I felt boundlessly connected to him. I kissed his sleeping form on the cheek before slipping away into the night, when another dream had startled me out of my sleep a few nights later. I'd somehow managed to sneak off with Jelly to the beach a block from my house without waking him from his deep sleep. It was a little too easy, as if fate had made it so.

The darkening sky was completely clear of all the clouds, and I felt in my soul that it was important for me to be here.

I found The Archer easily and closed my eyes, willing him to come forward. His constellation was shining the brightest out of all the stars above. I knelt down in the sand, grounding myself in the reality of the ocean speaking all around me. This was real. I was safe.

"Don't ignore me now," I commanded. "I know who you are, but not what you want from me."

I felt two familiar presences around me, but I didn't dare open my eyes. I couldn't afford to lose focus on the task at hand. I knew Freyja and Phoebe were on either side of me, called to this spot just as I was.

"Eferhild," the voice spoke, but no figure came forward. His voice was the stars, and the stars were his voice—infinite.

"The Archer," I whispered.

"Have you accepted your blood?"

I paused, not wanting to speak what I knew was true.

"Who am I, Eferhild?"

"You may be my blood," I answered. "But you are no father of mine."

"You are displeased with me, Eferhild," The Archer answered.

"Most kids want their father in their lives," I spat out, my wounded inner child activated.

"I knew you were important, my little bear. You've proven as strong as I'd always known you would be. I had to hide you for as long as I could. Until the time was right. I have loved you with all the power of the cosmos."

"I died anyway," I said angrily. "And I still might."

"You must accept your truth, little bear, or the celestials will ensure your death in the trials," The Archer said more sternly. "Be angry at me if that gives you purpose. Forge your fury or your fear, but you must embrace who you are."

"What does that mean? I know who I really am!"

"I believe in you, little bear," he whispered. "The trials are only the beginning."

I snapped my eyes open, heart pounding. Freyja and Phoebe knelt beside me, embracing me as the waterfall of tears cascaded down my face. I wasn't sure what I cried about. There were too many things going through my mind. I mourned for my father and what life could have been with him. I grieved that it was all for nothing. I'd still ended up right here, a pawn for the stars. When my tears could no longer fall, I wiped the remnants away, vowing that the stars would not define me.

"It was The Archer, wasn't it?" I asked Freyja. "Who told you to lead me to Elvy."

She nodded, seeming to hold back tears of her own.

"But if he is of Algol, why would he choose Elvy and not Oleander?"

"I don't know, Zoe. He only told us things in riddles."

"And you," I turned to Phoebe. "What role do you play in all of this?"

I took a long look at the gypsy woman, more closely than I ever had before. Her soul, her essence, was much more ancient and not of this world than I'd ever bothered to truly recognize.

"I've been faithfully serving The Archer for longer than your mortal realm has existed, child."

"Another pawn in the universe, then," I said.

"Do not get it wrong, Zoe," Phoebe replied, shaking her head. "The stars are for the dreamers still, but they are as imperfect as you and I. Any being will do hateful things in acts of desperation for those they love."

"And I'm the answer to their desperation?" I loathed to acknowledge that I related to their plea.

"No, child of the cosmos. You are their *creation*. I fear The Archer was just as much a victim in this story, though he refuses to see it yet."

“Don’t forget my mother,” I said, my gaze turning to ice. “My path was always to Emerge. No matter the choices I made, I was always going to end up right here—in this moment.”

Jelly laid her head in my lap, trying to stabilize my trembling frame, but I felt righteous fury growing within me. Perhaps my subconscious knew this was coming. Maybe that’s why I’d always lived like tomorrow would never come.

“Come back, Zoe,” Freyja whispered. “They haven’t won. Not by a long shot, but if you burn out now, we all lose.”

I breathed in the smell of the ocean water and tried to find the furthest wave in the distance to follow back to shore. This was real, and I had to face that fact.

“If The Archer is so mighty, why can’t he just fix everything?” I asked, frustrated.

“As he said, the trials are only the beginning,” Phoebe answered.

“Let me guess, if I survive that and choose the right path, then he’ll tell me what else he needs from me?”

“To heal us all,” Phoebe answered, as if it was that simple.

There was a whisper of familiarity about the way she said that, but I couldn’t quite place it. I scratched behind Jelly’s ears, settling into the enormous obstacle before me. Whether or not I was ready, what was coming was coming, and I had to be ready to face it head on.

“I better get back to bed,” I said, yawning. “Let’s go, Jelly.”

I bid my farewells to both Freyja and Phoebe and crept back into the seaside bungalow. Elvy was sitting up in the bed, waiting for me. He opened up the covers for us, and I snuggled into the form of his body behind me. Jelly snuggled closer to me on the other side.

“Do you want to talk about it?” he asked, pulling me closer.

“The Archer just confirmed he is my father,” I said, taking a steadying breath. “He was the one who told Freyja to lead me to you. I still don’t know what he wants from me or what the bigger picture really is. I feel completely out of control and angry.”

My fists were clenched, causing my nails to dig in painfully. He traced circles on the back of my palms, which allowed my hands to relax some.

“I understand your anger, Zoe, and the ability for it to be all-consuming,” he said in solidarity. “I’m always furious, on the edge of losing control, but I’ve learned to forge my fury into something powerful—something that is feared. My power, my true gift—it terrifies me. The lock I have around it, if I ever lost control...”

"I trust you, Elvy," I murmured, and I meant it. He pulled me even closer. "I just want to feel like I'm in control of my destiny," I whispered.

"You are life. You are the wind of the wildness of freedom that flows from the mountain to the sea. Ferocious and kind. You decide what happens next."

I closed my eyes, desiring to believe in his words. I believed in myself, but I felt a need to prove it more than ever before. Eventually, I drifted off into a needed peaceful slumber.

***

I was on my way to work a few days later when it happened. The thing they'd tried to warn me would occur if I pushed my gifts too far. I had no other choice, though. I would not stand still while someone else suffered.

The onslaught of nausea caught me off guard. I hadn't felt it this intensely since the first time I'd met Oleander. I quickly figured out where it was coming from and followed the path that emitted in front of me, silently swearing, as I knew I'd be late for work. I wasn't sure what I'd find when I arrived, but I knew if I didn't, someone wasn't going to just get hurt—they were going to die.

I was in a full-on sprint when the path suddenly stopped. It took only a breath to figure out what had happened. I stood before a house on fire, and it was burning fast, much too quickly to be natural. I noted the man that rushed up the street, dropping a gas canister as he sped away, probably frightened that I'd arrived unexpectedly.

Shit. Was I supposed to chase after him or was there someone else hurt? I closed my eyes in frustration, trying to figure out my next move, when I heard the screams. Too young to be an adult, but more than one voice was stuck in that house.

"Stay," I commanded Jelly, knowing she would obey.

The memory of Madison, the woman I'd met at the pier, and her family dying in a fire flashed through my mind. So much pain could have been avoided—even if I'd helped her find some peace that day by releasing the plants into the ocean. I silently cursed again, steadied my breathing, and leaped headfirst into the burning building.

I was met with so much smoke I could barely breathe, and I knew if I continued to inhale it at this rate, I would pass out before I helped get them to safety. I started crawling on the floor, making my way up to the second level, trying to ignore the stings of fire I felt as the ceiling started to crumble. We did not have long left.

I finally made it up the stairs, and the screams became louder. They were mercifully behind the first door I tried, and I ignored the searing pain in my hand as I turned the doorknob. Before me stood a female teenager, probably about fifteen or sixteen, and a young boy, probably aged ten. The girl was cradling her arms around the younger sibling, and the stillness of his chest indicated he wasn't breathing.

I knew going down the stairs was no longer an option, so I hoisted up the first piece of furniture my hands touched, and I smashed it through the window on the first try. I felt my body becoming tired, but I forced my fatigue to cease. I made quick work of throwing the two small twin mattresses out of the window to help break our fall. I'd never wished I had wings so badly in my life.

"Out the window now," I ordered the girl.

"I'm not leaving him," she shouted back at me. I understood her all too well.

"I've got him," I thundered back, trying to be patient despite knowing we had zero time for arguments.

She finally nodded and leapt out of the window, landing perfectly on the mattresses, though her limp showed it was still somewhat painful.

"Stay with me," I said, as I lifted the young blonde-haired boy into my arms. I wasted no time in wondering how badly this would hurt, and I bounded out the window, making sure the boy's body was fully protected.

I hit the mattress hard and saw stars in my vision as I tried to get my bearings.

"Is there anyone else inside?" I asked.

"No," the girl said, focusing on her brother.

I called for Jelly, and she came sprinting towards us.

"Please check on my dog while I take a look at your brother," I said, working through the physical pain.

The girl didn't argue and knelt next to Jelly as I examined her brother. He was breathing, but barely. He wasn't going to make it, even if I called an ambulance now. He had severe burn marks over the skin that was not covered in clothes. I saw the sorrow in his sister's eyes and the decision was made for me.

"Look away," I said, sternly. A crowd was gathering in the distance, but we had landed in the privacy of their backyard.

The girl hugged Jelly around her neck and began crying. I didn't blame her, and I hoped this would work.

I summoned that pull deep in my chest. I allowed the sounds of the ocean to drown out all other noises. I tasted the saltwater on my lips and felt the breeze of the ocean flowing through my hair. I pictured Elvy's face, knowing the decision I was about to make might never let me see him again, but at least I could give a proper middle finger to Vega and Algol before I went.

I placed a hand on the boy's head and encased his body in the gift of Vega. Without seeing it, I knew a liquid-like substance was moving across his burn marks, healing them fully. I envisioned it entering his throat, clearing his airways of soot. I felt his lungs breathe in a powerful breath of fresh air, and I smiled, knowing he would live.

Then I was burning... and everything went black.

21

Mortality

I wasn't dead… I didn't think so anyway. I was somewhat aware of what was going on around me. I heard familiar voices and footsteps pacing with concern. I was still burning, like acid coursing through my veins. How many days had it been? What happened to me?

Flashes of the brother and sister crossed my mind, and I winced. I knew I'd healed him, though, and I'd brought him from the brink of death.

Was the burning ever going to stop?

"Heal her!" a voice screamed—Oleander. It was Oleander shouting.

"Don't you think we've tried?!" Elvy yelled back.

"We've been trying for days," Blaz said, voice cracking. I'd never heard him so… helpless.

"Try harder then," Oleander said angrily.

"Can you reach her?" Elvy asked Oleander, ignoring his rage.

"No," Oleander said with a hint of sadness in his voice. "She's not dead or dying, it seems. The stubborn girl has her shields up… I can't see her future."

"So she will heal?" Imelda asked.

"Only the stars will reveal that," Oleander answered. "But if she has enough magic to shield… I'd say she has a fighting chance."

I hated the idea of my mind being trapped in a lifeless body more than dying. I would fight to break free of this, but the burning had to stop. I had no plans of dying just yet. I had work to do, and the answer to my path was becoming clearer to me now.

"She's so still," Elvy breathed, holding my hand. I could just barely feel Jelly lying next to me.

I wanted to tell them to be patient, that I was coming. I just had to figure out how to wake myself up. I didn't know if it was time that I needed or some kind of jolt of energy, but I wasn't going down without a fight, not when my life hadn't even really begun. Not when I'd never truly been the master of my path.

I flashed back to the day I'd helped Madison say goodbye to her daughter and husband. I knew that had partially been my motivation to save these children. No parent should have to do that, and if I could take away their pain, then I was glad to have done it. I'd also seen Freyja in that teenager, ready to die alongside her brother. I couldn't ignore them.

Wake up, I screamed internally.

Fatigue eventually washed over me, and I fell asleep. It was just a dark void of nothing, no dreams or nightmares or hallucinations, only darkness.

"Fight, Eferhild. You are as lethal as a bear. Fight like it," The Archer commanded me, before fading into the abyss of whispers that was my current frame of mind.

I awoke to Elvy holding my hand, murmuring softly to me. I couldn't make out what he was saying, but I felt the wetness on my hand and knew he was crying. The burning had lessened, and I felt I would wake fully soon. I only needed a little more time. I wished desperately I could tell Elvy that, to let him know I was going to be okay.

I was lulled back into another dark sleep, and I prayed to whatever God or star was out there on my side that I would return to my mortal body. I even pleaded my case to Vega and Algol, despite my current irritation with them.

"Look, I know we aren't on the best of terms right now," I began. "But I've wished on the stars all my life, always feeling more connected to the night sky than the Earth beneath me. You know we aren't finished. Not yet."

They didn't bother to give me a reply, but I believe they heard me all the same. Whether they answered was beyond my control.

The next time I woke, I didn't feel anyone next to me, but I sensed a presence near. My eyes fluttered open, and I winced at the sudden awareness. The brightness was overwhelming.

"Zoe," Elvy said, racing over to me. "No, no, don't move."

I tried to sit up, but the room started spinning around violently. My throat was so dry, it was difficult to speak.

He handed me a glass of something that tasted like it had electrolytes. It took every ounce of self-control I had not to down it in one gulp. I didn't think my stomach would be too happy with me if I did that.

I realized we were not alone, and I took in the smiling faces behind Elvy. All of them, Delmira, Clodovea, Finnian, Imelda, and Blaz were there, along with Oleander, Zadie, and Freyja. They had all been waiting to see if I pulled through.

And they were all dressed to the nines. Even Freyja.

"Glad you could join us, sleeping beauty," Blaz said, playfully, but my heart was pounding.

"Tomorrow is the Winter Solstice," I said, noting their attire. "I was out that long."

"You don't have to go tonight if you'd rather just stay and rest," Elvy said, tucking a section of hair behind my ear. I hated to think what state my hair was in or how I probably smelled.

Even though I had been "asleep" all this time, I was still so tired and drained. *Way to completely diminish your energy before the trials, Zoe,* I chastised myself.

Looking into the eyes of all my friends, I knew that I needed to go with them. Not only for their sake, but for my own.

Seeing the decision in my eyes, Elvy nodded.

"We will help you get ready," Clodovea offered, stepping forward. She wore an A-line flowing white dress that made her look like an artist's depiction of an angel. It was beautifully contrasted against her dark skin.

I nodded weakly, taking her hand to another area of the lighthouse I'd never been to.

All the girls except Zadie followed Clove and me down a flight of stairs and into what looked like someone's bedroom. What I assumed was my dress hung in a bag on the rack.

While the rest of the girls started getting things squared away, Freyja hung back, wanting to speak with me. She wore a tight-fitting fiery orange dress with jeweled flames shining throughout. I thought it suited her nicely.

Jelly stayed planted at my feet as well, apparently unwilling to let me out of her line of sight. The girls of Vega did not pay any attention to who I now spoke to, even though I felt like they probably knew.

"That was very dumb," Freyja said, cutting me off as I was fumbling with an excuse. "But very brave. I knew you always had that kind of fight in you, and I'm glad you fought for life, despite the risks."

My voice caught, unsure of what to say.

"I love you, Freyja," I said, wanting to wrap my arms around her.

"I know," she answered. "Now, let's get you ready for the rest of your life."

After what felt like hours of primping and scrubbing and loads of coffee to fuel me, Imelda seemed pleased with her work on my face. It was a true test of her talent given the canvas she had to work with after the length of time I'd been out. I wouldn't think laying comatose did wonders for the skin. Imelda wore a halter style, floor-length gown that held all the pastels of the rainbow, intertwining together whenever she twirled. It complimented her well.

"You look hot," Delmira said, as a matter of fact. Delm had gotten her wish and was the only one not wearing a dress. She wore what looked like violet leather pants with a suit jacket that showed off her curves and flowed just shy of the floor.

"Have you tried looking in the mirror?" I teased.

I had yet to turn around to the full-length mirror to examine the woman who would be there. Jelly wore a sea-foam scarf around her neck with black beading that sparkled in the light. She seemed very proud of her accessory.

"It's time," Freyja said, knowing I was the only one to hear her.

I slowly turned around, and I couldn't help the smile that formed or the tears that brimmed in my eyes. Isabella was worth every penny.

At the base of my mermaid bodice dress, the sea-foam green encircled the flowing satin material, which she had somehow designed to mimic the ocean, especially as I twirled the fabric. As the dress moved up, the green faded into a deep rich black that was encrusted with a constellation of stars. Six huge stars spread throughout my chest—one for each star in the kingdoms of Canis and Algol. The dress had sparkly, translucent sleeves, and I felt like a warrior in it. It was designed to go into battle.

"Ready?" Clodovea asked.

"Yes. I am."

I trailed behind the rest of them as they made their way up the stairs and into the living room, full of smartly dressed gentlemen. There was only one pair of eyes that I searched for as I crossed the last step into the open floor of the lighthouse.

I locked eyes with Elvy, tuning out the rest of them, who I noted were conveniently stepping away. Even Oleander. I did not shy away in embarrassment as Elvy took me in, letting his gaze flow from bottom to top, savoring every inch of me. He wore a tux that matched me in every way. His suit incorporated a continuation of the night sky across my dress and the ocean that lay below it.

"What do you think?" I asked, baring myself to him.

"I'm thinking that if you were a goddess, I'd get on my knees right now and worship you," he replied, with a hint of playfulness in his eyes.

"A Lord Astral on his knees for a mortal... the stars may combust at the thought," I said, gazing into his eyes.

As if to prove a point, he got down on both of his knees and wrapped my thighs in his embrace as he leaned his head against me.

"They'd get over it," he said firmly.

I tried not to imagine how upset Imelda might be with me, but I got down on my knees with Elvy. He planted a generous kiss on my lips, and I wished we could stay right here forever.

"Let's live in our moment tonight," I whispered. "Let's forget all the rest."

"In this moment for you," he answered.

***

As we made our way to the ball, we ran into the last person I expected—Emma. She was averting her gaze in case I didn't want to speak with her, but I desperately did.

"I'll be right back," I told Elvy, as I approached Emma.

"Hey, Emma. I'm so sorry I missed our last appointment. I had an... emergency."

"I'm just glad you are alright, Zoe," she replied politely.

"I may be gone for a little while," I admitted. "I am so thankful for all that you have done to help me. Truly."

"Is everything alright?" she asked, concerned.

"Yes. It is," I said with conviction, even though I wasn't sure that was the case at all. "I just have things that I need to do." I couldn't stop the glance towards Elvy, and Emma followed my gaze.

"I see," she said, smiling. "My goal was always for you to eventually not need me, Zoe."

"Thank you, Emma. I'll check in with you when I get back, alright?"

"Take care of yourself."

I walked back towards Elvy's outstretched hand, knowing I was embracing the path to my future.

22

Winter Solstice

Mom and Grant had truly outdone themselves. The event was held at the Elysian again, but instead of their event hall, it was in their botanical gardens. The space was crawling with fauna that would not appreciate the cooler temperatures outside. Every shade of the rainbow represented itself amongst the flowers. The night sky easily showed through the glass ceilings, and the full moon was blindingly bright tonight.

"You can see Vega from here," Elvy whispered close to my ear as he pointed to one of the biggest stars in the sky.

It twinkled back at me as I pondered whether it would be my home soon. There was a part of me that still harbored anger towards the star, but I couldn't help the kindred spirit I had for it as well. Perhaps we could grow to understand each other, and they would listen to me. I'd make sure of it. The curious dreamer in me wondered what the realm could look like, but I supposed it was beyond what my mortal brain could comprehend on its own.

A crowd had gathered around on the other side of our enclosed space, so we made our way there, looking for my parents. Jelly trotted along beside us, eyes alert while in the crowd. I savored the glittering gowns and the sharply dressed men. Their eyes were so full of excitement, and I wanted to feel the same easiness tonight.

When we passed the threshold into the crowd, the putrid smell hit us first.

"What is that?" I asked, trying not to gag.

"That, my dear, is called a corpse flower," Oleander answered, appearing right behind me.

"Why are so many people standing around something so foul?" I asked.

"It's a rare sight, Zoe. The flower only blooms every decade or so, only when it has enough energy to do it," he explained. "Look past the smell."

We made our way through the crowd, and I stood before the towering flower, soaking in its beauty. The bloom was magnificent to see, standing at least ten feet tall in front of us. I'd seen nothing like it before. There was nothing inherently special about its color, but I admired the grit it seemed to have in standing tall after so many years down.

"How long will it bloom for?"

"Not more than a couple days," he answered, but I felt his eyes on me, not on the flower.

"You're missing out," I chastised him.

"No, I don't think I am," he stated, and I ignored the grunt Elvy produced beside me.

I turned to look at Oleander, who was still gazing at me. He wore a black suit with silver and blue accents I noticed matched my dress, though much more subtly than Elvy's. He was brilliantly beautiful by immortal standards, and a god amongst mortals, I was certain. There was no tug to him, though, nothing but the bantering friendship of sorts we had gained over the last months.

"You remind me of it—the flower," the Lord Astral of Algol said, as if he knew what my soul felt.

"Be careful, Oleander. Someone might think you have a heart," I answered.

"We can both keep pretending to loathe each other if you wish. If that makes you stronger," he replied, and I believed him.

"Do I really stink that bad?" I asked, feigning hurt, returning to his previous comment about the corpse flower.

"No, you keep rising against impossible odds… and when you finally bloom, everyone is there waiting to see you shine, no matter how long it is. You are the center that holds—despite all of it."

I saw the admiration in his eyes and felt the tears swell in my own.

"For what it's worth, Oleander, I couldn't imagine my life without you either now," I said, placing a kiss on his cheek.

He bowed, leaving Elvy and me alone again once more. I watched his retreating figure rejoin Zadie, who seemed enthralled with something Finnian was showing her. Delmira and Blaz were already on the dance floor, moving surprisingly gracefully with one another. Clodovea and Imelda were huddled together on a quiet bench, whispering to one another, lost in the intimate moment.

Freyja was wandering around, moving unseen and silently. I was about to go join her, but Zadie dragged Freyja over to her group and got her talking, though Finnian still couldn't see her.

"He thinks highly of you," Elvy said, leading me away from the corpse flower.

"And I of him," I admitted.

"He's changed," Elvy acknowledged. "Or maybe I never really knew him."

"We all live in the gray, Elvy," I said, wondering if the Lord Astrals were moving towards settling their differences.

Mom and Grant finally made their way over to us, and I tried to commit the smile on her face to memory, the crow lines by her eyes, the wrinkles around her cheeks from years of laughter. I wanted to remember this—all of it.

"You look like a dream," my mother said, as she made me twirl around. "You've really grown up... I wish Freyja was here."

I glanced behind my parents to see Freyja look up at me. She had just laughed at something Oleander or Zadie said, and I tucked that laughter away to hold on to—to the very end.

"She's always here," I murmured, giving both Grant and my mother a hug. "Just as I will always be, no matter what."

"We love you, kid," Grant said, voice breaking only slightly.

"But I wanted to tell you some exciting news," I said, an idea forming. "Elvy's invitation to Alaska has turned into a lengthy extension. His family needs our help with a business they run there. I could be gone for a little while, and the service isn't so good."

I was saying goodbye, though she did not know it. She wiped the tears from her eyes and fussed over her smudged makeup.

"That sounds like an adventure. Just like you used to go on, Zo. I never knew where you were half the time," she answered, seeming genuinely happy for me. "You'll take care of her, Elvy?"

"I'll look after her, Vivian. You have my word," he swore.

"I love you, dear. Now go have fun, you two. It's a party, after all," she said, dismissing us.

"Alaska? Is that right?" June asked, dressed in a beautiful, soft blue, floor length dress.

"It's all kind of last minute," I fumbled, surprised to see her here.

June didn't seem to necessarily believe me, but she didn't pry.

"No, don't apologize, Zoe. Dr. Malik and I have things well under control. You go make some new memories. Make mistakes. Piss a few people off. Never forget who you are though and what you had to do to be here," June said, offering her words of wisdom that so often endeared me to her.

"Thank you, June. For everything," I said, hugging her goodbye.

The familiar smell of lilies engulfed me as I embraced her.

"I'll see you again, Zoe. I've got a sense about these things," she said, squeezing me one last time before walking away.

A slow song came on, and Elvy held out his hand in invitation.

"May I have this dance?" he asked.

"And every one after," I answered, as he guided me to the floor.

Elvy expertly led me across the dance floor, holding me tightly, as if I might disappear right before his eyes. I felt no fear of embarrassment as he twirled me around, a move that was beyond what I had ever done. He radiated confidence, eyes shining with something deeper than desire or admiration. *Love.* I wasn't sure what was holding either of us back from saying it, but I wanted to scream it from every rooftop in the city for all to hear.

Before I could get the caught words out, the song changed to something fast, and Blaz slammed into us.

"Group dance," Blaz said, pulling us to the rest of our friends, including Oleander's court and Freyja. Jelly even joined in the fun.

I relished their euphoric expressions and thrills of laughter, no trace of my impending trial shown through any of their faces. Even Freyja seemed to enjoy herself, face full of life in the way it used to be. If this was the final night of my mortal life—if the worst should happen—it was a night well spent.

I knew I would fight to get back here to these faces. All of them. I would not accept my mortal life any longer. I didn't have the faintest idea what would happen in the trials, but I had every intention of *Emerging*. Emerging as what, though, I didn't know.

When we could no longer push away the heaviness of the last strike of midnight, we stepped back into the night to meet my fate.

Elvy cradled both me and Jelly in his arms as he flew us back to the lighthouse. He soared just above the ocean water, as the moon's light rippled across the waves, creating the illusion of rays emitting from it.

Much too soon, he guided me to the living room where the entourage awaited us.

"It's time," he said, hands shaking slightly.

He helped me lie comfortably on the large couch and placed a last kiss on my forehead. I called Jelly into my arms as I prepared for the fight of my life.

"We'll be waiting here, watching over you," he promised, squeezing my hand.

Both Oleander and Elvy stood over me, ready to initiate the trials.

"Will it hurt?" I asked.

"It'll be as easy as falling asleep," Oleander said.

"To help you travel between realms and induce the meditative state needed, we will each put a piece of the essence of Vega and Algol inside your soul. Your mortal body will stay here, but your mind will be in the realm of the trials. We will not be able to communicate with each other while you are gone," Elvy explained.

I nodded my understanding. My heart threatened to combust. I breathed deeply into my lungs and focused on the crash of the waves. This was real. I was safe.

Each Lord Astral pulled a piece of their essence from themselves and held a small ball of light in their hand—Oleander's black and Elvy's sea-foam green.

"Ready?" Elvy asked.

"To whatever future," I said, nodding, refusing to say goodbye to anyone in this room.

I let my eyes drift to Freyja's face as the Lord Astrals plunged their lights into the core of my being.

Just before I left the mortal plane, The Archer whispered, *"Fight ferociously, little bear."*

Instead of a peaceful drift, something slammed me into a level of consciousness I didn't know existed, and I was soaring into the night sky above, leaving the mortal realm behind me.

23

The Trials

After rising, I started falling, plummeting into an unfamiliar plane. I assumed it was Vega or Algol, but I had no way of knowing. A body of water was approaching fast, much too fast. Oh *shit.* This was going to hurt. So much for entering my trials with grace.

I was right. It felt like slamming into concrete, but I began wildly swimming to the surface, one kick at a time, guided by the moonlight peeking through the water above. I heaved a sigh of relief as air filled my lungs. After taking a steadying breath, I noticed a light coming from the shore and began swimming, fighting the fatigue.

While the dress I wore was beautiful, it didn't help against the sloshing water, but I had little faith I would be able to get it off without drowning myself. The lights were getting closer, so at least I was making some progress.

Finally, I made it to shore and slumped into the damp sand, panting.

"Hello, Emerging, I've been waiting to see you again," an unfamiliar voice spoke from above me.

I rolled my aching body to the side and found a woman standing over me. She wore a white, flowing dress with a plunging neckline that rested at her navel. Her hair was a pale white, like the color of the moon, and tattoos of a language I didn't recognize adorned every inch of her pale skin. Her smile was not unkind, but I wouldn't call it friendly either. Her eyes stopped me from any other movement. In them rested an infinite cosmos swirling where her pupils should be.

"You have nothing to fear, Zoe Eferhild," the woman said.

"You said *again*," I answered.

"We've met once when you were in the inbetween and you accepted the Emerging gift."

"Who are you?" I asked.

"That was the first question you asked last time," the woman chuckled.

"Are you God?"

"No. I go by many names, child, but you can call me Nova."

The name did not sound familiar to me, but I took her outstretched hand as she helped me off the ground. My spirit wanted to cringe away from her, but also get as close to her as possible. It was an odd, conflicting feeling.

"Where are we?"

"Everywhere and nowhere," Nova answered, clearing absolutely nothing up. I assumed that was by design.

I followed Nova as she guided me away from the shoreline and up to what I could only describe as a palace carved from marble. It reminded me of the Greek architecture I'd seen in my travels during my mortal life.

"Is this part of the first trial?" I asked warily.

"Rest, child. We haven't gone over the rules yet. It would be unfair to proceed until you've eaten and slept. A consciousness that has traveled this far needs to replenish itself."

"My physical body is back on Earth. This isn't real," I said, confused.

"Isn't it?" she said, smirking.

I couldn't hide the fatigue and soreness in my walk and knew she spoke the truth.

I continued following Nova through the palace doors, mesmerized by the *otherness* of it. It did not possess the feel of home. Every piece of gold furniture and intricate architecture was meant to impress those who walked before it. Gold and silver accents were placed with methodical detail throughout. Jewels were interlaced into every structure, as if there was no end in sight. All of this was still not the oddest thing, though.

We were completely alone. There were no staff in these magnificent halls, yet I smelled the scent of something delicious as Nova led me into what I assumed was a dining hall. Only two place settings were out, even though fifty people could easily fit comfortably. She motioned for me to sit down, and I obliged, unsure of what else to do.

With a snap of her fingers, an enormous amount of food piled onto my plate. Perfectly cooked meats, colorful vegetables, and what had to be the largest potato I'd ever seen plopped onto my plate. There was even freshly cut fruit that I couldn't place. Too hungry to question whether it was safe, I speared a piece of chicken, and it melted warmly into my hungry mouth.

"Thank you," I said, finally remembering my manners.

"Of course, Zoe, The Emerging of Legend. Realm-Healer, I think is what Elvy named you."

"Is that who I am?"

"If you choose it," she answered, eating her food more slowly than my ravenously hungry body would let me. "I believe it is his hope, as well as many others."

"I'm still trying to decide if this is real," I admitted, my stomach straining in fullness.

"You must have questions," she stated, with those never-ending eyes. "Now would be the time to ask them."

"I don't suppose it will matter in the end, if I can't remember anything once I leave here."

"Our experiences carry into our subconscious. Whether we remember them or not, they are stored in us and marked on our body in other ways."

I licked my finger and took a long sip of the strange, sweet substance, and briefly wondered if this was the nectar of the gods I'd read about in mythology. My translucent scar caught my attention, and Nova's words struck me deeply.

"You mentioned rules earlier," I said, trailing off.

"That is as good a place to start as any," she nodded. "It's important that you listen to me carefully, Zoe Eferhild. You will face three trials while in my realm should you accept the path of an Emerging. You can choose to opt out at any time. If you choose this course, you will cease to exist."

"Failure isn't an option," I said firmly, as the faces of my loved ones flashed across my eyes.

"You say that now because you are not in any pain yet, Zoe," she said, her voice not unkind.

"What exactly are the purposes of these trials?" I asked, wanting to understand the endgame of all of this.

"All three tasks are designed to test the truth of your mind, body, heart, and spirit. You will need to use all four to accomplish them. The first trial is to prove you are truly worthy of the Emerging," she explained. "Most don't make it past the first task."

Emma passed through my thoughts as I knew I would face my worth here more than I ever had while still mortal. I only hoped I had the courage to believe it when it counted. I would be brave. Embracing my courage might save my life here.

"And will the last two help me decide between Algol and Vega?"

"Perhaps, yes. This is a unique trial. You are the first Emerging to be touched by two stars. I believe if you make it through to the last trial, a path will become clear, and you must make your choice between them," Nova said with commanding clarity.

"What would you choose?" I asked, knowing I would not get an answer. There was no flip of the coin for me, not this time.

"The stars can give you life, but it is only you who can claim it," she answered.

"I'm scared," I said, exposing my vulnerability to this being.

"Every creature has a fear, Zoe. Forge your fear correctly, and it will give you purpose," she encouraged, mirroring what Elvy had said to me.

"You seem to root for me to succeed," I said with a secret smile.

"Not even I wish to see an Emerging with your potential fail," she admitted, with that *other* smile that was kind yet unkind. "The trials build on each other. If you pass the first and proceed to the next, I will provide more information then."

I only nodded, closing my eyes, leaning my ear to the sound of the foreign waters crashing into the strange shore. Even here in this realm, I was at peace knowing that this was real, whatever reality I was in. I felt the foreignness in the air, but it was the silence that seemed to be all-consuming. No sounds of traffic or the other telltale sounds of life were to be found.

"What now?" I asked.

"Rest, Zoe. You will appreciate the sleep when you wake," she said, with knowing eyes. "Anything you require while in this realm will be provided to you. You only need ask for it."

Nova led me down another hall and opened the door to a room that was half marble and half glass, looking out to the ocean. The bed was luxurious, with a material I couldn't place for the sheets and comforter. I turned to thank her, but she was already gone.

I stripped my gown off, gently placing it on the chair beside the massive bed. I felt protective of it—my last connection to my home. Rummaging through the wardrobe, I found some sturdier clothes to wear. I settled on a pair of green hiking style pants with breathable fabric, but plenty of pockets if needed. I paired it with a black athletic shirt, and I enjoyed the familiarity and comfort something like this could still provide me in this unfamiliar place.

Easily finding the open shower, I let the water get hot enough to burn and leave my skin raw. I traced the jagged scar on my left arm, kind of glad this part of me followed my consciousness into this battle for my life. I glanced down at the rest of my scars—not my stab wound—but the marks that had been left from the wild life I'd once lived. I would not give up.

I quickly dried off and opted to sleep in the clothes I'd picked out, just in case I needed to fight something while I was in the world of dreams. Before I laid down for the night, I looked up at the stars, thinking of Elvy and Freyja. Just for a moment, so fleeting I knew I'd imagined it, I felt them there with me, murmuring words of encouragement. Whether it was my mind losing its grip on reality or it was real, I needed it.

I crawled into bed, knowing I would face the rising sun, a warrior prepared for battle.

24

Beginning

Only the sun never rose. When Nova came to wake me from my peaceful slumber, the stars still crawled across the night sky, unwavering. I panicked, thinking I didn't get any sleep, but my body felt rested, more so than it had in a while.

"The sun does not rise here," Nova explained. "It is always night in the realm of the stars."

"Why?" I asked.

"So they can always lead you home."

I wondered silently if that was true, but I liked the sentiment either way. She offered me a quick breakfast before we headed... well, I didn't know where we were destined. I ate slowly, savoring every bite, and sighed at the last drop of coffee. Praise Vega that this realm had decent coffee or I might've failed before I'd even started.

I only looked into those unnerving eyes when I was ready, and she seemed to see the decision in mine.

"Come, Zoe Eferhild. It is time."

Nova stood elegantly from her chair and led the way out of the palace and up the shore of the beach that transformed from exquisitely soft sand to rocky terrain. The further we walked, the harder it became to climb, as it became steeper with every step. Nova slowed to my pace, and there was no sign that this was difficult for her. The rocks eventually turned to grass, and I realized we were on the edge of a sea cliff at the end of our trek.

It looked like we were standing on the edge of eternity. The waters went as far as my mortal eyes would allow me in this night sky, but the moon was full and the stars provided plenty of light to guide the way. It reminded me of my travels in Ireland. There had never been more stunning seaside cliffs.

"The Cliffs of Three," she said, motioning her hand around us.

"Three trials," I said, understanding.

"Yes, Emerging," Nova replied. "I will return once you have completed your task or you call to cease."

"But what do I do?" I asked, confused.

"Into the stars. What feels like the end is often the beginning," she said, before disappearing.

I braced for the onslaught of warriors that were sure to come to demolish me, but none came. I focused on my breathing, halting my panic. Panicking got you killed, and I couldn't afford to die yet.

Into the stars.

I looked up at the dazzling night sky, wishing I had the time to stare at it in wonder. She couldn't have meant flying into the stars. I had no wings. For a foolish moment, I strained my brain, trying to sprout wings from my back, but that only gave me a headache.

Frustrated, I sat down on the edge of the cliff, watching the moon's light ripple across the ocean. The stars gleaming in the water created an exact mirror image of the sky. I think I knew what I had to do, and I prayed I was right. Standing firmly on the edge of the cliffs, toes in line with the solid rock beneath me, I stared into the dark abyss below me. I couldn't wonder what would wait for me at the bottom.

With a steadying breath to rally me, I leaped into the unknown. I jumped to live and prove my worth—all of it—in this pivotal moment. My braid swirled around me, but I did not let an ounce of fear break through. I only closed my eyes just before I crashed beneath the surface.

The water did not feel like any ocean I'd ever swum in. It seemed to caress me in a warm embrace, and power radiated in every atom around me. I felt the *otherness.* No sea monster attacked me, but I didn't rule that possibility out.

I saw a brilliant light below me, and I took as large of a breath as I could muster and plunged beneath the surface of the water again. Somehow, the ocean seemed to be made up of the stars themselves, guiding me further down, closer to my destiny. The light was getting brighter, but it was too deep for me to reach. I paused. If I turned back now, I'd have enough air to make it to the surface, but I knew I had to keep going, pushing.

With my lungs still burning, I kicked myself deeper, propelling myself forward, towards the light. By the time I reached it, I was fading out of consciousness, but that tug in my chest that reminded me of Elvy and all things good lurched my fingertips forward so that they embraced the starry flame.

I held the light between my palms and suddenly, I could breathe, but I was no longer in the depths of the ocean as I took in my new surroundings. I was staring back at me, but not me right now. I was younger here. I wanted to look away and shove the ball from me. I made myself hold firm.

Until the end, I chanted.

I got this sense that I was not alone, and I dug down deep into my courage. *Breathe.*

I'd heard about people having their life flash before they died, like they relived their most treasured moments before they passed. That wasn't what was happening to me. It was slow and tortuous. The orb was showing me every moment of my life—the good and the bad. Everything I held myself responsible for. Every wrong I had committed was on display before me. Every doubt in myself, every bad thought I believed about who I was raged through me like an unforgiving riptide. I refused to let myself look away despite the burning ache to toss the star from my hands.

I needed to vomit. I wanted to scream at the girl in the flame, hurting herself on her thighs so that no one would see it the next day. I crumpled at the lies I told myself—the lies I had told everyone—even to those I loved the most. If I could just claw my eyes out, this would be over, but I glued my hands to this cruel ball of light. I wouldn't have to relive this anymore if I could just break free.

I hated the person staring back at me, and I loathed the girl I was about to see. The girl who let her sister die in her place. It was too much. It was all my fault. The burden was too great for anyone to bear—the guilt and shame that thrived within me, sinking into my bones. The knife going into my arm, trying to give into the tendrils of shame.

When would this torture end? It only kept replaying over and over again. No matter how much I begged for it to end, it would not relent.

What feels like the end is often the beginning. Nova's words burned through my mind. I had come to the end many times. I had to face the beginning.

So, I turned back to the flame of light. With fresh eyes and newfound resiliency, I watched again. I saw myself heal. The fight in my green eyes stared right back into the drowning soul holding the star of light. I witnessed myself break through the cycle of trauma and learn to trust once more. I saw myself being remade, the fissures of my brokenness closing through the love of others—but not just their love, my own. For every awful moment that had threatened to overtake me, two good ones took its place. I saw the joy in the eyes of the child I used to be, whispering adventures underneath the glow of the stars. I saw Freyja and I dancing on top of a mountain, dangerously close to the edge, high on the ecstasy of living fully. Again and again, I saw the wildness of the freedom that had always been lurking within me.

I loved myself. All of me. Every broken shard of glass that made me uncomfortable, I loved it even still. I was enough and worthy. I was the only person dead or alive who could decide that. I claimed the life of the stars for me—no one else.

With a resounding declaration, the star I grasped onto guided me gently to the surface, warming me the whole way, as if to say *well done.*

Gasping, that breath of air as I emerged from the waters below the Cliffs of Three filled my lungs with radiant joy. With tears in my eyes, I nodded my thanks to the stars shining above and swam quickly to shore to find Nova waiting for me. She neither smiled nor frowned, but stood resolute, timeless.

"You have shown your worth to the stars," Nova declared.

"I only had to believe it for myself," I answered.

"Come, child of the cosmos, it is time to rest and replenish for your next task."

"How long was I under?" I asked, unsure. It'd only felt like a few hours, but I doubted that to be true.

"Time works differently in this plane, but in your mortal time, one week."

"A week?" I asked, surprised.

"It will only get longer, Zoe Eferhild. The trials will take more from you and will be more alluring in ways."

"And what is the next task supposed to prove?"

"The intentions of your heart—your spirit," she replied, as she crossed the threshold to the same room I had stayed in... a week ago. "Eat, rest. I will come for you when it is time."

I allowed myself to soak in the grand bath, somehow not turned off by being immersed in water. I didn't let my mind wander to those waiting for me back in the lighthouse. I dared not give into that hope. Not yet.

The water never cooled, despite how long I stayed submerged in its comforting steam. I wrapped myself in a fluffy robe and braided my hair down the length of my back. A pile of hot food and, much to my happiness, a large pot of coffee awaited me beside the bed. I savored the taste and smells, wanting to remember this night—this moment I had survived.

I easily fell asleep in that never ending midnight, dreaming of the starlight water wrapping me in its soothing embrace.

25

Pieces

The next morning was much the same. The night sky shone brightly, providing life to the lands below. Nova had already gathered me, and we now stood before the Cliffs of Three again, and I awaited any words of wisdom that she might depart to me.

"You needn't any," Nova said, seeming to read my thoughts. "You realized you have the power to choose how you view yourself, who you truly are... the stars gave you a second chance to claim your life, Zoe Eferhild—Emerging of Legends. Remember that gift and why they chose your heart, your spirit. You choose how that power is molded."

I nodded, trying to absorb every word she said, knowing I might need it later.

"Forge my fear or my fury," I said in thought.

"Is fury not but fear, Zoe Eferhild?"

I understood what she meant, but I still didn't know what to do with the information. Could I be both—choose both emotions?

"I'll see you on the other side," I said, jumping headfirst into the starry abyss below, spearing my body towards the glowing orb of light.

If I wasn't mistaken, just before I broke the water's surface, I thought I heard Nova whisper, "I hope so, too."

I didn't hesitate as I clutched my hands around the orb of light, ready to face whatever it showed me. Only this time, I was not merely watching my life. My consciousness seemed to be thrust into the orb, as if it launched me into a simulation. However, as soon as I rationalized, this wasn't real that thought and realization left me.

I was back on Earth, but I couldn't remember why I was there. I wore unfamiliar clothing, and Jelly wasn't with me. How odd?

I wasn't in Saint Andrews; this city was much too big for that. I began jogging through the alleyways, trying to catch my bearings to no avail. I was pretty certain I had circled around this same sign a few times. A task. I had something that I needed to do, but I couldn't quite put my finger on it.

Before I could dwell on that thought any longer, voices up ahead pulled me towards them, desperate to figure out why I was here. Every time I got closer to the voice, it seemed to jump further away. I did not give up though and kept chasing after the people, knowing in my gut they could help me on my way to what I needed to do.

Finally, I tracked the group to a bridge with a deadly drop off into the water. I went still as ice at the scene before me. Four men were taunting this man to jump as he stepped onto the railing of a bridge with a lethally steep cliff below. I recognized their faces and wanted to buckle with grief and sickness.

I had burned their faces into my memory from the night of the attack, and I wanted—*needed*—to tear out every single one of their throats. My rage boiled, and I had a beeline focus for destroying these men and everything they stood for. Vengeance—my blood ran hot with it. I completely forgot about the man on the railing.

In that moment, my power—my essence—had been remade into pure fury. I refused to look past my rage. I would not look deeper into their intentions. It was pretty obvious they were only there to cause harm. Why would I show them mercy?

My need for blood payment blinded me to the man on the railing. No thought of healing entered my mind for him. I would help him by destroying those who would treat him this way. Oleander had never taught me how *divine* the darkness could taste, nor had Elvy. This enraged me even further. I sauntered over to the four men with a gleam in my eye that surprised them. They would not overpower me. I wasn't only connected to the spirits of the dead, but I was death itself. I was the reaper who had come to deliver a killing blow and thrust them into an eternity of torment, just as they had tortured me long after their hands had left my body.

Before they could even speak, I let the dark tendrils creep from my fingers, enslaving their minds to me. If I could shield my mind, then I could crush the minds of others... I just had to reverse what Oleander had taught me. How dare he not teach me to be this weapon of justice?

"Who are you?" one of them stammered.

How dare they not know my face? No worries. They would memorize every surface before the night was over. Somewhere in the back of my mind, I could hear the man on the rail screaming, edging closer to his fate. A task. I had a task.

But then one man made the mistake of speaking without being spoken to.

"We don't want any trouble," another sorry excuse for a human said, lips trembling.

"But I do," I said, snarling. I wanted *all* of the mischief.

I unleashed my darkness on them, filling them with nightmares even the devil would flinch at. I tossed my head back to gaze at the stars as I relished in the bliss of their pain.

"You're killing them," a soft voice said. Who was that?

I looked back down to find the man on the rail pleading for their lives.

"You wish to have mercy on the men who want to see you dead?" I asked, angry at his pathetic weakness.

He nodded, still moving closer to his deadly jump.

"Why?" I asked, eyes still full of my wrath.

"Because they are me!"

This guy had lost his mind. He made no sense. The men wrapped around my dark tendrils looked nothing like the guy on the bridge. One glance at him, and I was full of heavenly spite again. He would die first.

I picked him up by his throat and dangled him in the air, ready to claim and destroy his mind. There would be no healing—no mercy.

"If you kill him, I will surely die," the frail man on the bridge said.

"Then you will die," I snapped, my voice unrecognizable.

I brought my first victim down to my eye level so I could watch the life force fade from his eyes as I snatched it from him.

Just as I was about to deal the death blow, I glimpsed myself in his eyes. I did not know the woman who stared back at me. It was me, but I had no carefree easiness about me. I was shrouded in darkness, consumed by it. There was no room in my heart for the love that had moved mountains to fight for me.

My grip did not slacken as I took a steadying breath, forcing the Zoe I loved fully to come back. This darkness was a part of me I loved—yes, but it did not define me. It was not my identity. I would fight it. I would not become my enemy.

I set the man down on the ground and allowed myself to see with clear eyes.

I didn't recognize this man or the three men with him. They truly did not know me, nor I them. I blinked rapidly, getting clarity into my thoughts. I glanced back at the man on the bridge who had stopped moving. He seemed to huddle behind the pole in fear, too afraid to come to me and not ready to give up enough to jump.

I would save him. If he would let me.

A task. I was here in the realm of stars. This was a trial, and I had almost let my savage temper allow me to fail. I'd almost lost control.

I glanced back at the four men nearest me, and they were identical replicas to the man who stood on the bridge—pieces of him. His darkest pieces had been taunting him over the edge.

"I can help you," I said at last, knowing what I needed to do for him.

"I'm afraid," he said, barely audible.

"Me too," I answered, the most powerful words in existence at that moment.

I approached the man like a newborn animal, afraid to scare him away. He stood as still as a statue, as if waiting for me to show the monster that lurked beneath. She was buried deep within me—for now.

"Take my hand," I said as softly as I could muster. "I'll help you face it. We'll do it together."

"You'll stay the whole time?" the fragile man asked, before taking my hand in trust.

"Until the end," I promised.

I helped the shaking man step back over to the edge of safety to help him face the parts of himself that he feared the most. I swallowed, understanding his fear far better than he realized.

"How will it work?"

"We'll face them together. One at a time. We'll heal each of them. I'll take as much pain away as I can," I explained.

The man nodded with tears in his eyes, gripping my hand.

"Be brave," I encouraged. "Whenever you're ready."

I knew his fear as if it were my own. I would forge my power in my fear with all the might that my fury had just displayed.

The first of his dark spirit self approached, and the man squeezed my hand tighter.

"I am your body who you have betrayed," the mirror image said. "You must face me first."

The shaking man nodded, and I held the hand of his mirror and a jolt of darkness went through me and into the man. I wanted to run at the terror he was facing, but I didn't let go, even when he clutched so tightly through his screaming that I thought the bones in my hand would turn to dust.

Once the screaming ceased, and his mirror image was now a part of him once again, the next took its place.

"I am your heart who you have shattered. You must now face me."

I repeated the same process over again. The screaming did not lessen, but grew in sound as every piece of himself was made whole once more. The man became so weak that I helped him stand, and it was an honor to do it.

"I am your mind who you have let torment you...." Another round of screaming and exhaustion from the man. Even acting almost as a conduit, I was feeling just as fatigued as the man I helped, but I would bear this with him.

Finally, the final mirror image took my hand.

"I am your spirit who you will forget no more."

At the last of his wails, I sat down on the ground and cradled the sobbing man on my lap, gently brushing his hair as a loving mother would do. I placed a hand on his bruised face and cut arms, willing them to heal at my touch. The wounds listened to my magic sing, and I made him as whole as that gift would allow. I gave him all the strength I could conjure from my depleted reserves. I knew I'd made him strong enough to face life. He only had to reach into his courage.

"You are worthy," I said, whispering to him like a prayer.

Then I was suddenly jolted to the surface of the water, back to the land of Nova. The orb seemed to nod to me in satisfaction as I swam the short distance back to shore again.

"I am glad the true Zoe Eferhild made it back to me," Nova said, with the faintest smile on her lips. "Realm-Healer."

"What did that prove?" I asked, voice full of exhaustion.

"That your creed is true of heart," she said, pointedly.

"But how did I know to do those things? I had no idea if it would actually work," I said, craving reassurance.

"You are Zoe Eferhild—Emerging of Legends, Realm-Healer. Have you learned nothing, child? Your magic is a part of you that molds to your needs, Daughter of Algol. Placing limitations on yourself will not bode well in the end."

"You know about The Archer?" I asked.

Nova only looked at me with those cunning, endless eyes.

"Well then. How long was I out?" I asked, remembering why and who I was fighting to get back to. My strength was completely gone. I would need to dream and think of them tonight if I was going to continue.

"A month," she answered, turning her back for me to follow her.

"Do they—do they know I'm still alive?" I asked, petrified of the answer.

"They stand guard over your mortal body, even now," she replied. "They know you are still on the path of Emergence or your body would have turned to stardust."

I frowned at the thought, but I was glad they knew I was still fighting.

"You will need more rest before your final trial," she said, walking me into the familiar bedroom. "You will have three days to rest before you enter the cosmos below the Cliffs of Three. There you must choose your fate."

"Thank you, Nova."

"Thank the stars, Zoe Eferhild."

26

Twin Palace

Three days to choose my end. Three days to say goodbye without getting to actually say it. An impossible decision, but one I had to make. I knew I would choose to accept my place among the Emerging, but I didn't know which path to choose between Vega and Algol. Oleander had been right... the stars could have a twisted sense of humor.

No matter which I chose, I would lose someone. Not only would I lose the people that held my heart, but I would lose a piece of me along with it. I longed to see Freyja again. Even though she belonged to the world of spirits, I could keep her in my life, but she would not really be living. I didn't know if I possessed the will to lose her again.

With Elvy it was a different pain to think of losing him. He had etched out a place in my heart that belonged solely to him. My life became... hopeful again when he entered it, and I didn't mean that gentle kind of hope with small wisps of energy. I meant that kind of hope with sweat on her brow, that rose back up no matter how many times she crumbled to the ground. The kind of hope you would cross realms for, tear down mountains for. It had always lived in me, but Elvy drew me from that stagnant valley of just surviving, never daring to fully live again. Having him ripped from my life would surely tear me apart.

Both would accept whatever path I chose. It had always been about my choice. However, I couldn't only factor in the personal reasons for choosing the Emerging star. There was also a darkness in Algol, something much darker than Oleander let on. Looking back on how I had planned to rip those men's flesh into ribbons still haunted my thoughts. The image was difficult to shake.

Elvy had mentioned that Earth was tethered to these five elemental realms and whatever happened in them would have a domino impact on the mortal realm. The thought of that darkness leaching into my home made me shudder. Maybe Algol had chosen me because it *needed* me just as much as I needed it. Perhaps Algol was calling me home as a true

Daughter of Algol. On the other hand, maybe it chose me because it saw my potential for all-consuming darkness.

And what of Vega? What did Vega see in my future? Vega had blessed me with the ultimate gift of healing, but I was just one insignificant mortal. I could not heal nations. I could not give all of me, no matter how much I wanted to. I'd nearly died bringing that human boy from death's clutches. What did Vega expect of me? Did Vega really believe that I could heal realms?

I stood on the balcony of my room, gripping the cool marble railing beneath my fingers so tightly it hurt. I gazed into the world of stars above me and screamed for the answers to be revealed until I was hoarse. It was all for nothing. No answers came. I had not felt this alone in... I wasn't sure I'd ever felt this alone.

The only other being on this island was Nova. No other souls to speak of had shown themselves. What did Nova expect me to do for the next few days? Stew over my decision? Write goodbye letters to those who I would not go back to? Was the waiting some sort of test of discipline to see if I went mad?

I climbed into bed, exhausted from the second trial. I was too tired to eat the food that appeared and didn't bother changing from these worn clothes. Sleep called to me like a sweet mistress in the night, and I gave myself fully to her.

***

The next morning, I awoke to fresh food by my bedside, and my stomach groaned at the soothing smell. I ravaged the buttery soft croissants and barely paused enough to breathe as I forked in the rest of the meal. I wanted to kiss Nova as the waft of coffee finally caught my senses. I greedily drank from the cup that didn't seem to have an end.

After my belly was full and hunger satiated, I slid into the bath wondering what I would do with this day that was also night. I let the tug in my chest think of Elvy as I bathed, and I remembered him massaging my scalp as he worked the shampoo through my hair, bringing me peace. I would love to feel those calloused hands on me now, bringing me peace as he once did.

If I closed my eyes long enough and listened with all my might, I could trick myself into hearing him whisper soft words to me, though I couldn't discern what he was saying. I wanted to believe that he still waited by my mortal body, hoping that I would return to him. In the privacy of those moments, I knew he would also feel guilty in wishing for that.

If by some miracle my soul made it back to him, whether it was in this life or the next, I would tell him I loved him, though *love* didn't seem like enough. I would find him again, though. My will was strong enough to cross whatever realms I had to—if only to glance at his face one more time.

I stayed in the bath until it was uncomfortably hot, the water never cooling here, as if they designed this place for whatever I needed. I quickly dressed in hiking pants and an athletic shirt and trailed my way back to the first entrance Nova had led me through.

"Going somewhere?" Nova called from behind me, reminding me of the many times Freyja had snuck up on me in her ghostly form.

"I thought I'd have a look around. Clear my head," I answered, pausing before opening the door. I didn't feel like getting killed after all I'd been through.

"The island is yours to explore," she said. "If you should need something, Zoe Eferhild, you need only ask for it."

"Thank you," I said, darting out the door before she could give me any more cryptic messages.

I followed the beach to nowhere in particular, looking for something to catch my eye or draw me from my swirling mind. It wasn't much of an island to speak of. Apart from the palace, there was not much else except vegetation.

Deciding there was probably something more interesting in the palace, I turned to head back that way when my foot stepped on something smooth. I bent down to find a patch of white marble, far too big for me to lift. The more I pushed the sand away, the larger the stone seemed to be. I eventually cleared enough to see the section was at least as big as my own body.

You need only ask for it. The words rang in my mind, and this was a magical place. I had never been one to ask for help, but I was supposed to be remaking myself, right?

"Reveal yourself," I said to the stone, feeling absolutely ridiculous.

Nova appeared beside me instead. She did not speak, but motioned her hand and the sand began pulling away, revealing a marble path that disappeared into the ocean.

"What's down there?" I asked. "Is it safe?"

"The answers you seek," she replied, unwilling to give anything else away.

"You can't tell me what's down there."

"I cannot interfere," she confirmed.

I nodded, taking a deep breath. I'd been able to breathe underwater with the Cliffs of Three. I had to believe I could do the same now, no matter the fear I held inside.

I sloshed down the path, my body becoming heavier with each step. I guess I wouldn't be swimming. Taking in a large gulp of air, I submerged myself completely. I was met with a path to what looked like an identical palace on the surface, as if they were twins tethered together. The cosmos in the water easily provided enough light for me to explore this unexpected turn of events.

Vega lives in me, I thought. *I am of the water, and the water is of me.*

I took a small breath to find it... comfortable. Yes, I could breathe in this star-filled ocean thanks to Vega. I reminded myself that time worked differently in this water, and I would need to hurry. I didn't think Nova would take kindly to my being late for the trial that decided my fate.

To my surprise, I could move easily and found myself sprinting towards the palace door, unsure of what I was looking for. Something that would help me choose. The palace seemed to be laid out the same as its counterpart above the surface, but I had only ever seen the dining hall and my room.

I focused on the power of my discernment, hoping it would emit a path of light to my destiny. Much to my happiness, a bright light shot out of me. I moved as quickly as I could through the mirror palace and found myself in a library. I took it as a sign that I'd found favor with the powers that be and was on the right track. If I could figure out what they really wanted from me, that would aid me greatly in deciding my fate. I chose not to question how books stayed in this pristine condition while underwater, and I began fingering through the spines, attempting to figure out how they were organized.

Even in the realm of the stars, alphabetical seemed to be the standard. Minding the time, I quickly grabbed a book on Algol, hoping my discernment led my hand to the right one. Then, I plucked a book on Vega, praying for the same thing.

I scoured through the Algol book first, trying to find something, *anything,* that would help me. Nothing jumped out at me, so I turned to the book of Vega, desperately searching for my purpose, only to come up short again. I didn't know why I'd thought it would be that easy. Out of anger, I thrust the books off the table I'd been using and immediately regretted my actions. I never wanted to act out of anger. That was a good way to lose control, as I'd so clearly demonstrated in the second trial.

I bent down to pick up the discarded books when the ceiling caught my eye, only it wasn't a ceiling at all, but a moving swirl of the stars. They reminded me of Elvy's chest tattoo, showing the five courts under the Kingdom of Canis.

I laid down on the floor of the library and gazed up at the ceiling as if to say, *Yes, you have my attention.* I centered myself as Oleander had taught me so many times, leaning into what the universe wanted me to know, what it wanted me to change. The power of discernment lived within me and I with it. I did not need the pull of sickness to guide me, I only needed to listen—with my whole, worthy self.

It only took a moment to understand what the living stars were showing me, and my heart saddened. The ceiling had been turned into a retelling of the history of the stars. The story took me back to the moment that Algol was ripped away from Canis, severing their ties to the balance of the other sources of life: fire, water, air, and ground. It didn't show me how the bond had been slashed, though, as if the image was cloudy. I noted that as significant, but kept pushing on, knowing there was more I needed to understand. While all the other elemental realms were shining brightly, Algol's light was dimming. I had this gut instinct that Algol was dying, untethered to a mortal plane or elements of life, and its slimy tendrils looked like they were searching for something to revive it. The moving cosmos did not show me what, or maybe it couldn't because even it didn't know yet.

A flash of The Archer's constellation shone above Algol, shining the brightest on his bow and arrow. Of course, it was related to my father. If I remembered correctly, The Archer's arrow had been the string to tie the realms together as one, making them more powerful than any other dominion out there. This was much bigger than I or anyone could have anticipated.

I had a feeling if Algol was destroyed, Freyja's spirit would die with it. Maybe even Oleander and the rest of Algol's immortals... maybe even me, or at least a part of me. I wasn't sure if it was my gut or my discernment, but I understood that if Algol was reattached to Earth before it healed its growing void of destruction, the darkness would shatter the realms encompassing every court and world in shadows, perishing the light with it forever. I had to reattach it, but not as it was now. And it wouldn't last much longer without a new tether, either.

Algol was calling me home. Could I answer the call to the realm of shadows? *The darkness isn't always bad.* The mantra ripped through me. No, it wasn't. The dark made us human; the dark made us look up at the stars and dream for a better tomorrow. The darkness demanded to be felt, but allowed us to balance it with the healing of the light.

I knew what I had to do. I just prayed I wouldn't die living in my true courage.

27

Stardust

I ordered the cosmos of the water to take me to the surface. Kneeling before Nova, I tried to slow my racing mind. I knew what I had to choose, and I was prepared to face the consequences of that choice. I only hoped that my shields would hold long enough to see my choice through to the end.

"You are ready, Zoe Eferhild," she said, with those knowing eyes, staring deep into my soul.

"You knew exactly how long it would take me, didn't you?" I asked, pointedly.

"I hoped."

"How long was I in the water, Nova?" I asked, though I knew the answer.

"Exactly three days," she replied, holding out her hand to guide me to the Cliffs of Three.

We walked in silence, and she paused just before we touched the edge.

"Will I survive?" I asked.

Her eyes swirled faster than I'd ever seen them. Without speaking the words aloud, she entered my mind saying, *You will burn, Zoe Eferhild.*

"I've burned before."

I said that more confidently than I felt. I knew I may not survive the jump I was about to make. I didn't want to die, and I knew I'd fight what was coming with all the fight of the bear my father thought I possessed. Allowing the faces of Jelly and my mortal companions, the Court of Vega, and the Court of Algol to flood through my mind, I said goodbye to each one of them, lingering on Elvy the longest. If I didn't survive this, I hoped he would find me again.

I let my last thoughts drift to Freyja and Jelly. The two that held me together when I was at my most fragile. I owed them my life, and now I was willing to freely give it if it came to that, not because I sought death, but life.

"It is time, Zoe Eferhild—Emerging of Legends, Realm-Healer," Nova commanded, motioning towards the water below.

I would not fear this fall. I would not yield to the panic. Not tonight. When I jumped, I would own every second of it until I Emerged.

"I am enough," I said, clearly.

Breathe.

"I was chosen for this. Born for this *moment.* And it is not insignificant."

Breathe.

"This is not the end, but the beginning."

I dove into the cosmos, mind, heart, body, and soul. I would burn so brightly even the stars would bow to the power of my name. I thrust my impenetrable shields into place, knowing they would not break unless I commanded them so. With one last breath, I laid eyes on my target.

I didn't hesitate to clasp my grip firmly around the orb, and I welcomed it like an old friend as it transported me to my fate.

The orb dropped me onto the surface of what looked like moonstone, which seemed to encompass the entire planet, and the night sky was somehow more wondrous than the realm of Nova. There were so many stars that the darkness of the universe barely showed through them.

I stood before two figures. The being to my left was neither male nor female—it just *was.* They were shrouded in darkness and the fortunes of the universe. It was not a sense of evil, but of the embrace of free will. I knew before they spoke who this figure was—Algol.

The second was much the same, neither male nor female, and water and lights of gold gleamed through the surface of their skin. All life and healing and love seemed to drip from them, desperate to leap into the world. This was Vega.

It was interesting to see the darkness cling to Algol like an obsessed lover while the life emitting from Vega longed to experience freedom, not knowing the turmoil it may face.

"We've been searching for you," both Vega and Algol said in unison.

So like what Elvy had revealed to me, that he had been searching the realms for me, not knowing who I was yet to be.

"You've found me," I said, my mental shields stronger than ever.

"What have you decided, Zoe Eferhild?" Algol and Vega asked.

"Are you real?" I asked no one and everyone.

"We present to you in a way you can understand us," Vega answered, voice infinite.

"Why me?"

"You have the strongest scent of an Emerging in our histories," Algol replied. "You are a true daughter of Algol. None can match your power to turn the current course of destruction coming to the star realms and the mortal world."

"But I must choose between you."

I felt them trying to pry my shields down, but I would not waver. I'd made my choice.

"As one chooses between life and death, so must you choose between which star you will serve," Vega demanded.

"What if you're wrong?"

"There must be balance," Algol and Vega answered. I heard their impatience growing in the tone of their voices. I doubted they were used to being questioned. "You must choose, Zoe Eferhild, or you must join your sister Freyja in the world of the spirits."

"Why don't you just fix this mess yourselves?" I asked them.

"A celestial's direct power cannot touch another celestial, child of the cosmos."

"How do I choose?" I asked, no longer willing to prolong my fate.

Both Vega and Algol reached inside themselves to produce an orb of light, much like Elvy and Oleander had done to send me to this realm.

"Absorb the one you choose," Vega stated.

Here's to hoping I did not turn to stardust.

"I'm ready," I said, voice solid, commanding.

The majesty of the stars approached me until they stood side by side. Their otherworldly body language suggested they didn't enjoy being so close to each other.

"Choose," Vega and Algol said in that unnerving unison voice.

Breathe. Life was about moments. I was about to leave my mark amongst the stars.

"I choose me," I said, grasping both orbs with each hand and slamming them into my chest at once. "I choose all those who came before me who did not get this second chance."

The sheer force of the orbs knocked me to my knees, but I did not relent.

"How do you plan to survive this, foolish girl?" Algol spat.

"Recklessly. Confidently. Without the shame of my past and with forgiveness in my heart," I said, with resiliency coursing through me. The wind whipped my hair wildly, knocking me to all fours.

"You will burn," Vega said, not unkind, much like Nova had foreseen.

"Then I will burn until my last ember flickers out."

I clenched my chest as I felt the orbs battling for control of my mind, body, heart, and soul, but they only belonged to me. Only I determined what entered or escaped them. They would consume me or become me. It was *their* choice.

"I'm the daughter of The Archer. I am unmatched. I have proven my worth. My creed is true. You will not alter my fate any longer. I. Choose. *Me.*"

My entire body lit up into conflicting glows of black and white, but even then, I did not falter. I embraced the balance of light and dark in my body. I needed both for my mission, should I survive this. I only hoped I could remember my task when I returned.

I pictured Elvy's gentle touch and Freya's exhilarating laugh and commanded my grip to hang on until the end. To a better future. For the rising sun and moon of another tomorrow.

"You will not hold them both," Vega warned.

I rallied all the forces of hope to my aid, preparing them for their last battle.

"Be brave," the army of hope seemed to chant.

The glow surrounding my body turned to flames. I screamed in pain but refused to give in to the fight within me. They would meld together or I'd die for it.

"You want me to believe in you?" I screamed to the stars before me. "Believe in me!"

Neither Vega nor Algol could seem to watch their champion Emerging end this way. Through the pain, I felt them place a hand on either side of my temple until...

Stardust.

28

Phoenix

Stardust.

I was covered in it.

Where was I? I gathered my senses, trying to figure out where I was. The smell of home... of saltwater in the ocean flooded through me, and I felt the warmth of the sun on my skin more intensely than I ever had before. I had just been burning. Such a terrible nightmare.

"Zoe?" A loving, angelic voice spoke my name. I would know him anywhere. My soul called to his essence fervently.

Slowly, I allowed my eyes to open to find the face of the one I loved. There were tears in his eyes, and my heart stilled as I took in his face with my immortal gaze. I saw the storm in his gray eyes more clearly now, as if a hurricane dwelled just on the edge, begging to come out to play. Were my eyes different? Everything seemed so *intense*.

"Elvy," I said, voice smoother, steadier than the mortal girl that I'd left behind. No, not behind. She was still there, cheering me on with tears in her eyes. She was the stars, and the stars were me now. Infinite.

He had not approached me yet, and I was desperate for him to close the distance.

"You—it's been months—you were gone, stardust," he said, sounding unsure of himself.

A dawn of clarity swept over me.

"I have been remade," I stated.

"Like a phoenix rising from the ashes," he breathed.

He dropped to his knees before me, clinging to my new form, as if he wanted to make sure I was really there in front of him—in this moment.

"The others are waiting," he said.

I knelt down next to him so that I was at his eye level.

I cupped his face into mine and kissed him slowly, intentionally. I never thought his lips could feel any more wonderful, but it felt like kissing him for the first time all over again. Wherever I touched him, shining stardust lingered. Some part of me was aware that I was naked except for the dust that covered me, but I did not cower in shyness.

I grew that kiss into a hunger that was led by love. The groan in his throat told me he needed me just as much as I needed him. The tug for Elvy I'd known as a mortal was still there, but was intensified and almost painful to ignore. My heart pounded, as if readying for a war. It would find its mate at any cost.

Elvy came up for air and held my face in his hands.

"You're real," he murmured.

There were so many things I wanted to tell him right there, but I knew the others were waiting for me. The words paused in my throat as I thought of Freyja and Jelly. I needed to lay eyes on them.

"Let's get you cleaned up," he said, as if reading my thoughts.

He easily lifted me into his arms and carried me into the shower. He didn't let go as he turned on the water. I think he would've gotten in the shower with me fully clothed if he didn't have to let go of me. The storm in his eyes never wavered from mine. I felt entirely safe, confident. Remade.

"A shower usually works better without clothes on," I said, pulling on his shirt. "You are not leaving my sight."

He sat me on the bathroom counter and ripped his clothes off as quickly as possible, tossing them to the floor. Standing bare before me, he took my hand, guiding me into the warmth of the rainfall from the showerhead. Even the heat of the water felt different in this immortal body. Before I had time to ponder it much further, his lips were back on mine, and I gladly succumbed to the blissful peace he brought me.

I gently traced the tattoos over his chest, pausing at each star, as if I knew them better now. Perhaps I did understand their purpose, even if I couldn't quite remember mine. I swallowed down that train of thought and returned to Elvy's ministrations of my body.

"At this rate, we will never leave this shower," he said, kissing my neck, frantically moving to other parts of my body with desperation.

"I'm okay with that," I said, tugging on his hair in response to the taunting mouth he had on my core.

"I can't be selfish with you, Zoe," he replied, eyes full of conflict.

"I guess there's always later..." I said with a frown, trying to be reasonable.

"Later," he agreed, voice gravelly, as if it was painful for him to get the words out.

"But there is one thing that can't wait," I said, hoping he understood.

I turned to face the wall, so that my back was bare to him. I gently took my hair and pulled it to the side so that it flowed down the front of my breasts. I held out my hand, and he placed his outstretched palm in mine.

Without hesitation, I placed his hand on the parts of me I had allowed no one else to touch, not even him. I sank into the tender touch of his hands on the back of my neck and upper back. He trailed kisses on every inch of that exposed skin, appreciating the trust, but I think more than that, he was happy I was healed in that way.

"I hope you like the tattoo on my chest..." he began as he massaged my neck.

"I am a fan, yes," I said, leaning into his touch.

"You've been marked with a nearly identical one on your back," he noted, tracing the stars that now lay across my shoulder blades. I couldn't help the smile that played on my lips.

"Nearly?"

"Vega and Algol are bigger than the other stars and..." he paused, tracing a pattern higher above the rest. "There are more threads between the elemental realms."

"Another mystery to be solved," I said, sighing.

"It can wait another day," he reassured.

He began washing my hair again and did not stop caring for me until every fleck of stardust was off my skin, placing kisses down every inch with only fondness in him.

"Be careful where you kiss, Elvy, or we really will never get out of here," I said, only half joking.

He laughed with a carefree ease and grabbed a towel to dry me off. He stood me in front of the large floor-length mirror, wrapping his arms around my toweled frame.

"Are you ready to see your immortal form?"

I nodded, and he gently unveiled my body slowly.

I gazed in curiosity at my reflection. It was me, but not me. The lines were slightly sharper on my jawline, and I looked *healthy*. Like I had a glow of life about me now. My brown hair now had streaks of gray in it, just like Elvy and the other Shadowed I knew. I turned slightly in the mirror to glimpse the tattoo of the elemental stars on my back and instantly fell in love with it. I'd done it. Somehow, I knew deep down that whatever I'd done in the trials would cost me.

"I'm Shadowed?" I asked in surprise.

"Yes, Zoe. You are. Beautifully so."

"I have wings?"

"Yes," he said, laughing. "It may take some practice to get the hang of them. And we better not do it inside."

"Right," I agreed, smartly.

I continued to check out the differences in my immortal body, but didn't find many. I noted the jagged scar that still adorned my left arm; all the others had gone away when I'd been remade—even the one that had adorned my abdomen, and I smiled that those vile men no longer marked me.

"I guess some things will always follow us," I said, tracing the line of the scar along my forearm, wondering why the stars had left it there.

"To always remember where we came from," he replied, placing a kiss where I traced. "Take another look with your immortal eyes."

I focused on the jagged lightning shape, and it changed—moved. It was as if the cosmos now lived in the lines of my scar... and there was something familiar about the constellation that was shimmering back at me.

"The Archer," I breathed. "It seems he is not done with me yet."

"Let me see," he said, examining the moving stars beneath the surface of my skin. "I've never seen anything quite like this."

"That can't be good," I responded, trying to hold back the nerves.

"Unique doesn't equate to foreboding," he disagreed. "Here, look at this." He directed my attention lower.

At the end of the lightning bolt, right where my wrist was, a fresh scar had appeared. No, not a scar—a tattoo in the shape of a star with eight points, four smaller than the other cardinal directions.

Elvy held out his wrist, shaking away the glamor of his own tattoo, revealing his own similar star. While mine swirled with blues and blacks, he had only the colors of the ocean—the element of life.

"It marks us as immortals. It's like an aura of sorts, connecting us to our chosen star. As long as our star lives, light will shine. I've never seen one like yours, though," he said curiously. "Two distinct colors and integrated into your own scar."

"Algol and Vega," I said, feeling the conviction. "I did it. I defied the stars. The prophecy was right."

The question was... what did that act cost me?

"That's not possible..." Elvy answered, voice shaking and eyes full of fear.

"My defiance will come at a price, won't it?"

"We don't know that. I knew you were extraordinary, Zoe. I can only marvel at your true strength now. You are a perfect balance... life and death," he whispered, reminding me of how I'd lived my mortal life, wavering on the cusps of both.

"I—I can't remember," I said, straining to remember what had happened during the trials, but it was like looking through a thick fog. I couldn't quite grasp the images, but I could feel them brimming beneath the surface.

"You're not supposed to," he said soothingly. "We'll get Finnian to help with the research in Vega. You're not alone in this."

"I think I am supposed to... there's something important."

"We will figure it out, Zoe," he promised, holding me snugly. "Together. Always together."

I couldn't shake the feeling, but I wanted to rid that worry line from his forehead.

"Should I join the others naked, or do you have clothes for me?" I asked playfully.

He joined in my laughter, and it was a glorious sound.

"It's so nice to hear that," he said, handing me clothes to pull on to meet the rest of the immortals.

"The marks, scars, whatever they are... they're kind of distracting," I said, glaring back into the light show swarming my arm.

"Here," he said, swiping over the light, turning it into what looked like a mortal's tattoo. "Let me show you."

He briefly demonstrated how to change the marks from their true form back to the stability of the tattoo, then how to put a glamor over it. I seemed to take to it surprisingly quickly.

"Remarkable," he said, tracing along the marks again.

The tug in my chest had me back in his arms before I could think about what I was doing. I kissed him, forcing all the love I had for him into the embrace, needing him to know the fight I had in me to get back to him.

"Later," he breathed, voice husky. I knew he would hold me to that.

29

SIMARGL

Elvy brought me to the rocky, secluded beach where we had first flown to meet up with the rest of his court. My stomach filled with butterflies as we neared, and I was nervous to meet them in my new form. I had grown to cherish each of them and was fearful of seeming too different to them.

One look at Blaz told me all I needed to know.

He aggressively wrapped me in a bear hug as if he hadn't seen me in months, and I guess technically he hadn't, even though it hadn't seemed that long to me.

"When I heard you turned to stardust, I thought we'd lost you for good," he said, wiping an actual tear from his eye. "Me and Jelly were beside ourselves."

Just as he said her name, Jelly came bounding into my arms, recognizing me with such love and fierce loyalty. I couldn't help the tears that sprang to my eyes. I laid down on the hard, wet ground, not caring one bit at the discomfort as Jelly pounced on me, licking my face repeatedly.

"I missed you too, my good girl," I said, giving her all the belly rubs and ear scratches, not caring who was there to see it.

Delmira embraced me next, eyes full of pride.

"It's about time we outnumbered the men," she said, smiling mischievously.

"Like it would do you any good!" Blaz teased back.

"Always in a cat fight," Imelda said, approaching me next with Clodovea in tow.

"We are so proud of you," Clove said. "Elvy wasn't the only one who needed you back here."

"It still feels like a dream," I admitted.

"I felt the same way for years," Finnian chimed in, pulling me into an unexpected hug. Physical affection had never appeared to be Finnian's thing. "Me and Delm will help you learn everything. Being born immortal and remade as one comes with its learning curves."

"I am thankful for it," I said, genuinely grateful he had thought of it.

Oleander and Zadie stood before me waiting... for what, I wasn't sure.

"Your mark. Let's see it then."

I ignored him as my eyes fell on the figure behind him. Zadie and Oleander stood almost in a protective stance around her. My knees wanted to give out at the sight of my sister. Some force unknown to me kept me standing in that moment. I could *see* her.

I forcefully shoved them out of the way without a second thought, which seemed to catch the mighty Oleander off guard. I didn't care. I wrapped my arms around my sister and cried into her shoulder, in gratitude that I'd made it back to her.

"You can see me?" Freyja asked, surprised. "So you picked Algol."

I felt everyone staring behind me, waiting for me to speak. I glanced at Elvy, and a silent message passed between us, as if to give me an extra bit of strength to be vulnerable with this new life.

I waved a hand over my tattooed mark to reveal its true form—*my* true form. The cosmos eagerly lined the chasm of my scar while the blues and blacks lit up my immortal mark. Freyja's eyes widened, and I was sure I heard Oleander swear underneath his breath.

"You insane woman. You could have died!" Oleander exclaimed, exasperated. "That explains your scent... I've never smelled anything like it before. You are both Algol and Vega."

"Zoe is Realm-Healer for a reason, Oleander," Elvy responded.

Those words struck a chord deep within me. He'd called me that once before... but I'd heard it somewhere else. I couldn't place the source frustratingly enough.

"Realm-Healer," I said, testing the words out. "What does that mean?"

"It's a tale as old as time," Oleander said, shaking his head.

"One you believe in," Elvy replied, pointedly.

"Even as an immortal, your bickering is annoying," I said, sighing. "Realm-Healer, what does it mean?"

"It's a prophecy—ancient," Finnian piped in. "Everyone thought it was only a fable until Algol separated from the other four elemental realms. Our oldest and brightest immortals started looking for answers and came across one about the *Realm-Healer.*"

"And let me guess, this Realm-Healer would be one of the strongest Emergings ever created?" I asked.

"No," Finnian disagreed. "*The* strongest."

The Archer had warned me the trials were only the beginning. I had a feeling that I'd just won the battle, but war was soon to come.

"It appears so," I said, unable to deny the truth in my gut.

"How did you do it?" Oleander asked with fury in his eyes. "Take in both stars?"

"I think I might have... I burned," I said, as a few tinges of the memory scraped my mind. It still wasn't clear, but I felt the flames over my body.

"She was remade, Oleander," Elvy said, moving only slightly in front of me. "Reborn from stardust."

"I've never heard of an Emerging being transformed like that," Delmira stated, face full of concern. Finnian's mimicked hers. In fact, they all seemed worried, unsure of what they were dealing with.

"You cannot serve two stars," Oleander said, determined to drive home the point. Apparently done with niceties, I felt his gifts probing my mind, but my shields were more impenetrable than he could ever hope of conjuring himself.

"I serve no master," I snapped, suddenly full of rage that seeped from somewhere.... dark, deep. "I burned for those in the darkness... those in the light owe everything to the void of the dark. The beauty of life cannot be seen without it. I choose them. All of them."

I didn't know where the words came from, but they poured from me, ringing with truth. I felt the heat swelling in my chest, and I feared I might burn again.

"Careful, Oleander," I warned. "I'm stronger than you now."

He conceded apologetically, pulling his black tendrils away from my mind.

You will burn, Zoe Eferhild.

The voice was familiar to me. She'd warned me but did not stop me. Maybe she knew this would always be my fate. I felt the power—the gifts—roaring inside me, desiring release. I was nothing more than a ticking time bomb.

"Zoe," a voice whispered.

The voice that could ground me when no others could reach me.

"Come back to me," Elvy whispered.

I knew this wasn't over. I felt it deep down that I had a mission that went beyond me and this group of those I loved. I didn't want to let go, but it wasn't time yet. Soon, but not yet.

I shook the seduction of the gifts away from my mind, bringing myself to the present. Elvy stood closest to me, with Freyja right behind him. The rest had taken a protective circle around me as if to contain me should I explode. I doubted even their magic would hold me if I ever let go of the power inside me.

"Your eyes," Elvy said. "They glowed."

I rubbed my eyes, checking to make sure every ounce of that surge of power was gone.

"The colors of the star realms," Oleander noted.

Elvy shot him a snarl, ordering him to be silent.

"Your commentary is not needed," Clodovea said, stepping in.

"She is part of the Algol Court whether or not you like it," Zadie said, defending her Lord Astral. "Cruel though the stars are, it seems we will need to play nice with each other. We need an alliance."

"I have to remember what happened while I was... away," I said, unsure how to explain it. "I can't shake this feeling that I have to do something. I don't think I took these powers freely."

"We'll figure it out together," Elvy assured, squeezing my hand firmly. The tug in my chest lit a fire at that simple gesture, but I held on despite it.

"What now?" I asked, uncertain.

"We go home," Elvy answered. "To the realm of the stars."

"To Vega?" I asked.

"Only if you want to," he replied.

I wanted to go with him, but my gaze fell on Freyja, then to Jelly. No matter my choices, I didn't want to leave them behind. Freyja's gaze met mine.

"It's okay, Zo. Go, live. I'm only a realm away, right?"

Jelly pawed at my legs, and I couldn't take it. Something inside me broke.

No. No more choosing. I'd given enough.

I flung my arms around Jelly and sobbed into her soft fur. I invoked the two gifts within me, taking from them once more and gave a piece of myself over to Jelly. I constructed and created new life in her anatomy to cross realms as I could now. I felt the anger leaking from the sources of my power, but I did not care. My will alone transformed her, but I knew it would come at a cost later. Right now—in this moment—I could get drunk on this power. I felt an ember of my magic transfer to Jelly, and I gave it readily. I called on the truth that my power would mold to my will—limitless in the possibilities. Before I dove any deeper into the void, I pulled free, jetting back up to the surface of reality.

When I opened my eyes and pulled away from my companion, Jelly stood before us with silver streaks in her fur and wings as soft as rabbit's fur sprouting from her back.

"Did you just... make Jelly a Shadowed?" Blaz asked, a gleam in his eyes.

"No, no. Not entirely Shadowed," Elvy responded. "Jelly is a Simargl—a protector of life."

"No one has seen a Simargl in several millennia. I thought they'd all died out," Oleander noted. "The last in Arcturus—fire nation."

"I have remade her," I said, quietly, but my focus was on Freyja.

"It won't work on me, Zo. My spirit is already in the realm of the dead. I cannot come back."

"I could try." I started towards her, but stumbled from the power I'd just exerted.

"No, Zoe. You can't. The risk to you and the balance is too great," Freyja said. "There are some laws of nature that even you cannot change."

Not yet, I thought.

"I'll figure out a way," I swore. "To bring you back."

I knew Freyja saw the promise in my eyes, and she had a faint glimmer of hope that I had enough fire in me to make it happen.

"Freyja is welcome in my court," Oleander said. "If she wishes."

The sadness in Elvy's eyes nearly tore me apart. I saw in his frown that he wished desperately that he could offer me the same thing, even though he couldn't see Freyja himself.

"Go with him," I encouraged.

"What about Mom and Dad?" Freyja asked. I felt like this was more of a stall tactic than anything. Freyja had checked on them some when she first started revealing herself, but she had seemed resigned to accept their grief.

"Just as you have told me to move on, so must you, Freyja. I'll deal with the parents," I answered, though I didn't know how I'd manage it. "Besides, I have a feeling I'll be required in Algol before you have any time to miss me."

Oleander only smiled at that, as he knew the truth in it. I was part of Algol, and Algol was part of me. I was a true Daughter of Algol. It called to me the same as Vega did now.

"Alright," Freyja conceded, taking Oleander's outstretched hand.

"We look forward to welcoming you, Zoe," Oleander said. "Very soon."

Oleander gave me a pointed look before he disappeared between realms, with Zadie following in tow. What had seemed like just shadows when I was mortal was actually colorful portals between realms that seemed to flare open when the Shadowed called on them to do so.

"I really hate that guy," Blaz stated, eyes glaring at where the trio had just disappeared.

"We must have peace with Algol," I answered, unsure of where that sentiment came from, but Elvy nodded in agreement.

"The stars know something is lurking. They have been... generous with Zoe... almost in desperation. Something bigger is going on."

"We have to get my memories back," I said, voice shaking.

30

Goodbye

I wasn't ready to part completely from my mortal life. Maybe in time I would be, but I didn't want to give up my quaint bungalow where I'd learned to love myself again. I didn't want to let my parents think I'd died... not yet. Elvy told me he'd kept in touch with them on my phone for me while I was gone, which I was grateful for. I didn't want them to worry. I knew my journey on Earth wasn't finished, even though I also knew I was needed somewhere else right now, if only to help prolong this world a little longer.

I stood in the entrance of my house soaking in every detail. I smiled at the kitchen sink where Elvy had washed my hair for the first time. I grimaced at the coffee stain I'd never quite gotten out of my beloved couch. I thumbed through some of my favorite novels on the dusty bookshelf and chuckled at the fantasy books that had been leafed through so many times. Here I was now, living some of the things I'd only dreamed about in stories.

I knew Elvy was behind me without turning around. My spirit was tuned to whatever frequency he ran on. Jelly remained outside and out of sight with the rest of the court as she proudly showed off her new wings. She seemed quite fond of them, as if she knew she was part of some ancient lineage.

"We can stay here a while longer," he said softly, mistaking my hesitation for a desire to stay.

"No, I'm more than ready to start living for the reason I fought. I'm reminding myself of that, of what I've earned."

He slid his arms around me, holding me there, knowing he was the only soul alive allowed to touch me like this. The pull in my chest tugged tighter, as if wanting me to be even closer to him.

"Do you still feel it, too?" I asked, only slightly afraid he might think I'm crazy. "The pull."

"Yes," he said, kissing my neck gently.

"What is it?" I asked.

"The stars," he answered, trailing his nose along my shoulder.

"You know I'll want further explanation," I murmured.

"I know." I felt the smile on his lips.

A new presence entered the room, interrupting our solitude.

"Alright you lovebirds, are we ready to go to Vega?" Delmira asked, clearly ready to be in the comfort of her home, mission complete for now.

"I just need to make a couple of calls and arrangements," I said.

Elvy and Delmira took the hint and waited outside while I prepared myself to lie through my teeth to my mother and to June. I couldn't disappear without a trace. I wouldn't do that to them. I took a few mind stilling breaths and dialed my mother's familiar number.

She answered after the first ring.

"Zo? Is everything okay?" Her voice was curious, but not frantic. Elvy had done well.

I swallowed the guilt down.

"Have you been in Alaska all this time? Surely, you are tired of it by now. You didn't even answer on your birthday. We wanted to celebrate with you."

I'd forgotten that the trials had lasted until nearly springtime. Glancing at the digital calendar in the kitchen, I realized my birthday was a week ago. I spouted my well-rehearsed lie, hoping that she would buy it.

"Sorry to worry you, Mom, but you won't believe it," I said, forcing a chipper voice through the phone.

"Well, what is it?"

I launched into a story of getting chosen for a rare marine research study that required me to be out on the seas for an undetermined amount of time. I told her of how I met a research group passing through the town Elvy was from in Alaska, and how it all had fallen together so perfectly. I explained my phone had gotten soaked at some point, and we'd just returned to a docking port for a replacement. I let her know I would be out of range most of the time, but that Jelly was able to come with me. This seemed to make her happy, at least.

"You'll get to see so much of the world just like you used to do," she said, voice full of genuine happiness.

"I hope I didn't cause you too much worry. I'm about to get the adventure of a lifetime, I think," I said, meeting her enthusiasm.

"Grant and I are so proud of you, Zo. I never worried too much about you when you were traveling. It just seemed like where you were always meant to be, you know? We will check on your house and take the Jeep for a spin while you're away, if you'd like. I know how much you love that house."

"Thanks, Mom," I said, voice choking. "For everything."

My next task was calling up June to give her a similar reason for my absence and a thousand apologies for abandoning the work they were doing at the rescue. June seemed to be thrilled and a little jealous of my adventure, but she didn't scold me for even a second, which I was thankful for. I didn't want to disappoint her. I promised to keep in touch the best that I could and thanked her for the years of support she'd given me.

I only had one more goodbye left in this mortal realm, and I did not hold back the tears as I wrote a letter to Emma. I thanked her for not giving up on my stubborn ass. I thanked her for sitting with me in the silence when that's what I needed. I thanked her for not trying to fix me, but for allowing me space and room to grow and heal. I owed her my gratitude in ways I couldn't repay her directly. I only hoped that I could pay it forward.

I placed the letter in the outgoing mail and locked up the house one more time, unsure of when I would visit it again. Something told me I'd be called back here before I knew it.

Elvy leaned against the porch post, eyes shining with wonder, it seemed.

"Do I get to fly now?" I asked.

He laughed and swept me into his arms. "Flying between realms should not be your first experiment with wings, Zoe."

"So you're saying I need training wheels before I launch myself on the realms?" I asked, eyebrows raised.

"Of sorts," he laughed. "We've got nothing but time."

I wanted to believe that, but something in me knew that wasn't true. I think he knew that, but I shoved that problem way down, determined to enjoy and savor every moment of what was about to happen. Delmira, Clodovea, Imelda, Finnian, and Blaz appeared around us in a circle as they always moved. Blaz had Jelly in his arms and she was licking his face.

"She's not ready to travel between realms either," Blaz said, laughing.

I was grateful to be alive. I was thankful I had fought the uphill battle, even though I knew my real fight had just begun. I'd take every blow that came. I'd fight for those I love—to tomorrow's rising moon.

"Before we go..." Elvy said, pausing. "You failed to mention your birthday was on the second."

"I was kind of unconscious," I pointed out.

"I have something for you." Before I could protest, he placed the necklace he'd given me at the pier around my neck with a swift kiss.

"Thank you," I said, clutching the familiar pendant. I thought I'd lost it forever.

"Are you ready?" he asked, those gray eyes full of excitement and desire.

"Always," I said, placing a kiss on his lips.

Then we were soaring.

31

Home

I clung to Elvy's neck as he lifted us high above Earth's atmosphere; then he started plunging us faster than mortal eyes could see towards what looked like a swirling, colorful fissure in the night sky. I knew from below we must look like shooting stars or comets until we disappeared into nothing once we entered the bridge between realms.

I kept my gaze on him as those gray eyes filled with something more than joy—exhilaration. All the colors of the rainbow seemed to whirl around us. In what felt like seconds, his focus narrowed, and we were racing towards another colorful rip between worlds, which I could only assume led us into the land of Lyra and home to the Court of Vega.

As we crossed the barrier, the rushing of the wind ceased, and it was only calmness that surrounded us. Beneath our soaring figures, a city full of life sprawled below with lights twinkling everywhere, as if the city was an entity itself. In the distance, the formation of an enormous mountain range and a star shining brightly enough to illuminate the ocean that lay beneath it met my gaze through the misty clouds. The sky was filled with night and swirled with purples and greens dancing across it, similar to the northern lights I'd heard of, but had surprisingly never seen on Earth.

"Vega," he said, motioning to the brightest star in the night sky. "Our life source."

I noticed a moon hanging in the sky, but it wasn't quite the same as the moon of Earth. It seemed more translucent, not as tangible. The air smelled of the sea, fresher than I'd ever experienced on Earth. Even though the sky was dark, I could see the crystal blue waters gliding below us, as if welcoming its Lord Astral home.

Elvy took us through the city, and I couldn't compare it to anything I'd seen before despite how much I'd adventured while still mortal. It seemed to be a mix of ancient architecture, but there was something new about it, too. Some roads seemed older than others, the paths cobblestone, while others were much smoother and metallic. There were townhomes nestled nearer to the mountain range. Skyscrapers seemed to reach higher than was safe, and off in the distance, near the shore, I saw a mansion of a home. It immediately drew me to it, wishing to explore what could be in its walls.

Fortunately for me, we seemed to be heading that way. I allowed my eyes to drift and noticed no one drove vehicles here. They all seemed to be walking, flying, or using the seemingly intricate waterway system. I briefly wondered if that was what helped keep the air so clear despite the bustling city. Out of the corner of my eye, I caught the flash of a train, but it was unlike any I'd seen before. It seemed to move soundlessly and fluidly.

"It runs on water," he explained, catching my gaze.

He gently descended on the mansion's front garden. It was filled with exotic plants I had no prayer of naming and best of all, I could hear the ocean. I closed my eyes, smiling. This was real. All of it. *Home.*

The mansion itself seemed to be made of moonstone or something similar to it. It glowed under the light of Vega, but it still possessed this air of warmth and light. I vaguely noticed the others land behind us, with Blaz and Delmira tearing off with Jelly hot on their tails, wings flapping in the wind.

"This is our home," he said, gesturing to his Luminaries—his family.

"Everyone lives here?" I asked.

"If they choose to," he answered, laughing. "Sometimes, we all need our own space. Even here, it can get a little crowded with the hotheads in this group."

"I can only imagine the repairs over the years," I said, noticing the differences in material in various places that somehow still fit perfectly.

He led me to the porch, which seemed to wrap around the entire building, and stood before the massive navy-blue door. Elvy's wings vanished as he paused outside the entrance.

He hesitated, seeming a little nervous. I squeezed his hand, excited to see the place he called home. He tucked his long curls behind an ear and led me inside.

It was nothing like I expected. It was more quaint and charming than the massive outside indicated. The mansion seemed to be divided into three levels with a downstairs, the main floor, and upstairs. The stairs were on either side of the foyer, making quite the grand entrance, which seemed to be made of that same moonstone material, lined with blue and gold hues that led up and down. There was no fancy chandelier, but warm lights lined the hallways, creating a more rustic seaside feel.

"Would you like a tour?" he asked.

"If I'm to live here, I suppose I need to know my way around."

"I'd like for you to live here," he admitted, voice full of sincerity. "We have condos in the city, if you would prefer it."

I didn't have any desire to live away from him, though perhaps my own space at first would be nice. I'd chosen this life, and I was ready to fully embrace that without the fear that had once kept me from living.

"The tour, Lord Astral," I said, teasing him.

Elvy greeted me with an easy smile and guided me down the first hall. He showed me the massive kitchen, which was bright and open with enough equipment to easily feed a thousand, which I assumed came in handy for a Lord Astral. Then, he pulled me further down the hall to a dining room, which was clearly for important functions. It felt more stiff and formal, but still had the same touches of whites and blues.

"We don't eat here unless we are conducting business," he said, confirming my thoughts. "Through that door is the grand hall. We use it for bigger functions and balls."

I peeked my head through the door and my mouth unceremoniously fell open at the sheer beauty of it. The ceiling was translucent, allowing the night sky and Vega to show off to anyone below it. The designer of this room knew what they were doing and understood the importance of impressing others.

A sly smile crept across my lips as I thought of dancing with Elvy here. I tucked that image away for a later day, and I let him continue showing me my new home.

"I'm excited to show you the next room," he said with the excitement of a child in his eyes.

He led me down another hall, and I found myself staring at two massive, white wooden doors that seemed to be aged with time. I could only imagine what lay behind it.

He excitedly pushed open the doors to reveal a massive library. There was no one else around, and I freely gaped, wondering how I'd ever get through every book stored within these walls. There had to be tens of thousands of books. The ceiling was translucent, like the grand hall, but this one formed a dome at the very top, as if framing Vega.

Elvy twirled me around, enjoying the glee on my face, and I kissed him fervently.

"This is incredible," I said, genuinely happy.

"I'll bring you back when one of the Keepers is on duty," he said. "A librarian of sorts. They can show you how everything is organized."

"I'd like that," I admitted. "Is this a private library?"

"No, anyone is welcome. The public has a separate entrance outside."

"Good," I said. Knowledge should be shared freely with others.

"Come on," he said, pulling me away from the trance of the books.

Elvy led me up the stairs and pointed down a few halls, describing where some bathrooms and bedrooms were.

"The upstairs is strictly the living quarters. No one is allowed up here without my permission," he said, not unkind. I'm sure safety precautions were necessary even amongst the immortal.

He paused outside of a door, unsure of how to proceed.

"Out with it," I encouraged.

"This is the room I had prepared for you, if you want it. I thought... you might want your own space, while we figure it all out," he explained, tucking his hair back again.

I knew he meant *us* when he said *it*. The tug in my chest pulled me closer to him, and I threw my arms around him, wanting him close. I did value having my own, safe place as we continued to navigate the love between us, even if I ended up never using it.

"Thank you," I said, kissing him softly.

The room reminded me of my own in my beloved beach bungalow. The room was covered in shiplap from floor to ceiling, painted in the dark blues and gold of this court. There was even a bed for Jelly beside mine, which made my heart heat with warmth for him. I was also impressed that he either had that much faith in Jelly coming with us or his communication to his court was exceptionally quick. A few bookshelves filled to the brim with books ready for me to explore took up the length of one wall and another was filled with pictures of the sunny beaches of Saint Andrews. It was perfect in every way.

"One door is a closet, and the other is a bathroom," he explained.

"Clothes would be good," I said, realizing I only had what was on my back.

"Would you like to rest?"

"I'd like to see your room," I said, wondering if he would allow it.

"Of course. You don't have to ask that," he replied without hesitation. His eyes suddenly filled with hunger. He'd been patient with me, I realized.

"It's later now," I said, kissing his neck.

"Indeed it is," he answered, pulling me into his arms as he threw the door open across the hall with some force of magic I didn't see.

Elvy's room mirrored my own in a lot of ways. There were books lining the plethora of shelves on the walls, but this room was clearly lived in. There was a fireplace already roaring with a blue-green flame and a skylight above that let the light of Vega shine through the room. There were papers scattered across a desk and discarded journals tossed haphazardly around. Then, there was the bed—it was massive and took up most of the room. The white sheets looked so soft to the eye, and I wanted to curl up in them.

My throat felt dry as I tried to swallow down my nerves. I wasn't scared and had no fear, but I was nervous. The tug in my chest overpowered those nerves, wishing to join with the pull I had towards him. His gray eyes were on me as he laid me gently on the bed, letting me decide, as he always did. I was right about the sheets, luxury I'd never felt before, but my focus was on the man before me, who I had fought so hard to reunite with.

Pulling him to me, I stroked his brown-gray hair as he trailed kisses down my neck to my collarbone. I knew my eyes matched the desire in his. I closed them, letting my heightened sense hear the ocean as if we were right beside it. This was all real.

Elvy helped me pull his shirt off after he realized what my searching hands were trying to do. He ripped my own open down the middle savagely, exposing my bare skin. I couldn't stop the yelp that escaped my lips, and the exhilarated laughter that followed.

Feeling his skin on mine so unabashedly sent that fire inside me burning throughout my whole body. I could almost see silver flames in his eyes, such a contrast to the hurricane that usually lived there, and I knew he felt it too by the set of his jaw.

"What is this?" I asked desperately, placing my hand over his pounding heart. I felt almost frenzied with desire, creating as much friction between us as I could.

"You're my flame," Elvy said, voice deep, almost animalistic, primal. "And I am yours."

"Flame?" I questioned, but I already suspected the answer.

"Mortals call it a soulmate," he replied, not taking his eyes off me.

You will burn, Zoe Eferhild. The voice whipped through my mind. Maybe I'd burn in more ways than one.

"What does that mean?" I asked, voice tight as I continued to find new ways to touch him.

"It means, Zoe, that the stars have fated us. A rarity."

"So we have no choice?" I asked, growing more wary, but still resolved to embrace this.

"You don't have to accept me as your flame," he said, eyes vulnerable, as if it would kill him if I didn't. For all I knew, it might.

"Do we accept it by..." I trailed off, motioning towards the space between us.

"No, Zoe. Making love will not make us flames," he answered. "But it will start the process. There's a ceremony that must be done for it to be official."

The burn had not left his eyes, but he was the picture of patience as I asked him these questions, which only made my desire for him increase tenfold. My control was coming to a feverish end.

"But there are perks... to being flames," I said, eyes feline.

"More than you could possibly imagine," he breathed, kissing my neck, needing me the same way I needed him.

I would not be forced to make more decisions placed on me by the stars tonight, but I would choose Elvy in this moment.

I saw the question in his eyes, and it wasn't about being his flame. He wanted me right now, and I greedily replied, "Yes, all of me."

He needed no further words as he shredded the rest of my clothes off, kissing every inch of exposed skin. Not a hint of anxiety filled me, only my passion for him rang through me. I fumbled with his jeans and slid them down with immortal expertise, taking his underwear with him and exposing his hardened length.

For a brief moment, we just stared at each other. With no rush to meet someone else's expectations or looming decision over us. We simply gazed, each appreciating the other. The burn in me could only look so long before I needed to feel him. He seemed to have the same sentiment.

I pushed him aggressively to the bed, straddling him as he dug his calloused grip into my hips, sweeping his lips along my neck to my chest. His eyes pierced through me, making sure I was okay before reaching his hand to drag his fingers down the back of my neck and the length of my spine. I shivered, relishing in the touch.

There wasn't a part of me I didn't want him to see or touch. We took our time exploring each other, teasing each other, making the buildup that much sweeter. Everywhere he touched, my skin seemed to blaze with pleasure—*need*. He slipped two fingers inside, finding me wanting with the love I held for him as he teased the peaks of my nipples. His tongue was tortuous in its rhythm as he ruined me greedily—and repeatedly. This moment was branded on my flesh and within my soul as I lost myself to him completely.

"*Mine*," I said as I arched my back for him. No matter what the future held, he was mine, and I would always find my way back to my flame.

"Yours," he promised, teasing my entrance with his fullness before thrusting inside me—claiming me in the way I needed.

Joining caused the burn in me to flame hotter than I could contain, and I knew my eyes were no longer the pale green they normally were. They were green flames once more, needing to find the release that was consuming me. His pace was unforgiving, and I clawed at his skin to get closer to him.

Elvy flipped my hips sideways, continuing to thrust, as his tongue claimed my hardened peaks once again, biting them gently.

“I’m so close,” I yelled, and he caught my claim with his mouth. I pushed against him so that he was underneath me now, meeting him thrust for thrust as he dug his fingers into my hips.

This only seemed to drive Elvy wilder and his wings burst from him at the same time I found my euphoria. For just a moment, I felt my wings flash as I claimed my pleasure from him, too. We both glowed in our embrace, and it had nothing to do with my powers or his that I still did not fully understand.

It was just… us.

32

HALL OF MEMORIES

Elvy and I had exhausted ourselves, but neither of us was tired enough to lull ourselves to sleep. My wings had vanished, only lasting a second, but his wrapped around us as our limbs tangled together. I never wanted to leave the bliss of this moment. A moment I never thought I'd reach after what had happened to me. Some small part of me was proud of myself and the resilient fight I'd endured to have this.

He trailed gentle fingers down my arm as I twirled my own through his locks of hair. I loved him, but some part of me feared voicing that, even though we'd both just shown it. I decided it was okay to take my time.

"Tell me more about these flames," I said, snuggling closer into his frame, if that was even possible.

He tucked my head under his chin, gently stroking my hair.

"As I said, they are rare—true flames. The last flamed pair are the current monarchs of our kingdom. Queen Farron and King Aldrich, they were flamed several millennia ago, long before they ruled Canis."

"You said there were perks? Beyond... all this," I said, referencing our joining.

Elvy laughed, nuzzling my neck. "Yes, Zoe, perks beyond our lovemaking. Flames are connected on a spiritual, primal level. We can communicate through the connection in our souls, we can heal each other if wounded beyond what those of Vega can do. We can always find each other, no matter the distance, and we have a stronger connection to the stars..."

There was longing in his voice, as if he had waited a long time for this.

"You said you had been searching for me when we first met. That Lord Astrals rarely go looking for the Emerging."

"I was pulled to you even then, before I knew for sure. There had been rumblings for a long time about an Emerging, one that would turn the tides of fate, an Emerging of

Legends. Like we said, no one really believed in all of that until Algol. I told myself that's why I had to come. To ensure Vega's future, but as soon as I laid eyes on you, I didn't care about any of that. Once I caught your... scent," he said, looking sheepish. "I knew you were my flame. I felt the faintest ember ignite, and I was yours. Right there in that moment."

"But you so easily made it known that it was my choice... that I could have chosen Algol, despite how you felt."

He tucked a few stray hairs away from my tear-filled eyes as I took in the sacrifice he was willing to give... to just give me the freedom of choice.

"There was nothing easy about it, Zoe. I wanted to tell you. Hell, I wanted to shout it across the realms, but I would not influence your decision like that. You owed me nothing. You still don't. After all you've been through, I couldn't be another man forcing some expectation on you," he confessed, pulling me closer.

"And if a flame rejects its soulmate?" I asked, not sure that I wanted to know the answer.

"I honestly don't know," he said. "I imagine it to be painful."

He had let me go into the trials, knowing that I may not choose him without knowing what would happen to him if I chose Algol. The dark part of me I'd carefully tucked away wanted to lash out at him, but I steadied myself with some deep breaths. If I rejected it now, he would take it. I didn't want that though, but I wasn't sure I was quite ready to do the ceremony yet either. The rest of eternity was a long time, and I was just getting used to my new reality. I realized he knew this, which was why he made sure I had my space to figure myself out. I'd never seen myself even getting married, and to have my soul joined with another... that was a whole other level.

"We're in no rush," he said, noting the flurry of scenarios running through my eyes. "I'm more than happy to accept whatever you are comfortable with now, but just know that I would be very honored to be your flame."

I gingerly kissed his lips and let my mind rest. I eventually succumbed to my fatigue and fell asleep peacefully wrapped in his arms.

***

The next morning, I woke to Elvy at the desk in the corner, going through a pile of intimidating documents. At least, I thought it was the morning. The night sky still glittered through the room's windows. It would take time to get used to eternal night.

"Good morning," he said, setting down a large stack of papers. "Sleep well?"

I stretched out my arms and noticed I felt more rested than I had in a while, though there was a hint of soreness in some unexpected places, making me smile at the memories.

"Yes," I said, patting the space beside me.

"I have something for you. Close your eyes," he commanded, and I obeyed.

I heard him open a door and sit gingerly on the bed. I thought I smelled something burning.

"Open your eyes," he whispered excitedly.

I opened them to find Elvy holding a white cake with candles and a *"Happy Birthday, Zoe"* written on top.

"I know we missed your actual birthday with the trials, but you are worth celebrating."

Tears filled my eyes, and I happily blew out my candles, wishing on the stars themselves. Elvy scooped up a piece of icing with his finger and brought it to my mouth. I eagerly sucked it clean, laughing.

After indulging in the best chocolate cake I'd ever eaten, he wrapped me in his arms, kissing me.

"Elvy, I meant to ask about... Do we need to take precautions?"

He seemed confused at first, but quickly caught on. "Oh, no. I take a tonic for that."

"Do I need to take one, too?"

"You can if you'd like, but it's not needed."

I nodded, scooting in closer. I wasn't ready to bring new life into this realm whatsoever and was glad, at least, one of us had thought ahead.

"What's on the agenda today?" I asked, feeling unsure of myself. I didn't exactly have a clue what to do with this new life, but I wanted purpose.

"I have some court business to tend to. I thought you might spend some time with Finnian and Delmira to help you adjust."

"Can Jelly come?"

"If you can pry her away from Blaz," he teased. "Clodovea, Blaz, and Imelda will actually be with me today."

"Sounds serious," I prompted.

"Oleander might be better than I want to give him credit for, but there's a growing problem with Algol since it parted from Canis."

The familiar gut feeling swept over me, just long enough to make its presence known. My gift of discernment wanted to break free, as if it called for me to remember something. I centered myself as Oleander had taught me so many times, leaning into the discomfort in the knowledge of the future. Nothing came up or made itself known to me, but my intuition didn't waver. I had a feeling Elvy was right to be worried.

"You know something," he stated.

"Know something—yes. Remember it—no," I said, frustrated.

"It's alright, you were able to wield both gifts while still in mortal form. Those gifts will be magnified now and harder to control at first. It will come."

I wanted to shy away from the confidence in his eyes. He truly believed I could do this, whatever it was I had been called to do. I would not fail him or myself. Not again.

"Where should I meet Finnian and Delmira?" I asked.

"They should arrive soon," he said, not loosening his grip on me.

"I'm afraid you'll have to let me go then," I replied, placing a kiss on his bare chest. "I'll see you tonight?"

"Tonight," he agreed. "But I think we've got just enough time..."

I broke free, pouncing on him in answer to what he wanted. I let him lead me into his desires, which only created more longing in me. He seemed to know just the right place to have me breaking repeatedly with trembling legs and a desire to never part from his embrace.

"Ethereal," he said, panting heavily.

"My turn," I said, taking control of him, which seemed to only delight him further as he smirked down at my eagerness. I would taste the deliciousness of *him* breaking this time.

Before long, we were both lost in ecstasy, and I'd forgotten all about the worries of today. Eventually, time caught back up to us, and the reality of the realms came flooding back into our consciousness.

"Tonight," Elvy murmured, giving me one last kiss before I forced myself from the comfort of his bed.

He gave me a quick wink before I sauntered off to my room to freshen up before the rest of the group arrived.

The first order of business required me to shower. Even though it was perhaps the most luxurious shower I'd ever taken, I didn't linger longer than necessary to scrub myself clean. I wrapped the fluffy white robe around me and combed through my brown, gray hair. I quickly formed it into two braids until I was satisfied with the volume. I tried not to notice the green fire of my eyes in what used to be only pale green smudge.

The walk-in closet was filled to the brim with endless clothes. From sparkling ball gowns to casual jeans, t-shirts, and everything in between. I always felt more comfortable in sturdier clothes when I had no idea what I would be getting into. I opted for a pair of dark blue pants that resembled leather, but also didn't. They seemed stronger than leather, but more flexible at the same time. I found a matching, long-sleeved shirt that reminded me of the usual athletic attire I was accustomed to. For shoes, I donned a pair of sturdy boots. I felt prepared for anything, which gave me the confidence to step out of the safety of my room.

"Nice choice," Blaz said, bumping into me, wearing a near exact match to my outfit. In fact, so were Clodovea and Imelda.

"It's the uniform of the Shadowed Legion," Imelda explained, undoubtedly seeing the curiosity on my face. "It suits you."

My cheeks flushed red with embarrassment. I wasn't sure if it was from the compliment or that I'd unknowingly put on a uniform that I wasn't technically part of yet.

"You could start training with us," Clodovea offered. "Learn to fight and fly for battle. We could help teach you to control your gifts better without letting them consume you."

"You're more powerful now in this body," Blaz said. "More dangerous, especially wielding both."

"Blaz!" Imelda chastised.

"No, it's alright. He's only echoing what we all are thinking. What we fear," I answered, remembering my conversation with Elvy.

I knew nothing about fighting strategies other than the boxing classes I'd taken. The embarrassed part of me did not want to show my weakness in a ring full of experienced soldiers, but the loyal warrior in me craved to know how to fight, and not just with my stubborn inability to give up.

"I'd like to take you up on that, Clodovea."

"We are otherwise engaged this morning, but I can have Delmira and Finnian meet us at the training center after the twelfth hour," Clodovea suggested. "Speaking of, we need to collect Elvy and head to the city center. See you soon, Zoe."

"Jelly's in the backyard when you're ready," Blaz mentioned before following Clodovea and Imelda.

Eager to see my companion who had followed me across realms, I raced down the stairs to find Jelly playing with Finnian and Delmira in the ocean just beyond the gates of the estate. I stared for a moment, in awe of her and my magic that brought her with me. I missed Freyja, but I shoved that thought down, knowing I would find a way back to her.

Jelly sensed my approach and tore off in my direction, half flying, half running. It was hilariously cute to see her trying to use her new wings. I'd have to research what a Simargl really was, but she was just Jelly to me. I was grateful the stars had allowed me to bring this piece of my humanity with me on this new adventure.

"Hey, good girl," I said, scratching her ears. "Are you ready to do some work?"

Jelly barked in response and panted happily.

"Finn and I are ready when you are," Delmira added. "We thought we would start off with the history of this place and answer any questions."

"Alright," I agreed, following them down the cobblestone path, leading me to a seemingly more rustic part of town.

"What would you like to know?" Finnian asked, hands folded behind his back.

"What did Vega gift you?" I asked. "It'd be connected to water, right? Please tell me you can communicate with sea life. That would be so cool."

"Well," Finnian answered, nodding to Delmira. "You're not far off. While Vega and Algol both seemed to give you a magnitude of power from their stars, unlike anything we've ever seen, ours are a little unique all their own."

"Our gifts require both of us to use either," Delmira said. "I have... influence, persuasion over others. Similar to telepathy, but I can't read thoughts, just influence them."

"Wait—you two are telepathic? How is that connected to the water element?"

"What we do is rare. Even for Vega's Emergings. It's a similar concept to how whales communicate. We can read and influence the vibrations in the psychic field... which mortals have not yet accepted as reality."

"I'm sure that comes in handy serving Elvy's court," I noted, trying to act nonchalant.

"It can. Only in dire circumstances. I'd never attack an innocent with it," Delmira said, shuddering, eyes clearly lost in history.

I could relate to Delmira's thoughts. I tried not to notice the slight nods of recognition from seemingly every immortal we passed going down the street. Everyone must know who they were, and their eyes lit up with curiosity once they found mine.

"Vega would not gift us something that we could not control," Finn said soothingly. "I do the opposite of Delm. I can pull thoughts from others. Take their memories."

"So, you can read my mind now by taking my memories?" I asked, cheeks blushing from the thoughts I'd likely had around him. Finnian looked sheepishly away, as if the question had embarrassed him.

"Just tell her," Delm said.

"Even when you were still mortal, I could not cross the barrier to your mind. That has only strengthened in your immortal form."

I was not angry that he'd tried and was thankful to know my mind was not free game to anyone. I recalled attempting to break through Oleander's mist of a shield when I was still mortal. While I was grateful to have developed into a powerful shield, I wanted to be a weapon. To use my gift in its entire capacity, I would still need to learn how to break through barriers like that.

"I'd like you to show me how to break through them—the barriers of the mind." Maybe I could surprise Oleander the next time I saw him.

"We'll add it to the agenda. I can teach you what I know," Finnian replied.

"Battle is more than physical," Delmira said, coming back to the present. "In fact, I'd argue it's mental above all else."

Finnian and Delmira paused in front of a building that seemed to buzz with the energy of light. The material was the familiar moonstone I'd grown accustomed to in this realm; the stone seeming to be interlaced with the stars themselves.

"This is the Hall of Memories," Finnian said. "No Emerging has recovered their memories from the trials, but maybe something here can help."

The silence struck me as we entered the grand area, filled to the brim with scrolls and works of art. I couldn't hear the ocean, the first time in a while. I swallowed my fear and continued to follow them.

"What's different about this place compared to the library?" I asked.

"The Hall of Memories is an energy source. The memories come from the artifacts stored here. They can't be read."

They led me to a massive painting that reminded me of the tattoo now resting across my shoulder blades and a map of their worlds. It showed the stars and the kingdoms, along with the tethers, to each other. At the top lay the Kingdom of Canis, its power source Sirius, the brightest star, which encompassed the rest of the courts that surrounded it in a semicircle, forming a crescent moon. On Canis' right was the Air Elemental—Court of

Canopus, in the realm of Carina. Next to this realm lay the Ground Elemental—Court of Rigil in the realm of Centaurus. The Fire Elemental—Court of Arcturus resided next in the realm of Bootes. Then, there was the Water Elemental—Court of Vega, resting in the realm of Lyra. Finally, to the left of the Kingdom of Canis lived the Spirit Elemental—Court of Algol in the realm of Perseus.

A tether of light held each court, connecting their life sources together, which Earth absorbed on the opposite side of Canis. I brushed my hand along the lines of Algol, searching for the answer I needed, trying to understand the magic beyond my wildest ideas.

"We Emerged many lives ago, Zoe. Even then, it was bad. Algol had already disbanded from the Kingdom of Canis at that point. There has been no peace since."

"Oleander seems... reasonable," I said, fighting for the right word. Dangerous, maybe. He was not evil, though. I was certain of that.

"Oleander is playing a game he can't win," Delmira said through gritted teeth. "There are those in the Court of Algol that want to tether to another world, effectively destroying the remaining Courts of Canis and Earth with it, though we have no idea how she'd do it."

"I thought Oleander was the Lord Astral."

"He is," Finnian explained. "But he was not responsible for the separation. He serves under a vile queen."

"Hesperia," Delmira said, anger in her eyes. "She was once the Lady Astral of the Court of Algol. She murdered her weaker husband and Lord Astral. No one saw it coming before it was already done."

"Why?" I asked, head spinning. "How is Oleander related to her?"

"That's the thing, he isn't. He rose to that power from Algol," Delmira described.

"We can only guess her true motive," Finnian said. "No one can get close enough to know for sure. We think she has her sights on binding to a more beneficial mortal realm, or maybe a new one she can remake in her own image."

"Beneficial?" I asked, confused.

"Some of Hesperia's sympathizers believe in reversing the tethers," Finnian explained. "In theory, we could suck a planet dry of its usefulness and move onto another world once it no longer served a purpose for us, and continue consuming other realms."

"She's a snake," Delmira said, rage continuing to boil. "It's blasphemous what she did, knowing it would affect Earth and the other realms."

"Then why hasn't she?" I asked Finnian. "And I thought the five courts provided the essential life elements to Earth, not the other way around?"

"To Earth, yes. Our purpose is to strengthen and protect this mortal realm... but there are other worlds that we could take from, that are more *advanced* and able to stand on their own without other aid," Delmira said, illustrating the complex rules around the vast universe.

"Perhaps she can't," Finnian said, pondering why the queen hadn't made a move yet. "Maybe she needs something else... or someone else, someone chosen to help her bond elsewhere."

"That's why she sent Oleander," Delmira suggested. "To collect her prize. She was not expecting it to take this long for the right Emerging to come along."

"I am no one's prize," I said, a tinge of flame in my eyes. I knew there was more to Oleander. My gut—my gift—told me as much. I would have to arrange a meeting with him. Soon. "I would have no idea how to do what she wants," I said, trying to shrug it off.

"It doesn't matter," Finnian said, shaking his head. "She does, or *thinks* she does, which is just as dangerous. We still aren't sure how she broke the bond in the first place."

"Elvy called me Realm-Healer," I said, heart pounding.

"You cannot be one without the other," Finnian mused. "If you can heal tremendously, you can destroy on a detrimental scale."

I had not gone to the bottom of hell and clawed my way back up to be someone else's pawn. That queen had another thing coming if she thought I'd lift a finger to help her. I had to get my memories back. There was something I needed to recover. Something *vital*.

33

Wings

Unsuccessfully, Jelly and I had tried to lean into my gift of discernment for hours after I'd sent Delm and Finn away. The stars didn't feel like revealing themselves to me today. I didn't give up hope though and knew I would try again the next morning. They had warned I'd likely not be able to recover these memories, but they had given me this magic for a reason. They had granted both gifts to me in the end, and I believed I was destined to heal the realms, not break them.

"I'll figure it out," I muttered to myself. Growing frustrated would not do me any favors. "Now would be a great time to come out and give me mysterious answers, Archer."

"Delmira said we'd find you here," Imelda said, sitting beside me on the cold floor. My back had stiffened painfully. "It's beautiful, isn't it?"

I followed her eyes to the painting of the realm of the stars. A beautiful mystery that I intended to unravel. If only I could persuade them to tell me their secrets.

"Whatever is going on, you were meant for it," Imelda said, leaning her head on my shoulder. I surprised myself by not jumping at the unexpected contact.

"I fear failing," I admitted quietly.

Jelly placed a heavy head on my lap as if she sensed my worry.

"You may be the key to saving the realms, Zoe. But you are not responsible alone. You have us. All of us."

"No pressure, right?" I nudged her, wanting to lighten the mood.

"Ready to have some fun?" Clodovea asked, leaning against the doorway.

"Is training supposed to be fun?"

"Depends on your definition of fun," Imelda replied, smirking.

I knew I wouldn't be having any fun then.

***

Clodovea landed with me in her arms at the training center, which was nestled between the mountains and the ocean. Imelda had carried Jelly and had tried unsuccessfully to get her to fly on her own. I was grateful to hear them roaring with laughter after such deafening silence in the Hall of Memories.

Lights were flashing all around us as the immortal marks put on a glittering light show from those in the training rings. A smattering of matching tattoos adorning chests and backs were joined with the flecks of gray hair that shined with each movement of the Shadowed training. Swords were clinging everywhere, and I noticed sharp weapons of varying degrees in length strapped to most of the Shadowed here. I was clearly among elite warriors, who moved gracefully and fluidly with one another. I wasn't confident my body would ever move like that.

"It's best to train in true form," Clodovea explained. "It's where our power comes from, especially the healing."

"Convenient," I noted.

"We need to figure out what you can do first before we start you on a regime," Clodovea decided. "Though we already know you can fight well."

"Alright," I said, not letting my fear show.

"Let's see what you've got now that you are immortal," Blaz said, coming to stand beside me, eyes full of cunning delight. He would enjoy this a little too much.

"She might surprise you, Blaz," Clodovea taunted. "We don't know the full extent of her Emergence."

I prayed my boxing skills would show up, even if on a small scale.

"Both Delm and Finn Emerged with new strength," Imelda offered. "Didn't Delmira knock you on your ass, Blaz?"

"Lucky shot," he muttered.

"Come on, Zo. We'll warm up together," Clodovea decreed. "Elvy should be here later this evening. Finnian and Delmira are with him now."

Much to my surprise, Blaz was the picture of a professional. He was the essence of patience, and his usual playful banter was kept to a minimum. So much so that Clodovea and Imelda left him to work with me one-on-one after our warmup jog around the track to get the muscles activated.

"Call me over if I need to put him in his place," Imelda said, laughing. "Clove and I will be over there working with some squadrons who need to fall in line."

"First things first, you need to be in your authentic form. Punching and kicking with wings is like learning from scratch. Come on, mark and wings," he said, shaking his stagnant tattoo into a glowing emerald blue. A map of the star realms spread across his chest. Massive wings, similar to the wings Elvy bore, erupted from his back, which seemed larger than life compared to Jelly's, who was dutifully standing beside me. She seemed to stretch her wings in response, wanting to impress her friend.

"Good girl," Blaz praised, petting her head. "Let's see them, Zo."

"I don't know how to... summon them," I admitted, eyes down. "Not on command."

"It's like flexing a muscle. Think about pulling your navel to your spine, bearing down," Blaz explained, happy to go over the process. "Good, then flex your shoulders back, like you were correcting a slumped posture."

I did as I was told, and nothing happened.

"It's okay. She'd kill me for telling you, but it took Delmira weeks to sprout her wings without tumbling over," Blaz said, smirking.

"You trained her too?"

"And Finnian," he added. "For that matter, I trained Imelda and Clodovea, too."

I hadn't considered that Blaz was older than the rest of them.

"Shouldn't that make you Elvy's second?" I asked, curiously.

"He offered it, but it's not the kind of work I enjoy doing," Blaz answered, motioning his hands around him. "This is where I belong. And I'm good at it. Though Clodovea and Delmira can more than hold their own in battle."

"I can't imagine Delmira being an eloquent politician," I said, as I continued practicing the flexes Blaz showed me. He never touched me without asking, which I appreciated.

"She's not," Blaz agreed, laughing. "But she can make the hard calls... there's a balance to her that is only manifested in true leaders."

"And Clove?"

"She can mesmerize foes to their knees without lifting a finger."

I could see that in her. There was no one more graceful, even here in the training arena, than Clodovea. If I stared too long, I found myself in a trance watching her.

"I see what you mean," I said, wondering if I'd ever develop that kind of smoothness.

"Focus," Blaz said, bringing me back to his lesson. Sweat poured down my back, and it was gathering uncomfortably in my eyes. I'd done nothing but flex, and I was worn out.

"You're doubting yourself," Blaz suggested soothingly. "Find your center."

I was reminded of the times Oleander had instructed me to do the same. Closing my eyes, I drowned out the chirps of birds, the grunts of the warriors behind me, and any other distraction that was not the sound of crashing waves. I found the furthest wave that was beginning to cap, listening so closely that I knew the moment it washed to shore, bringing peace along with it.

I followed his instructions and felt my wings make their grand entrance. It didn't hurt, but I knew I'd be sore and take some getting used to. They were light as a feather, but my vertigo felt off adjusting to them. I felt the breeze flowing through them as if they were an extension of me. Each flex of my back operated a part of the wing. I understood why Jelly was not in full flight yet.

I opened my eyes to find Blaz staring, mouth slightly ajar.

"What is it?" I asked, worried there was something wrong with them.

"I've never seen anything like them, Zo. Elvy's got to see this."

"Is something wrong?" I asked, whipping my head around, nearly knocking myself over. "I think my wings flashed for a second last night, and he didn't say anything."

"I'm afraid I was distracted at the time," an unexpected voice said right beside me. How did he get here so fast? "Absolutely nothing is wrong with your wings, Zoe Eferhild."

Elvy placed a caressing hand on my waist, guiding me to the mirrors lining the arena walls. I almost stopped walking as I took in the image in front of me. I'd thought Blaz's wings were big, but mine were at least double the size, and combined both my Emergence from Vega and Algol gloriously.

The wings were a deep void of black from where they sprouted out of my back and developed into a turquoise ombre in the middle, then faded to white. The most striking part was that each wing had a jagged line down the middle that seemed to match my scar, which the cosmos swirled in, much like my forearm. They had the same texture as Elvy's and the rest of the Shadowed instead of the feathery softness of Jelly's. My wings seemed to possess an almost sentient air about them.

I had a feeling the rest of the arena wanted to stand still and admire the wings, but their training kept them focused on their tasks. I was sure it helped to have the presence of the commander and Lord Astral to keep their gaping mouths closed tightly.

I almost let myself believe for a moment that I was not worthy of something so otherworldly beautiful. I slashed the thought from my mind, reminding myself of the madness I had traveled through to find myself and believe that I was enough, just as I am.

"The light darkness has longed for," Elvy whispered, brushing his fingers along the apex of my left wing. I shivered at the intimate touch, glancing down with flushed cheeks.

With a slight nod, the spectators in the arena dispersed, leaving me utterly alone with my Lord Astral. This steady vibration of belonging washed over me as he cupped my face, pulling my soul into those gray, stormy eyes.

"Why do you look away?" he asked, eyes unreadable.

My insecurities wanted to rip out of my chest, screaming obscenities at myself, but I shrugged them off, wishing to silence that darkness inside me forever.

I took a deep breath of the ocean breeze, choosing to tell him my heart.

"Even now... in this remade form... I can still feel this darkness in me. I may not remember why I chose both Vega and Algol, but part of me is disappointed in knowing I could not let go of the remnants of who I was, of who I had to become to survive."

I met the intensity of his gaze, as if to say, *"This is who I am, take it or leave it."*

"Zoe, I've often found the light easy to love. I look up at the stars and the moon in wonder of the illumination and power they give us," he paused. "If I look long enough, I can't help but love the darkness surrounding the celestials even more because we would never appreciate the magnificence of the stars without it. We owe our existence not to the light, but to the darkness that makes it significant. Remember, the darkness is just the shadows of ourselves that we've rejected. They don't have to be a bad thing."

I didn't hold back the tears that threatened to flow from me. I embraced them in my vulnerability of courage. With all the uncertainties of the world right now, I had the greatest gift in being *known.* To truly be seen by someone for who I authentically was, and loving the scars I wore as a badge of honor in battle. The pull in my chest wanted to engulf us in the flames they fated us to be.

"I think I've been waiting for you. All this time," I whispered softly.

Elvy grasped my hand in fervor, kissing me roughly and with intent. I bit his bottom lip and enjoyed the breathy gasp that rocked through him as he pulled me against his solid frame. "Mine," he claimed. He tilted my chin to gaze up at the stars, and my eyes followed his.

"For the heart of the new moon," he breathed.

"And the life in the starlight," I answered, wrapping my arms around him—my flame.

34

Little Bear

My abdomen and back muscles were unexpectedly sore from the seemingly insignificant training I'd been enduring the past week. I'd mastered summoning and banishing my wings almost every time I flexed those muscles correctly. Blaz had warned that I would still need to get used to the balance of them before launching into more rigorous training—swords, which I was inclined to agree with. It was so strange to have something so delicate affect every movement of my body.

Elvy had slept in my room last night and had already left for the day on more court business, which left Jelly and me to get ready alone. We were gearing up to head to the Hall of Memories to hopefully crack my forgotten time and were due to meet Blaz back on the training grounds after lunch. I have disliked every moment spent in the Hall of Memories and hoped that I would get answers soon.

I slipped on similar clothes from my first day on Vega and sighed longingly at the unused library as we left through the nearest exit. I was pretty confident in my ability to retrace the steps from the mansion to the Hall of Memories. Despite having gone there everyday, I was struggling with remembering my way around the city. The immortals of Vega politely stared at the sight of Jelly, but struggled to keep their shock when they met my gaze. You would think that a dog with wings would be far more interesting than the likes of me.

I found the ornate building fairly easily and was again startled by the lack of noise once I entered the hall. Forcing my mind to calm, I propped myself up against the same painting as always, trying to find my center and lean into my gift.

"I'm trying to connect with you, Algol." I whispered, closing my eyes. "The least you could do is show up."

I practiced the five-senses grounding technique that Emma and I had done so many times when I was becoming overwhelmed with my emotions. However, it was the opposite in this room. I couldn't hear or feel anything but the silence and coolness of the floor. Jelly propped her head on my leg, reminding me she was there and giving me a surge of self-efficacy.

I thought of Freyja and my promise to her and all the people who were suffering deeply from the impact of the unrest between the courts in these realms. I had to give them a fighting chance. Then, I could start doing the actual work. At least, that's what I told myself and echoed what Emma had explained when we first started therapy.

Emma said I had to stabilize in my immediate needs and safety first before we could start doing the nitty gritty, deep trauma work. As much as I wanted to return to Earth and continue the work I'd started while still a mortal Emerging, I had to stabilize the tethers first. I had to fix whatever that queen was doing to our worlds.

I pulled my racing thoughts back, demanding my discernment guide me to what I already knew was inside me. I couldn't help but think back to Emma's words about our body storing memories in the darkest parts of ourselves, even when we couldn't consciously remember them.

"Breathe, Zo," I said, voice echoing within the walls. I wouldn't yield to my panic or frustration.

By the time lunch rolled around, I had made no progress. Exiting the Hall of Memories was like stepping into a storm of sensory overload. Not wanting to overwhelm my senses, I honed in on the one that always centered me, finding the rhythm of the waves crashing to the nearby shore.

The mental strain had caused me to lose my appetite, so I opted for a stroll on the shoreline with Jelly before heading to the training center. I decided on the private beach in front of the mansion, wanting to be away from everyone else. A part of me knew I sought solitude because I didn't want to admit defeat when the literal world was depending on me.

I plopped down on the damp sand and Jelly joined me in examining the stars above us. I let my thoughts drift to Freyja, missing her terribly. It felt odd not having her with me after all this time. I'd grown so used to having her with me at a moment's notice. I'd find my way back to her and keep the promise I'd made. The universe owed me that much.

You will burn, Zoe Eferhild.

The voice came through me, invading my mind. The hair on my neck rose and the swell of discernment rolled over me. It seemed the universe wanted to speak back. As Oleander had instructed many times before, I didn't shy away from the discomfort that roared over me. Instead, I leaned into it, ready to face what came.

My mark burned and burst with light without my command to do so, and what was once my jagged scar seemed to lengthen up my arm, expanding up to my bicep. The cosmos swirled dangerously beneath my skin, then faded into a void of black. A sense of sorrow washed over me that was deeper than even death itself.

"Show me what it means," I said, back dripping with sweat. It took all my focus to cling to the *sight*.

Somewhere in the distance, I heard screaming. It took me a moment to realize it was my voice that echoed across the ocean. I had to let go or the warning may come true, and I couldn't afford to burn yet. I forced the sensation out of me, belonging to only myself again.

I hesitated to examine the scar, unsure if I hoped to see its new development or not. My heart sank, but my mind was relieved to find the dark tendrils still there, lurking within my skin. The cosmos still shined brightly where the original scar had been and my immortal mark blazed in blues and blacks.

"So, I'm not crazy. That did just happen," I muttered to myself as Jelly pawed at my leg.

The new marks made little sense. They didn't seem to be in any particular pattern, but they reminded me of a hand reaching out, searching for something. That was the feeling I got from them, anyway.

I breathed in the ocean's smell, smiling at my center, which had held me through my darkest times.

"It's you, isn't?" I asked the ocean. "You're what I need to get this to work," I continued, pointing at my head.

I didn't need the empty walls void of life in the Hall of Memories. I needed the soul of the ocean and the life it brought to shore with every crash of its waves. Vega seemed to wink at me in the never-ending night sky as if to answer my question.

I placed a hand over the black tendrils along my arm, hoping to heal them, but they now seemed a permanent part of me, cracks in my armor.

I sighed, flinging myself down onto the sand. My head was pounding, but I didn't feel finished. Not yet.

"Little bear."

I'd know that voice anywhere.

"Of course you come now," I mumbled.

"You are harder for me to reach in Vega," The Archer stated.

My head was screaming, but I shoved it aside for just a minute longer.

"What do I do?" I begged, unsure of what I should ask for specifically. How do you ask how to save the world?

"Daughter, you must go from where you are descended. The answers you seek lie within the heart of Algol."

"Which answers?"

"Algol, little bear. Find that which was stolen. Only my descended can wield what is true and not meet death. This is the beginning to mend what was broken."

The pounding in my head released suddenly as I felt the weight of The Archer leave me. I didn't know what he was referring to or how I was supposed to train for the rest of the day, but I got up and put one foot in front of the other. The rest would come.

Much to my happiness, Blaz didn't ask questions once ascertaining that I was okay. He agreed to wait until I had a chance to tell Elvy this evening before pressing further. He remained focused on my training, giving me instructions on maneuvering different stretches with my wings out. I tried not to groan or let the pain flash across my face as I winced at the tender parts of my muscles. I didn't even see a point in healing the muscles, as they would just be sore within the next hour.

"It'll ease, the more you do it," Blaz offered with knowing eyes.

"I look forward to that," I responded, leaping off an elevated platform without busting my ass on the way down.

"Barely off center that time," he encouraged. "Now, jump back up."

My legs were screaming, but I nodded. My wings caught under my heel, almost making me fall flat on my face. I caught myself at the last minute, which had Blaz yelping in satisfaction.

"Don't tell them I said this, but you're learning much faster than the rest of the Luminaries," he said, signaling for us to begin our cool down.

"My lips are sealed," I said, not believing it for a moment.

"I'm serious. Most would have cursed me already."

"Maybe I do on the inside," I suggested, laughing and moving to the next stretch.

"It's okay to not be okay," he stated, suddenly serious. "Whatever you might need to throw at me—whatever you need *me* to be for *you*... this is a safe space. I'll do it. I remember how focused you got when Imelda and I stayed over that night. You were centered while throwing punches. Even if it's not punching things, we can always go for a run."

I understood what he meant, and I had a feeling I'd take him up on that.

"Thank you, Blaz. I don't know what to feel sometimes."

Blaz nodded, seeming satisfied that I had taken his words to heart.

"I promise... you'll be the first I punch if my hands start getting twitchy." I gave him my best winning smile.

"I'll walk you back home," he replied, giving Jelly her obligatory belly scratches. "Elvy called a family dinner."

"Why do I have a feeling he already knows what happened to me?" I asked, more curious than anything.

"It's the flame," he explained. "You two are connected even without the joining ritual."

I thought back to the fear that must have consumed me and what must have shot down our flame's tether to each other.

"He didn't come to me though," I pointed out.

"I've known Elvy for a long time. If I had a guess, he wanted to give you the chance to stand resolute on your own. I'm sure he was nearby if you needed him."

I smiled, knowing he was right. A gentle caress seemed to warm through me, as if to let me know I was safe and cared for. I squeezed the embrace back, hoping it hit its mark.

35

Library

"What does it mean?" Imelda asked, studying the black marks that now adorned the length of my left arm and shoulder. They hadn't spread any further since my time on the beach.

"I don't know," I answered. "Based on what I felt when it marked me, it's nothing good."

"You said *it.* Why say it like that?" Clodovea questioned, hand clasped in Imelda's. Worry was etched on both their faces. My heart was saddened that this was causing either of them distress.

"That's what it felt like. Like something specific looking for something. It needed help, I think. I just couldn't contain it long enough without..." I let the thought trail off.

"Burning," Elvy finished. His face mirrored Clove's and Imelda's.

I nodded and stroked Jelly's soft fur, wishing the shadows would swallow me. I had never felt more cared for as I sat around this dinner table, and the weight was almost too much to handle.

I also really didn't want to say the words that were about to come out of my mouth.

"I think I need to go to Algol," I announced, following my gut. I hadn't yet mentioned my little talk with The Archer. I wanted to give them one blow at a time.

"Not happening," Blaz said, clearly not fond of the idea. Elvy shot him a glare, silencing any further outburst.

"Look, all of this is tied to Algol. I think Oleander can help me figure it out. For my gift to work, I think I need to be at the center of it. I need to see Hesperia. I'll be able to feel her true self."

"And you can't do that from here?" Elvy asked.

"I don't think so... or maybe the stars don't want me to for some reason." I took a breath before continuing. "The Archer visited me after this appeared." I pointed to the new marks on my arm. "He said I have to find something in Algol. Something that was stolen."

"You are not The Archer's errand girl," Blaz argued.

"I'm tied to him whether I want to be or not. It's not about that. It's about saving the realms, right? Do you think he means his bow?"

"No," Finnian piped in. "Not his bow. It's been lost, not stolen... his arrow though. There's been questions about it. I know I've read something about the arrow in the Hall of Memories."

I shuddered at the name. I had not enjoyed that experience and did not wish to go back there if I could help it at all.

"Perhaps the Hall is kinder to me," Finnian suggested, smiling. "It seems you were called to the place where the wilder spirits need to be."

"Sorry, Finn. That place gives me the creeps," I returned.

"It does for most of us," Blaz agreed. "Are you sure your gift can't work here, Zoe?"

"Finn, Delmira?" Elvy asked.

"Her gifts could work similarly to ours," Finnian mused, nodding his head. "We have to be in closer contact with our target."

"Finnian couldn't get past Hesperia's shields," Delmira said, stating this fact. "We may be risking a lot for Zoe to not be able to get in her mind at all."

"Zoe is learning to break through shields... but I'm not sure it matters for Hesperia," he said, lips pressed in thought.

"I don't read minds," I replied, my gift coming into more clarity after thinking back to the mortals I'd helped. "I see their essence, their souls or auras, I guess. Oleander said I could discern someone's intentions. Oleander can shield from me. We don't know if Hesperia can. Reading minds and *seeing* the future aren't the same magic. I need to find out her intentions and how she broke the bond to Canis. But I don't think it's a distance thing for me... I just know I need to be there."

"Hesperia likely can't shield from that kind of power—a soul power," Finnian said. "But we also do not know what Hesperia's true power is."

"No one does," Elvy agreed.

"So, we just let Zoe walk into the lion's den by herself?" Blaz asked, visibly frustrated.

"I won't be alone. Oleander will be there," I answered. This seemed to only make Blaz angrier. "I don't think he has any love for Hesperia."

"I think you're right, Zoe," Elvy admitted. "He showed his true colors to you while in Saint Andrews. If you trust him, that is enough for me."

"I will go with her," Finnian declared.

"Then I'm going with you too," Delmira added.

"No," Elvy said, making his voice clear. "I can't have my second in command go there right now, and you are too volatile towards Oleander's court. Clodovea?"

"I will go," Clove conceded, and Imelda sank back in her chair at this.

"I'll send word to Oleander tomorrow to secure safe passage. He'll need some time to figure out how we want Zoe presented to Hesperia. We won't be able to hide that you are coming. She will want your power, so she won't object," Elvy said, nodding his thanks to Clove. "I expect you will depart in within the week."

I wanted to leave right then, but I understood the need to prepare and loop Oleander into this. I would get to see Freyja soon, which lifted my spirits somewhat. Dinner fizzled out soon after this, and I found myself wanting to seek the comfort of solitude. Elvy and Delmira seemed to be in a heated discussion, so I found my way to the library with Jelly trotting behind me.

The library took my breath away as it had the first time I'd seen it. I thumbed through the shelves, looking for nothing in particular. The smell of coffee filled the air, and I felt like I was home. I followed the scent and discovered a fresh brew sitting in a lounge area of the library, but no one was anywhere in sight. Unable to resist the aroma, I made myself a cup and my taste buds found pleasure in it.

"I'm glad someone appreciates my coffee the way I do," a voice behind me said.

I turned to find a petite girl with blonde hair and freckles smiling back at me. No silver streaks in her hair. Jelly wagged her tail, excited to meet a new friend.

"It's arguably the best I've had," I admitted. "I'm Zoe."

"I'm Octavia, a Keeper here."

"It's nice to meet you," I admitted. "You'll have to show me around sometime if that would be okay? Actually, I was hoping you could help me research something now?"

"What can I help you with?"

"I'm looking for any information you have on a simargl. I kind of made my dog into one and don't really know what it means," I said, pointing to Jelly.

"Of course! I will get right on that," she said with enthusiasm. "Come find me the next time you're around."

Before I could ask how I would find her in this labyrinth, she was skipping away from me, but she'd, at least, left the pot of coffee.

I picked up a nearby book that was lying on one of the coffee tables. There was no bookmark or any owner around, so I flipped through the pages, wanting to calm my nerves. The smell of the book reminded me of the serenity the ocean brought me. The novel was about nothing extraordinary or profound, but it had my interest from the start.

I wrapped a velvety soft blanket around my body as I settled into a comfortable couch, and I soon found myself immersed in the fictional world of this mystery. I barely noted Jelly snoring below me. The book reminded me of the writings of one of my favorite classic authors, which only had me turning the pages faster.

I was so entirely wrapped up in the novel, I nearly flew out of my seat when a familiar touch gently tapped me on the shoulder.

"I'm sorry to disturb you," Elvy said, a smile playing on his lips. "You look invested in the fate of those characters."

"I just needed to escape for a moment. Shut my brain off," I explained.

"I get it," he answered, sliding in next to me. "Would it be too distracting if I sat here with you while you finished?"

"Not at all," I replied, inviting him under the blanket with me. I leaned my head back on his chest as he wrapped his arms around me. He didn't breathe another word until I was finished with the book. I wasn't sure if he read along with me or was simply lost in his own thoughts. I occasionally stole a glance towards him and immediately blushed, having been caught. He probably needed the closeness more than anything.

When I downed the last of the coffee and closed the book, he swept me in his arms, carrying me to his bedroom with a fire in his eyes.

Only when he was out of sight of the others did he show his true fear of us going to Algol. He sat down on the edge of his bed, hands pressed to his face. I knelt down in front of him, leaning my head on his knees.

"I'll be okay," I said, attempting to bring some kind of comfort to him.

He took my hands in his, holding them close to his heart. His stormy gray eyes held me in his gaze. There was no force in this universe that would make me move. There was nothing I wouldn't sacrifice to protect him.

"I just found you," he said, voice cracking. "It is infuriating to know I am helpless in this—when it comes to you." The rumble of his true power rippled through the air around us like lightning.

I understood his desire to have control, and I admired the courage it took to let it go. I was sure there was a part of him that wanted me safely tucked away next to him at all times, but he had always let me make my own path, even when it meant sacrificing his needs.

"You didn't volunteer to go," I questioned.

"It took all my willpower to keep my mouth shut, Zoe. If you give me the word that I am to come with you, I will, but I could feel what you wanted. To do this. I'd like to say it is for the immortals in Vega that I must stay, but deep down, it's you."

"I'm going to be okay," I said confidently. "Whatever this bigger picture the stars have planned for me, it will not end in Algol. I will come back as soon as I get what we need."

"This scares me," he admitted with strain in his voice, tracing the black lines embellishing my skin with trembling fingers. "But I trust you."

"For the heart of the new moon," I reminded him soothingly.

"And the life in the starlight," he murmured.

I saw the love in his eyes and knew mine mirrored the same. Neither of us had ever uttered the words, and I wasn't sure I wanted to hear them now when I knew he was afraid he may not see me again. I didn't want it voiced in fear of the unknown.

"Please stay," Elvy said, pulling me closer.

I wasn't sure if he meant in Vega or in his room tonight, and I doubted he really knew either. Regardless, I straddled his waist, pushing him to the bed in need of him the same way he needed me. The heat flared between us, our flames aching to be joined in whatever way we would give them in that moment. We soon found ourselves in a familiar rhythm, though we both clung to each other with unrestricted desire more than ever before.

He was mine. And I was his.

As we both found our release, our marks flared brighter than the stars themselves, and I knew I was home.

36

REUNITED

We all anxiously awaited word from Oleander for the next several days, but Elvy never faltered in his self-assured demeanor around the others. I realized that he often shouldered the weight of things alone to protect his family from the burden, much like I had always done. I swore he would never have to bear any of it alone again.

The Keeper Octavia had thankfully found me one day while I was in the library to sneak some more of her coffee. She'd given me the books she could find on the simargl, and it was a significant amount of lore to read through. A visit to Arcturus would probably be necessary to understand Jelly's new form the best.

Finnian had been working hard with me to improve my ability to break through shields. It was much more difficult than manifesting one, and the progress was slower going than I'd like.

Elvy and I came together every night, throwing our fears to the wind, finding a blissful safe haven in each other. Thinking of him made my core burn, and my eyes automatically found him. As if he read my mind, he glanced up at me and the tug in my chest blazed brilliantly through my core. He seemed to feel the same as he subtly rubbed his chest, soothing the burn away. The entire crew was at the training grounds, trying to instill in me any last tips they could before we headed for Algol. We'd held off trying to recover my memories until I returned, which I agreed with. I had a feeling Algol—not the Hall of Memories—would have the answers we needed.

Blaz and I had gone on a twilight run not long ago, and we were already drenched in sweat. I'd become anxious about the mission, and he'd kept his word to bear it with me as we ran in silence together, pushing each other to our limits.

At the end of the run, he'd decided I'd gotten my balance good enough that I could try flying, which I was stoked about. This meant that I was one step closer to learning how to wield a sword. Jelly had become a competent flyer with the encouragement of Blaz, and

I wanted to feel that kind of freedom myself. With my shield impassable to those who would dare try, it was more important to focus on physical training for now.

Elvy, Finnian, Delmira, Clodovea, and Imelda all watched from the sidelines, likely bracing to watch me make a complete fool of myself.

"Don't pay attention to them, Zo," Blaz commanded, calling my focus back to him. "They're just pissed that you will fly faster and longer than all of them. Except maybe Elvy."

"So what do I do?" I asked, wings flared, ready to go.

"Think of your wings more like a helicopter than an airplane. You don't have to get a running start, you just have to build up enough speed or power in your wings to launch yourself into the sky. You will jet off with barely a second thought."

Blaz demonstrated what he meant, and he was off the ground in one strong flap of his wings. Jelly was now hovering around us, moving her wings effortlessly. Such a showoff.

"Do they really have to stare at us?" I asked, stalling for time.

"If you want them gone, they are gone. Elvy included," he said, completely serious.

I glanced over at Elvy to find his eyes full of encouragement and love. He was laughing with the others excitedly, and they all seemed to root for me to succeed.

"No, it's okay," I responded, swallowing down my fear.

"It helps if you have a center," he explained. "Whenever you're ready."

I nodded, extending my hearing to the ocean, allowing it to consume every molecule of my being. Never in my wildest mortal dreams did I think I would fly, but here I was living despite it all.

I began flapping my wings, choosing to trust in them and in me, that they could carry me. The flaps were slow at first as I adjusted to the feel of them, but it didn't take long before they became a blur. My feet lifted from the ground, and I kept my eyes closed, listening to the ocean. This was all real. All of it a gift.

"Open your eyes," Blaz said, voice beneath me.

"I'm afraid to," I admitted.

A calming sensation burned through my chest, and I knew Elvy had sent it. Taking a deep breath, I opened my eyes to find Blaz yelling incoherently down below. I slowly turned my head to find the others cheering and clapping. I couldn't help but join in on their joy and found myself laughing along with them.

Blaz joined me in the sky, giving me further instructions. Jelly stole a few licks before Blaz shooed her away for distracting me.

"Now, before you learn to move around, we need to learn to land," he explained. "That's the hard part."

I gulped, realizing I did not know how to get down. Blaz gave me clear directives and clasped onto my hands, guiding me down effortlessly. I somehow landed on my feet and not face first, which I was proud of.

The rest of Elvy's court surrounded me, and I let myself embrace the good feeling. We all seemed to pause at this moment, smiling.

"Much better than Delmira," Blaz joked, punching her shoulder.

"Not all of us can be perfect at everything," she snapped back playfully. "Finnian was way worse than me, anyway."

"I was on your side, Delm!" Finnian answered.

Clodovea and Imelda strode up to us hand in hand, movements graceful. The angels among us.

"Excellent work," Clodovea praised, admirably.

"Blaz may be a prick, but he knows his stuff," Imelda agreed, flashing a winning smile towards him. "Most of the time."

"Ever I aim to please, Imelda," Blaz answered, joking back.

Elvy slipped an arm around my waist, easily navigating past my wings, pulling me close.

Heat flared across my skin, and I placed a quick kiss on his lips. I banished my wings so I could get closer to him. His gaze suggested exactly what he had in mind as my reward for completing my first successful flight.

"Get a room," Blaz said.

Elvy snarled, which only made him laugh.

"Blaz is just mad he isn't getting any," Delmira offered.

"And you are?" Blaz questioned, fire in his eyes. Delmira's eyes seemed to soften at this, and I couldn't help but wonder if there had ever been anything between them.

Before I could question further, I felt Elvy tense beside me. A familiar face came striding forward across the training field, escorted by members of the Shadowed Legion.

"I hate to break up the party, but I've come to fetch you," Zadie said, hands on her hips.

"Always a pleasure to see you," Elvy replied, smiling, but I saw the rage broiling beneath the surface.

"Lord Astral," Zadie answered with a slight bow. She turned her attention back to me. "I trust you are prepared?"

"I am," I answered, without a break in my voice. I would succeed, no matter the cost.

"Then let's go," Zadie said, turning on her heels, which left little time for goodbyes.

"You stay here with Uncle Blaz and Aunty Delm, okay?" I said, patting Jelly on her soft head. Jelly looked about as equally put off at staying behind as Blaz and Delmira did. Without knowing more about Jelly's powers, I refused to put her at risk.

"We'll take care of her," Blaz promised.

Delmira whispered something to Finnian while Clodovea and Imelda gave each other a parting kiss. Elvy pulled my face to his and planted a firm kiss on my lips as I wrapped my arms around his powerful torso.

"Are you sure we shouldn't go together?" I asked, second guessing my earlier confidence.

"Say the word, and I'm yours," Elvy promised, and I knew he meant it. However, that would leave Vega vulnerable, and he'd been gone for long enough pursuing me. I couldn't ask this of him.

"I'll be with you again soon, right?"

"I am with you always," he said, speaking so low only I could hear. "When you feel the cold wash of doubt in yourself, you do not relent. Let them fear the burning fire within you."

"So bright that even the stars will remember the power of my name," I said, with a sense of familiarity and foreboding.

Elvy reluctantly let me go, as I let myself be swept into Clodovea's arms, trailing behind Zadie's retreating figure. Finnian trekked beside us, a fierceness in his eyes. In what felt like seconds, we were crossing the shadows, flying to the unknown of Algol.

"How do you know where you're flying?" I asked Clodovea through the sounds of the wind between realms. We were surrounded by darkness, but swirling vortexes of light passed us by as we plummeted at an immeasurable speed.

"You just have to let the stars guide you. You'll learn to navigate them, but you will always be able to find home, Zoe. It'll call to you."

Upon breaching the Court of Algol, I was met with heartache. The eternal night sky in the realms of the stars was as devastatingly beautiful as the Court of Vega. There was no life here, though, and the swell of power in my *sight* roared within me the moment we crossed the threshold. The good part of this meant that I was in the right place, but it didn't ease my wariness. I forced down the trickle of sickness, ordering my body to no longer need it. I could find what I needed.

My body seemed to listen, and I let my eyes drift down to the barren land below. There were remnants of a once thriving city, but it looked as if the center had lost its heartbeat. Zadie seemed to lead us to what looked like a small castle, like the many I'd seen in my mortal life while traversing through the United Kingdom. I prayed beyond hope we could speak to Oleander before meeting with Hesperia.

"She's not in there," Clodovea said, leaning in close.

I nodded and allowed myself to relax a fraction, but I still kept my guard up.

We landed on one of the four pillars of the castle, and Zadie didn't slow as she sauntered through the closest door, leading us down a narrow passageway. Even inside the castle, I felt its emptiness, void of life. My heart broke at what used to be a thriving empire at one time.

Zadie led us through another door, and I couldn't help the smile that crossed my face upon seeing Freyja sitting on a red parlor chair. She leaped up at the sight of me and we bounded across the distance to each other, wrapping each other in a ferocious embrace.

"When I realized there was something gravely wrong going on here, I was worried you weren't safe," I said, not letting go of my sister.

"Your faith in me is as always astounding, Zoe Eferhild," Oleander said, displaying his familiar, charming smile. Oleander snapped his fingers and the glamor of what was a dank living area became one of modern majesty. I briefly wondered just how far his glamor extended and if it was strong enough to hide an entire city.

"Just ignore him, Zoe. I have learned to," Freyja suggested, breaking our embrace.

Oleander feigned hurt and welcomed the rest of us into his home as a gracious host.

He had a calming effect on the tension that was radiating from those from the Court of Vega. I sadly realized they still couldn't see my sister, but they put on brave faces.

"We will meet with Hesperia tomorrow night," Oleander stated, explaining our plans. "She has agreed to a dinner at her palace."

"And how do you plan to keep Zoe safe?" Clodovea asked, slightly placing her body in front of me. Even though she couldn't see my sister, Freyja placed herself in a protective position alongside me.

"I trust Zoe can take care of herself," he replied pointedly, noticing Clodovea's stance. "However, my sources say the queen is more interested in keeping Zoe alive than killing her. She will try to win you to her side."

"Bold of her, really," I stated.

"Hopefully, she reveals what she needs you for," Finnian mused. "Something she can't do on her own."

"I won't do it. Whatever it is," I said with conviction.

"Don't underestimate her, Zoe," Oleander cautioned. "She can be quite persuasive."

"I only belong to me," I answered, voice unwavering.

"We need to decide what the aim of this mission is," Clodovea voiced.

"Yes, we will get down to business, but please rest for a moment. We can go over the logistics at dinner like civilized allies," Oleander said smoothly. "Zoe, I can show you to your accommodations for the night."

"Thank you," I replied, nodding to Clove. Freyja followed us as Oleander led the way.

"How are you settling into Vega?" he asked pleasantly.

A blush creeped along my neck as I thought of just how well I'd been settling into my new home. A pang of guilt rippled through me, but I shoved it away, knowing I was here to fight for the realms.

"It's going well. I've started training with the Shadowed Legion."

"It suits you. You seem stronger."

"I don't know if it works that fast," I dismissed. "But thank you."

"I didn't mean just physically, though that is nice too," Oleander chuckled. "I meant your shield... it seems stronger. More powerful."

I noticed Freyja listening intently, but she remained mute behind me.

"I guess it is. Sometimes I think it's there to protect me or maybe it's biding its time to break," I said, thinking of the trials. Attempting to remember what happened had left me slightly mangled.

"The trials. You're trying to remember?" Oleander guessed. I chose not to attempt breaking his shields despite my curiosity at his true thoughts.

"I think it's imperative that I do."

"How do you feel now that you are in Algol?" he asked.

"Like the answers are here. Like I'm on the cusp of something, but I have this sense of dread... like there's something I'm missing."

I knew in my gut there was a reason my arm was scarred black now... but I was afraid to think too much about it, not when I'd finally found some sense of happiness. I had this unshakeable feeling that the stars didn't want me to remember or put it together until they were ready for me to give them something in return.

"I don't suppose you have any insight?" I asked him hopefully.

"My time away from Algol was not good for my immortals. My attention has been focused solely on them." The irrational part of me wanted to be angry, but I'd seen the same dedication in Elvy. They'd sacrificed a lot to come to Earth to help me. I couldn't ask more of them when they had given so much, which was why Elvy was safely back in Vega, even though I knew it destroyed him to let me go.

"Here we are," he said, pulling me from my thoughts. "They will serve dinner in three hours. We will make our preparations then."

"Thank you, Oleander," I said genuinely, as Freyja and I closed the door behind us.

***

Freyja and I used the time before dinner to catch up with one another, even though it hadn't truly been that long. I told her everything that had happened between Elvy and me, and she gushed right along with me at some of the more intimate details. She seemed to live vicariously through me, but there was not one etch of jealousy coming from her.

"You've earned it, Zoe. This happiness."

"I believe that most of the time," I agreed.

"So, what are you going to tell him? About the flame?"

"It's not like he's asked me formally or anything," I said, twirling my thumbs.

"You love him," she stated.

"Yes," I nodded. "It just seems like I'm waiting for the other shoe to drop. Maybe I'm just trying to make sure that this isn't some dream I'm going to wake up from. I just have this feeling like something bad is going to happen, Freyja. The *sight* is not being very forthcoming, though."

"You can't spend the rest of your existence waiting for some perfect time or opportune moment, Zo. Sometimes you have to take that leap and not fear the fall."

"I really hate it when you're right," I answered, sighing. "So, what have you been doing here in Algol?"

"I think it'd be easier to show you," she said with hesitation. "Throw that cloak on and follow me."

Freyja led me outside the door and through passageways that seemed like they were tucked away for discreet purposes. Eventually she led me out of the castle and along a tree covered path through the forest to what had looked like an abandoned town while we were flying above it earlier.

The closer we got to the town, the more I wanted to turn right back around. It almost felt like a command.

"It's glamor, Zoe. Oleander. Come on," she said, dragging me through the protective shield around the town.

The stench of death hit me the moment I crossed the threshold. There were immortals here, but they were not well. The gift of Vega rumbled beneath my skin, aching to break free and get to work.

"What happened to them?" I asked, assessing the situation.

"We can only guess, but we think with Algol unattached to the other elemental realms, it has caused catastrophic consequences... the magic here is all but gone. Oleander is one of the few who still has power at all."

"Why didn't he tell me?" I demanded angrily.

"He'd be asking a life sentence from you... healing them won't cure them. This sickness... it'll just come back. You would be drained of power constantly. He is here, though. All the time. He does what he can to help them."

"None of the other courts know," I guessed.

"No. No one knows."

I slid the cloak from my face with determination in my eyes. I didn't know if this was why I was called here tonight, but I'd do everything I could to make these immortals comfortable.

"Let's get to work then," I said, walking towards the first building housing the immortals Oleander was protecting. This was going to be a long night.

37

Seduction

Freyja and I had spent nearly every available minute healing the refugees of Algol. A few of the Sublunary—the rebels—stood guard while I worked. I guess they didn't fully trust me and with good reason. I'd have to ask Oleander about his relationship with them. By the time they expected us at dinner, I could barely walk on my own. I could've really used those healing powers from my flame right about then.

"You used too much magic," Freyja chastised.

"Nothing a good night's sleep and a cup of coffee can't fix," I waved off, but I knew she was right. A knock sounded at the door and I stifled a groan at the severe reprimand I was about to get from Clodovea or Finnian.

"Zoe, open this door or so help me, I'm coming through it. Manners be damned."

Oleander. Of course, he would've heard about our little adventure. I begrudgingly opened the door and tried to hide the wince of the soreness of my muscles. My gift always made me physically fatigued.

"What were you thinking?" he asked, a breath away from my face.

"I was thinking that there were sick immortals and I could heal them. So, I did."

"You shouldn't have done that. We don't know what tomorrow will hold. We need you at full capacity of your power."

"You're welcome," I said, slumping down to the bed, too tired to argue. "It was the right thing to do, Oleander. I couldn't turn a blind eye... not when I could do something about it."

Oleander sighed and sat beside Freyja and me on the bed.

"How many did you heal?" he asked, resigned that what was done was done.

"All of them," Freyja answered.

He whipped his head around at that in obvious exasperation.

"All of them?"

"Yes, every single one of them," I confirmed. "I probably still have some magic in the tank if I really needed it."

"Impossible."

"You should know by now not to use that word around me, Oleander."

"You're right," he said, offering his hand as he stood. I grasped it, already feeling a little more sure on my feet.

"You're working with the rebels? The unallied?" I questioned.

"I had to find help where I could. I was able to plead my cause to some of them," he admitted, as he steadied my shaking form. "Come on, we need to get going... unless you want to explain to Finn and Clodovea why you can't come to dinner?"

"Nope, I do not. Lead the way, sir."

Finn and Clodovea definitely suspected something was up, but they didn't press when it became clear I wouldn't be talking about it. Whatever reason Oleander had kept this secret, I would respect that he knew what was best for his subjects—for now.

I ate more than I ever had before, each bite seeming to replenish a bit of my gift's reserves. I drank the coffee Oleander provided by the gallon, and everyone seemed too scared to mention that I might not be able to sleep after so much caffeine. Amateurs.

"What story did you tell Hesperia about Zoe coming here?" Clodovea asked, pulling me from my caffeine induced bliss.

"Hesperia and I have a mutual hate for each other, but she seems to think I have loyalty to her out of fear. I've played my part well since she severed the bond to Canis."

The hint of shame rolled through Oleander's eyes, and I tilted my head curiously. My discernment told me he'd given much more of himself to Hesperia to protect his people than anyone realized.

"I told her that Zoe would serve her cause well and she would do it because she loved me."

"She won't believe that," Finn responded.

"She will," I said with conviction. There was a fondness for Oleander that I held dear to me. I would show that part of me proudly tomorrow.

We concluded that tomorrow, we would focus on figuring out what Hesperia wanted from me and finding the source of Algol's severed tether. Oleander had a good idea of where it was, but he had learned that the magic around it created illusions to where it was truly kept. Every time he'd gotten a lock on it, it had disappeared. We hoped my enhanced Algol gift would lead me right to it. No pressure.

Once we found where it was, we could secure it away from Hesperia. It wouldn't fix the problem, but it would hopefully keep it from getting worse until we found a more permanent solution. One step at a time.

I stopped Oleander in the hall before heading to my room for the night.

"You're risking a lot if we fail," I said softly.

"I'll be alright, love."

"You don't have to be brave for me," I replied, squeezing his hand firmly.

"You saw the devastation. You forget that Algol was stolen from its immortals, too. We never wanted this. It's a risk I have to take, Realm-Healer."

"I vow to give all that I have to see this mission through," I said, kissing him on the cheek before heading down the hall to my room. I silenced his protests as I slammed the door.

I cuddled up next to Freyja in bed, feeling full and content. I would let the anxiety and racing thoughts about everything that could go wrong tomorrow greet me in the morning. Tonight, I would keep my sister close and find my peace in dreaming of Elvy and a better world.

***

"Little bear," The Archer called to me, disrupting my one desire to have a restful sleep.

"I'm a little busy here," I said, trying to go back to the dream I'd been having of Elvy.

"Do not forget your true purpose tomorrow. Find what was stolen, Eferhild. Do not get distracted by the pull of your heart. Your creed is true, little bear. Do not let it cost you. It is not yet time to mend the broken," The Archer whispered through me. "You are my daughter. You are capable of great things... but I do not wish to see you perish for them."

"Any other cryptic demands?" I asked. "Don't suppose you want to come fix this little situation yourself?"

"I would trade places with you if only I could, little bear. Never doubt that. I'm with you. Always."

I wondered if The Archer was capable of speaking without creating more questions within me. Unfortunately, I had little time to ponder what he meant as he seemed to lull me back into the things I'd rather dream of.

***

Freyja helped me into the night-blue dress that was beaded with the glitter of stars, and I opted to let my scarred arm show and wore my marks like a shield of armor. The back of my dress was opened, allowing me to easily sprout my wings.

"Royalty suits you, Zoe Eferhild," Oleander said, leaning in the doorframe of my guest room.

Oleander wore a perfectly tailored black suit, fit for a king himself, and the carefree smirk on his face showed he knew he wore it well.

"I will escort you to dinner. Zadie will follow suit with Finnian and Clodovea. Freyja must stay behind."

Freyja and I both nodded, understanding the immense risk we were about to take. There was no room for argument here while the fate of the realms was at stake. I trusted Oleander.

"It's important you play your role well tonight," he said, gently reminding me. "You will see things you do not like. That I do not like. Remember the purpose of tonight. No matter what comes, we cannot fail in uncovering what Hesperia wants from you or where she is keeping the heart of Algol."

"I don't have a good feeling about this," Finnian mumbled.

"I will not yield until it is finished," I swore, remembering Elvy's words, and the whispers of The Archer. Oleander didn't know about my other mission from The Archer, but I would see it through despite the irritation his visits brought me. I knew he was on my side.

I couldn't doubt my ability to do this. I would pry into the soul of the dragon and would stand as loyal to my conviction as a lioness to her cubs. Glancing out the window, I found Algol winking back at me, as if rooting for me to succeed. Perhaps it was The Archer trying to help guide me to the secret mission he sent me on tonight.

"Heed my warnings, little bear," The Archer said, breezing through me silently.

"It's showtime," Oleander said, extending his hand. I kissed Freyja on the forehead, murmuring a goodbye and joined Oleander.

"When we land, show your wings. It will only make her want you more," he instructed.

"Have you been keeping tabs on me?" I asked.

"I always protect my investments, Zoe."

Before I could explain that I was not his investment, we were shooting across the sky, followed by three winged figures, all dressed in their respective court regalia. Oleander led the entourage to an onyx palace that seemed to be part of the mountain itself, overlooking the dark city below. This felt like a fortress more than a place to rule from. The nausea dared to creep up as it got closer to what Algol wanted to show me.

"Breathe, Zoe. I've got you," Oleander said, as he hovered just above the landing point. "They can't see us until I say so. Summon your wings and we will land together."

There was no roaring ocean to help center me, so I focused on the burn that had not left my core since I parted from Elvy. I allowed the warmth to fill me from head to toe, and my wings broke free.

"Zadie did not do them justice," he whispered, admiring my wings. "Are you ready?"

With everything to lose, I wanted to fly far from the ominous darkness, but I knew if there was no light to be found within its walls, I would have to let it come from me.

"Yes," I said, voice steady.

He nodded, snapping his fingers, and we descended upon the landing point that was encircled by guards. I didn't panic, as Oleander had warned me of this.

"Queen Hesperia always sends such a warm welcome committee," Oleander drawled, keeping my arm wrapped in his. Our wings touched slightly, but I kept my balance.

"Follow me," the one in charge said, apparently not finding Oleander as charming as he found himself.

I kept my eyes alert, and senses keyed into anything that might be useful. The walls were void of any decorations, keeping in theme with a black nightmare. The feeling of death seemed to radiate through the walls, and every single survival instinct had me wanting to escape its clutches. I remained resolute, ready to serve the purpose I'd been remade for.

The guard eventually led us to a grand dining hall with ceilings so high I could barely make out the top. This was a show of power. Hesperia had chosen her field well. There was no one seated at the dining table yet, but the guards showed us to our seats, instructing us to stand until the queen had arrived. Hesperia did indeed know what she was doing, and I almost wanted to applaud her for it.

It appeared the queen would be seated at the head of the table with Oleander at her left, me beside him, and Zadie on the other side of me. Clodovea would be seated to Hesperia's right and Finnian beside her. The queen kept us waiting in silence long enough to be annoying before she graced us with her presence.

Hesperia had sickly, long black hair with snow white skin that contrasted considerably with the blood-red lips she had chosen to wear for this dinner. I noted there were no streaks of silver in her hair to mark her as a Shadowed. The A-line dress she wore was a lacy black with a red slip underneath it. I had to work hard to keep the snarl from escaping my lips. Clodovea gave me a slight nod, reminding me to keep my face pleasant.

The queen looked to each of us with her cold, dark eyes as she stood in front of her ornate chair, grander than the rest. Oleander had been right about my wings. Her gaze lingered on them longer than the others, with greed in her eyes. She motioned for us to sit, and we followed her lead. The chairs accommodated a Shadowed's wings, much to my happiness. I would've hated to fall over and give a weak impression.

"Oleander, what have you brought me?" Hesperia asked, drinking from a golden goblet.

Ours remained empty on the table, and I felt my fingers curl, ready to punch her delicate face.

"Algol's Emerged," Oleander said, picking up his glass. "Surely we can all drink to that."

Hesperia gave a tight smile, analyzing us. She snapped her fingers and wine filled to the rims of our goblets. No water was offered, so I would have to pretend to drink. My *sight* had been screaming to come through since she'd arrived, and I'd kept it down.

"Hello," I said, turning up every ounce of dark charm I had without letting my lurking beast out to play fully. I felt Oleander's pride next to me, so I knew I'd at least accomplished my outward charisma. "I'm Zoe."

"And what brings you to my realm?" Queen Hesperia said, taking another long sip. I noticed the ripple of anger briefly flow through Oleander.

"I'm not sure I find Vega to my liking," I said, glaring at Finnian and Clodovea. "I certainly don't need these two breathing down my neck."

This seemed to please Hesperia, but I knew we still had much work to do.

"We felt representation from the Court of Vega was pertinent to this meeting since she is also Emerged from Vega," Clodovea said, pleasantly.

"You don't have to talk about me like I'm not even here," I snapped.

Clodovea winced, but kept her face cool and collected.

"With your permission, your grace, I was going to offer her a place in my court," Oleander said smoothly.

"I'm sure you would like to keep her all to yourself," Hesperia said, noting the hand Oleander had placed on my thigh, inching higher to my apex.

He had discussed this with me prior, and I'd agreed to go along with this plan. I saw the briefest of apologies in his eyes as he squeezed my thigh. The flame inside me wanted to incinerate his hand, but I instructed it to play nice with the brooding Lord Astral.

"Perhaps she could help us have better relationships with Vega," he suggested, winking at Clodovea.

"I had the understanding that pitiful excuse for a Lord Astral, Elvy, was keen on Zoe," Hesperia said, eyes raised knowingly.

"He wanted more than I could give," I answered, hating the lie spilling from my lips. I let the seduction of my darkness leak out just a little to take the pain away.

"I can personally assure you, Zoe, that Oleander is a fantastic lover. You would not be disappointed," Hesperia promised, lust lacing her words. I wanted to squeeze Oleander's hand in solidarity, but stayed true to our mission.

"I like this one myself," Zadie purred, leaning towards Finnian. Even though they both had a part to play too, I had a feeling neither minded very much. Clodovea openly scowled at the pair.

With Hesperia turning her attention to Zadie and Finnian, I slowly relinquished my power, letting the path of light flow from me undetected and into the most secret parts of her shadows. Oleander continued stroking my leg, pretending to drink his wine sloppily. The discernment sung within me, louder than it ever had before. Whatever reason Algol wanted to bring me back for, my answer was here.

Zadie and Finnian continued a show that would make anyone blush as I continued to see into Hesperia. There were no barriers around her. They'd been right. There was no magic that could keep me from touching her soul. I was met with a black heart and unyielding lust for power. I understood she would savagely do anything to get what she wanted, but I needed to go deeper.

A flash of a room appeared. It reminded me of a cave with a pool of darkness in the walls, like a large mirror. I saw Hesperia kneeling over it, trying to manipulate it. She stuck her hand in the water, and black marks that looked like tree roots started up her arm, and she screamed in pain, clutching her hand back to her chest.

I ignored the sweat forming on the nape of my neck and tried to hold the image, but Hesperia snapped her fingers, drawing me away. Food filled the dinner table, and she made no indication that she was aware of what had just happened. The sense of unease did not leave me, though, so I might have to take my chances. I would need to get Oleander alone to see where the room from my vision was located.

I didn't know what I'd been expecting of the food, but it was an ordinary dinner with chicken and vegetables drizzled in a lemon garlic sauce. I didn't bother to taste it as I silently chewed, wondering what Hesperia was up to. If I found the room, then I might not need to touch her essence again. Where did I fit into her scheme? I wasn't sure which was the bigger risk.

"I'll take your request under advisement," Hesperia said. "We are only interested in those with true power, though. What is it that the stars have gifted you?"

I could lie, but I had expected this question even though I wish she hadn't asked. It felt like I was giving something away.

"I can heal on a pretty substantial level," I admitted.

"You're being very modest, Zoe," Oleander said, grinning as though I hung the moon. "Magnificent truly. Nothing as powerful in our recorded history."

"Surely not that impressive," Hesperia said, lips pouting at the sight of Oleander praising me. Jealousy seemed to only make her desire me more.

"And that's not all," he said, leaning closer to me.

"Oh?"

"Her shield is incredible. Even I can't get through it now," he said, frowning. We did not want to give Hesperia any sign that I had the gift of *sight.* We wanted her to desire me, not want to kill me.

I felt the tendrils of her power reach out to me, but my mind was solid, unrelenting. It would not allow her to pass.

"I must say I am impressed, Zoe," Hesperia stated in a way that was almost insulting. "How do I know you are serious about joining us here in Algol permanently?"

"Surely there is something I can do to prove my loyalty to Algol?" I asked, desperation in my voice.

"Perhaps there is," Hesperia agreed. "You all must stay here tonight. You can prove your worth in the morning."

I didn't want to stay in this place overnight. The sense of dread had only increased since sitting here through dinner. Nothing good would come of this, but it gave us the opportunity to get to that room.

"Zoe, you haven't touched your wine," Hesperia said, raising a brow. "Please, if we are to be allied, you must drink to my health."

Letting more of the blissful darkness consume me, I picked up my glass and drank. I begged the darkness to shield me. Hesperia laughed, as if she was aware of the torment inside me.

"You all have proved quite entertaining. Especially you two."

Zadie planted another kiss on Finnian to drive home the point.

"How generous of you," Oleander said, nodding his hand in thanks.

"How many rooms shall I have made up for you?" Hesperia asked, dismissing us.

"Three will do," Oleander said, pulling me closer.

"Three then. I trust Oleander to show you just how grateful Algol would be to have you, Zoe," Hesperia said, and her guards were on us again. Each led us to a secluded wing of the castle where our rooms were prepared. Oleander played up his drunken swagger until we had closed our bedroom door behind us.

I was about to speak, but he placed a finger over my lips, and tossed a piece of his shield around us, shrouding us in darkness.

"Well?" he asked.

"One, you have got to teach me how to work one of these shields like that," I started. "Two, her motives still aren't clear, but it's not good. I got a flash of something though," I said, explaining the vision of the room to him. I shook my head, trying to shake off the lingering cloud over me.

He sat down and his face told me it was grim.

"I know it. It's a sacred space, and she is defiling it. It's not unexpected."

"Can you get me to it?" I asked.

"Yes, it's in the mountain, where the power of Algol connects to the realm of Perseus. That's likely where she would have broken the tether to the Kingdom of Canis. It sounds like she's still trying to do something else."

Our worst fears could be confirmed tonight.

"This could be a trap," I said, trusting the hesitation in my gut.

"It probably is, but we have no choice. We have to know how she broke the tether… we have to secure it."

"Hesperia… she's forced you to do things you didn't want to," I stated. Oleander looked down, not answering. I threw my arms around him, pulling him close. He stiffened at first, but he returned the embrace with fervor.

"I'm sorry she made you drink," he murmured. "Here," he said, holding out some type of candy that he must have slipped in his pocket from dinner, and I popped it in my mouth, grateful.

Before I could think more about what she'd made me do, a knock on the door sounded, and he stepped away from me to let in Zadie, Finnian, and Clodovea.

"What's the plan?" Zadie whispered, even though Oleander had extended his shield to them the moment they entered the room.

"Zoe and I will go inside the mountain. To where it all began," Oleander confirmed.

"She's not going without one of us," Clodovea stated firmly.

"I can't shield us all. Not for the length of time it'll take us to get there. Not with the state Algol is in now."

Clodovea didn't like this, but she didn't like the idea of me not being shielded at all even more. I had a feeling Oleander would be powerful enough to shield us all if he wasn't exerting so much magic in protecting the other immortals. He wouldn't compromise them.

"If we get separated, Zoe. Remember, the stars will guide you home, okay?" Clove asked.

"I can do this," I said, exerting the confidence I didn't feel. I hugged her fiercely and allowed Finnian to join in. "You can't be caught with me, Oleander. The immortals who have not fallen to her in this realm need you."

"Then we better not get caught, Zoe Eferhild," he said simply.

"This might be the most reckless thing I've ever done," I said, steeling myself.

"I'm honored to be a reckless fool with you," Oleander returned, leading me out the door.

38

Creed

Oleander led me easily down several passageways I would have no hope in retracing. The only sense of direction I gathered was going deeper into the belly of the beast with my *sight* reinforcing that we were on the right path. The air became inhospitable, and the ocean was nothing more than a distant memory. The fiery embers in my chest did not lessen, and I knew Elvy was still sending me every bit of him that he could. Oleander kept a vise grip on my hand until we made it to our destination.

"Through there," Oleander said, pointing to a door carved from the mountain itself.

I trusted Oleander, but I still let my gift unravel around him, reassuring that his heart was pure, and I found his soul to be unscathed by the darkness. I realized I could only see this part of him because he allowed me to do so, though I felt I was probably strong enough to crumble even his shields to dust now.

"I'm on your side," he promised in hushed tones. "Your destiny is in there. If we make it out of this alive, Zoe, I swear I'll teach you everything you want to know."

I nodded and led the way into the cavern, and was greeted with a familiar sight.

"This is too easy," I said, my gut warning me.

"We still have to try," he encouraged, sealing the door behind him.

I slowly approached the swirling darkness that tethered this realm to Algol, which gave Perseus its power. Though from the looks of it, Algol didn't seem so strong. On the other side of the wall, parallel to the living darkness in front of me, lay a barren, shattered orb. What shocked me more was the large, metallic arrow sticking out of the living star. The arrow called to me like a siren's song. My discernment was ignited within me.

"The Archer," I breathed. "He sent me here for this. That's his arrow."

"That's where Algol is supposed to be connected to Sirius, the star of the Kingdom of Canis. The histories say that his bow creates the tethers... to use it to destroy a bond would cause catastrophic consequences. I don't understand how Hesperia got it or used it."

"Stole it," I said, teeth clenched. "What would it take to reconnect the tethers without it?" I asked, tilting my head on the cusp of something.

"The Archer's bow and arrow has been the only source of a permanent cord. It would take more power than I have. Maybe with all five Lord or Lady Astrals, we could create a temporary bond, but they would have to give a piece of themselves and their star with it. It's some dark shit and unstable at the best of times."

I turned my attention back to the wall of Algol, my eyes staring into its soul as if it was a living thing with a beating heart. The Archer had warned me to only take what was stolen, but after seeing the devastation of Algol's people, I could not ignore the call of Vega to heal. Even though I was still somewhat drained from the healing I did yesterday, I had to try. Even if it only bought us a little time. My decision was made. I was a loyal Daughter of Algol, and they needed me. The blood of The Archer ran through me. I would be the light when all hope seemed to be hidden. What I was about to do was reckless, and I had a feeling this moment was what the stars had tried to protect me from. I'd never listened to them before... why start now?

"*You will burn, Zoe Eferhild,*" a familiar voice whispered through to me.

"So bright that the stars will remember the power of my name," I replied to the void.

"Wish me luck, Oleander," I said, as I plunged my hands into the liquid darkness, allowing it to ensnare its dark claws up my arm just as they had with Hesperia.

And then I remembered.

The memories of everything from my time in the trials flooded me in a sensory overload, and the warning Nova had given rang true. She hadn't just warned me what it would cost me when I chose both Algol and Vega. She was warning me of this moment. My creed was true, and she believed I would not walk away from this choice.

I remembered seeing Algol dying and knew that it would be fatal for everyone if we reconnected Algol to the rest of the kingdom before it was healed. Before *I* could heal it. Algol was not bad in itself, but the one who manipulated it like a puppet was making it into something it was not. We would need the weapons of creation that belonged to The Archer to truly bring this world back to balance, but we didn't have time to wait for that. This was my blood right, and only I had the power to do the unthinkable.

Oleander was shouting my name, but I blocked out the screams, letting Algol consume all of me. I felt the flame from Elvy giving me every morsel of power he could send.

I guided Algol's damage through my veins, willing my magic to heal it. It was almost like a blood transfusion. Some conscious part of me was aware that Oleander could not get near me because of how brightly I was burning. I did not surrender. At the expense of all I held dear, I would not cease. The pain and sorrow of Algol filled every atom of me, and I buckled to my knees.

I called on the spirit of Vega, who lived in me, and commanded its magic to heal its sister star. Vega had no choice but to obey me, breathing life back into Algol through me. I did not yield my magic until every last drop of death had left Algol, and I did the ultimate thing that would give Algol and its inhabitants their best chance until we could find The Archer's bow. I shackled Algol's life force to my own.

Only the child of The Archer could withstand this strength of magic, and even I wouldn't be able to hold it forever. Algol's fate was now my own, and my fate was that of Algol's. What happened to Algol happened to me. I collapsed onto the hard, rugged surface beneath me. Oleander caught me just before my head crashed to the rocky ground.

"Zoe," he breathed, tears in his eyes. "Please tell me you're alive."

I gave him a weak nod, unable to speak. I wept in his arms as the sickness of Algol swirled beneath my skin, forming a permanent tattoo down both arms. Like my scar, the cosmos seemed to swirl within them.

"What did you just do?" he asked, fear in his voice.

"I healed it," I muttered, voice barely a whisper. "Algol."

"Realm-Healer," he whispered.

"We aren't finished."

"You were on fire," he said, almost angry.

You will burn, Zoe Eferhild.

"I bought us some time. To find The Archer's bow. Algol's life source is connected to me now. As long as I'm breathing, it is safe."

Oleander's face faltered in wonder at the magnitude of power I'd just possessed and the sacrifice I'd just given for his realm. I didn't know how long I'd be able to hold this source of power for Algol, but hopefully, it would be long enough.

"They're coming. I couldn't contain your magic once you... burned," he said, looking as helpless as Elvy had.

"Go," I demanded. "You cannot be seen down here with me. You must protect Freyja and the rest of this realm. Don't let my gift be for nothing."

"No," he said with defiance.

"I swear on the stars if you don't get your ass out of here, I will never forgive you," I said, voice getting louder.

"If you don't leave this cave alive, I will gladly let Elvy kill me after he finds out I left you alone down here."

I heard footsteps closing in—they were at the door and would be on us any second.

"Believe in me, Oleander."

"I'll keep my shield over you for as long as I can," he promised.

"Thank you," I answered. "I can do this. I have to face her true nature."

He was poised to argue, but we didn't have the time.

"Now," I said, voice pleading.

Oleander placed a swift kiss on my forehead and disappeared into the shadows, just before Hesperia breached the threshold of the door, a gleam in her eye.

I used the cool cave wall for support as I gave the most menacing expression I could muster. I was living on a prayer that my strength would return or the stars would save me one more time before Hesperia ended my existence. Algol was resting inside me, but I knew my power would be nearly infinite once it woke.

"I thought I might find you here," Hesperia said, gliding towards me. "Where are your friends?"

"I came alone. Algol called for me," I answered, only half lying.

"I doubt that," Hesperia said, examining the new mark of the stars on my arm and the arrow next to me on the floor. The magic still flared within the new markings, leaving them in their moving form instead of a solid tattoo.

"You truly are a wonder, Zoe," Hesperia said. "I see you took care of one problem and failed my test all in the same blow."

Hesperia moved towards our tie to Algol, finding the star completely healed from the damage she had caused. I wanted to get in between them, protective of the one who had deemed me worthy of life. She didn't seem to understand or recognize that Algol's life force was now connected to me. I prayed she never found out.

"Pathetic," she announced to the guards around her, kicking me away from her prize. "I, unfortunately, still have a use for you."

I winced at the assault and tasted blood on my lips where she'd landed her blow.

"I will not help you tether back to Earth," I said, spitting my blood in her face in an act of defiance. We couldn't do that until we had destroyed her.

"Oh, I will, Zoe. But not for long," Hesperia said. "I think we've wasted enough resources on that pitiful planet. No offense."

"There are good people there," I responded, astonished at the casualness in her voice.

"And so they will die," she said dismissively. "They are insignificant."

"Their lives are worth living. You do not get to decide they aren't, so you can feed some narcissistic agenda. You are not a god."

"Are we not gods?"

I had fought to believe in the worth of myself and humanity for too long to have some bitch throw it all away. I would wipe that smile from her face if it was the last thing I ever did. The rage that roiled in me gave me flashes to the second trial and the venom I had wished upon those men. I doubted there was anything worth saving in this queen, but my soul was indeed worth keeping sane. I would not yield to the wrath that threatened to consume me. At least, not in this moment.

"Don't worry, Zoe, it'll be over quickly."

"You can't do anything without the other Lord Astrals," I answered, stalling for time. My strength was almost enough to fly, though I wasn't sure how to navigate through the shadows. I prayed the stars would guide me home as Nova and Clodovea had promised they would.

"What they do not provide, I will take," she promised, smiling. My illusion of being weak let Hesperia's guard down just enough. I flooded my magic through her once more, letting the path of light guide me through her soul. Her heart was on full display for me, like a lover desperate for affection. She was too enraptured with herself to realize what I'd taken. I *saw* part of what she planned to do. I had to warn the others.

"Do you ever get tired of hearing yourself talk?" I asked, knowing what I had to do to get out of here. It was going to hurt like a bitch.

She responded with several blows to my face, my eyes swelling in response.

"Most immortals speak to me with a little more respect," she spat.

"Not respect," I disagreed, knowing I was about to get hit again. "Fear. I do not fear you though"

Hesperia kicked me in the ribs, and her guards seemed to wince, but they didn't come to my aid either. Her magical pull with them was too strong.

"Hold her down," she commanded, and the guards obeyed. I focused on staying present in this fight. I was not in my past being held down by a different set of hands. For some unexplained reason, I felt multiple calming presences kneel resolutely beside me, keeping me steady. Their features were unclear to me as I focused on my assailants.

"You realized you weren't strong enough on your own after you severed the bond from Sirius?" I questioned, trying to probe for the truth. "How that must have ruined your ego."

"You think you are stronger than me, Zoe," she laughed darkly. "You are in this room because I let you see what I wanted you to see."

I swallowed down my first taste of terror.

Hesperia pulled out a silver dagger and kneeled next to me with a smirk on her lips. "I think it's time for your darkness to really come out to play," she purred as she sliced my bared skin. Whatever this knife was made of scorched my skin. I swallowed back my screams, ignoring the feeling of blood pooling around me. Hesperia leaned closer to the green of my eyes. I felt the shadows swell beneath me, wanting to unleash. Whether it was to answer Hesperia's call or protect me, I wasn't sure. All I knew was that she wanted it for some purpose that couldn't be good, so I couldn't let it out.

I used the only tool available to me. I head-butted her aggressively, which knocked her back, causing her to drop the knife. The guard on my left fumbled, and I snuck the arrow in my gown in one fluid motion. Swallowing down the seduction of my fury, I stared at her defiantly.

"Get her out of my sight," she barked. "You will come to my side by the end, Zoe. Do not doubt that," she promised, as one guard supported my weight and started leading me down the passageway.

I could barely see in front of me, but I could just make out the darkness I needed to escape through the shadows. Just as we crossed it, I summoned my wings and shoved the guard with all the strength I had left, ignoring the pounding in my head. What I would give to be able to heal myself right now. The celestials had seemed to think that too much power.

Taking a leap of faith, I shot into the shadows that provided the way to the fissures between realms. I would keep my promise to Oleander and Elvy.

I floated through space and time, unsure of how to find my way back to Elvy, so I listened to the flame within me, praying it shot true. I was fading fast, operating on autopilot as I broke through the familiar comfort of Vega. Too weak to fly, I spiraled down to the ground, but before I hit the bottom, loving powerful arms wrapped around me tightly, bringing me to safety.

"I have to tell you something, Elvy," I mumbled, consciousness barely holding on.

"Later. Just hold on to me," he replied, soothingly, and I felt his healing power work through my tired body as he flew me home.

39

Bubbles

The familiar smell of the warmth and life of the Vega mansion was the only reason I knew where I was. My eyes were sealed with weighted fatigue, and I wanted to give into the feeling of the dark void. If I just slept for a couple of hours, I would be okay.

"Stay with me," Elvy whispered.

"What happened to her?" Blaz asked, voice as steady as the captain of a sinking ship.

"I can't heal her on my own," Elvy said, frustrated. "Not without the flames bonded."

Even though my eyes were closed, I felt the familiar bodies surrounding me, my friends—my *family*. I must warn them. I had to wake up. The darkness reached out to me, caressing me into a comfortable sleep.

NO. I screamed at it.

I felt hands all over me, but I didn't flinch or fear them. Soft fur was under my right hand, pawing for me to stay with her. Warmth and light moved slowly from the hands on me, expanding until every inch of my body was consumed by it. I felt the warm waves of water filling me with life, healing me from the inside out. This is what peace felt like. All the worries of the world drifted from my mind.

"Zoe?" Elvy asked, barely audible.

The voice that would always call me back home.

My eyes fluttered open, and I was met with the concerned faces of the family that had welcomed me so easily into their world.

"Elvy," I croaked, and relief flooded through all their faces.

"I'm right here," he replied, clasping my hand.

"Freyja? Oleander?" I asked, trying to sit up. They were not among the faces staring back at me.

"Safe," Finnian said with Zadie beside him, holding his hand. Apparently, their ruse had awakened their true feelings for each other.

"Oleander's wards are unbreakable in his castle. Even Hesperia cannot cross them," Zadie explained. "He sent me to ensure you came back in one piece."

A sense of dread filled me as I remembered the promise of Hesperia's words.

"I wouldn't count on that," I said, swallowing. "Hesperia is coming. War is coming."

"What do you mean, Zoe?" Elvy asked, face serious.

"If the Lord and Lady Astrals do not agree to help her tether and consume another mortal plane, she will take everything from them. She wants to suck the Earth dry of its resources first."

"That's not possible," Delmira said, muscles tensed to fight. "Not permanently, anyway."

"She seems to think it is," I said. "Oleander had mentioned some dark magic that could make it possible, but it would come at great cost. I think it would do the opposite of what The Archer's bow and arrow does. Our worst-case scenario is here. It would allow her to consume a mortal plane... instead of giving it the power of the elementals."

"No one would agree to that," Imelda said, but there was some uncertainty in her eyes that said enough.

"Everyone has a price," Finnian replied. "The devastation in Algol is worse than we suspected. The realms have reason to fear her. A promise of power could persuade the other Astrals."

"In more ways than one," I whispered, barely detectable.

"What exactly happened, Zoe?" Elvy asked, gripping my hand tightly as if I might slip from existence.

"I healed Algol," I stated, rubbing the new tattoos up and down my arms. "But that's not all."

"You can tell us," Clodovea said, stepping forward as tears threatened to roll down my flushed cheeks.

"I bonded Algol to my own life force. The power is in my blood right as The Archer's daughter," I explained, taking a breath. "Our fates are now intertwined. Mine and Algol's."

The terror in Elvy's eyes was palpable, but so was the pride in what I'd done.

"If the other Lord Astrals heard about Zoe wielding this kind of power... we could face a civil war," Blaz said, already in strategy mode.

"I'm more concerned about Hesperia. She'll take it all for herself, ripping away the hopes and dreams of the stars and cosmos, filling all who stand in her way with eternal suffering. She only wants to consume other worlds, make herself a god. And she wants to start with my home. Then, she will make a new world in her own sick image."

"But if we can link Algol back to the Kingdom of Canis and Earth, we can stop her," Finnian explained.

"Not without ensuring her death first," Delmira confirmed what we already knew.

"I just have to try not to die in the meantime," I said, trying to lighten the mood, but the joke did not take to the Luminaries well.

"What's to stop her from severing the tether again or even other realms?" Imelda piped up as she clung to Clodovea's side.

"We obliterate her to stardust," Blaz said nonchalantly.

"Her influence is strong. It will take more than just killing her," Elvy answered.

I pulled the arrow away from where I'd secretly stashed it in my cloak from Algol.

"There's also this. I took away the only weapon that can sever a bond—The Archer's arrow. He wanted me to get this for him. I suspect we will need the bow next. Hesperia's got a dark power. She knew I was *seeing* her at the dinner. We have to be careful."

I twirled the arrow that had caused the realms so much damage, wondering how something so seemingly insignificant could end up changing the fate of the realms.

"We have to mend the hearts she has damaged. I think I have the power to break that magic," I said, realizing the truth of my words. "I saw it in their eyes when she was beating me. There are some that have not succumbed to her black magic. With the refugees now healed and under Oleander's protection... we might form some sort of rebellion. They have some hope now, I think. Even the Sublunary are aiding the cause."

Elvy winced at the image, and I was sure he had a few choice words for the guards that hadn't stepped in to prevent my potential demise. I held no ill will towards them, understanding their need to fight another day. Perhaps he was more frustrated at the amount of magic I'd been wielding in the two nights I'd been away from him. He may never let me out of his sight again.

"You speak of Algol as if the star is alive and has a conscience," Clodovea pointed out.

"They do, Clove. The stars live on the dreams of all those who wish upon them," I said, smiling. "Even Algol. Where do we start?" I asked, wanting to launch into planning mode. Everyone looked to Elvy, ready to leave right now if that's what he decreed.

"Hesperia isn't going to conquer the universe tonight. Let's rest and regroup in the morning. Zadie, you are welcome to stay and bring Oleander up to speed when you return tomorrow. Delmira and Blaz, go check and reinforce the shields around Vega before settling in for the night."

Everyone seemed to take this as their dismissal, leaving Elvy and me alone with Jelly laying down nearby. I half expected him to scold me for putting my life in danger, but only gratitude was shown in his eyes.

"What you did..." he said, struggling to find the words.

"Was completely stupid and egocentric?" I offered.

"No, it was the most brave, remarkable, selfless thing I've ever known someone to do," he stated, stroking the lines of the mark of the death star.

"Algol was reaching out to me for help. That day on the beach." I clutched the hand that stroked my arm. "I had to invoke Vega to heal Algol. Vega answered."

"Remade by the stars," he murmured, placing his forehead on mine.

"Take me upstairs," I said, voice trembling.

He swept me in his arms and carried me up the stairs. Jelly didn't follow. I briefly wondered whether she was picking up on those social cues or if Blaz had stolen her attention away again.

I didn't have long to wonder as Elvy expertly slipped my dress and cloak off while turning on the faucet to the enormous bathtub. Steam filled the room and the sweet smell of the sea filled the air. My exhaustion was slowly leaving me, and I couldn't help the laugh that escaped my lips as he poured bubbles into the water. It was something so silly and mundane... and it was important that we lived in it—this moment.

I helped him slide his clothes off, and he gently lifted me into the boiling hot water, laying me against his chest. I welcomed the sting of the water, relishing in feeling alive. He took his time seeking every inch of my body, which proved to be distracting in getting us both clean. We didn't seem to mind.

I arched my back as he pinched my hardened nipples while sliding teasing fingers lower to my apex. He swallowed my moan with a kiss as I ground my ass closer to him, enjoying the feel of him against me. Soon, my worries were blissfully lost to the musings of my Lord Astral.

Determined to remind him of who I was, I flipped so that I faced him in the water. With a smirk, I began fisting him, savoring the feeling while memorizing every detail of the one who was my flame. When he was about to find his own release, I bit his peck savagely, following his ecstasy through to the end.

"Fuck," he said, pulling my hips up so that I straddled him.

I rested my head above the beat of his heart, and he gently trailed his fingers up and down my back, making me shiver.

"For however long I have with you, I want you to know that I didn't feel like I was truly living until you came crashing into my life," he said softly. "I am so damn glad you are mine, baby."

"I dreamed of you the first night you were on Earth searching for me. I'd been looking for you ever since that moment, but I didn't know it at the time," I shyly replied. I'd been dreaming of those six stars shooting across the sky in Saint Andrews for months before I found them.

He lifted me out of the still warm water of the bathtub, wrapping me in a fluffy towel all in one fluid motion. He guided me to the bed and laid me down gently. With a snap of his fingers, the air warmed, and he ripped the towel away from me, desire in his eyes.

Kneeling before the bed, he placed my thighs on his shoulders, devouring my slit with a merciless rhythm. I gripped onto the comforter, then his hair, pulling him in closer. I felt him slide two fingers inside, and all I could think was *more*. As if he could read my mind, he reached his free hand up and kneaded my swollen breast, tipping me over the edge.

Aggressively, I pulled him onto the bed with me, needing to feel him inside of me. *Now*. He met my silent plea and thrust into me as I rode him through another orgasm. He flipped us again, never ceasing the thrust of his hips, as he sucked and teased each of my nipples. I gripped onto his shoulders tightly, crying out for him like a prayer.

Somewhere in the fray, Elvy's wings had burst from him, and they were closing around us, keeping us safe. As he continued to thrust, I gently stroked his wings, and he cried out my name in his own euphoria.

Elvy collapsed on top of me, and we just breathed each other in.

"Zoe," he murmured.

"Elvy," I whispered, stroking his hair.

We were lost in each other the rest of the night, unable to get enough of the pleasure in being joined with each other. We moved with the fierceness of the ocean, working through our fears of what had happened and what was to come. Then, we became more gentle as if willing ourselves to live in the hopes of the stars and the dreams of our future.

40

Preparations

I awoke to find Elvy still sleeping. His curly hair softened his worried expression. I imagined the weight he must carry as a Lord Astral, responsible for so many souls. He'd never really shown me all the power I knew lurked beneath his tamed demeanor. His power did not matter to me, though. I would love him all the same.

I tucked myself back into his chest, and his arms instinctively wrapped around me. I would never need the calm of the ocean again if I could always feel the beat of his steady heart. Jelly perked up from the foot of the bed, having found her way in the middle of the night. I motioned for her to scoot in closer and after a few twirls to find just the right spot; she wedged herself in between Elvy and me.

I kissed the bite mark I'd left on his chest, grateful to add this moment to my ever-growing collection of memories. This stirred him awake, and he pulled me into a gentle kiss, cupping my cheek.

"I hope that is Jelly I feel on the bed," he murmured, laughing.

"Well, I don't think it's Blaz," I said, teasing back.

"Don't give him any ideas," he replied, nuzzling Jelly. She only snorted, not opening her eyes.

"The horror," I agreed, hiding my face.

"I have to run out before we meet with the others. I'll see you soon?"

The last thing I wanted to do was let him out of my sight, but I conceded, rolling away from him.

I whistled in appreciation as he stood erect from the bed, which earned me another kiss before he darted off to the bathroom to get dressed. Jelly took the opportunity to move into his spot and I snuggled closer to her.

"Traitor," Elvy said, giving me a swift kiss goodbye with a promise to see me soon.

Jelly and I lounged in bed for a little while longer while I built up the courage to brave the day. I stretched my muscles, surprised to find any trace of the brutality I'd endured yesterday gone.

Stealthily, I made my way to my room and rummaged through the closet to find something comfortable to wear. I opted for a pair of dark leggings and a casual jean jacket. I tamed my hair into a braid and looked myself over in the mirror.

"Ready?" I asked my reflection, and she seemed as ready as I felt.

Jelly followed me down to the library, where I found another pot of freshly brewed coffee by the smell of it.

"I found a few more books for Jelly," she said brightly.

"Thank you, Octavia. I'll grab them on the way back down if that's alright?"

"Absolutely. If it is not too bold to say, I'm glad you made it back."

"Not at all. Someone has to be here to drink your delicious coffee," I joked, trying to lighten the mood. She grinned, and I nodded my thanks to her and headed to the secure meeting room on top of the mansion, where Elvy had flown me to safety yesterday.

"Well, don't you look happy?" Blaz nudged me, winking.

"Don't even go there," I responded, rolling my eyes. "Can't a girl heal the realms in peace for once?"

"Hey, I'm just glad the Court of Vega can provide you a service in our gratitude," Blaz teased further.

Delmira smacked the back of his head, and the two went at it, causing the rest of us to erupt in laughter.

"Children," Clodovea said, as I approached her and Imelda.

"Literal children," Imelda agreed, but there was joy in her eyes.

Zadie and Finnian joined us, and they seemed to have an air of satisfaction about them. I prayed Blaz would not stir up more trouble with them, but I wouldn't hold my breath. Delmira might actually kill him.

"Where's Elvy?" Clodovea directed the question towards me.

"I figured one of you would know. He said he had to run an errand or something this morning."

None of them seem to know his whereabouts, but before I could let myself panic, he joined the rest of us on the rooftop room.

"Are we ready?" Elvy asked, taking a seat in the middle of the table. We all followed his lead and took our respective seats around the circular table. Jelly laid down at my feet, tired from joining Blaz in fighting Delmira.

Elvy waved a hand over the moonstone table, and a translucent hologram of the courts and Earth filled the table, providing us with a map.

"Delmira?" he asked expectantly.

"We should send our emissaries to the joining courts to warn them what Hesperia plans to do and hopefully rally them to help us tether Algol back to Earth."

"What are the risks in doing this?"

"They could choose to side with Hesperia out of fear," Clodovea mused. "If we bond Algol back to Sirius before the threat has been eliminated, it will leave the realms vulnerable."

"She's been planning this for centuries. We don't know what kind of hold she might already have with them," Blaz answered, weighing the risks. "Now that Zoe has Emerged, she will enact her plan sooner rather than later. She'll come for Zo."

"She still needs me—wants me," I agreed. I shivered, remembering how euphoric it felt to surrender to the madness during the trials.

"It might be best if you stay in Vega," Blaz suggested.

"I'd be able to *see* the other court's intentions, though," I countered.

"We thought it would help persuade the other Astrals to see you... in all of the star's glory, but that would come with its own risks. We would need to be selective on what we shared with them regarding your uhm... situation," Delmira said.

"Situation? Really? That's one way to put tethering the life force of a star to my life," I said, amused.

"No, she needs to be working within the Court of Algol, undoing the damage Hesperia has already caused there," Clodovea responded. "She could be the face of the rebellion there."

"I agree I can't abandon Algol," I said. "But I see Delmira's point."

"Clodovea is right," Zadie replied. "I saw the change in those around Hesperia in the brief time you were there, Zoe. You gave them life and hope. Hesperia's fear took it back from them once you left."

"We will have to come to a compromise," Elvy said diplomatically. "Zoe has a say in where she goes."

I wanted to throttle Hesperia, but I kept the anger composed, remembering what it could lead to within me.

"What about the Sublunary?" I asked, recalling Elvy's explanation of the rebel group. "Could we call on them for aid like Oleander has?"

"I think we must," Elvy responded, with Blaz nodding his agreement.

"We'll need to reinforce our defenses around our bonds to the stars," Delmira stated.

"Any courts we think might be easily swayed?" Imelda asked, speaking for the first time.

"The Court of Canopus," Elvy answered. "Though if we can get the Court of Arcturus on our side, they are powerful allies."

"Strategically, it would be smart for Hesperia to go after those two. It would put them between us and the Court of Rigil, isolating two strong allies."

"I'll schedule a visit with Sierra and Terran myself," Elvy said.

"Hesperia will get all the pieces in place before she strikes, but she will hit Vega hardest and first," Blaz said, examining the playing field.

"She knows we won't willingly give up Vega," Elvy agreed.

"Or betray the mortals of Earth," Imelda added.

"If she persuaded the Court of Canopus and Arcturus to willingly give up their stars, she would only need Zoe with Algol strong enough to overtake us and Rigil. This would complete the needed five elements to reverse the tethers, and consume the stars and suck Earth dry if she wanted to," Delmira said, malice in her words.

"We need to figure out the exact components of the dark magic she wants to wield to reverse the tethers. If we can understand that, we might have a better chance at preventing it," Finnian theorized. "Nothing she does can be permanent without The Archer's bow and arrow."

"Not just the bow and arrow. She needs me to make it work."

"When do we tell Queen Farron and King Aldrich?" Clodovea asked.

"Once we speak with the other courts, I think. They are our last line of defense before all of this spreads to Earth," Elvy said. "They may be able to shield it long enough to buy us some time."

"Can we figure out where she wants to go after she destroys us all? That might help us," Imelda said.

"She will have the power of the five elemental stars; if she succeeds, she will overtake the powers of the Kingdom of Canis and its star Sirius. The possibilities are endless," Finnian said, defeated.

"We won't let it get that far," I said confidently. "The stars are on our side, but let's hope it doesn't come to that."

"Has The Archer talked to you since you returned?" Blaz asked.

"No, he hasn't. I supposed he's pissed at me for not listening to him. I will try to reach him to see if we can find a lead on where his lost bow might be. That's the key."

The truth in my words sung over us, and Vega seemed to shine brighter in the eternal night sky above. The marks that Algol had left on my body burned brightly with the life force of the cosmos.

"When do we move?" Blaz asked, ready to pounce.

"We have some time," Zadie offered. "Hesperia didn't plan on losing you and the power you could have held on the other courts so quickly. She doesn't know what you did, but I think she will figure it out sooner than we would like."

"A week from today," Elvy declared. "We take on saving our realms. Make the plans you need for your assignments. Blaz, let's make sure the Shadowed Legions are ready for battle."

Blaz nodded, a warrior rumbling beneath him.

"I'll go to Oleander and tell him what the plan is," Zadie informed, standing swiftly. I followed her and placed two notes in her hand before she could leave.

"One for Oleander and the other for Freyja," I said, eyes pleading.

"I will deliver them," Zadie swore, with a slight bow. "Thank you for saving my Lord Astral."

With those last words, she disappeared into the night.

The rest of the group had formed into pairs, making preparations for the coming days before we enacted our monumental plan to save the world. Blaz and Delmira were swooning over Jelly, filling my heart with joy in this difficult moment. Elvy joined me in staring at the stars, hands gripping mine as if I might disappear if he let me go.

"Walk with me?" he asked.

I nodded, following him down to the private beach below.

41

Starlight

Never letting go of my hand, Elvy stopped just short of the shoreline. The warm water splashed on our bare feet, and we sat in the comfortable silence of each other's humming energy. He seemed to work through something internally. I didn't pry, content to lean against him and appreciate the ocean's reminder that this was real—all of it.

"I never told you how my parents died," he started, still looking into the stars. "When an immortal dies, they become the stars."

I followed his gaze, wondering if he saw his parents every time he looked into the night sky. I suddenly felt very blessed to have Freyja in my life, even if it wasn't in the way I wanted.

"My parents were flames," he said, turning towards me finally. "They were the most in love, kind souls I've ever known. They were flamed even before the King and Queen. When Hesperia first severed the bond from Algol, they were the only ones who realized what was happening at first. They flew to Perseus and stood against Hesperia, knowing they would likely never return from it."

Squeezing his hand a little tighter, I recalled the essence of death in the mountain, wondering if his parent's last breath had been taken there. I was sure they had perished within those walls, and I recalled the shadows of strength that seemed to keep me going while I was fighting for my life. I'd like to think his parents lent me the last bit of energy they had.

"Hesperia killed them," he said, voice void of emotion.

I didn't offer any words of condolences, as I knew none would bring comfort to him.

"I wish I could have known them," I said, leaning my head on his chest, understanding what it was like to survive while the one you loved died. I now understood the animosity he had towards Oleander, though it was unwarranted. He seemed to have come to terms with that, and I admired him for that growth.

"There's a part of me that you don't yet know," he said, body shaking with the sounds of a low rumble in his chest.

"I'm all in, Elvy. No matter what."

"My power... my true power is *death,*" he said, as his gray eyes darkened to black and the realm itself seemed to shudder at his hidden magic.

I gazed into those hurricane eyes and saw the fury that swelled within the center of the storm. His fury was what he always tried to steady—forge. He'd warned me that he was dangerous, but I'd never felt safer.

"You don't want to know how?"

"It doesn't matter to me. When I said I'm all in. I didn't just mean the easy parts."

"All it takes is a nod of my head or a snap of my fingers, and all the water inside you is mist. Evaporated. Gone. An instant death to thousands if I choose it. It is my family curse," he said, hanging his head in shame.

"You can't scare me now, Elvy. I'm standing right here where I'll always be. Right by your side," I promised. "We both have the potential for great destruction. We'll keep each other safe."

"For the heart of the new moon," he answered.

"And the life in the starlight," I swore.

"Zoe," he mumbled, pulling my chin upwards so my green eyes met his stormy, gray gaze.

"Elvy."

"I don't care what is going on in the world. None of it means anything if I'm not with you. Watching you rise from the stardust, a warrior of the cosmos, I knew I'd spend the rest of my life loving you. No matter the darkness that threatens to pull you under, I know the light that lives within you is made of the stars themselves. I love you endlessly."

I took in all his words, allowing myself to accept his truth. My eyes filled with tears as he bared the unspoken words of his soul to me.

"I love you, Elvy. You live in my veins and there is no realm I wouldn't cross to find my way to you."

He wrapped me in his arms, swinging me around in the comforting waters of the galaxies. He sat me back down and knelt before me, placing his head against my middle.

After a few deep breaths, he gazed lovingly into my eyes and produced a ring from his pocket. The band of the ring was a smooth, rich color of midnight, and the white stone seemed to glitter with flames. Butterflies filled me as I realized what he was going to do. I joined him on my knees, always an equal with him. The moon seemed to show off in this moment for us.

"Zoe Eferhild, Realm-Healer—Emerging of Legends, would you do me the greatest honor of my existence in accepting our flame and joining as one with me?"

"Yes," I said, voice unwavering. I didn't want to wait another minute.

He slid the ring onto my left ring finger and scooped me up in another embrace. He leaned his forehead so that it met mine, and I found I could be happy getting lost in those storms for the rest of my life. We just had to save the realms first.

"How soon?" I asked.

"I'd like to do it before war consumes us," he said seriously. "It's not ideal circumstances."

"Choosing the one you love and how you get to love them is always ideal timing and never selfish," I replied, placing a kiss on his cheek.

"Nothing would make me happier than to love you eternally," he agreed.

I'd been told that I was a balance of life and death, but I held this truth in my heart that it was Elvy and me. We were the perfect balance between death and life—intertwined eternally. I let myself briefly long for the presence of my mother and Freyja, but I knew they would only wish to see me happy. Refusing to let the darkness cloud this moment, I returned to the one I loved—my flame.

"We'll tell the others tomorrow," I decided, wrapping my arms around Elvy. "Let's just have this moment—for us."

He kissed the top of my hair, dreaming of a better world with me.

I had conquered the madness of the shadows to find the light in myself. Elvy had stood by me while I had saved and chosen myself. This reckless love of his had kicked down every wall I hid behind, and he knew every lie I told myself. He still kept coming after me, lighting the way when I couldn't do it myself.

I would give all of myself to him because he would do the same for me. He would stand by my side as the world was consumed in darkness should we fail, but I would cling to hope as we fought to save the mortals of Earth and the immortals of the star realms. I would lend my strength to them when they faltered, as so many had done for me. I would be the starlight for the dreamers.

"Realm-Healer—Emerging of Legends," Elvy breathed, wrapping me tighter into his embrace. A glimmer of hope shone in his flamed gray eyes, and I welcomed it within me without the doubt that threatened to surface.

With the odds against us, that's what I fought for—hope. Hope in the dreams of the cosmos fueled by the ember of light within us all. For a healed world.

Moments.

42

Epilogue

Red. The sand was painted with the color. My hands were covered in the hue of death. But today was supposed to be the color of life with my flame by my side. Beneath the crusted blood, both of my hands were marked with intricate designs of the cosmos that weaved together in a flame that matched Elvy's. He'd explained that the seemingly random pattern of stars was actually a retelling of our own story, just like the stories the mortals had in the stars. The celestial map was only complete when our hands joined together. That had been such a surreal, beautiful *moment*.

Mom and Grant, nor any of the mortal guests in attendance, were none the wiser about the true nature of the ceremony they were attending. To them, it looked much like a wedding, but the High Priestess to the Court of Vega ensured the flame ceremony was done properly and hidden from prying eyes. Traditionally, the ruling Lord and Lady Astrals would be in attendance, but safety had been a concern for us. It only took a drop of our blood and words we both had to repeat. What had made it binding was the confirmation from the priestess in offering to the celestials.

He was mine. And I was his.

I was his Lady Astral, but, more importantly, I was now responsible for every soul in our court and beyond. And I'd already failed. Our cruel destiny had come like a thief in the night, stealing away one of the happiest moments of my life—our lives.

My dress had been beautiful. Designed by Isabella, I'd expected nothing less. It flowed lovingly around my curves and complimented the beach of Saint Andrews well. Elvy's beige suit had been the perfect match. Everything had been right. Freyja had been by my side, though unseen by those not of Algol. Even Oleander had joined Elvy's side, seemingly happy for us both.

Jelly had trotted down the aisle, proud of us. She and I had come a long way since watching volleyball games so long ago. Oleander and Finnian had worked together to create a shield over Jelly's wings so that she could be here today—a true gift.

I'd committed that moment to memory. Delmira, Imelda, and Clodovea were all dressed in neutral colors, standing by my side behind Freyja, as I became their Lady Astral of Vega. I'd given them all a pendent infused with my healing magic as a reminder that I swore to protect them just as much as they did for me. I'd even made one for Blaz and Finnian. The Luminaries had all bowed before Elvy and me before our flame ceremony, swearing the blood oath to this court and to me.

All I could see now was red, and the petrified, frozen faces of those I loved.

She was still warm in my arms, but I couldn't mend the gaping hole in her chest. There'd been no heart for me to resuscitate. Her last act had been to protect me. Even though she had no idea what was going on, she'd known something was wrong—a mother's instinct.

Grant's lifeless body laid next to his wife, clutching her hand, even in death. I couldn't allow myself to feel the agony or I would give myself over to the darkness that demanded vengeance. But Hesperia hadn't left it at that. She'd found Emma and ripped out her heart right in front of me. I'd tried to put her back together, but I couldn't. I don't know how she even knew about my therapist—one of the kindest soul on this planet.

It'd all been so fast—calculated. We'd planned for something like this. We didn't know how she'd broken through our defenses so fast. Elvy and I had decided it was best to join our flames as quickly as possible in case the worst should happen to me. If I died before Algol could bond back to Earth, he could still protect it now that my blood ran through him. I'd like to say that it was purely for selfless reasons, but that wasn't true. I needed him in every way the universe could offer me—including joining our flames.

"Zoe, you must flee back to Vega," a voice whispered, kneeling next to me. My hands still clutched my mother, and I couldn't seem to let go of her.

"I can't just leave her here," I said, lost in the chaos of fighting that was going on around me.

Somewhere, a part of me knew that the Luminaries, Elvy, Oleander, and Zadie were fighting Hesperia and her followers. I knew it wasn't safe for us, but I knew it wouldn't be safe for the mortals if we left them here to defend themselves.

"Honey, I'll take care of her. You've got to snap out of it, kid," she barked. June. That was June. I tore my eyes from my mother's face.

"How do you know about Vega?" I questioned, still holding onto my mom.

"No time for questions," she said, reaching out her hand. "You've got to go. I swear, I will take care of everything here."

"I can't leave them here on the mortal plane," I argued, as the familiar scent of lilies engulfed me as June tried to pry my hand from my mother. *Lilies.*

"You're not mortal," I whispered.

"Not completely, no. The Archer has been watching over you for your entire life, Zoe. Now, come on. I know this is hard, but you can do this. You must do this."

I looked back down at my mother's frozen face and closed her horrified eyes—an image that will burn in my mind for the rest of my existence. I kissed her forehead, promising justice and praying that her spirit was at rest. Jelly licked my face, reminding me she was there.

"Come on, Zo," she said, dragging me into the fray, towards Elvy. June was much more agile than I'd ever noticed. Elvy and Oleander were marching straight towards Hesperia.

Out of the corner of my eye, I saw Jelly surround herself in flames, knocking everyone from our paths with lethal fire. She had become a warrior. We were still learning about all of her powers as a simargl, but the stress of this situation must have ignited this gift.

"Elvy, call them back!" June exclaimed, but his eyes were dark, full of death. The storm forming over the ocean on what was just a sunny day moments ago was coming from him. If he unleashed his death blow now, every mortal within a fifty-mile radius would suddenly find themselves evaporated.

"Oleander, stop him!" I said, running at full speed towards them. Oleander heard me and grabbed onto Elvy's shoulder. Elvy only knocked him down, losing control.

I finally caught up to them as Freyja was helping Oleander up.

"Mom? Dad?" Freyja asked.

"I'm so sorry, Freyja. I couldn't—I tried to," I said, voice breaking. She flew into my arms, sobbing, and I didn't have the heart to tell her we didn't have time for this. I stroked her hair and passed her off to Oleander.

"I will make this right, Freyja. I swear it," I promised.

Oleander looked concerned for me.

"Your eyes are darker than I've ever seen them, love. Please be careful," he moved in closer to whisper, "Don't forget you hold the fate of Algol in you."

He kissed me on the cheek before placing Freyja behind him to guard her from the next assailant. His black sword easily sliced through the man before turning on the next. I turned towards Hesperia and Elvy, who were in the throes of battle.

"Come to play?" Hesperia chuckled towards me. "I wonder which of you I will break first."

"Elvy, we must flee to Vega. She will follow us and leave this plane. We cannot continue this fight here," I said through our flame.

Elvy's jaws clenched, but I saw his resolve start to come back to me. His knuckles around the grip of his sword were white from the strain.

"I've made you both little orphans now," Hesperia said, amusing herself.

The shadow part of me cried desperately for me to let it out, but I swallowed forcefully, unsure of what that kind of power would do, or if I could control it.

"Come on, Zoe. Let me see who you really are," she taunted further.

"I see you, Zo. For who you really are. I'll call the retreat," Ely said, voice clear.

I felt his command through the bond with the Luminaries. June was fighting alongside them, her own sword drawn.

"You may not get another chance at me," Hesperia said. "Destroy me now and your problems will go away."

I let a little of my black tendrils out, just as I had in the second trial in the star realms. They encircled her, which seemed to delight her.

"Come on, Zoe. Is that all you've got for me?"

"Stay with me, Zoe!" Elvy shouted.

"I can end this right now," I promised.

I ordered my magic to wrap around Hesperia's neck, lifting her up, as I dreamed of ripping her into ribbons of flesh. Why was she smiling? Jelly barked underneath her as her flames tried to break through to Hesperia.

Hesperia's eyes had gone as dark as I knew mine were, and my darkness seemed to see the kindred spirit in her, which frightened yet exhilarated me all at the same time.

"Vengeance, little bear, is not the answer," The Archer whispered through me.

"There she is," Hesperia purred, eyes ensnaring me in their trap.

"Zoe!" a voice called that I thought I would never hear again. "Let my daughter go, you bitch!"

My mother shoved her spirit between Hesperia and me, blocking her eyes from my own. I shook off the trance and found Hesperia screaming in rage at my mother.

"Mom! No!" I heard Freyja scream from behind me.

"Fly, Zo. I love you both," my mother whispered, before Hesperia incinerated her.

Before the shock could overwhelm me, Elvy snatched me up in his arms, joining the rest of his Court, transporting us into Vega.

I closed my eyes, and all I could see was red.

ACKNOWLEDGEMENTS

There are countless people that have contributed in some way to the creation of the world of Zoe Eferhild. I would like to take a moment to thank several who have had such a profound impact on this dream becoming a reality.

To my Heavenly Father for blessing me beyond the limitations I so often place on myself.

To you, the reader, I thank you most of all for taking the time to read Zoe's story. You are worthy, just as you are, and I hope this book has gifted you hope—I apologize for the emotional pain this book may have caused (IYKYK).

To my Mimi and Mom who were my Alpha readers (sorry for the sex scenes). Your feedback and support kept me going through all the cover changes and the development of this world of magic.

To my husband, who is not a reader, but is still my biggest fan. I'm so glad to have found my own Elvy in you.

Thank you to my long list of friends who have cheered me on from the beginning. I am in gratitude for you. When self-doubt threatened to creep in, you all were there to give me hope.

To my four dogs, who I could always count on to snuggle beside me when writing, if only you could see the joy your influence has brought to others.

To the entire Indie Author community and the readers who support Indie Authors, you have been such a light in this overwhelming process.

About the Author

E.C. Lawton is the author of *Emerging,* book one in The Zoe Eferhild Chronicles, which is her debut series. She writes books about mental health with a magical twist in an easy-to-read fantasy world. E.C. is also a psychology adjunct professor and clinical therapist. When not writing, she can be found nose-deep in a book, adventuring outdoors with her husband, drinking too much coffee, listening to true crime podcasts, and hanging out with her wolf pack.

Connect with E.C. on her socials at ec_lawton or the QR code.

Printed in the USA
CPSIA information can be obtained
at www.ICGtesting.com
LVHW070951250923
757542LV00033B/310